A PIRATE'S PRIZE

"There are worse things than being a pirate, Merry-mine," Devin said as he leaned toward her. "Much worse . . ." His breath brushed her heated cheeks like a cool, sweet zephyr.

She clenched the covers to her chin, his nearness wreaking absolute havoc with her senses. His eyes probed hers . . .

Was she going mad? Or was it the brandywine she'd imbibed? Or both?

He reached out and covered her hand with his own, then lifted it to his mouth. He turned it over and pressed his lips to her palm, his mist-blue eyes never leaving her face. Unconsciously Meredyth's other hand crept toward the coverlet she'd been forced to release, but whorls of hot desire invaded her middle, intense as fire, debilitating as a ball of searing iron shot to the chest.

His tongue replaced his lips. "Umm . . . brandywine and Merry-mine," he recited in a husky murmur.

A bolt of pure desire speared through her.

"We've a room all to ourselves," he said, as he lifted his face to hers. "Why waste it, sweet, when we both want the same thing?"

Other books by Linda Lang Bartell

TENDER ROGUE
TENDER MARAUDER
TENDER WARRIOR
TENDER PIRATE

S̸T̸ENDER SCOUNDREL

LINDA LANG BARTELL

ZEBRA BOOKS
KENSINGTON PUBLISHING CORP.

ZEBRA BOOKS are published by

Kensington Publishing Corp.
850 Third Avenue
New York, NY 10022

Zebra and the Z logo Reg. U.S. Pat. & TM Off. The Lovegram
logo is a trademark of Kensington Publishing Corp.

First Printing: January, 1996

Printed in the United States of America

Prologue

London—February, 1692

The rumble of ancient cartwheels reverberated through the winter air and caught Keir St. Andrews's attention.

"Speak o' the Devil! 'Tis *him,* Cap'n!"

In answer to his companion's emphatic words, the sixth Earl of Somerset narrowed his eyes against the bitter wind and the errant snowflakes dancing before its ferocity. A creaky wooden cart was approaching them in the near-deserted Holborn Street, carrying its inevitable load of miserable miscreants toward the imposing and forbidding stone edifice that was Newgate Prison.

"Who?" the earl asked, expelling a visible puff of breath with the pronunciation of the single, curt word.

"Devil Chandler! We were just talkin' 'bout him a sennight past, remember? Why just look at 'im!" Peter Stubbs's grin revealed one missing bicuspid from some long-ago brawl. "Only Chandler'd dare stand and give stare for stare, lookin' as if 'e owned London an' was bein' toted about in a bloody litter!"

Keir didn't hear the rest of Peter's words, for his gaze settled on one man among the dozen or so trussed and being hauled to the jail, the one man who remained standing, as if in defiance of the world, as if to see exactly where he was going and who he passed on the way.

He was tall and fair-haired, from what Keir could discern, his long blond hair blowing about his features and obscuring much of them. Chandler tossed his head now and then, obviously to rid his eyes of his unbound mane, but not for long. The blowing wind did nothing to help matters.

Keir could see that Chandler was hard-pressed to keep his purchase against the side of the jouncing wagon, yet he managed to remain erect in spite of his hands being manacled behind his back and the nasty-looking guards who rode on either side and the rear of the vehicle, shouting occasional obscenities at both the prisoners and the sway-backed nags that pulled them.

Devin James Chandler, Keir thought, memories suddenly sifting through him. If he was the man Peter claimed he was, then Keir had known his late father, James Chandler, Earl of Southwycke. He'd also briefly met the earl's natural son by an Irish woman, a lad who'd been brought to Southwycke Manor after his mother's death and against Chandler's wife's wishes. Images teased the edges of his memory—a shock of white-blond hair, freckles, a child's laugh . . .

Shortly after Chandler was killed in a hunting accident, young Devin disappeared. Twenty years ago, to be exact, and, according to Peter and other sources, he'd ended up a seaman roving the Spanish Main, a story heart-wrenchingly like Keir's own.

"Must be freezin' 'is arse off after livin' on the Main," Peter muttered, his words edged with empathy.

Keir nodded, thinking of the good-natured, jovial earl and his one-time admission while in his cups that the only woman he'd ever loved was the mother of his natural son. Elysia was her name.

Keir was suddenly tempted to halt the wagon, identify himself, and remove Chandler from the jurisdiction of the surly sentries. But he didn't dare in this case, for he suspected a man like Chandler, who no doubt harassed both the Spanish and the French to England's advantage (and his own), wouldn't be dragged across the Atlantic in disgrace for anything less than high treason.

"No doubt he's going to jail for treason and deserves what

he gets," he observed as the wagon passed directly across from where they sat their horses to the side of the street. "For a man who commits treason is a man without scruples."

Without warning, the whimsical wind blew Chandler's hair back from his face and for the moment that he was directly in line with Keir, their glances met. Chandler's eyes were narrowed against the wind, yet he stood straight and tall within the meager protection of what appeared to be a ragged cloak, his expression unreadable as Keir's assessing gaze held his for a steady moment.

There was definitely a resemblance to Lord Southwycke, Keir could discern it from where he sat his horse—Chandler's impressive height and the breadth of his shoulders, and especially his pale golden hair.

Peter shook his graying head with vigor at Keir's observation. "Not the Chandler I know. He may be many things—a rakehell, a trickster, even foolishly reckless—but not a traitor. I'd wager anything that 'e's been wrongly accused or betrayed by someone 'e trusted."

With a shrug of dismissal, Keir pulled his gaze from the prisoners and looked at Peter. "What more can you expect from a pirate and his crooked cronies?" he asked in a carefully neutral voice.

Peter bristled visibly. "Have ye forgotten yer own background, Cap'n? Or that a seaman who roams the Main ain't necessarily a pirate?"

Keir's green eyes narrowed at his former quartermaster, a short man in his sixties with wind-roughened features; despite his age, Peter Stubbs maintained a snap to his step and a nip to his bark. His frown of displeasure was obviously uninfluenced by Keir's presence, nor had he been hesitant to voice an opinion contrary to that of a peer of the realm.

But then, their friendship went back much further than Keir's regained title.

Keir suddenly blew out his breath in capitulation. "Well, I owe it to Southwycke's memory at least to speak to the king about this, learn why Chandler's being incarcerated, and go from there."

Peter nodded with what could have been interpreted only as smug satisfaction.

As they swung their horses into the wind that whistled down Holborn Street and away from Newgate and the jouncing wagon with its unfortunate occupants, Keir couldn't keep one corner of his mouth from lifting at the ease with which gruff, tough, and irascible Peter Stubbs—former seaman and sometimes reluctant manservant—could get his way with his friend and employer when he set his mind to it.

It was too bad, however, that Keir was sworn to absolute secrecy in a certain vitally important matter, a matter which was also the other reason he was duty-bound to save Chandler's neck.

Keir thanked God for Peter's excellent memory and timely recognition of the doomed Chandler, in spite of the fact that he knew nothing of Keir's real—albeit anonymous—connection with Devin Chandler, or of Woodrow Kingsley's frantic letter regarding the betrayal and capture of the late Lord Southwycke's bastard son.

The brigantine glided steadily toward them through the jade-blue waters. Devin Chandler watched it with eyes narrowed against the westering sun, his heart inching up his throat with the vessel's progress.

It flew no flag; gave no answer to his calls for identification through the ship's horn. Just moved inexorably closer . . . unnervingly silent.

The gun crew of the schooner Lady Elysia *had scrambled to their posts, already manning the first four of the eight small bore cannon and two of her four swivel guns. Elysia was heaving to, preparing to fight or flee. The air crackled with tension in the eerie silence as the brigantine's bow loomed larger.*

"I say let 'em have it," a voice said in Keir's ear. It was his

first mate, Giles Glasby. "Failure to hoist a flag is an invitation to fight. We can't wait much longer or they'll blow us out of the water!"

Sweat broke out across Chandler's brow, under his arms. What if the brigantine was English? He lifted the horn one last time: "Identify yourselves! This is Captain Chandler of—"

A cannon boomed, then another, their ordnance parting the glassy swells between the vessels with blood-chilling speed. One hit just below the Elysia's bowsprit, the other blew out a chunk of the lower foremast and blasted a hole in one of the lower sails, causing splinters to spray the forecastle deck.

Chandler quickly gave his waiting gunner the signal, and within seconds four of Elysia's cannon roared in reply . . .

The discordant screech of ancient hinges woke Devin with a start. The turnkey ran his club across the bars and sneered, "Wake up, Cap'n! Ye got a visitor."

Devin blinked in the light from the turnkey's lantern and willed himself fully awake. The stink of Newgate invaded his nostrils and threatened to turn his stomach. Hunger gnawed his belly, and his lips and mouth were dry as those of a man who'd foolishly downed seawater, for he'd refused the horse piss they had the gall to call water.

And cold. Christ above! If he lived to be a hundred, he would never be warm again. He couldn't seem to stop shivering.

A tall stranger moved past the heavyset turnkey after the latter swung wide the door. The lantern light limned his imposing form, but Devin could tell little else about him except that his bearing and dress declared him a nobleman.

And he obviously wasn't afraid to be alone with Devin and his cellmate, who huddled on his filthy, louse-infested pallet beneath a sorry excuse for a blanket. Devin suspected the man had jail fever and wondered how long before he succumbed to the same.

"Call when you're ready, guv'nor," the turnkey said without the slightest deference and slammed the door behind the stranger. The long-shanked iron key scraped in the lock and the jailer lumbered away, leaving them alone in the foul dimness of Devin's cell.

"Devin Chandler?"

He tried to flash a grin of utter inanity, but he couldn't make his facial muscles obey. "Nay, rather a leprechaun! Who the hell are you?" His voice, ragged from disuse, sounded like a beast's growl to his own ears.

The man moved forward, glanced at the pallet opposite Devin's, then held out his hand. "Keir St. Andrews, Earl of Somerset. And I hope you're Devin Chandler."

Devin didn't take the offered hand. Somerset was no doubt one of the pricklouses who'd engineered his capture and incarceration, a blueblood making thousands of pounds through the slave trade.

"I knew your father, lad, James Chandler, Earl of Southwycke. He was a friend."

Devin remained silent and stared at the opposite wall. Anyone could have made that claim, and it didn't matter anyway. He had no particular feelings for his late father, could hardly remember what he looked like.

"You and I met once, but you were quite young," Somerset continued. "I dandled you on my knee and told James what a handsome child you were."

What was he trying to do? Devin thought with a mental grimace, besides, of course, worm his way into Devin's confidence?

"Must be your stiff Irish pride."

Devin felt his mouth tighten in reaction, but he said nothing, refusing to rise to any blueblood's baiting.

Somerset stepped closer and lowered his voice. "If you need further convincing, he once told me about your mother. She called you Jamie after your father."

Devin slowly turned his head to meet Somerset's gaze.

"Elysia, I believe he said was her name." It was almost a whisper.

Silence gathered in the cell as their gazes locked. Devin's cellmate moaned in his sleep and flung his blanket aside; a raucous argument suddenly erupted between a man and a woman several doors down; the shuffling of feet sounded softly in the passageway, but no one moved past Devin's cell; and, of course, the continual mewlings of those who suffered from either hunger, illness, or acute loneliness were magnified by the lack of words between the two men.

Devin unconsciously pulled his meager cloak more tightly about him and ignored whatever was crawling across his bare ankle. There was something about the Earl of Somerset that drew him, inspired the barest inclination to trust him (or at least listen to what he had to say), in spite of Devin's earlier suspicions.

Mayhap, one part of his mind thought with irony, this inclination to trust a complete stranger was the result of three weeks of imprisonment in a place little better than the stinking hold of a slaver.

Devin finally spoke, wondering how Somerset managed not to gag at the stench around them, as did most upon first entering Newgate. He also wished he'd been clean and presentable. But that didn't happen in Newgate Prison unless one had a supply of shillings to bribe any number of turnkeys and inmates of some stature. "If you were a true friend to my late father, then get me out of here!" he growled.

Somerset nodded. "Only if you tell me your side of the story."

Devin stood and moved closer, studying the earl's shadowed face. He noted that Somerset didn't back away. "My schooner was attacked. The hostile brigantine flew no flag, nor did she identify herself, in spite of my having requested so three times. My men were at the ready, and we were heaving to. I foolishly gave no order to fire until the brig fired two volleys at us."

Somerset nodded. "It seems your first mate gave a different account."

"Glasby? God *damn* the man!" He flung up one hand in a disgusted dismissal. "No doubt they questioned him in Port Royal after he'd swilled his weight in killdevil."

"Whatever his condition, he purportedly swore the brigantine flew the British flag."

Devin swung away angrily. "Damn it, he lied! All they had to do was ask the others."

"You know a first officer's word would hold more weight."

"Then it looks as if I'll die in this hole," Devin bitterly threw over his shoulder. He felt as if the tenuous grip he'd had on a rescue line was slipping, threatening to send him into an abyss from which there would be no escape.

Somerset moved forward and put a firm hand on Devin's shoulder. "I'm willing to pay your way out of here—I've already spoken to the king—in exchange for a reciprocal favor."

Devin turned slowly, and the earl's hand fell away. Suspicion darkened his eyes, flattened his eyebrows. But well-concealed hope also fluttered to life within him as he repeated, "Favor?"

"Aye. My youngest daughter is on her way to Jamaica even as we speak. I gave in to her wishes that she leave England for a while because the man to whom she was betrothed ran off to France to marry another woman. Or so I told Merry." Somerset shrugged lightly and gazed unseeingly over Devin's shoulder for a moment. "You see, after I'd discovered how despicable he was beneath the surface, I set him up for a fall, then threatened blackmail after he took the bait. 'Twas most unfortunate that Meredyth thought herself in love with him."

"But what has all this . . . ? Devin trailed off, thinking suddenly that his weeks in Newgate had robbed him of not only his sense of humor but also his wits. Of course, he'd spent the last two decades on the Main. He knew Jamaica like the back of his hand, had a town house in Port Royal when he needed a respite from sailing.

The earl remained silent, obviously sensing Devin's

thoughts, his eyes steady on the younger man's face. "And you want me to . . . ah, keep her out of trouble?"

"A simple enough task, don't you think?" Somerset asked in reply. "Surely she'll tire of Jamaica before the year ends. If you promise to hold to your end of the agreement, I'll see that you get back to Jamaica, and I'll provide funds to help refurbish your schooner if and when you find it. In addition, I'll pay you the sum of 10,000 pounds once Meredyth is safely back in London."

Surely, Devin thought, Somerset was a trusting fool. Devin could have been Attila the Hun for all the earl knew, could take his ship and sail away to the Mediterranean and roam the waters off the northern coast of Africa.

As a matter of fact, he mused, that wasn't a bad idea.

"And should you decide to renege on the proposed bargain," Somerset added, as if reading Devin's thoughts, "or carry it out with anything less than utmost dependability, I do have other agents in the area who can look into your activities and either report to me or take over in your stead. Or both."

By the Mass! Devin thought. It wasn't Somerset's threat that disturbed him so much as the image of himself trailing around Jamaica after a pampered, long-suffering daughter of the nobility, a pitiful, martyrlike soul who believed her husband-to-be had run off with another woman. Surely she was undesirable as the day was long, for, in spite of the earl's explanation, what man in his right mind would leave the daughter of an earl at the altar unless she were absolutely hideous?

A powerful and determined earl could move mountains, if he so chose, reminded a voice. *A man of lesser station would have little choice but to go along* . . .

He sighed inwardly. Even if he accepted Somerset's offer, he most certainly would be the butt of every joke circulating around the Caribbean. Yet that wasn't his main consideration.

As much as Devin hated the thought of remaining in Newgate one more minute than necessary, he said, "Give me the night to think it over."

"As you wish." Devin could have sworn one corner of the earl's mouth quivered with subtle amusement. He couldn't know, however, that Somerset was thinking that he knew just enough about Devin James Chandler to suspect that the man would give his melancholy daughter something else to think about besides Lucien Pendwell.

"Until the morrow then." The earl held out one hand again, and this time Devin reluctantly accepted it. Somerset called for the turnkey.

As pride held Devin James Chandler moored to the spot while the Earl of Somerset left the cell, he wondered if he hadn't just committed the biggest blunder of his entire life. For any number of reasons, Keir St. Andrews could decide that his trust in Devin was ill-placed; therefore, what guarantee did he have that the man wouldn't reconsider his offer and fail to return in the morn? Or, even worse, that the entire interview and offer were nothing more than a sadistic joke?

After all, there were many who wouldn't hesitate to slit his throat and toss him to the sharks if they could prove what he'd really been up to these last few years on the Main.

One

"Christ, I *hate* snakes!"

Even as he muttered the words, Devin Chandler stared down in revulsion at the brightly colored reptile as it slithered across his boot and into the foliage that pressed in upon the path. Renewed sweat broke out across his forehead, but it had little to do with the steamy rain forest around him.

The knowledge that constrictors were not poisonous wasn't any comfort, either, and goosebumps pricked his flesh.

His face settling into determined lines, he pushed onward and upward, ignoring the lush flora around him. He loved the sea and the pristine beaches of sand and even the sheer, rocky cliffs; he loved the mountains and open fields and light woodlands. But he also preferred neat and orderly gardens of tropical hibiscus and poinsettia and orchids, with every creature in its place, menagerie-like, not popping out from the all but impenetrable depths of a hot and humid rain forest and offering the threat of sharp teeth and claws or venomous bites.

He hacked his way through the more overrun sections of the path that led upward to his destination, the machete and dagger in his belt his only weapons. A pistol was safely in the saddlebag on the single donkey that trailed behind him. He would have preferred to have it tucked into his belt, but it would have been too bulky and hampered his progress. If nothing else, he wanted to get to the mission high up in the Blue

Mountains where this St. Andrews woman was cloistered, take her measure and calculate his chances of successfully going on about his own business with only token participation in the earl's bargain.

Surely, if this Meredyth was content to remain secluded in the mission, there was little reason for his presence. And he had a score of more pressing matters to attend to, like contacting Woodrow Kingsley and finding his schooner, the *Lady Elysia,* and checking on the condition of his town house in Port Royal and the state of his belongings there, rounding up any of his old crew he could find, then hiring on any new men he needed.

As promised, the earl had provided Devin with transportation across the Atlantic. They'd set sail for Port Royal, and Devin had had much time to think on the voyage.

He had to be crackbrained to be chasing down some hoity-toity daughter of a blueblood, he thought with a grimace of disgust.

The sound of rushing water met his ears, and instantly he knew he was nearing the small river that cascaded down the mountainside. His spirits began to lift, for the mission wasn't too far from the stream.

Suddenly, a tremendous bellow shook the ground beneath him and brought him up short, machete poised in mid-air. "On Harry Morgan's soul," he said under his breath, "what in hell was that?"

"Cocodrilo," a voice said from behind him.

Devin started slightly, having almost forgotten the silent youth he'd hired to prod the reluctant donkey up the mountain trail and help with the cutting when the going got too tough. He threw a glance over his shoulder and met the boy's brown eyes. "Of course, 'tis a croc, but why in the hell is it bellowing like Armageddon was here?"

"Tal vez tiene hambre, Señor Capitán."

Devin slapped his palm to his forehead. "Hungry! Now why didn't I think of that?" He rolled his eyes and turned back to the path. "No doubt his wick is lit," he muttered under his breath, one corner of his mouth quirking in empathy, "but his chances of finding a lady love up here are a mite slim."

A sudden thought struck him. "But mayhap he'd be interested in the lady Meredyth." He laughed aloud and renewed his ascent with vigorous steps in the wake of his jest. The sound of rushing water in a swollen tributary became louder, the result of the beginning of the rainy season, and he knew he was getting close to Father Tomas's mission. It was a haven to many runaway African slaves, or Cimaroons, and a few Carib and Arawak Indians indigenous to South America and the Caribbee Islands. He'd sent a few himself to Father Tomas, on the sly.

The wily old Spanish priest kept a well-fed crocodile in the stream up ahead as a deterrent for those who hunted runaway slaves, and no doubt the lonely old fellow was randy as a sailor after six months at sea.

Another roar rent the air, sending birds scattering through the living emerald canopy above them. Hard on its heels came the desperate shout of a man. Devin began to sprint, as much as it was possible on a partially overgrown rain forest path that wound up a mountainside.

"Juan," he called over his shoulder. "Hurry!" His machete flashed in the lancets of sunlight irregularly piercing the trees as he battled the entangling foliage to get to the stream ahead. His face was bathed with sweat, his muscled right arm arcing and slashing relentlessly with grim purpose.

Another cry, closer to a scream this time, pierced the air, and Devin feared he would be too late to help the man if the latter had had the misfortune of tangling with a crocodile.

He emerged into a clearing, where foaming water burbled over smooth-worn rocks before pooling a stone's throw downstream. Devin instantly picked out an angry croc, his teeth sunk into the leg of a man clinging desperately to a tree branch overhanging the more placid waters. Another crocodile, slightly smaller, was slowly moving in the wake of the first.

"Jesus!" he swore softly. "One I can wrestle, but not two."

He swung back to Juan, who was huffing and puffing and yanking on the reins of the donkey, which obviously sensed danger and had firmly planted its hooves in the moist soil of the riverbank. "Can you shoot a pistol?" he demanded.

Juan nodded, though with less conviction than Devin would have liked. "Aim the pistol from the saddlebag at the second croc, and don't shoot unless he attacks. *¿Comprende?*"

"*Sí.*"

Devin paused just long enough to make certain the boy found the pistol, which was already loaded with powder and shot, then skipped nimbly across the row of stones that bridged the stream. He slipped only once and cursed his fleeting clumsiness while a man's life hung in the balance.

The man cried out again, in a language one part of Devin's mind recognized as either Arawak or Carib. As he reached the far bank, he glanced up at the struggling man and saw that his hands were slipping from the tree branch as the crocodile moved backward, pulling.

Devin withdrew his dagger and aimed it right at the croc's head, silently invoking a higher power to guide his aim. Although he was fairly adept at handling a dagger, he was more skilled with sword and pistol. Throwing the dagger forward, his aim went slightly wide and he ended up embedding the blade in the crocodile's left front leg.

At the same time, the pistol exploded from across the water, startling the wounded amphibian enough to make it roar in rage, thus releasing its hold on its victim's leg.

In a split second, Devin made a decision.

He couldn't count on the animal's retreat, which would have enabled him to reach the man and help him onto the bank. But Devin wouldn't reach the injured Indian in time to prevent his falling into the water.

He dashed toward the water and launched himself at the crocodile, boots and all, hoping that Juan would use his second and last shot on the smaller amphibian if it moved to attack him.

He landed ungracefully near the animal's injured leg, and as it turned in reaction toward the geysering water, its great jaw yawning before him, Devin dared to snatch at the upended dagger hilt. He tugged mightily, and it tore free. But the crocodile was now almost on top of him.

He had no choice but to drive the blade up through its lower jaw.

From across the stream, the pistol barked again. The crocodile swung away, his teeth inches from the dagger blade, before Devin could drive it home. The amphibian made a half-circle, and blood reddened the churning water. Evidently, Juan had hit him.

Devin silently thanked the youth for shooting the first croc rather than the second, as he'd originally been told, and scuttled away to the bank. Something came crashing down on top of him just as he began to straighten, knocking him off balance and pushing him back under water. He came up sputtering and spewed out a mouthful of river water.

It was the Indian, who'd finally lost his grip.

Devin glanced at the retreating crocodiles and saw Juan waving madly toward the closest bank, motioning him to get out. Devin flung his wet hair out of his eyes and grabbed the motionless Indian beneath his armpits. As he dragged him up the bank until he was completely clear of the water, he heard rather than saw Juan cajole and prod the recalcitrant donkey over the ford.

His mind was on the mangled leg of the man beside him. After one more glance across the stream to make certain the crocodiles had retreated to the far bank, Devin turned his attention to the Indian's wounds.

The dunk in the river had cleansed away much of the blood, but the two deepest lacerations were still bleeding freely. Thankfully, although the knee appeared injured as well, the man's thigh—in which any deep cut could have easily caused him to bleed to death—was untouched.

Devin tore off his light linen shirt and used his teeth to start several strips, with which he intended to bind the Indian's wounds. "What in God's name were you trying to do here, you poor devil?" he mumbled more to himself than the injured man. "These creatures are kept well-fed by those at the mission. Their purpose is to scare off snooping miscreants, not make a meal of those who seek shelter here."

The man's lashes fluttered, surprising Devin, for he'd thought him unconscious. As the victim's lids raised, Devin looked into deep brown eyes filled with pain . . . and something else. The stranger tried to speak, but Devin couldn't make out his weakly uttered words. Although he knew enough Spanish and French to get by—most English seamen did—he knew next to nothing of the languages of the Arawak and Carib peoples.

By this time Juan was at his side, hunkering down beside him and staring at the Indian. "Will he die?" he asked.

"Not if I have any say, but we need to stop the bleeding and get him to the mission. We're not that far away." Devin deftly wrapped one linen strip about the first gash.

"To . . . mas. Padre . . . Tomas," the Indian whispered. "You?"

"He thinks you're the old priest," Juan said, his young features somber.

Devin's eyes widened briefly, then he grinned good-naturedly and shook his head. "Not me, *amigo*. That croc must have injured your head, too, if you think me a man of the cloth." Then he added softly, "Although I've used that ruse to gain the confidence of a lady or two." His grin widened, turned wicked.

He knotted the ends of the first bandage, then tore another from his shirt. "Keep an eye on those crocs, boy," he told Juan, then asked the Indian, whose eyes were steadily, soberly, upon him in spite of his light-hearted banter, "Your name? *¿Como se llama?*"

"I am . . . Bakámu."

Devin nodded, glad that this Bakámu spoke some English. He pointed to his chest. "Chandler. Devin Chandler." He swung his pointing finger toward Juan. "Juan."

Bakámu nodded.

"Do you think you can ride to the mission?" He indicated the small, gray donkey with a tilt of his head.

Bakámu sent a glance toward the animal. *"Sí,* Chan-ler," then closed his eyes.

"Bring me the killdevil from the bag," Devin told Juan, and the boy jumped to do his bidding. Devin uncorked the bottle with his teeth, then slid one arm beneath Bakámu's shoulders, angled him upward, and put the rim to the Indian's lips.

Bakámu turned his head away in refusal. "Drink!" Devin ordered. " 'Twill help dull the pain."

Evidently Bakámu realized Devin wouldn't be denied, for he obeyed, spat out half of his first swallow, and was forced to drink again. Then once more. "The more, the better," Devin assured him.

Juan brought the donkey closer to the wounded man, and with the youth's help, Devin hiked Bakámu to the animal's back. His feet almost touched the ground, but the Indian riding the donkey was best for everyone under the circumstances. Except for the donkey, Devin thought wryly.

He looked up at Bakámu, holding tightly to the mule's mane. "Where'd you hit the croc?" he asked then, looking over at Juan, one fair eyebrow tented.

"The tail of *el cocodrilo* is shorter now, *Señor Capitán.*" And the boy grinned, revealing even white teeth against his olive skin.

In spite of the situation, Devin threw back his head and shouted with laughter, the rich sound of it causing a cacophony of flapping wings as parrots, parakeets, and hummingbirds scrambled through the verdant network of tree boughs toward the all-but-invisible sky.

If a man couldn't find humor in even the grimmest situation, Devin believed, then life wasn't worth living.

Meredyth gazed at the breathtaking waterfall before her, thinking of what her mother had told her of her long-ago journey to Jamaica with Meredyth's father . . . as his captive. The Countess of Somerset had blushingly admitted to her youngest daughter that she and the earl had made love beside the very pool at her feet and most probably had conceived Meredyth's older sister, Kerra, there.

It was ironic, she thought, that Kerra, conceived beside a waterfall in exotic Jamaica, was now happily married and raising a family just outside of London, while Meredyth stood near the very place of Kerra's conception, halfway around the world from her family and all she held dear. And by her own choice.

Memories of her family blurred her vision and tugged in her breast. She allowed herself the luxury of thinking of them—her mother and father, sister and brothers. But she doused the flare of self-pity that often accompanied her thoughts of the man who'd broken her heart by running off with another.

She raised her face to the light mist coming from the curtain of water cascading over the precipice above her, welcoming the coolness against the heat of her cheeks, a stinging warmth fueled by the painful remnants of humiliation that festered anew every time she thought of Lucien Pendwell and his abandonment.

Her chest began to tighten, her eyes stung, and Meredyth knew she had to redirect her thoughts and quickly, lest she cry more useless tears over a man who wasn't worth one of them, in spite of his laughing blue eyes, his sand-blond hair, and well-cut features, the undeniable charm that had taken her in like a fish sighting a juicy worm.

Her fingers curled at her sides in anger—at herself and at Lucien Pendwell. She would never again look twice at a handsome man, never again be counted among the legions of other women who would lust over that man and then try to lure him away from the woman who truly loved him. And if she were ever addled enough to consider marriage again, it would be to the ugliest and oldest man she could find.

A movement caught her eye suddenly, scattering her dour thoughts, and her gaze alighted upon a tiny lizard skittering along the smooth stone edge of the pool near which she stood. It was brightly colored and stood out against the dull hue of the rocky floor. Meredyth immediately thought of Carla, the little girl who'd lost part of one foot beneath a runaway boulder. The child loved animals, and Meredyth immediately dropped to a most unladylike crouch and began a slow, stealthy pursuit of the unsuspecting creature, who'd stilled near the rim of the pool.

As she edged closer, Meredyth identified it as a young anole, a relative of the chameleon. It was a male, she guessed, for suddenly its bright orange dewlap began to waver back and forth. Her new friend, Dionisio (a Cimaroon who'd known Meredyth's mother and father) had said that was typical of male anoles. She noted it could change colors, as many of them did. Now, against the gray slate beneath the creature, only the dewlap stood out as the pigment in its skin adjusted to its surroundings. Or mayhap it was a sign of fright, she thought.

She suddenly remembered her straw hat, the wide-brimmed, unadorned bonnet that Father Tomas insisted she wear to protect her fair skin from the sun, though she often forgot. She slowly reached up for it, but the shadow of her moving arm, or her proximity, evidently alerted the anole to danger and it tiptoed a few steps farther away.

With childlike exuberance (and an admirable agility), Meredyth swiftly launched herself toward it with outstretched arms, the hat forgotten even as it went flying off to the side. All she could think of in those moments was the joy that would light Carla's face when she saw the tiny creature. It didn't take much to amuse the child, and Meredyth found herself going out of her way to keep the little girl's mind off her tragic handicap.

She landed hard on the stone floor, her elbows cracking against it and her chin thudding with her landing. But triumph filled her as she felt the tickle of the little lizard against her tightly cupped palms.

"Ah-hah!" she exclaimed with soft-spoken satisfaction.

Devin watched from the pathway as Lady Meredyth St. Andrews inched herself back into a kneeling position, her bottom, most intriguingly outlined against the cotton of her skirt, unwittingly aimed straight at him. His first thought was that she was performing some kind of religious ritual, prostrating herself on the ground with such zeal. What would the Jesuit Father Tomas think of such pagan activities from a supposedly civilized Englishwoman?

He smirked, thinking he could understand why a betrothed with any sense might change his mind and flee to France (at the lady's sire's urging or nay!) after witnessing such queer behavior. Many nobles were considered "strange" (by ordinary people, at least) because some practiced interfamily marriages to keep their grand and ancient bloodlines "pure."

But as she sat back on her haunches and reached for her straw hat, her left hand held firmly to her chest, Devin realized she had managed to trap some hapless creature, clutching it to her breast as if it were Spanish treasure. Whatever for? he wondered as he watched her slap the hat back over her chestnut curls and slowly rise to her feet, her bare feet.

It certainly hadn't taken her long to abandon any ladylike behavior she would have learned in England as the daughter of an earl. Mayhap she was getting long in the tooth and strange in her ways, which would also explain her former fiance's flight.

He stood there, one arm crossed over his chest, his other elbow braced upon it, fingers stroking his chin thoughtfully.

Meredyth St. Andrews slowly turned away from the song of the water tumbling into the crystal clear reservoir below, toward the path, both hands still cupped about her prize.

Her hat was askew, covering her eyebrows and shading all of her features except her chin and the blood that trickled down it. She peered into her loosely curled hands as if to make certain her captive was still there, then started forward.

As she neared Devin, obviously still unaware of his presence (for God's sake, he could have been some n'er-do-well pirate looking for a bit of fluff and fun, he thought with disgust), she raised her cupped hands to the brim of her hat and impatiently pushed it back so that it settled properly in place.

"Have you caught your dinner, mistress?" he asked suddenly, laughter lacing his words.

Meredyth started at the sound, her eyes widening as they took in his tall, unfamiliar form so unexpectedly—and unnervingly—close to her.

She tilted her face upward to meet his gaze, and Devin encountered vivid green eyes; eyes that put emeralds to shame; eyes framed by dark, finely arched brows and thick, curling lashes and long lower lashes that spidered over the fragile flesh beneath like sable gossamer filaments.

Eyes a man could get lost in, he thought with one last remnant of reason in the face of this totally unexpected assault upon his senses, of the paralysis of his normally nimble tongue before this young woman he had so soundly dismissed as utterly unappealing in every way; this vision who, in his ignorance and, yes, arrogance, he'd convinced himself was not only undesirable enough to send a suitor running but also so lacking in assets that she'd hidden herself in the Blue Mountains of Jamaica with her father's permission; this vision he'd concluded was not worth his time or attention save for the opportunity to escape Newgate, return to Jamaica, and find his ship. And collect his 10,000 pounds within a year.

"Who are you?" she asked, alarm narrowing her striking eyes. Her query helped bring Devin back from the brink of a sweet, inexplicable madness. Not, however, before he'd taken in her small, straight nose with its sprinkling of freckles, her sweet, rosy mouth that had momentarily formed a rounded "O," and the blight of blood threading down her delicate chin. Her sun-kissed face bespoke a disregard for wearing her ridiculous straw hat and caused him to smile at the thought like a grinning Bedlamite.

Devin got the impression she wasn't so much afraid of him as taken off guard by his presence.

"Captain *Devil* Chandler, at your service," he said, recovering and bowing just enough to make a mockery of the movement.

Meredyth caught the implication and chose to ignore it. After all, what would a buccaneer know of manners? she thought with acerbity. And he was obviously a buccaneer, with that name and his single flashing gold earring, as well as his sinfully long (almost as long as hers), sun-bleached locks bound with a leather thong and hanging over one shoulder. He wore only half a shirt, the top half, leaving the flat planes of his stomach and navel exposed beneath a ragged fringe of what looked like linen. And a fine, dark-blond arrow of hair pointing downward toward his . . .

She dragged her eyes upward. Why, the posturing pirate! she thought in sudden irritation. Even his eyes—a pale blue or gray from what she could discern against the sun—were lit with arrogance or conceit or mocking humor or something much too openly appraising.

A tickle on her wrist made her look down. To her dismay, the anole had slipped between her unconsciously relaxed fingers and was skittering up her arm. She opened her mouth to protest as if the lizard would freeze in its tracks upon command. Instantly one large, firm hand was over her mouth, the other snatching the hapless chameleon from the area of her bare elbow.

"There's no need to scream and alert the entire mission," Devin said, close to her ear. His warm breath caressed her cheek, and Meredyth felt a sudden and very unwelcome spurt of sensation deep down inside.

"I wasn't going to scream, Captain *Devil* Chandler," she replied with an indignant lift of one dark eyebrow and began to all but pry his fingers from Carla's gift-to-be. "If you'll be so kind as to give me back my lizard, then you can go about your . . . business, and I'll go about mine."

"*Your* lizard?" he queried, bringing additional color to her cheeks.

"Aye!" she snapped, growing more annoyed by the moment.

He nodded somberly, yet she had the distinct impression he was humoring her like a spoiled child.

"Ah . . . I see. Why don't you carry it in your hat?" he suggested innocently. "You'll be less likely to crush it that way."

His whole body, indecently close to hers, exuded warmth and a magnetic maleness that made the memory of Lucien Pendwell recede like snow melting before a fire.

"Here." And before she could object, he bent and retrieved a storm-tossed palm leaf from the ground nearby that looked the perfect size for what he obviously had in mind. He plucked the hat from her head, dropped the anole inside, and quickly laid the leaf over it.

"I'll take it now," she said stiffly, reaching for the hat.

He held it away from her. "Ah, ah, ah. What of the laws in Jamaica against pilfering lizards? Especially those who are under age?"

She didn't notice the amusement in his eyes, so intent was she on removing herself from his presence, and she ignored the deliberately ludicrous reference to the anole's age and size. She'd come to the mission to get away from treacherous men, heartbreakers who thought they were God's gift to women. He was dangerous, she knew instinctively. He presumed too much and was brazen as a drunken sailor.

And she didn't like the way he made her feel inside when he was close to her, like some spinster time had bypassed, deprived of a man for decades, yet still possessing enough life to pant against her will over his masculinity like a bitch hound in heat.

And that thought not only brought renewed color to her face but stirred up memories of Lucien Pendwell's perfidy as well.

He watched with satisfaction as doubt flitted across her features. But his smugness was short-lived. "Then I'll appeal to Governor White, Captain Chandler," she threw back at him, "for the creature will help lift the spirits of an injured child at the mission."

She had absolutely no sense of humor, he decided, in spite of her looks, and that would definitely bore a man to death. After he'd sampled the delights hidden beneath her simple peasant blouse and full skirt, of course . . .

She held out one hand in expectation, her green eyes narrowing dangerously, and Devin suddenly thought of the Earl of Somerset and of how he might look when crossed.

"Now, for the last time, Captain *Devil* Chandler," she said levelly, "be so kind as to return my hat and its contents, won't you?"

"As you wish, mistress," he said with a sigh as sweet as that of an angel and did as she asked, making certain his hand lingered beneath hers for a heartbeat longer than necessary before withdrawing his fingers from the palm leaf. "But won't you tell me who you are before you leave?"

"That, Captain, is none of your business." She moved past him, her skirt swaying gracefully with her movements, her dainty pink toes and slender ankles peeping from beneath it with each step toward the path, leaving the sweet and lingering scent of violets in springtime.

Oh, but 'tis my business, Meredyth St. Andrews, whether

you wish it or nay . . . The thought came bursting through his mind from nowhere, making him temporarily forget his intention of circumventing his part of the bargain with the Earl of Somerset.

Two

To Meredyth's dismay, Chandler followed her to the mission. Not that it was so far away, but not once did any of the men who kept watch over the small settlement materialize out of the thinning forest to confront him, as they would any stranger. Father Tomas's flock was made up primarily of runaways—Africans and a few Arawak and Carib Indians. Some were outcasts, but all found a haven with the old priest.

For a while it didn't register in Meredyth's mind that Chandler might have been known to Father Tomas and those under the Jesuit's protection. The captain looked disreputable enough to pose a threat to those at the mission—perhaps he even dealt in the slave trade itself.

Yet another side of Meredyth, a fair-minded side that was inclined to give a man the benefit of the doubt (at least until Lucien had left her embittered and suspicious of any decent-looking man), conceded that many of the seamen who sailed her father's ships looked equally unsavory or threatening. And while they were not considered proper gentlemen in the genteel sense, every one of them who worked for Keir St. Andrews was as trustworthy and loyal as any European of rank and means, or he was swiftly relieved of his duties.

So, Meredyth reasoned as she hurried up the pathway, either he'd taken them all by surprise, which she doubted, or he was known to, and trusted by, Father Tomas.

She suddenly slowed her pace, ostensibly to show him that she wasn't fleeing like a frightened rabbit, but more realistically so that she could turn her head and listen to the sound of him following her and judge just how far behind he was.

But the forest was quiet—a thinner forest at this altitude made up primarily of conifers and less sumptuous foliage than the rainforest. It was rockier as well, and while one didn't have to be as concerned about snakes and the like, the footing could be treacherous.

Where was he? she wondered as she listened to the wind sighing through the trees, carrying the crisp fragrance of pine and fecund flora; the sound of the waterfall had receded to a vague whisper in the distance behind her, but there was no sign of anyone else around.

She felt the tickle of the anole against the palm leaf beneath her hand. That brought her thoughts back to her mission. Why in the world should she care what happened to the man? If he tumbled into one of the many gorges that sliced through the Blue Mountains it would have been fine with her. One less high-handed—

She abruptly shoved aside the thought and pressed forward once again. She was thinking more and more like a bitter shrew, she realized, and suspected that lately she was capable of sounding like one, too. It didn't sit well with her. One didn't have to become spinster-strange and waspish just because one had decided not to marry. Ever.

Ah, ah, ah . . . What of the laws in Jamaica against pilfering lizards?

Had there been a hint of mischief in his voice? In his eyes? She didn't know him well enough (nor did she care to) to be certain. But her own ludicrous reply kept echoing in her ears, making her wish she hadn't mentioned so drastic a measure as appealing to acting Governor White over proprietary rights to a lizard!

Only months before she would have laughed aloud at his absurd warning, no matter who he'd been, and dismissed it as a jest, for laughter and a sweet nature were an integral part of her disposition, inherited from her mother, or so she'd been told.

When Meredyth reached the mission, it was obvious something was afoot. No doubt it had to do with Chandler. That sour thought made her ignore the small group gathered around the infirmary that stood to the side of the mission church and march right up to the hut Carla shared with her mother.

The day was still warm enough for the child to be sitting out in the sun, but Meredyth found her inside the dim, one-room home. She paused inside the doorway, allowing her eyes to adjust to the lower light level.

The little girl was face down on her pallet, and soft sobs shook her small body. "Carla?" Meredyth said in a low voice as she approached the child.

Carla raised her dark head. Her eyes were swollen, her cheeks painted with tears.

"Look!" Meredyth exclaimed, desperate to make the little girl smile. She held out her hat, her hand still over the leaf that held the tiny amphibian imprisoned. "I've brought you a new friend. *Un nuevo amigo.*"

Curiosity immediately transformed the child's face as her gaze went to the straw hat. She pushed herself into a sitting position, ran one light brown arm across her nose, and gingerly swung her bandaged foot to join the other already on the floor.

"Your crutch," Meredyth reminded her and nodded in its direction. She swung away then, toward the door, and said, "Come outside, *niña,* and see what I have."

Once out of the warm, stuffy hut and beneath the benign afternoon sunshine, Meredyth felt her spirits lift. Fresh air filled her lungs. Marry come up! she thought, where was the child's mother? Or the other children with whom she usually played?

She remembered the gathering at the infirmary, but first wanted to give Carla her new pet. Just as Meredyth was wondering what was keeping the little girl, she came limping through the curtained doorway, leaning heavily on the hand-hewn crutch Dionisio had made especially for her. She paused just outside the door, her eyes going once again to the hat. "What's in there, Señorita Meredyth?" she asked. "And is it truly for me?"

Meredyth nodded, her eyes asparkle. "Come see for yourself."

Carla moved awkwardly toward her, then stopped. The breeze ruffled her blue-black hair and began to dry her damp cheeks as she glanced questioningly up at Meredyth again.

"Oh, very well," she said with a sigh of feigned resignation and slid the leaf over the slightest bit. "You may only have a quick peek, or he'll get away and go scooting off into the forest. Then the entire mission will have to chase after him! Can't you just see Padre Tomas a-running, his robes flying about his ankles?"

Something miraculous happened then. As Carla leaned to peek into the dim recess beneath the leaf, the anole's head popped through the small opening. Its tongue poked the air, eliciting a giggle from the child.

"Oh," Meredyth exclaimed and slid the leaf back in place. The sound startled Carla, but she'd evidently recognized the creature. "Anole!" Her face lit, exactly as Meredyth had envisioned.

"And he's small—not much more than a baby, so he'll need extra special care. Mayhap we can ask Dionisio to fashion some kind of cage for him, what do you think?"

Carla threw her arms about Meredyth's waist, allowing the crutch to fall and almost knocking the bonnet from Meredyth's grip. "Gracias, Señorita Meredyth!" she exclaimed in a muffled but definitely delighted voice.

"Still torturing that poor chameleon, I see," said a male voice from behind them.

Meredyth turned toward the owner, knowing who it was.

"I suggest you set it free and come to the infirmary, ah . . . Lady Meredyth, I believe the good padre called you? We've a wounded man there, who may lose his leg. Father Tomas says he can use your help."

His caustic remark stung, and dismay at his rebuke briefly registered on her features before Meredyth could think of an appropriate answer.

Carla unwittingly came to her rescue. "Señorita Meredyth would never torture anything!" she said stoutly in Meredyth's defense. "She's not torturing *la lagartija!*"

With a glance, Devin took in Carla's reddened eyes, her bandaged foot, and the fallen crutch. He nodded, his voice softening as he said, "I've not come to debate the issue of confining a wild creature, *niña,* but rather to fetch Lady Meredyth, who is urgently needed at the moment." He bent to retrieve the little girl's crutch.

As he handed it to Carla, a tall and slender African man came lithely striding up to them. Dionisio. Meredyth instantly sensed a tension between the two men but thought she could understand why anyone would take an instant dislike to Devil Chandler.

Meredyth's whole expression brightened, Devin noted, as she looked up at the Cimaroon, this man who was like some dark forest deity and who'd evidently taken it upon himself to be Chandler's shadow.

It's a wonder the man didn't follow me to the falls Devin thought with annoyance, probably had, just hadn't revealed himself.

What was it about Meredyth St. Andrews that seemed to appeal to the African's protectiveness? he wondered. And his increased animosity toward Devin? He wondered if the Cimaroon would ever trust him. Even a neutral acceptance would be welcomed, he thought with rue.

Unexpectedly, as if she read his thoughts, Meredyth said to Devin, "Dionisio is a dear family friend. He's especially close to my lady mother."

Now how could that be possible? Devin wondered, inwardly bemused.

"Will you make a home for Carla's new pet, Dionisio?" Meredyth asked the dark man as she handed him the hat.

He peered beneath the leaf, and a broad grin spread over his dark features. "Anole? For Carla, *si?*" He nodded. "Dionisio can make good one." He effortlessly picked up Carla with one sinewy arm, making her giggle again, and sending the crutch tumbling to the ground. Several other children gathered around them, and Devin swung away.

"I'll tell Father Tomas that when you're good and ready you'll—"

"I'm coming," she said shortly as, after a smile and a wave at Carla, she fell into step behind him.

"When are you going to clean the blood off your face?" he asked bluntly, barely turning his head to acknowledge her.

Meredyth's hand went to her injured chin, for she'd forgotten all about hitting it against the rocky ground. For some reason, the dried and crusty blood she felt beneath her fingers only increased her anger at Chandler. "And just how did you get back to the mission before I did?" she demanded in answer, for, her anger notwithstanding, she remembered her father often telling her taking the offensive was the best defense.

"I sneaked off into the forest, of course," he answered blithely. "Or, mayhap I'm a warlock and flew back." He shot her a covert glance.

But Meredyth wasn't listening to his words. "And how dare you tell me to set the anole free in front of Carla," she asked through set teeth. "Have you no sensitivity? Or did you lose it while doing your dirty work on the Main?" She tossed her head, freeing her cheek of several loosened strands of rich chestnut hair.

Devin couldn't help but note the way the sunshine emphasized the deep auburn tint in it. No drab sparrow, this, he thought with inexplicable irritation and silently cursed Keir St. Andrews and his bloody bargain.

He'd done his duty, having ascertained that the girl was beneath the benevolent aegis of Father Tomas and far enough away from rowdy and dangerous buccaneers to remain relatively safe. He could leave now, for she appeared content and seemed to fit right in. Prim, righteous Sister Meredyth.

And the sooner he departed, the better. He had a lot of unfinished business to attend to.

As they neared the infirmary, Devin stood aside and let Meredyth enter the cool, dim room off the mission church. He wondered how long it would take her to faint at the sight and distinctive smell of blood as he followed her inside.

The wounded man was conscious as Meredyth took Father Tomas's place beside him and began to bathe the lacerations. She couldn't help but notice how, after a glance at her, his eyes went immediately to Chandler, an almost worshipful look in their loam-brown depths.

"This is Bakámu," Father Tomas, a man in his sixties with a vitality in his eyes that belied his thinning silver tonsure, told her. "He was trying to reach the mission when he was attacked by one of *los cocodrilos.*" He shook his graying head and clucked his tongue. "Dionisio mayhap did not satisfy the animal's appetite this day."

Devin watched as a rush of color touched Meredyth's cheeks. "Dionisio has been feeding them for years, didn't you tell me so, Father? Surely he wouldn't be so careless." She rinsed the bloodied cloth in the pink-tinged water and moved up to Bakámu's mutilated knee. Her eyes on her work, she added, "He must have somehow antagonized the animals, provoked them to attack."

The censure that edged her words prompted Devin to ask with heavy irony, "And pray tell, milady, how one can accomplish such a thing from a tree?"

Meredyth ignored him, concentrating on her task. But Bakámu, who evidently understood what was being said, muttered something in what sounded like a jumble of his native tongue and Spanish.

"He says he'd taken a *siesta* in the tree. When he awoke

and swung down, he evidently stepped on what turned out *not* to be a rock, but rather *un cocodrilo*," Father Tomas translated.

Meredyth nodded. "And how did you find him?" she asked the priest.

"Capitán Chandler saved him and brought him here."

"Vision," Bakámu said. "Chan-ler . . ."

His words were lost on the others, however, as Meredyth turned a disbelieving look toward Devin. It quickly turned uncharacteristically disdainful. "You brought this man to the mission only to abandon him and go roaming through the forest, spying on people?"

Devin scowled at her accusatory tone. "Don't flatter yourself, Lady Meredyth. He was in good hands, and Father Tomas asked if someone would fetch you."

"Will he lose the leg?" Father Tomas asked, a frown of concern furrowing his brow.

"I don't think so, if 'tis tended properly," Devin answered for Meredyth.

"Vision . . ." Bakámu repeated, then mumbled a word in his native language.

But Meredyth's attention was still on Chandler, her anger growing every time he opened his mouth. "If you're a physician, then pray tell why you deserted your charge and—"

"I'm no physician, he's not 'my charge,' and I already told you—"

"Chan-ler," the charge muttered.

One of the women beside Meredyth spoke softly to Bakámu in Arawak. He answered, and Meredyth caught the name "Chan-ler" again. She realized she was allowing Chandler to distract her attention from the wounded Indian, and she returned her attention to the task at hand, asking for a clean needle and thread.

"What did he say?" Chandler asked, shifting his focus to Bakámu and dropping to his haunches beside the Arawak.

The woman, Maria, answered, "He says you are his vision

quest. He calls you by name, 'Chandler,' whose face he saw in a dream when he was but a youth."

The room fell silent, save for Bakámu's breathing. His eyes were locked with Devin's.

"Vision quest?" Meredyth finally asked, lifting her eyes from her work to meet those of Father Tomas standing behind Devin. His expression was very somber.

"Sí," the Jesuit told her. " 'Tis very important to the Indians. It means Capitán Chandler is . . . Bakámu's destiny. They are inseparably linked."

"Oh, for God's sake!" Devin said and straightened abruptly. "Indians don't have visions of white men—unless mayhap, 'tis a dream of vengeance against one who's an enemy. The man is fevered already!" He swung away.

Father Tomas's hand on his arm stopped him. "Surely you know how important the vision quest is for these people, Devin?" he said in a low voice. "Humor him, *por favor,* lest he die without—"

Meredyth caught the name "Devin" before his eyes widened slightly in surprise. "You of all people should dismiss it as nonsense, *padre.* 'Tis pagan!"

The priest shook his silvered head. "Not necessarily."

Several other women gathered around Bakámu, and as Meredyth stitched the deeper gashes, they carefully bandaged the wounds. But she caught snatches of the low-spoken, urgent conversation going on nearby.

She wondered how the priest knew Devil Chandler, but now wasn't the time to ask, nor did she wish to interrupt them. "I think you'll be able to walk again, Bakámu," she said softly, a gentle smile curving her mouth. "But your knee will be stiffer than 'twas."

She watched as the Arawak dragged his eyes from Chandler and Father Tomas. They met hers as the priest interpreted her words, and she detected weariness and pain in them but also a warm sincerity and immediately sensed that this man's friendship and loyalty would be an asset to anyone. *"Gracias,"* he murmured, his eyelids suddenly drooping.

"Have you given him aught to ease his pain?" she asked Maria, though the smell of rum emanating from the victim wasn't lost on her.

"Sí," the woman answered.

They covered Bakámu and began to clear away the bloodied shreds of his pant leg, the soiled cloths, and water.

"Give him more spirits, then let him sleep." Meredyth gave Bakámu a reassuring pat on the shoulder and a half-smile. She straightened slowly, one hand going to her back.

Father Tomas leaned over to speak softly into Bakámu's ear, and Meredyth went outside. She stood just past the doorway and drew in several breaths of fresh air, satisfied that the Indian would recover and that she could get away from the obnoxious Captain Chandler.

Father Tomas invited Devin to partake of the evening meal with him in his humble stone-and-thatch hut. To Meredyth's dismay, Devin (with a look of smug satisfaction) sat directly across from her on the hard-packed, earthen floor. There was no way she could avoid his bold perusal except to ignore him outright. And that went against all she'd been taught of courtesy.

Even though there were only eight people gathered in the room—including Dionisio, Carla and her mother, and Juan—Chandler seemed to fill the tiny hut, and Meredyth wished they were in a sea of people rather than so intimate a gathering. The openly assessing looks he gave her were unnerving, to say the least.

Mercifully, Carla asked if she could sit beside Meredyth, which provided the latter with a welcome diversion for a few moments, whether it was speaking in whispers with the little girl or exchanging smiles.

Father Tomas cleared his throat, waited for silence, and said

grace. When all bowed heads were raised, he smiled at
Meredyth, then Devin, and said, "In my concern for Bakámu,
I have been remiss in my introductions. Devin Chandler, allow
me to present Lady Meredyth St. Andrews. And Lady Meredyth, this is Captain Devin Chandler of the *Lady Elysia*."

Devin moved to stand, and Meredyth waved him down. "Pray,
Captain Chandler," she said cooly, "don't rise on my account."

"Devin honors us with his presence now and again," the
priest added. "He's a privateer, and makes his home in Jamaica
when he isn't sailing the Main."

You mean a pirate, Meredyth corrected silently, then realized
with dismay that if Chandler resided in Jamaica, the possibility
of running into him again was very real.

Meredyth's eyes met Devin's over a platter of grilled fish
being passed around, her thoughts obvious in the darkening of
her eyes.

"Just like your father, *niña,*" Father Tomas added with an
ironic lift of his silvered eyebrows.

Meredyth had already pulled her gaze away from Devin's,
but she could feel his surprise. "Your father, a privateer?" he
asked, exaggerated astonishment punctuating his words.

Her shoulders squared slightly, and her chin hiked a fraction.
"He was left for dead on a Bristol beach at the age of eight,
his birthright stolen from him. His circumstances have vastly
improved in the last twenty years, rest assured, Captain Chandler."

Well, well, he mused as he digested her revelation, his sun-
bleached lashes lowering momentarily to hide his expression.
Sister Meredyth evidently knew how to put one in one's place
and, to her credit, without dropping titles or boasting of her
antecedents.

He nodded, glanced at Father Tomas as one corner of his
mouth quirked, then asked her, "Pray tell me, Lady Meredyth,
what birthright he recovered, that another humble privateer like
myself may aspire to a similar rise in . . . circumstances."

Father Tomas stepped in for her. "Why, he's our sponsor,

Devin, and has been for many years now. He's the Earl of
Somerset," he shook one finger at no one in particular, "but
he puts on no airs! Keir St. Andrews does not measure a man
by his wealth or title."

Devin took a long draught of Father Tomas's delicious pineapple juice laced with rum. It went down so easily—as easily
as sin, he thought, but when one went to stand up . . . Well,
a man was reminded of his limits. He wondered briefly if
Meredyth St. Andrews had rum in her juice. He wondered
other things as well, but his wolfish thoughts were disrupted
by the object of his contemplation.

". . . to visit the mission?" she was asking him with a look
of bemusement. "You're a friend of Father Tomas then?"

In spite of her best efforts, Meredyth couldn't tamp the rise
of hostility and resentment at this interloper's intrusion upon
what she'd come to regard as the haven of the mission. After
a month there, she'd begun to grow accustomed to the simple,
spartan life-style and her increasing work with the children;
she found it somehow healing and uplifting to her heavy heart.

Meeting Devin Chandler, however, brought forth a totally
unexpected and even less welcome resurgence of disturbing
feelings.

"Indeed he is, child," Father Tomas answered for Devin, as
if trying to smooth over the almost tangible tension in the air
between them. "But I would know, Devin, if the rumors are
true? Were you taken in chains to England?"

Devin nodded, an almost savage glint suddenly leaching the
blue from his eyes until they appeared a dull pewter.

"Aye. I was betrayed by one of my officers. And someone
in command on a brigantine that flew the English flag."

For the first time since she'd met him, Meredyth felt a bitterness infuse his words and his actions, though he appeared
to be trying to suppress any outward sign of agitation. Com-
passion moved through her, in spite of her dislike.

"And how were you able to return to Jamaica?" Father

Tomas asked, his brown eyes full of empathy. "They didn't put you in gaol, did they?"

"Only clapped me up in Newgate, *padre,*" Devin said, grinning suddenly and turning the full force of his gaze on Meredyth, as if to witness her shock.

Meredyth was made of sterner stuff than that, however. "Betrayal of any kind is hard to take, Captain Chandler, but you obviously had the rare good fortune of being released from prison, or you wouldn't be here. The only way most poor souls escape Newgate is in a coffin."

She felt Father Tomas's puzzled glance touch her face, for in her weeks at the mission, she'd never had cause to be sarcastic or cynical. For whatever reason, it seemed that this man who had called himself Devil Chandler brought out the worst in her. She would have to watch her tongue, for her mother had told her not to judge all men by Lucien Pendwell's behavior.

Without warning, Meredyth turned to the priest beside her and gave him her most genuine smile. "Forgive me, Father, for my terse words at your table." She turned that stunning smile on the unsuspecting Chandler, her green eyes sparkling like emeralds spilling into the sunlight. "And, Captain Chandler, will you forgive me as well? Had you not been released from Newgate, I may not have had the pleasure of making your acquaintance."

Devin felt his jaw drop before the entrancing curve of her lips and the delicate color that tinted her cheeks as she complimented him with flawless courtesy. All thoughts of Giles Glasby's betrayal, of Newgate and its horrors, were temporarily wiped from his mind as he found himself basking in her bright and guileless smile.

He clenched his teeth together for pride's sake, and the result was a sterner look than he'd intended. As he watched her smile fade, he felt like a man seeking heat from a fire that was suddenly doused.

He forced himself to speak, recovering his wits as the words began to emerge from his lips. "No offense taken, Lady Meredyth." He offered her a shadow of his own smile. "I was very fortunate," he added, "to have had a peer of the realm intervene on my behalf. Now," he dragged his eyes from hers and addressed Father Tomas, "I must find the man who turned on me."

Father Tomas shook his head slowly. "Do not take matters into your own hands, my son. Leave it to the authorities—"

"There are no authorities on the Main!" Devin interrupted with a derisive laugh. "Or they are as crooked as the men they're supposed to be policing. I cannot depend on any justice but my own."

Meredyth studied him as he spoke. Either he was a courageous man in the face of what sounded like a nasty plot or an utter fool. She'd learned much about the ruthlessness of the men who sailed the Main from her father and Peter Stubbs. And recently from Father Tomas as well as some of those who lived at the mission.

"And what of you, Lady Meredyth?" Devin asked her unexpectedly, snagging her gaze with his and rousing her from her musings. "You're a long way from home, are you not? How is it that the daughter of an earl is hiding up here in the Blue Mountains of Jamaica?"

Three

He grinned to soften the words but instantly knew he'd made a mistake. The last remnants of her smile disappeared, and her lips tightened as annoyance flashed in her eyes.

"I'm not 'hiding,' as you put it, Captain."

"A most, er, unfortunate choice of words, Devin," Father Tomas interjected quickly.

Devin also heard the soft hiss of indrawn breath from Dionisio, who sat near the door. He looked straight at the Cimaroon and encountered angry dark eyes. What was it about Meredyth St. Andrews that drove the African to be so damned protective?

No doubt the same quality that reduces you to fawning and babbling, jeered an inner voice.

"My apologies," he said, not very apologetically.

"Mayhap 'tis the Cimaroon's gallant defense against the likes of Devil Chandler that causes you to prefer this humble and obscure mission to the ballrooms of London?"

"Dionisio knew and admired Meredyth's mother, Devin," Father Tomas explained patiently. "Both she and the earl were here some years ago, and at the time Dionisio was just as protective of the countess."

Outwardly Devin did little more than grunt in acknowledgment as he helped himself to a hefty portion of grilled fish from one of the platters being passed around. But he made a careful mental note of the revelation.

Dionisio nodded, his eyes on the middle distance as if he were picturing Meredyth's mother. *"Mujer con pelo como la puesta del sol . . ."* He looked at Meredyth and grinned shyly, strong white teeth standing out against his mahogany skin.

Devin swallowed a bit of fish and said, "I see. Your lady mother evidently has red-gold hair." He canted his head slightly as he boldly studied the fall of Meredyth's chestnut hair. It glinted in the candle and torchlight with a life of its own. No mouse brown this, he thought wryly. "Dionisio seems to favor women with Titian tresses, for the sunlight brings out the auburn in your hair, as well, Lady Meredyth." And the freckles sprinkled across your nose, he added silently.

Watch it, Chandler, came the inner voice again. You're dealing with the daughter of an earl here.

He ignored it. One wench was like another, highborn or nay. He knew enough to get himself into the good graces of any blue blooded woman, and there wasn't a mistake his mouth could make that his actions couldn't correct. Yet as he watched her, noting the becoming color that crept into her cheeks, he acknowledged he had no reason to question her so bluntly, so tauntingly. Good manners aside, he knew exactly why she was there; and no matter what reactions she elicited from him, there was no excuse for needling her.

He had to stop this nonsense, and stop it now. He had other matters to attend to that had nothing to do with Meredyth St. Andrews.

"Mother indeed has lovely red-gold hair," Meredyth acknowledged with a slight curving of her lips, "although 'tis threaded through with silver now."

Was that a glint of moisture he perceived along the edge of her lower lashes?

"And you miss her, child," Father Tomas said gently, echoing Devin's thoughts and reminding him that she was little more than a child.

It occurred to Devin, in light of what the earl had told him in Newgate, that Keir St. Andrews and his wife had probably encouraged their youngest child to leave England, that they were taking no chances this former fiancé might clandestinely seek out Meredyth and possibly whisk her away. The decision had been made for her own protection.

Why else would a loving family allow a virtual innocent to leave the security of her home and travel halfway around the world? And to the Caribbee Islands?

"I miss everyone," she admitted with a small sigh, and put one slender arm about Carla's shoulders, hugging the little girl close as if for comfort. Her chin rested briefly on the child's dark head before she straightened.

Devin found himself wishing he were in Carla's place.

"The children adore her and have displayed greater interest in their studies since her arrival," Father Tomas said.

"Señorita Meredyth makes everything fun!" Carla said with sudden spirit. Her cheeks pinkened then, as if she realized it wasn't her place to speak unless spoken to.

Or perhaps it was the stern look her mother gave her, or tried to give her. Loving indulgence tempered Concepción's look, surely, because of her daughter's bandaged foot. What had Meredyth said? Devin thought, *The creature will help lift the spirits of an injured child.* He wondered how serious the injury was, for the little girl was very thin, as if she'd been ill and hadn't eaten; but now was not the time to ask.

"When you're ready to return to England, milady," Devin heard himself offer, "perhaps I can be of service."

All eyes went to him. "The *Lady Elysia* takes on passengers from time to time," he explained, feeling foolish for blurting out such an offer. What had happened to his wits? Was it some kind of fever? Or Meredyth St. Andrews?

He certainly wasn't feverish, and if he were, the delirium was surely caused by this young and lively woman. This *dangerous* woman, he corrected.

Of course you would offer, fool, came the exasperated inner voice. Once safely in London she'd be off your hands and you'd be ten thousand pounds richer!

Meredyth touched him with her gaze, her mouth curving

sweetly. "Why, what a lovely name!" she said. "Derived from Elysium?"

Elysium? he thought in secret bemusement. What in the hell was that?

Educated by his experiences on the Main and the men who sailed it, Devin had had no formal schooling. He'd managed to learn to read and write—essential for keeping his ship's log—and could navigate a ship with a brilliance that came naturally. He could also exercise absolute authority over the rough crew of a privateer, or at least he had until Giles Glasby's mutiny. The ability to charm a female, any female, also numbered among his natural talents. But he was woefully ignorant of subjects so erudite as Greek mythology.

He would have walked the plank, however, before admitting such a thing to the lovely and lively Meredyth St. Andrews.

"Nay," he answered. "Rather, 'twas my mother's name."

Comprehension flared in Meredyth's eyes and Devin guessed she was about to offer him condolences in the wake of his use of the past tense, and that he didn't want. He never should have mentioned his mother—he could easily have said the schooner was named after another woman—for it was easier to keep weak emotion and soggy sentiment under lock and key in one half-forgotten part of his heart.

To his relief, however, she merely said, " 'Tis a beautiful name . . . an unforgettable name." She threw an apologetic look at Father Tomas—Devin was reminded of a guilty child peeking at a parent in anticipation of a negative reaction—and said, "Although some would say 'tis pagan, 'tis still melodic. It rolls off the tongue like music."

The Jesuit nodded in accord, obviously having taken no offense, while Devin sternly bade his leaping pulse to calm in the face of her delightful enthusiasm, his traitorous eyes to cease their gawking at the animation that lit her piquant features.

He either had to seduce the wench and thus remove the

challenge or, in a more rational approach, get away from the mission as fast as his feet could carry him.

In this case, he thought with regret, the former wasn't an option, unless he wanted the Earl of Somerset to track him down and have him hanged like some common pirate at Gallows Point. Yet hadn't he originally planned to leave the mission as soon as he'd determined Lady Meredyth was safe and well?

"Thank you," he tried to say with his practiced smoothness, but feared the words were garbled into an indecipherable grunt. He looked to Father Tomas. "And speaking of the *Lady Elysia,* I fear I cannot tarry, Father. As I said earlier, duty calls. Is there naught I can do for you in Port Royal or—"

"You cannot leave just now, my son!" the Jesuit interrupted him with spirit.

Devin opened his mouth to ask why, then suddenly realized with a sinking feeling in the pit of his stomach what the priest was referring to.

"You must at least remain long enough to make certain Bakámu recovers. You know how important a vision quest is to the Carib and Arawak!"

Meredyth looked questioningly at Devin over the rim of her cup, then lowered it and turned her gaze to Father Tomas.

"A vision quest is, for any native Indian, an important part of his life," the priest explained. "A young warrior normally goes out on his own to seek a vision of what will become his protector. To help things along, he may go to a holy place or pray or deprive himself of sleep or fast until his vision manifests itself."

Devin drained his rum-laced drink and reached for the ewer for more. The corners of his mouth turned down with irony. "Aye, but normally the vision that comes to a warrior is that of an animal as protector, like a panther or a shark or any number of animals. Certainly not a white man."

The priest frowned. "And who are you, Devin Chandler, to decide what is an appropriate vision for Bakámu?"

Devin paused in the act of raising the ewer and locked eyes with the older man. "Then is this vision quest some little-known ritual of Catholicism that you so staunchly defend it, Father?"

The sarcasm in his voice was not lost upon Meredyth, who drew her eyebrows together in bemusement. Father Tomas flushed, and Dionisio sucked in his breath sharply once again and impaled Devin with his dark stare.

"If my words seem harsh," Devin added more mildly as he refilled his cup and replaced the pitcher, " 'tis only because you imply that this man is my responsibility just because he imagines he envisioned me at some point in time. A most unsettling thought."

"Dionisio was present when Bakámu told one of the women that he'd come to Jamaica in his dugout canoe from a tiny island south of here. He landed in Port Royal and was drawn inexplicably into the mountains. Specifically, our mountain."

"And 'twas purely coincidental that I was on my way to the mission, that I happened to be there when he tangled with that croc," Devin said with a twist of his lips. He glanced at Juan, quietly eating his fill. "Juan shot the animal's tail off, not I. If not for him, Bakámu would probably be dead, and so would I."

All eyes went to Juan, and Devin immediately took advantage of the situation. "Mayhap the Arawak should be persuaded that the boy is his destiny and not me. Juan is the true hero here, the shaper of Bakámu's destiny and, of a certainty, his protector. Or mayhap even the crocodile who tried to make a meal of his leg."

"I am part Arawak," Juan pronounced with shy pride, "and part *español, también.*"

Father Tomas shook his head, his face settling into obstinate lines. " 'Twould be most . . . ah, inconsiderate of you, Devin, to leave before Bakámu is completely out of danger."

Devin was about to give in, for he could afford to wait another day or two, and although he would never put it into words, he was by nature kind-hearted.

Then he felt Meredyth St. Andrews's eyes on him and met them. They were slightly narrowed, as if she were assessing him by his reaction. Ordinarily, he could contend with the most unpredictable of females. And, under normal circumstances, he would have found humor in the fact that he'd inadvertently acquired the unwanted and ludicrous position as some man's totem.

But an unexpected flash of perversity struck him. In addition to the mute acknowledgment that he'd been acting the smitten stripling ever since he'd encountered the St. Andrews wench on the path, he'd been given the unwelcome burden of a wounded and delirious stranger naming him as his vision. Thus, Devin's reaction was completely opposite of what he assumed would please her.

He placed his hands on his knees as he sat cross-legged and leaned forward, toward Father Tomas. His crystal-blue eyes turned wintry as he spoke. "Even if the Indian were my blood brother, I'd not be his keeper! If you insist that I saved his life, then so be it. But I'll not linger here awaiting his decision on just how I can fulfill my supposed part in the Arawak scheme of things!"

"But—"

"The apparition of a parakeet or a frog would have served him better than the mug of an Irishman!" Devin cut across Father Tomas's objection.

There followed a quivering silence. Suddenly, Father Tomas burst into laughter, startling everyone. Tears crept into the corner of his crinkled eyes and leaked down his weathered cheeks. "Ah, Devin, Devin. . . . Only you would fight so hard to deny God's will and in so humorous a manner."

It was that very humor, irrepressible at the most unlikely times, that caused one side of Devin's mouth to lift against his will and eased the tension in the room. "Then God's will is to encourage Bakámu to continue his pagan ways?" he asked with a lift of his brows.

"You once told me," the Jesuit answered, "that 'twas the

supreme arrogance for one man to attempt to impose his religion upon another. Mayhap I'm considering the possible merit of your words."

Father Tomas had everyone's attention now, and surprise replaced the earlier tension. Devin gave him a sharp look. "Coming from a priest, that sounds perilously close to direct defiance of the Church, wouldn't you say, Father? I was under the impression that your task here was to convert the 'heathen' natives to Catholicism."

Meredyth's expression was bordering on shock. "Father Tomas and I often engage in rigorous discussions of religious philosophy," he added for her benefit, even though he'd decided only moments ago to be contrary for her benefit.

Father Tomas shrugged. "Almost two score of years here has . . . er, shall we say, enlightened me? I feel my first duty is to provide a haven for runaway slaves and the endangered Indians, for if they leave the mission, their chances of meeting with severe punishment and even death are great. What use, then, to try and save their souls if they don't trust me enough to remain here?" He accepted the platter of fresh-roasted meat that was being passed to him from Dionisio, before adding, "Therefore 'tis folly, in my humble opinion, to completely ignore the religious practices that have been a part of their culture for centuries. Rather, tis easier to slowly incorporate the ways of the Church into their lives."

Devin felt Meredyth's discomfort before she even opened her mouth, even without glancing her way, as if she'd reached across the spread of food and communicated to him directly by touch. Obviously seeking to steer the subject to a less controversial topic, she asked brightly, "Have you made a home for Carla's anole, Dionisio?"

As if on cue, the tiny lizard poked its head from a drawstring cloth pouch at Carla's waist. Carla's soft grunt of surprise made Meredyth look from Dionisio to the pouch and the creature evidently trying to crawl to freedom.

Carla slapped her hand over the top of the pouch, and

Meredyth inwardly winced at the child's inadvertent but less than gentle movement.

"Dulcemente!" Dionisio warned softly.

"Is he part of our repast?" Devin asked. "If so, I prefer my lizard cooked and unmoving."

Carla's look of horror at his words made him instantly regret them.

" 'Twas a jest, *niña,"* he said lightly. "Tighten the drawstring, *sí?"* At her nod, he leaned forward, hoping Meredyth St. Andrews wouldn't think his attention to Carla was for the purpose of gaining her favor. "What will you name it?" he asked, seeking to wipe the distress from the child's features.

Carla looked up at Meredyth, the lizard secure once again in the pouch.

"He's noble-spirited, is he not?" Meredyth asked the little girl with a smile. "And his coloring is so beautiful—"

"Why, he reminds me of a fancily dressed London fop!" Devin cut in. "His dewlap rivals the best-looking neckcloth!"

Carla broke into a tentative smile in the wake of the compliments directed toward her new pet. Obviously, she'd missed the sarcasm in Devin's words.

"Lord Someone?" she offered. "Or Sir? We can call him Sir . . ." She frowned. "Sir Lagartija?"

"How about Sir Hiss?" Devin offered and cocked his head in imitation of the anole.

To his delight, the name (or his antics) brought a smile of approval to Meredyth's lips and a look of wonder to Carla's face. She clapped her hands then and, face alight, exclaimed, *"Ahhh, sí, perfecto!"*

Laughter sounded throughout the small hut, and the conversation turned lighter.

Devin tossed aside the light blanket and stood. He couldn't sleep. His thoughts kept returning to the injured Arawak and the latter's expectations of him. "Vision, indeed!" he mumbled under his breath as he shrugged into his shirt. "And now I have a Jesuit priest insisting I go along with this protector nonsense." He strode from the hut, the whiplike movement of the doorway curtain emphasizing his agitation. "I should have let the croc take him and saved myself a lot of trouble!"

He marched straight to the infirmary, his shirt hanging outside of his breeches, feet bare, and hanks of his long hair escaped from their tether and blowing about his face in the night wind. He would set this Bakámu straight once and for all, although he didn't know why he was even bothering.

Except for his friendship with Father Tomas, and his cursed conscience and the impression he made on Meredyth St. Andrews—damn the saucy wench—he was a fool a hundred times over, a lily-livered, blarney-spouting Irishman, who was being taken in by a pretty Englishwoman and a pathetic Arawak as easily as a blissfully ignorant child.

If he had one smidgeon of common sense, he'd be heading down the mountain as fast as his feet could carry him.

He practically stormed into the infirmary, the pity he'd felt for the Arawak now turned to anger at the man's audacity. How dare he show any gratitude he might feel by bestowing so weighty a burden on his rescuer? And how dare Father Tomas interfere with his life for so blatantly pagan a practice? And Meredyth St. Andrews . . .

His eyes were narrowed ominously and lit with the fire of outrage as he was brought up short by the sight that greeted him: she was sitting beside the Indian, ministering to him by the light of a candle and a single wall torch. Soothing words floated to him where he stood, momentarily halted, then held him anchored to the floor. But it was the sight of her long, torchlight-burnished hair hanging loosely down her back that was almost his undoing. He felt his anger begin to fade as quickly as it had appeared.

You like blondes, Chandler. Remember? came his inner voice. Why this sudden fascination with brown hair?

Another softer voice added, Brown is an inadequate word for that beautiful mane.

". . . won't leave you," she soothed. "He's too good a man to run off while you are so ill." She leaned over and replaced the wet cloth resting on Bakámu's forehead. He appeared to be sleeping, for his eyes looked closed from Devin's vantage point.

"Why, he—"

"I'll speak for myself, thank you," Devin announced in a low voice as he moved forward.

She turned toward him, obviously surprised, and began to stand. He placed one hand on her shoulder and pressed her back to her seat. "Pray don't rise on my account, milady. I think you've already assumed much too much regarding my character and my behavior."

Her mouth tightened, and color spotted her cheeks.

Before she could say a word, however, with quick strides he moved around to the other side of the pallet and bent to examine Bakámu for himself. "He appears to be sleeping," Devin said, "but his fever hasn't broken yet."

"Why are you here?" Meredyth asked with asperity.

"And why not?" he countered, his gaze clashing with hers. "Is he not considered my charge by all of you?" He leaned toward her, infusing his next words with accusation. "The question is, rather, why are you here? Do you enjoy soothing the savage? Mayhap you find it titillating after your ho-hum balls and masques?"

She lowered her voice to answer, but her eyes flashed. "At least I'm not planning to run off and desert him!"

Devin's eyebrows tented. "Oh, so 'tis desertion now, is it? And just what makes you the authority on desertion that you can sit in judgment of another's actions? Just what do you know a—"

He halted mid-word at the sudden distress that darkened her fine green eyes and belatedly remembered the Earl of Somerset's explanation of why his youngest child had fled halfway around the world to the tiny island of Jamaica.

To make matters worse, in addition to the sudden and unexpected guilt that grabbed him, Devin felt a tiny but razor-sharp hook of feeling snag his heart, a painful pinch that felt suspiciously like jealousy, an emotion he'd rarely experienced in his twenty-eight years—jealousy that the mere thought of another man could cause the heretofore intrepid-seeming Meredyth St. Andrews such undisguised distress.

"I beg your pardon," he said abruptly and straightened, "but there is no way that I could desert him. We're all but strangers!" Bakámu muttered in his sleep, as if unconsciously objecting to the withdrawal of Devin's attention. They both looked at the Indian, and Devin could have sworn the man had sneaked a peek at him through one eye.

By the Mass, now he was imagining a deception by the Arawak. No doubt due to the infinitely unwelcome influence of the female across from him. For God's sake, he thought, irritation replacing his earlier remorse, there were women aplenty in Port Royal. Women who were any man's for the asking, and a hell of a lot more cooperative and uncomplicated than the woman across the pallet from him, more easily dealt with than the manipulative Lady Meredyth.

"You'll forgive the intrusion," he said in a flat voice and strode past pallet and patient and out the door before he could do any more damage.

He found Juan and woke him up. "Fetch the donkey," he ordered in a low, terse voice. "Nay, forget the animal. I'll buy you another, as many as you want, later." For a moment he thought the youth would object, and he conjured up his sternest look to discourage him. "Collect your things and meet me at the entrance to the mission straightaway. And make no sound, do you hear?" Without waiting for an answer or looking at Juan again, he began to tuck his shirt into his breeches and pull on his boots.

He heard the boy scramble to do his bidding, then exit the

hut. He bent to collect his own few belongings, mostly what he wore on his back—and followed in the lad's wake.

They had no trouble getting by the two guards standing sentinel at the mouth of the defile leading out of the mission, for Devin normally came and went as he pleased, though he had to admit to himself that he'd never left in so hurried and furtive a manner, like a thief in the night.

He'd done his duty, as far as he was concerned, regarding Bakámu. As for his part of the bargain with the Earl of Somerset, he'd never intended to carry out any more than token compliance. The earl's daughter was safely ensconced at the mission, and that was that. From time to time, depending upon events happening in his life during the next year, he would perhaps pay Father Tomas a visit, just to make certain. Or he could just as easily send up someone in his stead if his conscience gave him trouble, which he doubted.

As he and Juan put distance between themselves and the mission, Devin evinced a combination of relief and something he didn't care to name. He ruthlessly concentrated on the former, mentally enumerating all the things he had to do to make up for months of lost time.

The trip down the mountain was easier than the trip up. Although it was dark, the bright moonlight helped illuminate the path before they descended into the rainforest that cloaked the lower half of the mountain. Plus it was cooler, and the night breeze, which had been almost brisk at the mission, was beginning to warm yet was still pleasant.

He felt his spirits lift considerably as Juan called back to him, "We're not too far from the stream, *Capitán.*"

"Don't wake the crocs," Devin answered half in jest, feeling suddenly ebullient with freedom. "I want to reach Port Royal by dawn and preferably in one piece."

Juan's laughter drifted back to him in the clear air. It was youthful, exuberant, like Meredyth St. Andrews's had been. He frowned, pushing her image from his mind.

But if he succeeded in temporarily obliterating her image,

he failed miserably to guard against the words that floated past his mind's ear: *What a lovely name! Derived from Elysium?*

Now, of all the things she'd said, he thought with annoyance, why would those words come back to him?

Four

"And good riddance to the rascal!" Meredyth murmured as she turned back to Bakámu. Devil Chandler was the most irritating man she'd ever had the misfortune to encounter.

She bit her lip, however, wondering if she'd been too harsh in her spoken criticism of him. Mamma would have cringed, she thought suddenly, upon hearing her youngest daughter utter such rude words to a man who was almost a stranger to her. To anyone for that matter.

Her thoughts scattered as she noticed the Arawak's eyes were open. "Chan-ler," he muttered.

Meredyth allowed her mouth to curve in a smile of assurance as she once more replaced the wet cloth on his forehead. "He went to bed," she soothed. "He needs his sleep just as you do."

"Chan-ler . . . gone . . ."

She shook her head. "Not gone."

The Indian frowned in obvious disagreement, and Meredyth noticed sweat beading his upper lip. Was his fever breaking? She dared hope as she uncovered the arm closest to her and lightly skimmed her fingers over his flesh. It was clammy, and her hopes rose another notch. "I think your fever is breaking, Bakámu. Do you understand? 'Tis good."

She replaced the light cover and renewed her smile of reassurance.

His eyelids drooped tiredly. Then closed. "Must find . . . Chan-ler."

"Better yet, I'll bring him to you in the morn," Meredyth told him as she stood, one hand going to the small of her back. Bakámu appeared to be slipping into sleep once again, so she turned and stepped away from the pallet.

"Buenas noches," murmured a female voice from the doorway. "How is he?"

Meredyth looked up, her eyes widening slightly in surprise. It was Maria, Dionisio's Arawak wife, who'd obviously come to relieve her. "You need sleep, so you can work with the children *mañana, sí?"*

"And what of you?" Meredyth responded, trying to stifle a yawn. "You're with him more than anyone else."

Maria moved forward. "I do not mind. He is one of my own."

Meredyth watched as Maria bent to examine the Arawak, then said, "His fever is breaking. 'Tis a good sign."

"Gracias a Dios!" the Indian woman said in perfect imitation of Father Tomas. "Now, you go and sleep, *niña, sí?"*

Meredyth nodded. She would need all her faculties to do battle with the impossible and utterly outrageous Devin Chandler in the morning.

"¿Padre?"

The soft-spoken but insistent voice intruded into his dreams, and Father Tomas de Almansa y Espinoza grunted with annoyance and burrowed more deeply beneath the covers.

A hand shook his shoulder and brought the Jesuit out of his sleep. He sat up as quickly as his old bones would allow, for nothing short of an emergency would merit this unexpected interruption of his slumber.

As he squinted against the darkness to identify his visitor, Dionisio's voice said, "He's gone."

"Oh, 'tis you," the older man began, then stopped midsentence. "Who's gone?" His mind was still fuzzy.

"El capitán. Chandler."

Father Tomas fumbled to light a match, knocked the candle

off the sea chest beside the bed, and felt rather than saw the Cimaroon rescue it before it hit the dirt floor. Dionisio lit the candle for the priest and replaced it on the chest.

"What do you mean 'gone'?" Tomas asked groggily, but before the African could answer, he added as understanding dawned, "Never mind. I understand. Chandler is like the wind—you might as well attempt to catch and hold a mountain breeze."

"*Cobarde.*"

The priest shook his head and braced his arms on either side of his body for support. "A rascal he may be but never a coward." His head drooped wearily in spite of his words, for he felt suddenly like the weight of the world was resting on his age-worn shoulders. Once he was young and strong, strong enough to . . .

No! It wasn't his wont to feel sorry for himself. If he had to persuade the Indian Bakámu that God had sent him the wrong vision in Devin James Chandler, he would do it. And throttle Chandler later.

His eyes met Dionisio's. "You know better than that. He will return. Mark my word. He always does, eh?" He raised an eyebrow at the Cimaroon and couldn't suppress the glint of humor in his brown eyes. He wished he could tell Dionisio what he suspected—that Devin Chandler was a courageous man, for all his faults. He would have wagered his clergy's collar that the Englishman was a staunch enemy of slavery, had undoubtedly already paid a price for his role by being betrayed and then hauled off to England and jail.

"Sit, my faithful friend," he bade the African and patted the pallet. "How fares our Bakámu?"

"Maria says fever broken."

"Praise God!" Tomas said. "Now, we must get him back on his feet again and persuade him that Devin had important matters to attend to. That he will be back or—"

"Chandler not leave because of Arawak," Dionisio interrupted him softly. "Left because of *mujer.*"

Father Tomas's look turned astonished. "Meredyth? Why, what do you—"

Understanding came to him then, and a slow, knowing smile spread across his face. "Why, how perceptive of you, *mi hijo*. And if 'tis true, he will surely be back. And sooner than later, *sí?*"

"Afraid of feelings. Very stubborn. Has never loved from here." Dionisio placed one fist over his heart.

Father Tomas frowned. "And so he probably has not. 'Tis easier for him to hide his true feelings with outrageous behavior or humor." He pursed his lips and stared into the shadows across from him for a moment. "Mayhap," he said at last, his eyes looking directly into the African's, "we can help matters, *sí?* Mayhap we can enlist God's help and bring them together."

Dionisio shrugged and grunted, his long, slender legs folded like a great, dark grasshopper's. "Don't like Chandler."

" 'Tis because you're as proud and independent as he is. You tended to be protective of Meredyth's mother twenty years ago, and now you appear to feel the same way toward Meredyth, as well. You didn't like Keir St. Andrews either, did you?"

"He lied to his woman. White men have strange ways of showing feelings."

The Jesuit shook his head sagely. "Don't even try to understand, my Dionisio. Don't even try."

He shifted, swung his legs over the pallet, and rested his bare feet upon the floor. "Now we have two good reasons. So how can we lure our runaway *capitán* back to the mission?"

"By the Mass, Chandler! Are you going to sleep the day away?"

Devin fairly levitated from the mattress, scrambling against the entangling sheet. He grabbed for his cutlass, forcing his heavy-lidded eyes to focus.

"Easy, m'boy . . . 'tis only me. And damned glad I am to see you!"

By now, Devin was in a crouch, his sword pointed in his visitor's direction, a shaky position at best, considering he was in the middle of his bed.

"I've always admired your skill with a cutlass, lad, but 'tis even more difficult to wield from beneath a sheet. New style, mayhap?" the other man asked with a lift of one snow-white eyebrow.

In frustration, Devin sliced through the sheet rather than untangle the weapon from its folds, though his visitor was hardly threatening.

"In a foul humor you are, too," Woodrow Kingsley observed, his silver mustache quivering slightly. His blue eyes twinkled with mischief.

"I'm not in a foul humor," Devin said at last with a scowl. Then, realizing how his actions were contradicting his words, he lowered the cutlass and dropped down to a seat on the edge of the four-postered oak bed. He grinned sheepishly. "Damn it, Woody, had you just been through what I have, you'd be scowling, too."

The older man sobered instantly. He stepped up to Devin, put one hand on his shoulder, and squeezed with obvious concern and affection. "What happened, lad? I thought . . ." He trailed off, obviously unable to put his thoughts into words.

"That I was dead?" Devin grimaced. "And so I might have been but for the grace of God . . . and the Earl of Somerset who hauled me out of Newgate." Devin stood, stark naked, and strode to a handsome oak chest of drawers that matched the great four-postered bed dominating the room. He reached for a decanter and matching goblets on its top. "Sit," he directed Woodrow, "and we'll have a morning draught together."

Devin missed the look of pure relief that crossed Kingsley's features—followed by a flash of surprise and something more—and then was gone. "Morning?" the older man exclaimed mildly. " 'Tis nigh on three of the clock, m'boy! You never sleep this late . . . or has being to London softened you?" Once again, his eyes gleamed with amusement.

"Someone ransacked the place," Devin said with a grimace.

"Here? The town house?"

"Right here. I spent much of the night returning from the mission," Woody's eyebrows tented at this revelation, "only to return to find all my belongings tossed about like a devil of a blow had been through here . . . or an earthquake." Devin sighed heavily as he poured a glass of Rhenish. "Tired as I was, I couldn't go to bed in the middle of the mess."

"If I may be so bold, why in God's name did you go straight to the mission?"

"To look in on Somerset's daughter, who's up there trying to heal a broken heart—or so her father said." At Woody's skeptical look, he elaborated: "The earl said he'd have me released from jail if I promised to look in on the lady Meredyth from time to time."

"Ah! A bargain."

Devin nodded, his mind suddenly on Meredyth St. Andrews.

"What were the would-be thieves after?" Kingsley asked as he sat on the only stool in the room.

Devin dragged his thoughts from Lady Meredyth. He turned and handed the cup to Woodrow. "We must toast my return," he said, at first ignoring the question. "No puling excuses like the time of day." He poured a second one for himself and, since there was no room for a side table in the bed-dominated chamber, he set the decanter on the floor beside the chest of drawers.

"As for the object of their search, I can guess what they wanted. I don't know for certain, however, because the documents are still here."

Woody nodded thoughtfully. "If you're right, then you've been found out, and that's a death sentence, lad. You'll have to curtail your activities."

Devin shrugged, dismissing Woody's warning. "But only some spare coin was taken. Naught more."

Woodrow appeared to sag in the chair with relief. " 'Twas done only recently then because we kept a close watch over the town house until these last few weeks. My man was dealing with some personal problem . . . inexcusable of me not to replace him, I admit, and I'm sorry."

Devin waved one hand in dismissal. "You can't be everywhere, even if you employ informants. As for growing soft in London. . . . Well, if you must know, the turnkeys coddled me shamelessly." He watched as Woodrow, with great drama, juggled his walking cane and the wine between his knees. Although his expression was sober, all trace of Devin's former ill humor was gone.

"And you, no doubt, were a model prisoner." Woody tapped the end of his stick on the floor vigorously and had to swig his Rhenish before it spilled. "But enough of that. 'Tis good to see you, lad, and I hope you'll set aside any thought of vengeance." He was silent a moment. "I fear the ransacking of your home was tied in with the attack on the *Lady Elysia.*"

"No doubt it was, but since we're in wild Port Royal and well beyond the reach of any dependable authority, I'm forced to do my own investigating." He drew a deep draught of his own Rhenish, then frowned suddenly as he righted the goblet. "Don't think I don't appreciate your warning, by the way, but I'll not run like a cur with my tail between my legs quite yet. If I find Glasby I'll run him through on sight, no questions asked! There's a good place to start poking our noses," he said darkly.

Woodrow shook his head. "Someone's beat you to it, I'm afraid."

Devin frowned.

"His body was found stuffed in a barrel, his eyes, ears, and tongue cut out."

Devin paused in the act of drinking, his stomach lurching. "A definite warning. And a dead end for my purposes." Another thought struck him. "How'd you know I was here? In Jamaica, I mean."

"Word travels like wildfire around here—or have you forgotten already? One of my agents noticed the glow of candlelight up here between opened drapes, like those of a man too long away from the magnificent view of the harbor."

"Obviously, the man hasn't enough to do."

Woodrow took another drink, then shook his white-maned head. "Nay, lad. He's an excellent observer. I told him I'd give him a bonus if he notified me the moment he had word of your return."

Devin grinned. "You fox. And what of Jimmy? Did he desert me in my unexpected absence, too?" The grin faded suddenly. "Or . . ." He left his grim thought unfinished, hanging palpably in the air between them.

Woodrow looked at the floor for a moment and drew a deep breath. When his eyes met Devin's, they were troubled. "Your true friends never deserted you, lad. Now and again I'll get word of one of your old crew being in town, hanging about the docks and inquiring about you." He paused, then added quietly, "As for Jimmy, he's dead. They found him in the alleyway next door about a sennight after you disappeared."

"Jimmy?" Devin repeated in disbelief. He stood and strode to the window that overlooked bustling Thames Street, close to where it intersected King's Lane. He gazed unseeingly at the skyline, through a score of white sails of vessels that lined the wharves to the north. Masts and spars skewered the cloudless Jamaican sky, bowsprits lined the water's edge like an army of lances, and men of all colors labored beneath the unrelenting sun.

His profile was also unrelenting, and a tick worked along his lean jawline. "Why in God's name would anyone kill Jimmy? He knew nothing!" He spoke his thoughts aloud, knowing that any answer Woody gave him would be unacceptable.

"Devin . . . Devin," his friend soothed softly. "Innocents die when evil and greedy men are involved. You know that by now. 'Twas an act of the basest kind, but by virtue of your work, you put the life of anyone whom you employed in jeopardy."

Devin's mouth tightened. "I'll find Jimmy's killer if I have to comb the entire Caribbean!"

Kingsley shook his head. "I believe Glasby killed him, and you cannot seek retribution from a dead man." Devin's gaze fused with his. "Glasby was obviously only a pawn doing someone else's dirty work. Then, somehow, he outgrew his usefulness—mayhap learned too much and couldn't keep his mouth shut. You've got to be cautious, for if Glasby's actions were any indication, he worked for someone who suspects your . . . activities."

"Someone like Jean-Baptiste du Casse?"

"Aye. No lone, common thug would take such desperate and dangerous measures. Why not just have done with you and take the *Lady Elysia?* There are scores of ways, and 'tisn't an uncommon occurrence on the Main."

The sound of his ship's name broke through the haze of Devin's anger. "Where is she?" he said over his shoulder, dreading the answer.

"Docked just this side of King's Wharf, directly across from the warehouse so we could keep an eye on it."

Devin swung to face his friend, a spark of hope lighting his eyes. "Is she . . . ? Did you . . . ?" He trailed off, unable to speak around the sudden tightness in his throat. His beloved mother's namesake, his most valued and hard-earned possession. Even though Devin Chandler knew that people were important, not things, his feelings for the schooner were no doubt as close as he'd ever come to love, except for Woodrow Kingsley, of course, who'd been like a father to him for so many years now.

Inanimate objects couldn't betray or desert a man. The *Lady Elysia* was as dependable in her service and responsive to his hands on the wheel as any other single entity in his life.

"Aye to both," Woody said, in answer to his unfinished questions. "She's still seaworthy and moored here in Port Royal. I also took it upon myself to continue the lease on the town house." He leaned forward, his eyes glistening with obvious emotion. "Don't you see, lad? I counted on your return." He set his cup on the planked floor, stood before Devin could reply, and waved his cane. "Put on your breeches and come look for yourself."

He turned toward the chamber door. "We'll have it refurbished—we have more than enough funds—and see about getting you a new manservant."

"And a good crew?" Devin asked in a low voice as he turned away from the window.

"As I said, most of your men are scattered about the Main." Woody shrugged. "Loyalty doesn't put food in a man's belly, and even your staunchest supporters among the crew have probably hired on with other ships by now. It's been months, and you can hardly blame a man for wanting to earn a living."

Devin didn't necessarily agree, but he reached for his breeches, deciding to attend to first things first. For now it was enough that his friend and mentor had found the ship and had been generous enough to keep it in safe harbor for him.

Thank God, he thought with uncharacteristic humility, for it was a hell of a lot more than he'd dared hope while sitting in the bowels of Newgate.

As Woodrow preceded Devin down the stairs to the first floor kitchen and sitting room, the merchant hoped that his little surprise for Devin would remain silent and unnoticed. Devin would be spending some time in Port Royal while the *Lady* was being repaired, and in light of recent events, Woodrow surmised he would need some company.

Devin was always drawn to the underdog (if one could apply the word "dog" in this case), although loath to admit it, and the surprise resting quietly in the sitting room needed a home and a kind master.

The pair had possibilities, Woody thought wryly, if they could get through what he suspected would turn out to be a rocky beginning.

* * *

The sun was well past its zenith. It sat low above the harbor to their left, its golden glow warming the wood tones of the docked ships, including the *Lady Elysia*. The pristine expanses of canvas dress that made her a real lady were lowered. A jagged hole leered at them from just below the bowsprit and above the waterline, the damaged foremast leaned drunkenly, and a second and more gaping wound marred her stern. Yet, in spite of her condition, she looked majestic to Devin as she rocked gently within her moorings.

Emotion blurred his view of her for a few moments, until he determinedly blinked back the tears.

As a fierce pride drove through him, he turned to speak to Woody. But the older man was already commenting, "Still beautiful, isn't she? Despite her wounds."

In a rare snow of emotion, Devin wordlessly placed one arm about Woody's shoulders, the brief strength of his hug saying what his lips could not.

When they parted, Devin told his friend, "Come aboard with me. I want to see the full extent of the damage." Before Kingsley could answer, Devin had leapt across the narrow space between the dock and the vessel's hull to grab the ship's rope ladder like a clinging spider. From there he reached up and grabbed the freeboard, then vaulted up lithely and perched atop the rail.

He grinned down at Woody, the kiss of the ocean breeze firing his blood. He felt as if he could deal with anything, do anything, in those moments. "Well?" he said with a laugh. "What are you waiting for, a boarding plank?"

"Only the least exertive for me, lad," Kinglsey answered with a smile and watched as Devin scrambled to lay down a heavy boarding plank. His actions had already attracted a few glances from dockworkers, but no one seemed to be suspicious of his actions.

Just as Devin was wondering if anyone around might recognize him, a crashing sound startled both men. Devin was the first to look up. " 'Sdeath! 'Tis Devil Chandler . . . or 'is ghost!" exclaimed a booming voice from the other side of the dock.

Devin glanced over, his eyes narrowed against the shadow of the ship moored across from the *Lady Elysia,* and the speaker's wide-brimmed straw hat. Woodrow looked over his shoulder, his walking stick already tentatively touching the boarding plank.

Devin grinned suddenly in recognition. "I'm no spirit, Red Flaherty," he replied and bounded down to the dock, skirting Woody, who was in the process of swinging toward the new-comer.

Devin held out one hand as he approached the short and bullish seaman, who was pushing back his hat to reveal receding filaments of red hair. As if to make up for the scarcity at the crown, Flaherty wore a long, straggly horse's tail, subdued and waterproofed with a light coating of tar.

The men clasped hands for a moment, then broke the bond. "Thought ye was feedin' the fish at the bottom o' the sea, Cap'n," Flaherty said with a shake of his head. "Ye just disappeared with Glasby, didn't know who to tell 'cept Master Kingsley here." He added gruffly, "An' things ain't been the same since."

A fleeting frown registered on Devin's forehead, then was gone. He winked. "Glad to near that, Red." He turned to Woody, who'd come up behind him. "Woody, you remember my boatswain, Reed 'Red' Flaherty?"

"Indeed," Woody said, graciously extending a hand toward the seaman. "Master Flaherty and your quartermaster, Emil Rogers, came to me with the news of your disappearance and the disabled schooner. They managed to bring her into port."

Red nodded to the older man, then said to Devin, "What happened to ye, Cap'n? Rumors were a-flyin' after the *Lady Elysia* was hit. Glasby an' his cronies from that renegade brig rounded up the crew an' locked us in the hold!"

"Damn, but 'tis a wonder they didn't sink the schooner and you along with her!" Devin said, his fair brows drawn together ominously. "Pricklouses, the lot of them. I'll find out who's behind this if 'tis the last thing I do!" But as his eyes met Woody's, Devin knew it wouldn't be as easily said as done without putting himself in real jeopardy.

Not that he'd ever shied away from a challenge—that was part of the reason he'd gone into the hazardous business of informant to the small, anonymous circle of men who employed him. His recent abduction and subsequent stint in Newgate were the latest evidence of that very danger.

"Master Kingsley's been keepin' an eye on the *Lady* and pickin' up the rent fees," Red added. He looked past Devin at the schooner. "She's chompin' at the bit, Cap'n. A few repairs and she'll be ready to ride the wind again."

Devin nodded. "Woody and I were just about to board her and assess the damage—"

"Hey, Flaherty!" shouted a voice from behind them. "I ain't payin' ye to stand an' gawk at that wreck. Get to work!"

Had the insult been to his person rather than his beloved schooner, Devin could have taken it in stride. However, instead he stiffened and threw a narrowed glance toward the voice. But the man had already turned away to continue directing other workers under his command.

"Stick it, Van Horne," Red called back, "I'm givin' ye notice as o' right now!" He tipped his hat in mock salute to Van Horne's back before his eyes met Devin's. A hint of sheepishness danced across his weather-beaten face as he said with uncharacteristic tentativeness, "That is, if ye'll have me on the *Lady* again, Cap'n."

The offer effectively pulled Devin's attention away from Van Horne and his callous quip. "Why, Flaherty, you loyal old tar!" His face split in a happy grin. "Of course I'll have you back . . . as boatswain. Business as usual, eh?" He slapped Red on the back and threw a look at Woodrow. "Won't you miss some pay?" he asked the boatswain in a loud whisper near the latter's ear.

"Nay. Not even a full day. I think I can manage," he answered with a broad wink.

All three of them laughed aloud, and in unison, they moved toward the waiting schooner.

"He's back."

From the window on the second floor of a nearby warehouse on Thames Street, Luke Pelton stood looking through a small telescope. "I don't know how, but he's here in Port Royal again."

Jean-Baptiste du Casse—slave-trader, buccaneer leader, officer in the French Navy, and governor of the rowdy enclave of Saint Domingue—had been sitting astride a simple wooden chair, his crossed arms upon its back supporting his chin. At the Englishman's words, he raised his head with a jerk. *"Non! It cannot be! Not—"*

"Chandler. And, aye, the very same."

Du Casse stood abruptly, toppling the chair backward, as he stepped over it. *"Cet homme est comme une mouche!* A fly! You may shake him free of your arm, but he returns *toujours!"* Then, as if realizing he was showing his anger, he visibly drew in a deep breath and regained control. He took the offered binoculars and raised them.

"He's not really so important, is he?" Pelton asked. "They say he's an undependable knave. How can he harm us?"

Du Casse muttered under his breath with uncharacteristic irritation, his fingers momentarily tightening on the instrument he held. "I believe he has in his possession papers documenting conditions on slavers, many belonging to my friends of la Compagnie de Sénégal." He lowered the binoculars, his eyes narrowing in thought. "Yet, we searched his town house while he was on his way to England, and nothing was found. If only we could find some written proof, we could take more fail safe measures to do away with him once and for all. He's obviously ignored the warning, and there must be no doubt, *mon ami,* of what happens to anyone who would seek to destroy us and our enterprise."

The tall, even-featured Pelton shrugged as he followed the Frenchman's gaze. "We could always castrate him," he mused aloud, one side of his mouth quirking briefly. "Send his pickled balls to Somerset or—"

Du Casse's eyes met his suddenly. "Somerset? I wonder. . . . Mayhap he had some business in London to attend to while Chandler was imprisoned, *oui?"*

"Mayhap he visited some of his sainted relatives in jail and stopped to see Chandler while he was there." Pelton laughed harshly at his own black humor. "After what he did to me, it appears more than ever that he's part of our little clandestine fraternity of the self-righteous."

Du Casse eyed him speculatively for a moment.

"We could always ask Chandler, couldn't we?" Pelton added with a humorless laugh. "Not that he would tell us necessarily, even under torture, but 'twould be one way to dispose of him."

Du Casse's dark eyebrows flattened thoughtfully. "Maybe not . . . 'tis so barbaric!"

"What pirate or privateer isn't a barbarian?" Pelton asked sourly, then realized he was insulting many of du Casse's acquaintances, even the man himself.

But the Frenchman evidently took the comment in stride because he merely lifted his eyebrows and said, "I think, *mon ami,* that your pride has taken a beating, and your honor. *"Après tout,* you can always find another woman, they are half the earth's population." He touched his fist to the Englishman's shoulder. "But a man's honor is entirely another matter."

The younger man swung away from the window. He leafed through some of the ledgers atop the battered desk across the room, feigning interest. He suspected, however, that the wily du Casse wasn't fooled. But he couldn't meet the Frenchman's probing gaze just yet, for he feared the man would see the fresh pain conjured up by memories of her. And by the manner in which he had been set up, plain and simple, and had foolishly fallen for the ruse, throwing away his chances for happiness.

He could still picture the earl's outraged expression as he'd burst into the room above the London tavern and had caught Luke in bed with a woman, a beautiful woman of loose morals whom the earl had hired to seduce him, Pelton had later learned.

For that, he would never forgive Somerset. And one day, mayhap not soon, but one day before the breath left his body for the last time, he would make the man who'd tricked and humiliated him pay dearly.

Five

"Why, Devil Chandler, you're a sight for sore eyes!"

The fiery-haired woman threw herself into Devin's embrace with all the exuberance of a hurricane, almost bowling him over in the process.

"Ah, Maddy, m'dear," he sighed into her hair (which, he noticed, smelled of smoke and stale food) "ye make a man's heart do a jig in his chest."

She pushed away from him and gave him a look that said she didn't believe a word he said. "Faith, but ye're a charmer. Must be yer Irish blood, and that convenient brogue." Her brown eyes narrowed. "Although ye can drink with the best of 'em, I can vouch fer that!"

He threw back his head and laughed.

"Pretty cocky, ain't ye, Devil, when 'tis said ye were rotting in Newgate these last few months." Her brow creased. "I was worried about ye, luv."

"I'm not rotting anymore, lass, and I've missed that sharp tongue of yours."

"Is that all?" she purred, rubbing up against him suggestively.

He tolerated her behavior for a moment, for it was perfectly appropriate in a bawdy house like the Seaman's Folly. They blended in with the noisy, lusty crowd around them. It was early evening and several ships had arrived in the harbor earlier in the day. Devin could tell by the crowds of drunken men prowling the streets of Port Royal.

The barkeeps and serving girls, the prostitutes and pick-pockets, would be hauling in the gold and silver this night in every tavern and whorehouse in town.

For once, however, Maddy's attentions didn't arouse even a lukewarm response, and suddenly a dark-haired woman sitting in the lap of a buccaneer nearby caught his attention. His heart jumped to his throat for a moment. He couldn't see her face, but she reminded him too vividly of Meredyth St. Andrews. Yet he knew that it was only superficial. Up close her hair would be dyed, mayhap to hide any telltale signs of silver or its natural mousy color. Mayhap it wasn't even her hair, and he knew for certain if she turned around, her face could never be as sweet and exquisite as that of the woman staying at the mission.

Without warning, the woman in his arms aroused the first, faint stirrings of revulsion within him. Her ample breasts, which mounded over the black lace edging of her gawdy scarlet gown, didn't beckon his touch as they normally did. And the titian hair, he noticed for the first time, wasn't thick and shiny and, of a certainty, didn't exude the fragrance of wild violets.

He deliberately pressed his mouth over hers, as if the kiss could wipe his mind clean of thoughts of Meredyth St. Andrews. A few hoots of encouragement sounded around them, moving Devin to increase the intensity of the kiss, opening his mouth over Maddy's and plunging his tongue into hers.

The kiss was long and wet and rough. He briefly felt a stirring in his loins but not the degree of arousal he normally evinced after months without a woman. Maddy's hands were all over him, brazenly stroking his back and buttocks, before traveling around toward his . . .

He put her away from him and drew in a deep, ragged breath. "Not here," he said shortly, irritation edging his words.

Maddy looked puzzled, in spite of the passion that glazed her eyes. "Then up the stairs, sweetheart," she purred, "and we'll finish what we started here, ummmm?"

"Rum. I need rum first," he answered, thinking the drink would help. He was oddly relieved as, apparently seeing no serving girl close by, Maddy released him with reluctance and went to fetch the drink herself. She threw him a glance over her bare shoulder, her painted lips in a pout, her eyes smoldering with obvious desire and promise. "Don't go away," she mouthed then and disappeared.

Devin glanced around him, looking for a familiar face. Even the most reluctant tongues inevitably loosened with enough drink, and Devin had no doubt that he could discover something about Giles Glasby before the evening turned to morn.

Before he could spot someone he knew, however, the thudding sound of pewter hitting the oaken floor signaled trouble nearby. He turned automatically, thinking to move out of some drunken sailor's path, just in time to see Maddy waylaid by a huge and tough-looking buccaneer, the tankards she'd been carrying bouncing about the floor and spewing out their contents.

"Why, you drunken cullion!" Maddy shrieked at him as he proceeded to grab her around the waist and drag her into his arms.

"Let me—"

The man's mouth descended brutally to cover hers, cutting off her words, and he plunged one hand inside her gaping bodice.

Maddy was no angel; she was a hardened prostitute. But because she was a woman, and because of their long-standing, if casual and carnal, relationship, Devin didn't think twice about going to her aid. He leaped at the buccaneer; grabbed the long, tarred stretch of braid that hung down his back; and delivered him a stunning kidney punch.

"Let her go," he ordered in a steely undertone.

The buccaneer released Maddy with a grunt of surprise mingled with obvious pain and swung toward his attacker, his bearded face dark with outrage. But as the man turned, Devin kept his hold on the tarred braid, which acted like a noose about the ruffian's neck.

The man clumsily pirouetted about the other way, like a drunken dancing bear, and was greeted by Devin's fist in his belly. The miscreant folded in half at the waist like a broken spar, then pitched headfirst to the floor.

Devin cast a look about him, his expression calm but deadly. Oddly, no one seemed eager for a brawl, or else it was the sudden presence of Tom O'Shea, the burly barkeep, and two other hulking tavern employees that subdued the crowd.

"Don't want no trouble, Chandler," O'Shea growled as the other two bent to lift the downed buccaneer and drag him to the door.

"And don't you be a fool, O'Shea," Maddy said as she moved up to Devin, gratitude in her eyes. "That pricklouse not only made me spill precious rum intended fer a payin' customer here, but he was also interferin' with business."

"Jake would'a paid fer yer precious services, trollop," said a voice from off to the side.

Both Maddy and Devin turned toward the voice. Another wicked-looking buccaneer stepped menacingly close to Devin, one hand on the hilt of the dagger at his waist.

"Then he'd o' been wastin' his gold," Maddy snapped, "because from his paltry excuse for a kiss, and in his drunken stupor, he couldn't even've got it up!"

"Break it up here," snarled the owner, Samuel Threatt. As big as the men who worked for him, Threatt had the reputation of being able to handle any man who came into his place.

However, at the change in expression on Devin's face, he had second thoughts about his reprimand. "The no-brawlin' rule has no exceptions, Devil Chandler, not even you," he said, his gruff voice softening a trace.

"I didn't start it," Devin said tightly.

"I can vouch fer that and so can any number o' men here," Maddy threw in. "You know me well enough, Sam, to take me at my word." The words held a subtle challenge that Devin didn't miss. Maddy was one of the Folly's most popular whores, and Threatt would be foolish to lose her to any number of competitors lining the streets of Port Royal, especially over something so minor.

"All right then," Threatt said, not very apologetically. Then to Maddy, he added, "Get the man another drink . . . on the house."

Maddy grinned at Devin and winked, then sashayed away again.

As Devin nodded his thanks, a sudden thought struck him. "Say, Samuel?" he said before the big man could turn away.

Threatt frowned warily. "Aye?"

Devin motioned to the only empty table in the taproom. "Any information about the crew of the *Lady Elysia?* My former crew, that is?"

Threatt didn't sit but stood staring down at Devin, one hand on his hip, the other stroking his bushy brown beard. "Accordin' to the story, after they hauled ye off, most of 'em were ready to kill Glasby. But they couldn't find him. A few come in here, lookin' fer work." He shrugged. "Some are still about, I 'magine, but most found work on other ships."

Devin placed two pieces of gold on the bruised tabletop and pushed them toward Threatt, whose dark eyes lit. "I'd appreciate it if you'd keep your eyes and ears open concerning my crew and, just between the two of us, the departed Giles Glasby."

Threatt picked up the coins, pocketed them and nodded. "We c'n talk more when it ain't so busy, Chandler. I'd like to hear what happened in England." He gave Devin a sly wink. "And directly from the horse's mouth, eh?" He swung away then, just as Maddy came up with two fresh tankards of rum.

It was her anger that gave Meredyth the greatest impetus— that drove her to leave the mission in spite of Father Tomas's exhortations to do otherwise. "You cannot just march into the infamous Port Royal to find that rascal!" he'd objected, obviously bewildered by her intentions. Yet it was not only her outrage at Captain Devin Chandler's having gone against his word that prompted her to go. Her need to find him and tell him exactly what she thought of him, to berate him for his very cowardly and dishonorable behavior, was fueled on a deeper level by lingering pain and anger at Lucien Pendwell's betrayal.

The donkey ride down part of the mountain had been awkward and uncomfortable—and sharing the animal's back with two bundles of straw hats and other handmade trinkets from the mission to sell made it even worse—but Dionisio had insisted she ride. Then, as they'd made their way along the sand spit and toward the city itself, Meredyth was glad for the animal, for the sun and sand were burning hot by the time they'd begun this second phase of their jaunt.

Every time the sea breeze blew off her straw hat, Manuel faithfully retrieved it, and under Dionisio's stern gaze she would reluctantly jam it back onto her piled up hair. She'd already lost her bodkins in the rainforest, for anchoring her thick, heavy tresses under normal circumstances was a challenge for any hairpin, to say nothing of a bumping and bruising descent down a mountainside.

"Marry come up!" she'd exclaimed to the Cimaroon. "What does it matter? We're wasting precious time chasing that silly hat!"

His only response came, however, when, just before reaching the outskirts of Port Royal, he'd braided her hair with surprising gentleness and, using a piece of thin leather thong, somehow secured the braid to the crown of her head before plopping the hated hat over her hair one more time. "Must look like boy, not *mujer.*"

"You don't think your musket will ensure my safety?" she'd answered wryly, eyeing the European-made weapon he carried.

The Cimaroon had only shaken his head in answer. And

Manuel, if he had an opinion, couldn't voice it, as the Spaniards had long-ago cut out his tongue.

Meredyth's heart had jumped a beat or two in response, for she remembered docking in Port Royal and being whisked right through it by the men designated by her father to escort her to the mission posthaste. Yet it was excitement, not fear, that had brought on the surge of adrenaline.

Dionisio led them to the inn Father Tomas had suggested, and Meredyth was shown to the last room they had. She ordered dinner to be brought to her room and laid down on the bed exhausted.

Now a knock on the door roused her from her thoughts. "Who is it?"

"Dionisio."

Meredyth rose from the bed, casting a glance at the single window of the room and, realizing it was close to twilight, knew she must act now or remain another night in the inn before seeking out the elusive Devil Chandler. She didn't particularly relish the idea of staying any longer than necessary, in spite of the fact that the city fascinated her. In fact, if she hadn't desperately needed sleep, she would have inquired about Chandler's house and confronted him in his own home during the afternoon.

Dionisio, with Manuel behind him, presented her with a simple dinner tray, which, after she'd reseated herself on the narrow bed, she attacked with enthusiasm.

Once she finished her meal, they left their lodgings to seek Chandler.

Port Royal wasn't named the "wickedest city in the world" for nothing. Seamen of every type trafficked its streets, from elegant merchants to swaggering buccaneers to rowdy English sailors to the most unscrupulous pirates. The number of bawdy houses and tippling places, or taverns, was mind-boggling. Prostitutes of every race—their skin ranging from deepest ebony to red to olive to lily-white—openly competed with each other by brazenly advertising their charms.

One woman, whose origins were impossible to discern beneath her heavily made-up face, carmined lips, and poorly dyed brassy hair, eyed the three of them and, in spite of the two tall, stern-eyed escorts, boldly stepped toward Meredyth in the sunset-gilded, cobblestoned street.

Meredyth, who was leading the donkey, flanked by Dionisio and Manuel, was surprised at the woman's approach, momentarily forgetting her male attire.

Dionisio stepped between Meredyth and the woman, but Meredyth held up her hand to him and smiled tentatively at the prostitute. Pity rather than revulsion surfaced from the depths of her innermost self.

She opened her mouth to politely refuse the woman's advances, but was stopped before she could get out a single word. "Damn, but ye're a fine specimen of a male!" the bold prostitute crowed, ignoring the two men. "I like my men on the smaller side—can't hurt me so much if I don't please 'em." She gave Meredyth a grin, revealing rotting teeth in an otherwise comely, if overdone, face. "An' I like 'em young an' fine-featured like yerself, too."

"What's your name?" Meredyth asked in her deepest voice as an idea popped suddenly into her mind.

"Arabella," the whore pronounced proudly, and formed a pout with her outlandishly painted lips. She placed one nail-laquered hand on Meredyth's arm in an overtly provocative manner.

Instantly Dionisio's hand was on her wrist. His strong dark fingers curled over her bare arm like shackles and jerked the hand away from Meredyth.

"Not like your kind," Dionisio said flatly, his deep, accented voice punctuating the sudden unease that swirled about them on the street.

"Hey, Cimaroon," shouted a passerby who was obviously well into his cups. "Watch out fer Arabella, she'll steal yer boy from ye." And the dark-bearded, flush-faced buccaneer threw back his head and exploded into laughter, the scarlet red kerchief covering his hair fluttering in the breeze.

"What do you mean, don't like my kind?" Arabella asked with a speculative narrowing of her eyes. "Or is it other young boys ye like?" she accused.

A choked sound emanated from Manuel as Meredyth tried to hide her shock. She'd been warned not to go into Port Royal.

She shook her head, feeling the heavy braid shift slightly under the hat. Please, God, she silently prayed, don't let it fall and give me away.

After a darting glance at the buccaneer, who was weaving his way past them as laughter still erupted from his throat, Meredyth said to Arabella, " 'Tisn't that, Arabella. But I have need of your services . . . or rather your assistance in a matter that—"

"What?" Arabella asked, obviously suspicious now. "I do naught that's unnatural, I'll have ye know." She lifted her chin. "I do have standards!"

Distress flitted across Meredyth's fine features. "I'm sure you do, Arabella, and I didn't mean to insult you. But I'll pay you for your time if you'll just give me . . ." she lowered her voice, "a bit of information."

Arabella crossed her arms. "Lookin' fer work, mayhap?" she asked slyly. "Ain't as much work fer men as fer women in the profession." Disappointment crept across her features. "An' I was thinkin' ye was mighty fine-lookin' fer such a young man."

"Master," Dionisio began, a storm brewing on his dark countenance.

Meredyth slanted him a warning look. "I would know, Arabella, where a man was likely to go . . ." She felt heat creep up her cheeks. "That is, which brothel is considered . . ." She trailed off again, feeling indeed like a blushing, stripling youth about to ask for the favors of a female for the very first time. "You see, I'm looking for a certain man," she began again.

Arabella's disappointment was short-lived. Disinterest began to register on her features after another grimace of distaste, and her eyes began to rove, presumably on to more promising prospects.

Meredyth touched the woman's arm with urgency, her low-spoken words emerging in a rush. "I'll pay you for a night's worth of work if you can tell me what bawdy house or tavern a man like Captain Devin Chandler would frequent."

"Why, Devil Chandler," Arabella said, her voice sounding suddenly strident to Meredyth, even on the noisy street. She grinned. "Now there's a man!" She peered over the donkey's back, seemingly to get a better glimpse of Manuel. Meredyth assumed she'd already taken Dionisio's measure and realized the futility of attracting him as a client. "Let me see yer gold first," Arabella said, returning her gaze to Meredyth with unnerving swiftness.

Meredyth reached beneath the baggy shirt she wore and into a small, drawstring pouch at her waist. She quickly flashed the coin at Arabella, then closed her fingers around it. "Well?" she pressed, suddenly feeling conspicuous standing on a street in Port Royal and dealing openly with a whore.

"Try the Seaman's Folly," Arabella said, her eyes lighting at the sight of the coin. She jerked her chin to the side, indicating the direction. "On Thames Street."

Meredyth gave her the gold, wondering if the woman was deceiving her merely to get the money. But it was too late. Arabella snatched the coin and backed away. "Try there, my pretty lad. But I warn ye, Devil Chandler don't like boys."

"You up on your Greek mythology, Maddy?" Devin inquired with a lift of an eyebrow.

Maddy looked confused. "My what?"

He shook his head. "Never mind, m'dear." Had he left his mind in Newgate? What would ever make him think that a woman who made her living on her back in rowdy Port Royal would know anything about mythology?

"Do any of the ladies here have a formal education?"

Maddy leaned forward, her brown eyes twinkling with lusty mischief. "Oh, we all have an education, sweetheart. Come upstairs wi' me and I'll pass it on to you."

Devin laughed aloud. "Oh, you've taught me just fine over the years, Maddy, m'girl." He leaned toward her so their heads were close over the small table. "But I had some questions about more scholarly things."

Maddy propped one elbow on the table and dropped her chin into her hand. "Didn't know you was scholarly." She studied Devin for a moment, as if trying to decide if he was serious. "Well, there's a new girl here at the Folly, came while you were away in England." She placed both hands about her mug of rum and transferred her gaze to its contents, as if choosing her words with some care. Thoughtfulness creased her brow for a moment. "Name's Ember. She comes from a good family, in the Colonies I think. An' she talks like she's educated, though she's never mentioned 'er past." She looked up at him, her gaze narrowed with obvious speculation.

Her heavy perfume drifted over to him, in spite of the overpowering smells of sweat and pipe smoke and cooking food. Once again, without warning, he remembered Meredyth St. Andrews's scent, a fragrance that vividly reminded him of the Ireland of his early childhood and wildflowers. And his mother.

"You ain't tired o' me, Irishman, are ye?" she growled with mock sternness. "Lookin' fer younger blood and firmer flesh, mayhap?"

Deviltry danced in his eyes as he pressed his lips together to hide a grin and shook his head. "Never!"

Maddy sighed. She pushed back her mug and stood. "I'll find her, if she ain't busy, an' send 'er over fer a bit." She pointed a beringed finger at him. "But I'll be back, Devil Chandler, and my drink there can hold my place."

He nodded. "Of course. And Maddy? I'll owe you one."

She swung away, then paused to add with a lift of a painted eyebrow, "Oh, you'll owe me more than one, Chandler. She's a real looker, too, so make sure all ye do is talk." And with that she flounced away.

Maddy returned quickly with another young woman in tow. His mind suddenly went blank and his glib tongue deserted him as he was introduced to Ember, whose black hair and eyes suggested Welsh parentage.

Maddy neatly retreated before he could prevent it, and he either had to ask his nonsensical query about mythology or show a genuine interest in her as a female and risk insulting Maddy by taking another whore beneath the same roof.

Meredyth stood near the entrance, attempting to focus her gaze through the smoky atmosphere of the taproom. She had to organize her thoughts, form a plan now that she was actually at the Seaman's Folly, a plan that wouldn't cause any commotion or Dionisio and Manuel would come bursting in to her rescue and ruin everything. That is, if Devin Chandler was, indeed, there.

And the two men ran the risk of being punished, for it was risky for a Cimaroon—or any other runaway slave—to enter public tippling houses or brothels.

However, Meredyth's complete attention was caught by, and riveted to, the scene being played out before her. Women in various states of *déshabille* were lounging in men's laps and feeding or fondling them, engaged in raucous badinage or drinking contests, a few even involved in lively conversation.

It was a shifting scene of bright color and movement; the noise was overpowering to her sensitive ears, the smell redolent of food and drink and pleasures of the flesh. At first, Meredyth could only stare at the gaudily dressed prostitutes and the only slightly less gaily dressed seamen, merchants, and planters. Many of the men were clad in the very latest flamboyant and often foppish English fashion, while the more wild-looking men of the privateer and pirate crews created their own kaleidoscope of colors and styles.

Her anger and purpose temporarily overridden by her sense of curiosity and wonder at the animated mural of decadence being enacted before her, Meredyth gaped for some minutes.

And then, after quartering the room with her gaze several times, she spotted Devin Chandler. He was sitting with a dark-haired woman, their heads very close.

No doubt, she thought bitterly, discussing the evening's arrangements. Her eyes narrowed, and the sight of him blithely making plans with a prostitute while up at the mission a sick man was devastated by his desertion helped purge her of any emotion but anger.

Then, without warning, someone grabbed her around the waist and roughly hoisted her off her feet as if she were no more than a light bundle of kindling. She briefly thought of Dionisio and Manuel outside but, in spite of her surprise and shock, was reluctant to call out for them.

"Well, what have we here?" growled a gravel-rough voice in her ear.

Six

The voice sounded vaguely familiar, but Meredyth couldn't place it. She struggled in vain, ineffectively kicking her legs but managing to give her captor an elbow in the ribs.

"Oof!" she had the satisfaction of hearing in the wake of her puny but obviously unexpected blow. "Enough o' that or I'll truss you like a plump hen on 'er way to market!"

Meredyth twisted in his grip and caught a glimpse of dark, bushy facial hair and a red kerchief.

"Only ye ain't very plump," the man added, setting her down without relinquishing his hold and meeting her eyes widened with outrage. "But the Cimaroon won't mind if I borrow you fer a while, eh?" He winked lewdly, then lowered his voice. "I like a lad now and then—breaks up the monotony, if ye know what I mean—especially young and spare lads."

"Dionisio?" she whispered with a sinking feeling. "What have you done to him? And Manuel?"

"Let's just say they're restin' fer the moment, eh? Given their overprotectiveness, I decided a few cronies should settle 'em down fer a while."

She braced her knuckles on her hips, her lips tightening in anger, and gave him a glimpse of the St. Andrews fury. Part of that anger was directed at herself, as well, for if either man had been harmed, it was because of her and her reckless trek into Port Royal. "If you hurt them, I'll see that you regret it for the rest of your miserable days, cutthroat."

A frown chased briefly across his pockmarked forehead. "You threatenin' me, lad? An' callin' me a common cutthroat?"

"You'd better convince me of their safety or I'll announce to all and sundry that you're a sodomite."

She couldn't believe the coolness and audacity that had suddenly taken control, let alone her foolhardiness in insulting this dangerous man by name-calling. But Meredyth remembered overhearing one of her father's crewmen mention to another in the seaport of Bristol that sodomites weren't welcome in brothels that offered women. Few men—even toughened seamen—had any liking for men who used other men or, worse, boys. Especially if they were unwilling.

In her present predicament, she was willing to grab at anything. The miscreant gripped her by the shirtfront and pulled her toward him angrily. His breath seared across her face, making her stomach heave with revulsion. "You'll keep your damned mouth shut, boy, and mind your harpy's tongue or you'll not see another sunrise!"

"And I'll shout it this instant, if you don't take your hands off me," she countered in his face, finding new bravado in her desperation and hoping to attract attention.

By now, several onlookers had moved in closer for a better look, and Meredyth was sorely tempted to make good her threat.

Consternation flickered in the ruffian's dark eyes for a moment, and he opened his mouth to speak.

"Why, lad, how I've missed ye!" exclaimed a feminine voice. "What kind o' mischief are ye gettin' into this time?"

Meredyth looked into the face of a woman with flame-bright hair, who was gazing at her as if she were the most desirable male on the entire island. She barely caught the impression of fading beauty beneath the woman's heavy rouge and powder. A black beauty patch at one corner of her brightly painted mouth leapt out at Meredyth.

"And you, Aaron Davies, what're ye doin' brawlin' in the Folly? Ye know O'Shea won't tolerate it, or Samuel, neither."

She linked her left arm through Meredyth's as Davies released the latter's shirt, his mouth momentarily agape.

"Well," he began, thrusting out his chin as he quickly recovered his belligerence, "this young cullion was callin'—"

"Cullion?" she interrupted with an exaggerated expression of shock. "Why, ye're scarin' the poor lad—er, *Chad*—to death! Not much more than a virgin, he is, and Maddy here's takin' care o' that! I wager he was just comin' to see me, weren't ye, Chad?" she asked Meredyth with a melodramatic wink. "Continue our lessons o' love, ummmm?" She returned her attention to Davies. "Tsk, tsk, Aaron, ye brawny devil, ye know 'tis bad business to frighten away the customers!" She unexpectedly reached over to press the palm of her free hand to Meredyth's heart. "Why 'is heart's bangin' against 'is rib cage like a woodpecker against a decayin' tree!" She grinned. "No offense, sweetheart."

Maybe the vibration of her thumping heart was enough to distract the prostitute from her femininity, Meredyth thought as Maddy's hand moved up to briefly caress her neck and throat.

"You tell him, Maddy!" encouraged one of the men nearby.

The chastened buccaneer snapped his mouth closed and allowed Maddy to lead her client toward the bar. Meredyth expelled a breath of relief, even as hectic color spotted her cheeks at this ridiculous situation.

They neared the table where Chandler had been sitting, but Meredyth was too preoccupied with her predicament to notice that he was no longer there. Maddy grabbed a tankard from a passing serving girl's tray and shoved it into Meredyth's hands. "Here, lad. This'll shore up yer courage . . . and other things, as well," she said with a wicked dip of one eyelid, and then made Meredyth lift the vessel to her lips and take a swig.

Whatever it was, it jolted past her lips and down her gullet like molten lava. A cough gathered in her throat and her eyes watered, but she bit her tongue to keep from choking or spitting the last bit onto the planked floor.

"Good stuff, eh?" Maddy said with a knowing grin and, after placing an arm about Meredyth's shoulders, guided her up the stairs toward the second floor.

They traversed a dim hallway, decorated by small lamps set in the stained crimson and gold wallpaper. The smell of spirits, dampness, pipe smoke, and decadence invaded Meredyth's nostrils. The latter had the contradictory effect of repulsing and titillating her at the same time.

Before she could consider the strange sensations within her, they paused outside one of several closed doors. Maddy's arm fell away from Meredyth's shoulders as she motioned to the tankard still clutched in Meredyth's left hand and ordered, "Take another swig, girlie. Ye'll need it."

Meredyth's eyes widened at Maddy's word choice and she shook her head. "Don't be absurd! I'm not a—"

"O' course ye are," the woman said impatiently and pushed the tankard up to Meredyth's mouth. "My friend's taste runs only to females."

Dear God, had Maddy rescued her from the buccaneer only to give her to another man who liked women?

"Well, actually, I am a—" she began in alarm.

"Drink!"

Meredyth obediently took another gulp, wondering what was about to happen and deciding another draught might help her face whatever was to come.

Maddy reached around her and pushed open the door. "Go on in before Mad Dog Davies changes 'is mind an' comes after ye," the prostitute said. "He'd be mighty irritated to discover 'e was taken in." She gave Meredyth a firm shove, and the latter stumbled into the darkened room, the drink in her tumbler sloshing over the side and onto one wrist with the abrupt movement.

"But, I don't—" she began, turning back toward the retreating Maddy.

Her protest trailed off as the door closed behind her. She heard the scratch of flint, and a single candle flared. Then another in a three-candled candelabrum. The fragile, flickering light cast leaping shadows upon the face of the man looming over it, and Meredyth drew in her breath sharply.

"If for naught else but simple gratitude, pray tell me, Lady Meredyth, exactly what you're doing at the Seaman's Folly . . . and dressed as a youth?"

Meredyth fought for composure. Hadn't Chandler been downstairs? At a table with a bawd, and completely unaware of her entrance?

Unthinkingly, she took another drink, as if the liquid were an elixir that would magically change this suddenly topsy-turvy world back to some semblance of normality. It went down more easily with every swallow.

"Ah." He nodded, as if suddenly enlightened, then lit the third candle. "I see you've a taste for brandywine."

" 'Tis my father's favorite drink . . . and my lady mother's name," she blurted out, then wished she hadn't. She was supposed to be full of righteous indignation. She needed to take the offensive rather than allow him to put her on the defense.

And how did he know she was drinking brandywine?

"So 'tis a St. Andrews trait? And the countess of Somerset is named Brandywyne?" He frowned slightly, seeming to mull over these interesting tidbits. Then he raised his eyebrows and made a mocking moue. "That could explain why you're here, I suppose. I mean, peculiarity obviously runs in the family, as well as love of the drink." He moved forward, and Meredyth noticed for the first time that his shirt was off.

All intentions of verbally defending her family's honor fled.

She stepped backward toward the door at the thought of what normally took place in this room between a man and a woman, though that idea did wonders to bolster her courage and mobilize her tongue. "To answer your first question, Captain Chandler, I was looking for you."

He grinned wolfishly. "Really! I'm very flattered, for not

many women would risk life and limb to follow a man from the haven of a Jesuit mission to rollicking Port Royal." Then his grin disappeared and his eyes turned wintry. "And manage to almost get herself raped by a rascal who thought she was a youth. What would you have done had Maddy not gone to your rescue?"

"You sent her!" she exclaimed as understanding dawned.

His features relaxed a little, and one sun-gilt brow curved upward. "Of course, little Sister Meredyth. Did you think I'd risk tangling with the likes of Mad Dog Davies?"

She shook her head emphatically. "Certainly not. Cowards let others take the risks for them. And that's exactly what you are, Captain Chandler, a coward."

"Because I didn't wish to brawl with Davies?" He moved toward her again, but this time Meredyth didn't budge. Outrage anchored her to the floor, in spite of the scent of him that assailed her nostrils and sent a thread of arousal spiraling through her middle.

"You know, Merry-mine," he was saying, "that the better part of valor is discretion? Why should a man use his brawn when his wits can serve him just as well? Mayhap even better, as in this case?"

"Don't try to weasel your way out of it!" She clutched the tankard to her midriff as he moved steadily toward her and eyed her straw hat, which had miraculously clung to her head during the struggle thanks to Dionisio's earlier efforts.

The thought of the Cimaroon threatened to snag her concentration, for two men were possibly injured because of her. Yet Devin Chandler's nearness held her attention unwillingly captive. Just what was he about? A game of cat and mouse? "You sent a woman to place herself between that pirate and me rather than confront him yourself!"

He let out a heavy sigh, the very picture of indolence. "Very well, you've discovered my darkest secret. I'm the basest of cowards." He reached out toward her hat then, but she remained unmoving, too busy struggling with the odd disappointment sifting through her at the fact that he hadn't been willing to risk a fight to come to her aid. Yet he had rescued Bakámu, a stranger at the time, from an attacking crocodile. And at great peril, according to the boy, Juan. The man was an enigma, to say the least.

The hat moved but didn't come free. Devin stepped forward before she could move away and reached beneath it to free it from her head. He tossed it aside, and her heavy braid fell down her back.

"As I see it," he said, his fingers working to loosen the long, chestnut plait, "my plan worked beautifully. No brawl, no injury . . . except possibly to your feminine pride. And—"

She dropped the tankard and reached with both hands to remove his fingers from her hair. The vessel thumped to the floor, spewing brandywine as it rolled, while her hands encountered his. "Take your—"

The thud of the vessel hitting the floor was repeated outside in the hallway, but in rapid succession, someone's hurried footsteps.

Devin stiffened, his head canted toward the sound. In the next instant, he grabbed Meredyth around the waist and flung her none too gently onto the gaudily bolstered bed.

"What do you think—?"

His mouth slanting over hers cut her off, and, to her horror, he grabbed hold of her shirt and rent it down the middle, exposing her bound chest. He threw one leg over hers to pin her down, then grabbed and pulled at the bands of cloth that had been part of her disguise. His low curse revealed they weren't as easily shredded as the shirt, and seemingly from out of nowhere he produced a dagger and expertly slit the strips.

Meredyth began to struggle, though with little success, for the wine was producing an insidious languor. Nonetheless, the pressure of his mouth turned bruising in answer, as if he were punishing, or warning, her. "Shhh!" he hissed into her ear, freeing her lips for a heartbeat, "if you value your virtue!"

She felt the cloth bands about her torso fall away as the dagger disappeared and his fingers worked feverishly to fling them aside.

The boots pounding along the passageway stopped at the room just before theirs. A fist assaulted the wooden door, and a voice thundered, "Where's the boy?"

Chandler had warned her, and now Meredyth felt real fear. Instinctively following his lead, she wound her arms about his back and tried to relax against the mattress beneath him. It was easy enough, with the wine racing through her, robbing her of some of her maidenly inhibitions, and urging her to trust Devin Chandler, coward and scoundrel that he was, to take care of things.

The footsteps moved to the door of their room, and Devin awkwardly fanned her unbraided hair out across the mattress. She couldn't cry out against the tangles he encountered in his haste, for his mouth never left hers. Then, with his other hand, he jerked the coverlet from beneath Meredyth and stuffed it between them.

The door burst open and slammed back against the wall. It shook the entire room, and Devin dropped back against Meredyth with a swift but controlled movement.

She looked into his face as he pulled away from the kiss at the interruption. Although he somehow managed to look surprised and tousled, Meredyth felt the coiled tautness that suddenly stretched along the length of his body.

"Jesus, Davies!" he said with convincing irritation. "Can't a man enjoy his paid-for privacy for even a few minutes?"

At the same time, he unobtrusively relieved Meredyth of enough of his weight that she could draw the coverlet he'd bunched between their bodies far enough upward to hide her breeches and most of her exposed breasts.

She also now realized why Chandler had taken such pains to spread out her hair. That left only the straw hat to give her away. Where had he tossed it? she wondered, knowing it was too late now to do anything about it.

He sat up, his body shielding much of Meredyth from the buccaneer's gaze.

"Who's in that bed?" Mad Dog bellowed as he stepped forward, one huge hand going to the hilt of the cutlass at his waist.

Meredyth's heart leapt to her throat, and she fought the urge to shove Chandler to his feet.

"Aren't you being a bit rash?" Devin was saying, his voice calm.

"Get out of the way!" Davies demanded. He lunged toward the bed.

Just as Meredyth noticed Chandler's hand snatch at the dagger at the back of his belt, another voice roared from the door, "One step farther, and I'll blow ye to kingdom come, Davies!"

Mad Dog froze in mid-step.

"Drop the cutlass."

The weapon clattered to the floor.

"Now, turn around and see what's waitin' fer anyone who don't abide by the rules o' the Folly, caitiff!"

By now, Meredyth's curiosity exceeded her trepidation, and she sat up and peeped over Chandler's shoulder, covers still pressed against her bosom.

In the open doorway stood a behemoth of a man, holding a pistol aimed at Mad Dog's middle, and between his huge form and the doorjamb, a flash of flaming hair and wide brown eyes revealed Maddy peering into the room.

"Ye better have one hell of an excuse fer blunderin' into half the occupied rooms upstairs here like a lovesick bull, disturbin' my customers and causin' a commotion throughout the entire place!"

"Samuel, she was the lad I was speakin' to," Davies snarled, pointing to Meredyth.

"The boy was lookin' fer me when Mad Dog waylaid him at the door downstairs," Maddy shot back from behind the shield of Threatt's bulk. "I saw the whole thing."

"Waylayin' good-payin' customers, were you?" Threatt

growled. "That's like tellin' 'em to go elsewhere, whether by talk or by deed."

"But he didn't say he was lookin' fer Maddy," Mad Dog blustered. "He seemed content enough—"

"Whoever's behind Devil Chandler looks more like a fetchin' piece to me than a lad," Samuel rebutted. "And even if she turned out to be a he, you'd o' been put off the premises anyway fer intendin' to engage in unnatural practices beneath my roof."

"And I find this entire disturbance unwarranted," Devin said in a bored voice. Meredyth felt his hand slip from the dagger hilt and move unobtrusively to rest on the mattress beside him. "We've been up here for at least half an hour, Davies." As he held the nasty-looking buccaneer's gaze, one corner of his mouth slanted upward insinuatingly. "There isn't a masculine hair on my light o' love's entire body. I've gone over every luscious inch of it, you see." He shrugged and gave the fuming Davies an engaging grin. "You've obviously got the wrong person. But I'm a forgiving soul."

At the intimacies he seemed to delight in announcing, Meredyth pulled back. She jabbed him in the spine with a knuckle and took immense pleasure in feeling him jerk slightly in reaction. She'd show him "light o' love"!

The candlelight danced in the draft from the passageway. The muted noise from the taproom downstairs came to them through the cheaply carpeted floor. And then the stink of Mad Dog Davies came to Meredyth and brought with it the helplessness and terror she'd felt at his hands, in spite of her brazen show of bravado. She wanted to open her mouth and tell the blackguard to get out—all of them get out—so she could give Devin Chandler the tongue-lashing she'd been rehearsing mentally since she'd discovered he'd gone sneaking off like a thief in the night.

But she wasn't that foolish. She kept quiet and stayed where she was, praying the other three would make a quick exit. She had no doubts as to the owner of the establishment's willingness to use the pistol and didn't want to contribute to Davies's death.

That is, until she remembered Dionisio and Manuel.

Just as Mad Dog was moving toward the door, his hands in the air, Meredyth said, "Master Samuel?" She felt, rather than heard, Devin's indrawn hiss of breath.

The buccaneer halted, and Threatt looked over at her. "Aye?" he rumbled.

"There are two injured men, my friends, somewhere outside your establishment. He—Master Davies—implied that he had his cronies hurt them so they couldn't come in after me." Her voice wobbled when she pronounced the word "hurt."

Samuel Threatt's brow darkened even further. He looked at Maddy and motioned toward the stairway with his chin. "We'll see that they're tended to."

Maddy disappeared down the hallway with light footsteps.

Samuel shook his big, shaggy head. "I ought to shoot ye right here, Davies. How dare you accost two potential customers outside the Folly's door?"

"She's lyin'. She can't prove aught!" Mad Dog huffed as he glared over his shoulder at Meredyth for one uncomfortable moment. "An' 'twas only a Maroon an' a deaf mute Arawak, anyway," he added sullenly.

Meredyth felt Devin stiffen. She glanced at the devil-handsome profile, but there was no other sign of his feelings.

"If they like women," Samuel said, "they're welcome as customers. I'll decide who ain't fit to enter the Folly, Davies, and not you." He motioned to the buccaneer with the pistol barrel. "Don't ever show yer face in here again," he pronounced harshly, "or I'll blow ye all the way back to England."

"Now, you say you were looking for me?"

Meredyth met Devin's gaze as he looked over his shoulder. There was a glint of humor in his crystal blue eyes and a tilt to one side of his handsome mouth. He looked like a fair-haired devil, Meredyth thought again. His sobriquet fit him well.

The scent of him filled her senses—she was still seated intimately close to his naked back—and threatened reason once again.

"Aye," she snapped, rousing herself from the increasingly erotic web he seemed to be unconsciously weaving about her. With an effort, she reached deep within and drew on her anger. "But 'tis no compliment to you."

He turned toward her, and Meredyth scooted backward. The more space between them, the better.

"Ah, yes. Something about my lack of courage," he said with sham solemnity.

" 'Tis bad enough you sent Maddy to my rescue, but I'm here to take you back to the mission! How could you desert a dying man?"

For a fraction of time, his teasing look remained. Then, as her words registered, it slid from his face. "Dying?"

She swallowed her guilt. Even with his fever broken, Bakámu surely could still die. Couldn't he?

But Devin Chandler didn't know the Arawak's fever had broken.

"Indeed," she said with a righteous tilt of her chin.

She thought she discerned a flicker of genuine concern in his eyes, but it was gone before she could confirm it and she suddenly had other things on her mind. Like the state of her borrowed shirt.

"That's unfortunate," he said unexpectedly. "I could have used him as my manservant here in Port Royal."

Her look turned incredulous. "What use would a—" She closed her mouth with a snap, appalled at almost having voiced her caustic thoughts aloud.

"There are worse things than being a pirate, Merry-mine," he said, as he leaned toward her, obviously unperturbed by what she implied. "Much worse . . ." His breath brushed her heated cheeks like a cool, sweet zephyr.

She clenched the covers to her chin, his nearness wreaking absolute havoc with her senses and causing his endearment to go right over her head. His eyes probed hers.

Was she going mad? Or was it the brandywine she'd imbibed? Or both?

"As for Bakámu, I say you're lying," he continued in a calm murmur. "If the Indian were dying, you would assuredly be at his side, like a proper zealot bent upon righting the wrongs of the world."

Their gazes still fused, Meredyth felt as if a great wall were collapsing onto her chest, trapping the breath in her lungs. No, she had the presence of mind to think, it was her hand pressing against her breastbone with a strength born of panic.

He reached out and covered her hand with his own, loosening her crabbed fingers, one by one, then lifted her hand to his mouth. He turned it over and pressed his lips to her palm, his mist-blue eyes never leaving her face. Unconsciously, Meredyth's other hand crept toward the coverlet she'd been forced to release, but whorls of hot desire invaded her middle, intense as fire, debilitating as a ball of searing iron shot to the chest.

Deny it . . . deny it! whispered a voice. But she was incapable of uttering a word in those moments.

His tongue replaced his lips. "Umm, brandywine and Merry-mine," he recited in a husky murmur.

A bolt of pure desire speared through her.

"We've a room all to ourselves," he said, as he lifted his face to hers, obviously having dismissed her claim of Bakámu's near-death status. "Why waste it, sweet, when we both want the same thing?"

Seven

His lips moved inexorably toward hers, his eyes drawing her closer with all the potency of a sorcerer.

"W . . . want?" she managed to stutter as his words penetrated her sensual fog. "Nay! You. . . . You presume too much, Captain!" But her outrage was tempered by brandywine and the powerful effect of the quintessentially masculine flesh and blood figure before her. Her memories of Lucien Pendwell were like dim shadows compared to the living, breathing man holding her like an unwitting fly in the proverbial spider's web.

Bakámu. Think of the Indian . . .

It worked. At least enough to make her turn her head just before his mouth met hers. "The only thing I want, Captain, is for you to return to the mission," she managed to say through lips that still tingled with anticipation of his kiss. "You've a responsibility there, and I'm not leaving without you!"

She dared to look at his face, so close to hers. To her dismay, he was grinning. *Grinning!*

"I do believe, Lady Meredyth," he said in a low, seductive voice, "you've developed a . . . *tendre* for me. Admit it. That's why you came chasing down the mountain after me."

"You are *vile.*" How could he make fun of her precipitate actions? Deliberately misinterpret them when she'd—

How can he come to any other conclusions, insisted an irksome voice, *when you hied yourself into Port Royal against Father Tomas's wishes, against your own better judgment?*

Weren't you really doing what you've wanted to do for months to Pendwell? Chase down the knave and confront him? Give him, at the least, a verbal set-down?

"And full of yourself," she added for good measure, fighting to dissolve her wine-induced euphoria.

Devin watched her lovely eyes darken with ire and knew the moment was past. "Oh, hell!" he said in frustration and pushed himself to a sitting position. "You, sweetheart," he pointed a finger in her face, "haven't the sense of humor of a . . ." He searched for a properly denigrating word and thought of the anole. "Lizard! Why, even your fa—"

He snapped his mouth shut, inwardly appalled at what he'd almost revealed.

He, who made a lucrative living by risking his life to investigate and then record—for a small, anonymous and select group of interested parties—the treatment of slaves and the living conditions aboard slavers, he was allowing his attraction for this young woman, whose activities he was supposed to be secretly monitoring, to weaken the strict guard he was forced to maintain for his personal safety.

Little Sister Meredyth, it appeared, had no need of anybody's protection and obviously hadn't inherited any of the earl's ability to see the humor in things. And from his brief dealings with Somerset, Devin had caught at least a dry sense of humor in the man.

Her eyes narrowed at the insult. "And you, Captain Chandler, are a grinning buffoon! I believe you missed the opportunity of a lifetime by not applying for the position of jester in some nobleman's household."

He stared at her for moment, a suspended look on his features, then startled her by throwing back his head and laughing aloud with gusto.

Just as quickly, however, he brought up his head and caught her gazing at him in rapt contemplation. "So you do possess a sense of humor! Possibly even the ability to laugh and—"

"I did not laugh," she corrected him and immediately felt

silly at the petulant sound of her words. In an effort to gather what little was left of her dignity, she tipped up her dainty chin the slightest bit.

Devin noticed the small cut still visible there, threading its way downward and marring her peaches-and-cream complexion.

"Now," she said, pulling him from his brief musings, "if you would kindly remove your presence from this room while I attempt to put myself together, Captain Chandler, I'll go see about my friends downstairs."

He watched her eyes darken to the deep green of a forest glade, obviously with concern. "Very well, Merry-mine. But I'll turn my back rather than leave the room. After all, sweet, you barged in on me, bringing in your wake, I might add, one of the worst ruffians to roam the Main." He pushed away and stood, and his words, rather than inflaming Meredyth, reminded her that, indeed, Mad Dog had attempted to confront Chandler because of her.

She jumped on the thought that if it weren't for his cowardly actions, she wouldn't have marched into Port Royal and the Seaman's Folly in the first place.

Her lips thinned. "You, sir, are no gentleman," she said through set teeth, pushing away from the headboard with one hand while maintaining the shield of the bedclothes with the other.

He walked over to retrieve her hat from where it had landed behind the door. As he turned back to face her, he said easily, "I've never made claim to that title. But I would think that a proper lady would show some gratitude for my having saved her virtue . . . to say naught of her very life."

Color bloomed in her face as he tossed the hat onto the bed and moved to retrieve his shirt from a corner stool. Not to be outdone, however, she retorted, "Maddy saved my virtue and not you, Captain. As for my life, I hardly think it was ever in real danger. Surely, one such as you can only be expected to exaggerate such things."

Devin paused in the act of donning his white linen shirt and spun toward her. As he approached the bed with slow but deliberate steps, Meredyth couldn't help but notice the contrast between the dark musculature of his chest and the pristine garment he held against it.

He leaned toward her, making her mouth go dry at his nearness.

"In spite of the shrewish tone of your comments where I'm concerned, Lady Meredyth, I feel it my duty to remind you that you're not at Whitehall in London but rather a brothel in Port Royal, a town notorious for its egregious traffic. The worst criminals in the world are drawn here by virtue of the fact that Jamaica is the hub of an extremely lucrative, thriving commercial trade. Rape by a man like Davies, be you male or female, would have made you wish you had taken your life, instead."

For once he wasn't grinning or speaking with his typical mocking indolence, and Meredyth didn't have an answer ready. She pushed to the edge of the mattress as he spun away and scrambled to gather what was left of her shirt and put it on.

" 'Tis futile," he said, as if he read her mind, for his back was turned. "So it seems you'll get your wish, for I must leave the room to find you some proper clothing."

"Wouldn't I be in more danger dressed as a woman, considering we're in a brothel, Captain Chandler?"

Meredyth couldn't see the look on his face as he answered, "You may not believe it, sweet, but you are safer with me than any other man in the Folly . . . except, possibly, the two men from the mission. And their ability to safeguard your person is, at best, if they're yet alive, questionable."

He slipped his stockinged feet into silver-buckled leather shoes and, clad only in shirt and breeches, swung toward the door. As he pulled it open, he paused and glanced back over his shoulder. "Slide the bolt behind me, and don't let anyone in but myself. Do you understand, Meredyth?"

Once again, that uncharacteristically sober tone.

Rather meekly, in response to his stern mien, she nodded.

Devin couldn't help but be reminded of a lovely, innocent child—flushed, her lips in a pout, her beautiful hair a disheveled umber halo—as she stood quietly in the incongruously gaudy surroundings of the Seaman's Folly. He could just make out, even from where he stood, the sweet sprinkling of freckles over her small, straight nose.

She was all woman. There had never been any doubt of that.

With a shake of his head, he stepped through the doorway and shut it firmly behind him. She was enough to drive any sane man to the questionable haven of the Hospital of St. Mary of Bethlehem.

Bedlam.

Meredyth stared down at Manuel's body and admitted silently she'd made a horrible mistake. Nothing had gone right since she'd entered the Seaman's Folly, but this latest and most sobering tragedy drove home the point as nothing else could.

Emotion clotted in her throat, tears burned the back of her eyes. Guilt weighed heavily upon her soul, for she was ultimately responsible for Manuel's death. He'd not survived the assault of Davies's minions. Evidently, he'd been attacked from behind with such force that he'd crashed into the side of the Folly, crushing his temple.

She watched in silent misery as Devin and Dionisio, who sported a bandaged head and a nasty-looking black eye, wrapped Manuel's still form in a clean sheet and carefully lifted and draped his body over the donkey. The animal stood patiently as it received its grisly load.

Meredyth bit down on her lip, sorrow and regret overwhelming her self-consciousness at the borrowed deep purple silk gown. With one hand, she clutched the edges of her light fichu to her chest, not against the night breeze but against the emotion that threatened to overcome her.

Dionisio kept glancing at her, but she wouldn't meet anyone's eyes in the light flickering over them from the windows of the Folly.

Devin, however, was dealing with his own demons and paid Meredyth no heed as he went about his task. "How is your head?" he asked Dionisio in a low voice just before the Folly's door burst open, letting an explosion of noise burst into the otherwise serene Jamaican night.

Dionisio gave him a hint of a nod, as if it hurt to move his head, which no doubt, thanks to little Sister Meredyth, it did mightily, Devin thought with heavy irony. He hoped she'd learned a lesson. She had had no business sticking her nose into his, or anyone else's, affairs and, in the process of interfering, jeopardizing the lives of two men.

What in the hell had the Jesuit been thinking, allowing her to leave? Had she been brazen enough to defy the priest? Or had she sneaked off? Something was festering deep inside her, he sensed, that only inflamed her determination. More than likely, the sour taste from having been jilted.

"I suppose it would be too dangerous for you to go after the culprits," her voice interrupted his thoughts. Especially irritating was her tone.

Dionisio shook his head without waiting for Devin. "Bad men. Return to mission with *mujer*. Take Manuel home to *el padre*."

"Even the *padre* can do nothing for him now," Devin said bluntly. "And you neatly left me out of things, Cimaroon," he added with a twist of his lips. "I don't like to rub salt in the wound, but you're in no condition to protect the lady." He tucked in a stray end of the sheet and stepped back to survey their work. "By the Mass, man," he said then, looking at the African, "it pains you even to shake your head. You cannot deny it. And they took your musket, did they not? How could you defend yourself, let alone her?"

" 'Tis the least you can—" Meredyth began, indignation adding a spark to her low spirits.

"Will you keep out of this?" he growled at her. "From

whence the unexpected boldness? A moment ago you were quiet as a mouse, reflecting upon, one would hope, the results of your rash actions. Mayhap even asking God for forgiveness, though the good Padre Tomas can always intercede for a fair damsel, can't he?"

The sarcasm in his words was not lost upon Meredyth.

"We don't need you!" she pronounced, her eyes suddenly taking on the light of battle.

"My, my," he drawled, "was it only moments ago that you said you weren't leaving Port Royal without me?" He motioned to Dionisio, who took the donkey's reins and began walking down Thames Street, away from the Seaman's Folly. Meredyth moved past Devin in her ludicrous purple dress. She'd been too rushed to plait her hair, and it fell in long, dark waves about her shoulders. From behind she could easily have been mistaken for a choice morsel working in any of the whorehouses in Port Royal.

He wondered how Dionisio would be able to aid him should some random rowdy approach them, thinking her a prostitute. Or, even worse, a group of miscreants. And, as much as Devin would have liked to teach her a further lesson by forcing her to make the trek back to the mission in the dead of night, his softer side reasoned that she was suffering enough from guilt.

Devin made a sudden decision.

"Cimaroon!" he called softly.

He saw Meredyth noticeably stiffen as Dionisio halted and turned back to him. "I've changed my mind. We're going yonder," he pointed in the direction of his town house, "for the night. Where this street meets King's Lane. No arguments."

Dionisio looked as if he would have argued, in spite of Devin's emphatic order, but was momentarily diverted by the door of another tippling house opening and spitting out several enthusiastic celebrants. One barefoot sailor in baggy red silk pants and flimsy vest over his bare chest led the way up the street, raising a bottle of spirits to the sky in some kind of drunken salute. Two other, less gaudily dressed buccaneers, followed, arms about each other's shoulders. The second and third men were singing some bawdy chantey as they staggered in their colorful leader's wake.

Swiftly, wordlessly, Devin shoved Meredyth toward Dionisio, who pushed her around the donkey and its burden, putting the animal between her and the roistering seamen.

Meredyth lost her balance, brushed against the sheet-covered corpse, then came up against the donkey's flank with a soft exhalation of breath. Devin gave her a warning look but then saw there was no need. She realized, apparently, the danger close by.

"Go!" Devin commanded the African in a low voice.

This time Dionisio didn't pause to argue. He jerked the animal's reins and headed toward the corner Devon had indicated. Meredyth stayed on the far side of the donkey, out of view of the men, who initially ignored them.

Then, as they moved away, one of them shouted, "Hey there!"

The leader echoed, "Aye, izzzat Devil Chan—ler?"

"Nay," Devin called over his shoulder without turning around. " 'E's dead, didn't ye hear?" He wished now that he'd thought to take along Meredyth's hat, bothersome as he'd considered it earlier. His exposed bright hair probably shone like a newly minted doubloon in the velvet black of the night every time they passed an establishment whose front door was illuminated by lantern light.

He quickened his steps in response to the donkey's gait as Dionisio pulled its halter rope without mercy. Just then, Meredyth peered over Manuel. "Stay down!" Devin hissed out of the corner of his mouth, "lest they see you and develop an appetite for more than spirits."

The slurred replies of the three men faded in the distance as the trio from the Folly neared the intersection of Thames Street and King's Lane.

* * *

Devin inserted the key in the lock and turned it. The town house door swung open with a soft wince.

"All hands on deck! Pirates! Pirates!" someone cried from within.

Devin started, his hand going instantly to his cutlass hilt. His abrupt halt caught Meredyth off guard. She blundered into his back, her jaw solidly connecting with his rigid spine.

Dionisio, who stood holding the donkey's reins and surveying the shadows around them, raised his head, muttered something unintelligible and stepped up to Meredyth protectively in reaction to the eerie noise and Devin's sudden movement.

"Henry Morgan says kill the Spanish swine! Greasy riffraff! Squaaawk!"

There, on a wooden cross-bar perch, sat the shabbiest-looking bird Devin had ever seen. Or was it a bird? His eyes narrowed as he wondered briefly what manner of creature it was.

A parrot, it looked like.

A parrot?

He stepped closer and allowed his hand to drop from his sword as he reached for flint and steel. He lit the two-foot-high ship cabin lantern hanging from a hook on the nearest wall and beheld the owner of the shrill voice of doom.

"Man yer stations, mates! Squaaawk! Henry Morgan ain't afeared!"

The bird bore no resemblance to the brilliantly colored parrots indigenous to the Caribbean. It was gray in color—that is, where it had feathers. Aside from a short red tail and, of course, its thick, hooked bill, it could have been some bedraggled bird of no particular interest, and it listed slightly, like a drunken sailor, to one side.

Meredyth peered around him and instantly felt a bubble of laughter form in her throat. In spite of the fact that a man was dead and that she was being unceremoniously escorted to the mission looking to all the world like a prostitute (and without necessarily having achieved her original goal), she felt an irrepressible urge to laugh at Devin Chandler's reaction to a parrot.

"Pray, Captain, don't run him through," she said, her voice quivering with poorly suppressed mirth. "He's unarmed."

"Squaaawk! Female aboard! Bad luck!" the creature shrilled. "Throw 'er overboard!"

"What the devil?" Devin said under his breath. "Where in the world did that come from?" He heard a muffled giggle from Meredyth and spun around, surprised and suspecting that she was mocking him.

But her features were lit with merriment, her hand over her mouth in an obvious attempt to snuff her laughter.

When he beheld her glowing green eyes, he lost his urge to silence her. He wanted to hear her laugh fully, in that delightful way she had. But then he wanted to take her into his arms and kiss her until her mind was free of all thought save him.

Christ above! Was his mouth falling open like that of a moonstruck lad? He caught himself with alacrity and decided he couldn't do what he really wanted to do. Instead Devin threw her a menacing scowl and, with a sense of loss, witnessed the captivating expression slide from her face. "If I'm any judge, I don't believe you have aught to laugh about, Lady Meredyth," he said. "Manuel's body isn't even cold, and here you are giggling over a parrot."

He swung away and cautiously searched the two rooms on the ground floor, sword drawn.

"Mayhap he brought a companion or two," an imp prompted her to add, in spite of his damning reminder. "With pistols."

The look he shot her would have turned a lesser person to whey.

"Watch your back," he said curtly to Dionisio and moved toward the stairs.

"Henry Morgan says guard yer back, mates!" the parrot screeched again. "Pirates on board!"

Meredyth moved toward the bird, fascinated by its ability

to speak. She was vaguely aware of Devin's steps overhead, but something much more intriguing had caught her attention as she moved toward the bird and its perch. One leg had only two talons instead of four.

"Bird was hurt," Dionisio's deep voice said from behind her.

"I believe you're right," she replied. "No doubt he lost part of his foot but then he was rescued and tended by some kind-hearted person."

"That kind-hearted person should have done the bird a favor and put it out of its misery," Devin said as he descended the stairs. He sheathed his cutlass and stepped toward Meredyth and the parrot, the lantern light muting the brightness of his hair to burnished gold.

The look of disbelief on Meredyth's face mirrored her shock at his callous statement, and Devin suddenly felt foolish. He didn't normally dislike animals.

The creature observed him with bright, beadlike eyes, an alertness that was almost uncanny. "Pricklouse!" it pronounced without warning and then pecked briefly at a place beneath its wing.

Meredyth's pale cheeks lit with embarrassment.

"What an ugly parrot," Devin observed in an attempt to get the bird to say something more appropriate for a lady's ears.

"Squaaawk! Ugly parrot. Ugly pirate, mates!"

"And with a sassy tongue, to boot." He leaned toward it and pointed a finger. "They should have named you Peg-Leg. What is your name, anyway?"

"Name? Squaaawk! Henry Morgan's me name. Huntin' treasure's me game!"

"Henry Morgan?" Devin repeated in surprise. Then chuckled, without looking at Meredyth. "You're a sorry namesake for the old pirate."

The bird recommenced its preening, ignoring Devin, who noted the feathers on its head were so pale a gray as to be almost white, as were the longer feathers at the bottom of its back, just above its slightly fanned, red tail.

He turned back toward the door, shaking off thoughts of the bedraggled bird. "Help me take the body into the cellar," he told Dionisio. " 'Tis shallow but cool, and 'twill serve our purpose until the morn. Then you can see that the donkey is fed and watered." He paused and looked over his shoulder at Meredyth, who was still standing near the parrot. "The bed is upstairs, milady," he added with a twist of his lips. "You'll need your rest before the trip into the mountains."

But at the mention of Manuel's body, Meredyth's distress, which had been lurking just beneath the surface in the wake of the saucy Henry Morgan, returned to claim her attention. Mayhap she was losing her mind, she thought, for by some kind quirk of fate, never in her nineteen years had she been forced to deal with death. And now it couldn't be closer, at least physically. It had been beneath her very hand as she'd walked beside the donkey, keeping Manuel's body in place.

"I can tend to the donkey," she said, a frown creasing her forehead. "Dionisio's been through enough—"

"And you're not in charge anymore," Devin cut her off. "You're under my protection, and therefore you'll obey my orders to the letter, until we reach the mission on the morrow. My patience is running low where you're concerned, _Lady Meredyth_."

Her eyes narrowed. Orders? "You're not my commanding officer, Captain, however you may see yourself. And as for your patience, I wasn't aware you had any to speak of."

He put one hand on her arm and gave her a light shake. " 'Tis for your own safety," he said in a low, taut voice. "You don't know how close you came to getting yourself ravished this night, even killed. One man is dead because of you, and I'll not tolerate any more of your defiance."

An ebony hand on his own wrist silenced Devin for a moment.

His eyes met and held Dionisio's. His words, however, were

for Meredyth. "If you insist, then fine!" He inclined his head the slightest bit, the gesture containing more derision than words could ever convey. "Hie yourself off through Port Royal in the dark of night dressed as a bawd. You're more than welcome to leave here with your weakened and lone bodyguard." With an abrupt motion, he shook off the Cimaroon's fingers and swung toward the door.

"I warrant you'll find my bed," he threw at her over his shoulder, "with or without me in it, preferable to that of some rough and hungry sailor fresh from a long stint at sea."

A short time later she had to admit to herself that his bed was heavenly, even though it was ludicrously large for the room. Meredyth supposed that after the confined space and narrow bed of a cabin on a ship, Devin Chandler craved the luxury of a huge, four-postered bed.

It smelled faintly of him, which she found irritating and, at the same time, comforting.

Deciding to remain in her borrowed dress, which, if nothing else, was at least clean, she stared at the ceiling for a long time before exhaustion overcame her. It was easier to give in to fatigue than to allow her thoughts to whirl around in her brain, sucking her down into a vortex of despair.

She was sound asleep when Devin finally came in to check on her. He hadn't intended to, having decided to sleep with Dionisio on the floor in the sitting room. But something drew him up the stairs long after the Cimaroon was asleep and anchored him to the floor beside the bed.

She looked lost in that huge bed, a small figure huddled beneath a light blanket, the garish purple of her gown an incongruous blotch against the sweet expanse of flesh on one exposed arm, neck, and face. The wealth of rich, dark hair, which managed to shine defiantly with a life of its own, even by the meager light of a lone candle, was spread out beneath her head in startling contrast to the pale pillow beneath. Rather than making Meredyth St. Andrews look wanton, it emphasized her innocence.

A slight frown marred her peaceful countenance, and it came to Devin once again how very hurt she must have been to leave the security of home and family to journey halfway across the world to live on an island of scoundrels and savages. If truth be told, Jamaica was more than that, but for a young woman her age to venture forth from England's embrace, from the very lap of luxury, her wound must have been deep.

His fingers toyed with the edge of the blanket, and Devin was suddenly struck by an odd sense of satisfaction that she was in his home, in his bed.

But why would he ever experience true satisfaction? he wondered, genuinely perplexed. She was a total enigma to him, possessing the courage of any man he'd ever met. *And the tongue of a termagant,* his darker side prompted him. The face and form of an angel, yet also the tangible presence of a boiling anger just beneath that exquisite exterior.

"Damme!" he whispered to the sleeping girl. "I'd like naught better than to put you on the next ship to England!"

But if he was adept at lying to others when it suited his purposes, he never lied to himself, at least not consciously. And whether he wished it or not, Devin James Chandler knew that he was, indeed, trying to convince himself of something that hadn't a shred of truth to it.

Little though he wanted to admit it, he wasn't quite ready to watch Meredyth St. Andrews walk out of his life.

Eight

They buried Manuel almost immediately upon their arrival at the mission, less than twenty-four hours after his untimely death and after a simple mass said by Father Tomas.

Meredyth felt a childish urge to throw herself into the arms of her mother or father. As they stood beside the humble grave, she tried to fight off the guilt, for she'd never experienced the like before.

Neither had she ever been, directly or indirectly, responsible for anyone's death. It was a huge and onerous burden to bear, but she accepted it and didn't make any excuses for herself, for that wasn't her way.

Later, in the dispensary (and after discarding the clothing from the Seaman's Folly), she sat beside Bakámu and talked quietly to him, Carla by her side. Excited though the child had been to see Meredyth, she obviously sensed her friend's troubled frame of mind and played quietly with Sir Hiss in his small wicker basket.

A very subdued Meredyth somehow found a little solace in being with the Arawak. She determinedly put the trek from Port Royal from her mind. They'd left just before dawn, using the cover of darkness for Meredyth's own safety, according to Devin. It had been humiliating, and she'd guessed that Chandler had wanted her to suffer some kind of punishment to atone, in part at least, for her rash sojourn to Port Royal and its tragic consequences.

"Not only are you responsible for the loss of a life," he'd

told her as she'd labored up the mountain, "but you've managed to earn me a new enemy for life. And one not to be taken lightly, in spite of his obvious lack of intelligence." His eyes had bored into hers, reflecting the deeper hue of a royal blue silk scarf he wore like a cap, and knotted carelessly behind his head. His expression had been cold and she'd thought at the time that he resembled a cutthroat crony of Mad Dog Davies. "Just what I need after having had my ship practically blown out from under me and myself dragged in manacles to Newgate."

And to make matters worse, he'd once more made her responsible for seeing that Manuel's body remained secure atop the donkey, which no gentleman would ever have even considered doing. No doubt, she reasoned, because of what he thought had been her refusal to accept the man's death. If she'd sought refuge from her guilt by indulging in laughter at the pitiful parrot and the way it had taken Captain Devin Chandler off guard, she hadn't done it out of disrespect for Manuel, or because she didn't profoundly regret his death.

"Chan-ler come back," Bakámu said, breaking into her thoughts.

"Aye," she answered with a ghost of a smile. "But you must concentrate on getting back on your feet and on with your life. Devin Chandler is not very dependable. Mayhap you are following the . . . er, wrong vision quest. Captain Chandler—"

"Can speak for himself, thank you," said Devin from behind her.

Carla looked up and Meredyth stilled. Bakámu's face lit.

"A dying man, I believe you said?" he added, a hint of menace underlying his deceptively light tone. He moved forward, around the end of the bed, and faced Meredyth.

"How are you feeling?" he asked Bakámu as the Arawak's obvious enthusiasm all but made him jump from his sickbed.

"Leg good, *si?*" He thrust aside enough of the light cover to show Devin his wounded leg. It wasn't the angry red that went along with a festering wound, and between that and the

Indian's demeanor, Devin felt a slow anger build inside him at what had obviously been a blatant lie.

There was no way on earth the man could have gone from death's door to such an improved state in twenty-four hours, he thought, his lips compressing. Not even in a Jesuit priest's mission, where an occasional miracle might be said to occur.

"Chan-ler come back for Bakámu, *si?*"

Devin didn't answer but placed the palm of one hand to Bakámu's forehead. No fever, as far as he could tell.

His eyes sought Meredyth's across the blanket, but her gaze was lowered, riveted to the Indian's other sheet-draped leg. "You cannot even look me in the eye in the wake of your outright lie, can you?" he said softly, ignoring the Arawak for a moment. "Why exactly did you follow me to Port Royal against all common sense? Could it be that you were getting some manner of vicarious revenge on the man who jilted you?"

Meredyth's face flamed, for he'd hit the nail on the head. Whether she would acknowledge it earlier or not, now she had to face the truth: she'd been taking out the fury and frustration she felt for Lucien Pendwell on Devin Chandler, had rashly and recklessly gone chasing after him the way she'd wanted to pursue Lucien, to catch and then vent all her pain and outrage on him.

Why hadn't she seen it earlier?

Manuel would probably still be alive if you had, she thought.

For a moment, she couldn't speak around the tightness in her throat. And the accusation in Devin Chandler's eyes acted like a cauterizing iron, searing across her conscience. God in heaven, what had she done?

Devin watched the play of emotions across her face and was caught between anger and regret. She was made to love, not accuse and deride.

Now where in hell had that thought come from? the outraged part of him wondered.

"I accept full responsibility for Manuel's death," she finally managed. "And no one regrets my very rash and inexcusable behavior more than I." The last words emerged in a husk of sound.

"Well," he said, suddenly feeling his ire replaced by awkwardness, "as I mentioned before, it does so happen that I need a manservant." He looked at Bakámu. "When you've mended, you can come and live in Port Royal with me. While I'm at sea, of course, you'll be alone and in charge of my home."

Mayhap the Arawak wouldn't like that, he thought suddenly. Mayhap he fancied himself going on voyages with Devin and would be so insulted that he'd refuse the offer.

"Bakámu go big village with Chan-ler?" His teak-toned face split into a happy grin.

Devin nodded. "Aye. If your heart's still set on it. But only as my manservant, *comprende*? Naught more."

Bakámu nodded eagerly, which caused Devin to wonder how much the Arawak had actually understood. But his main interest at the moment, against all his instincts and his better judgment, was Meredyth St. Andrews. He supposed he should acknowledge her acceptance of responsibility for her actions and possibly soothe her conscience somewhat. After all, the blame should have been shouldered directly by Mad Dog Davies and his henchmen. Yet he couldn't help but feel an odd disappointment, on the one hand, because she hadn't gone chasing down the mountain after him for his masculine attributes and an equally strange admiration for her boldness and selfless concern for Bakámu, on the other. If that had truly been part of it.

Devin Chandler was accustomed to women chasing him, women of all stations, although, he had to admit, never down from the Blue Mountains of Jamaica and into an infamous den of iniquity like Port Royal. He'd always thought it amusing, if not downright degrading, for a female to do so and preferred to do the pursuing himself.

The thought that Lady Meredyth St. Andrews had been vent-ing her spleen on him when it was meant for another wasn't very complimentary. Hence his disappointment, he reasoned.

He glanced at her, but Meredyth was deep in thought, present only physically, it appeared, until little Carla touched her arm. The two put their heads together for a brief and quiet exchange. Meredyth took the anole from Carla for a few moments, while the girl fidgeted with something in the tightly woven basket that was its home.

A shadow appeared in the doorway, capturing Devin's attention. Father Tomas. He moved up to Meredyth and put a sympathetic hand on her shoulder, his gaze going briefly to Bakámu, then Devin. "Manuel wouldn't have wanted you to feel responsible," he said quietly. "And only a simpleton would say that I had no part in it . . . and Devin, himself. But the greatest burden of blame belongs to the men who killed him."

Meredyth didn't answer, her gaze lifting to one whitewashed wall behind Devin.

"Would you like to go to the chapel to be alone?" he asked her gently.

Her unfocused eyes cleared for a moment, and she nodded her head. "Thank you, Father." She replaced Sir Hiss and stood, one hand reaching out for Carla's. The child awkwardly got to her feet as she wedged the crutch beneath her arm, and the two left without a word.

"You are too hard on her, Devin," the priest admonished.

Devin glanced at Bakámu, whose eyelids were beginning to droop. "I only spoke the truth. She set things in motion."

Father Tomas shook his head as he moved up to the bed. "You set things in motion." He frowned. " 'Tisn't like you to avoid blame, Devin. And 'tis especially cruel of you to do so in this case. I don't understand your actions, when you are the one who came directly to the mission upon arriving in Jamaica. Why did you come here, anyway?"

Devin paced a few steps, then returned to the bed, debating whether to tell the priest the truth. He glanced at Bakámu once again, but the Arawak appeared to be sleeping. "If you must know, *padre,* I was fulfilling a promise I'd made to her father in London."

"Keir St. Andrews?" he asked, obviously shocked.

Devin nodded. "He managed to get me released from Newgate in return for a favor. A small favor I thought 'twould be, but it appears that anyone who enters Lady Meredyth St. Andrews's life, no matter how peripherally, is in for more than he bargained for."

There followed a long silence before the Jesuit finally asked, "Does Meredyth know?"

"Nay. And so I would have it remain. She harbors enough ill-feelings toward me without learning that her father set me to keeping a watch on her."

"Then why don't you try being kind to her?" Father Tomas said unexpectedly. "She needs kindness more than ever now."

Devin's eyes narrowed. What was the good *padre* up to now? "Just because you believe Manuel would have forgiven her, you need not presume I'm so soft-hearted. What she did was inexcusable . . . childish. And ultimately cost a man his life, no matter where else you try to lay the blame, Father."

By this time, Bakámu was softly snoring.

"Had you not left so abruptly, *mi hijo,* when the child thought Bakámu needed you, she would not have followed you. She is *muy* . . ." he frowned as he searched for the right word, "vulnerable, at this time. *Frágil.* Surely, Keir St. Andrews told you why she is in Jamaica in the first place?"

"Aye, but—"

"As for being a child," the Jesuit cut him off gently but firmly," she is one still, *muy joven*—young—to be half a world away from her *familia.*"

"But I'm not responsible for her feelings! Nor am I her confessor." He plowed his hands through his hair in agitation, inadvertently sending the blue scarf tumbling down his back.

Father Tomas shook his head slowly. "When you entered into the pact with Keir, you accepted responsibility for Meredyth, whether the thought occurred to you at the time or not." His eyebrows tented. "Although I suspect that his reward was . . . enticing enough to mayhap cloud your thinking where the daughter was concerned. Don't disappoint me, Devin or, *muy importante,* the Earl of Somerset. He entrusted his own daughter to your care."

"Bakámu go boat with Chan-ler," the sleeping Arawak murmured at that moment, a dreamy smile softening his mouth. "Sail big water . . ."

Devin bent to sweep up the discarded scarf and was sorely tempted to wrap it about the Indian's neck and squeeze.

Instead, he slapped it over his head, the knot drooping carelessly over one ear, and said through his teeth, "I'm sorry I ever told you about that accursed bargain, *padre!*" He threw a murderous glance at Bakámu. "And I'm even sorrier that I told this conniving Arawak that I needed a manservant. The next thing you know he'll be taking over as captain of the *Lady Elysia*—in league, of course, with the innocent and ill-used Lady Meredyth."

His body emanating anger, he stalked from the dispensary, fully intending to go straight to Port Royal, swill himself silly in rum, and never set foot in the Blue Mountains again.

But Devil Chandler, in spite of his nickname, was not one to harbor anger for long. And as he passed the hut where Carla lived with her mother, he noticed the child was alone with the basket Dionisio had made for her pet. She looked forlorn, and Devin evinced a sudden, premonitory flash of insight: Meredyth St. Andrews flinging herself from a mountain precipice or drowning herself in a still, deep pool beneath some cold mountain cataract.

He abruptly swung toward the path that led to the pool beside the waterfall where he'd first met her and moved with swift strides toward it, all manner of horrible images conjured up by his wriggling conscience. He was a fool ten times over for feeling such concern for the troublesome, quarrelsome jade, but that thought did nothing to slow his pace.

In fact, he began to run.

* * *

Meredyth stood before the waterfall, the cool spray from it misting her face and arms. Gooseflesh prickled her skin, for it was growing cool as the afternoon waned.

And she felt cold inside. Numb, but not quite numb enough to cover the pain that pulsed through her with every beat of her heart. She was a murderess, in every sense of the word, and she had had no business going off after Devin Chandler. In fact, if she were honest with herself, she'd had no real reason to run off to the Caribbee islands in the first place.

No doubt many women—and men, for that matter—had lived through the loss of someone they loved after being forsaken. But most people didn't have the urge (or the means) to hie themselves off to the other side of the world, and now she could see why. Running away from all that one knew and loved didn't ease the pain or eradicate the memory of the source of it. New surroundings might help keep one's mind occupied, but memories were always lurking around the edges of her consciousness, her companions when she went to sleep or had any idle time.

She had to exhaust herself to the point that she couldn't even think about England or her family or Lucien's betrayal when she dropped to her pallet at night.

And most people hadn't the misfortune of encountering a man like Devin Chandler, she thought miserably, to press home her sins, as if she needed reminding.

Tears filled her eyes, dribbled down her cheeks. She couldn't blame her actions on Chandler. If she'd had one bit of self-discipline, if she hadn't been so appallingly righteous, she would have conducted herself with better control. It wasn't Father Tomas's fault or Devin Chandler's, tempting as it was to shift the blame.

No, she was responsible for Manuel's death.

She stared unseeingly at the curtain of water rushing over

the precipice above, desperately seeking a solution to a solutionless problem.

Go home, a voice whispered. *Home to Somerset Chase, to the haven of your family.*

" 'Twould be running away," she said, her voice a tortured whisper. "And Father taught us to face our problems, not hide from them."

But how could she face Manuel's family? And Father Tomas? And Carla? And all the others at the mission whom she'd failed? She was to have been an asset to the small settlement—as beneficial to it as the experience was to be to her—yet it hadn't taken her very long to turn a potentially good thing into a tragedy.

She sank to her knees, allowing her face to seek the cradle of her hands as she wept softly, the sound swallowed by the roar of the falls. Unconsciously, she rocked slightly back and forth, a silent keening filling her as she allowed her ceaseless motion to express her burden of grief.

Manuel's face appeared in her mind's eye. His hand touched her shoulder.

"Meredyth?"

She stilled.

Someone pulled her hands from her face and lifted her to her feet. She raised tear-filled eyes to meet Devin Chandler's anxious look. The concern in his eyes, and something infinitely more subtle and profound, caught her off guard, and she found herself moving into the security of his offered embrace as if it were the most natural thing in the world for her to do in that moment. It felt comforting, and right.

She felt his lips against her hair, his breath tickle her scalp, as she felt rather than heard him murmur her name again. "Weep until the pain eases, Merry-mine," he encouraged gently. "There's no shame in crying."

She found it too easy to do as he bade her and allowed her face to nestle in the cay where his neck met his shoulder. The upper portion of his shirt became wet with her tears as one of his hands glided up and down her back in a surprisingly soothing motion.

Meredyth wouldn't have dreamed him capable of such tenderness, but in those moments she didn't bother to analyze his behavior, didn't dredge up and examine the animosity that dominated her feelings for him . . . and vice versa.

Devin found an immense satisfaction in holding her in his arms, albeit for reasons of comfort rather than anything sexual. His experience hadn't included much comforting of females—rather, he had sought them out for his own physical surcease and a break in the monotony of the exclusively male companionship that went with the life of a seaman.

In his efforts to avoid emotional entanglements, Devin trafficked mostly with women of ill-repute. And because of a personal fastidiousness, he was very selective.

Thus, he certainly wasn't in the habit of comforting any of the women who pleasured him. In fact, on occasion, the opposite was true, especially when he'd had one rum too many and chose to complain about his burdens as ship captain.

The crystalline water sang as it tumbled over the edge of the rocks above and into the pool; the breeze brought the fresh scent of pine and falling water, the fecund fragrance of the mountain floor. Slowly, Meredyth's shuddering sobs subsided, and Devin became aware of her heartbeat next to his.

"Are you better, Merry-mine?" he murmured, his mouth still against her hair and near her ear.

She nodded and shifted slightly. His arms tightened in reaction. He wasn't ready to let her go just yet.

Surely you're going mad, taunted a voice. *Lost your mind in Newgate.*

He ignored it as Meredyth lifted her face to his. If he was mad, it was all the more remarkable for its sweetness, he thought as he looked into green eyes luminous with fresh tears. He pressed his lips to one tender cheek and tasted the salt of her tears. Something rendered deep within him and his arms tightened protectively about her.

His mouth moved to her brow, then the tip of her nose.

Strangely, mayhap because of his unexpected and almost worshipful gentleness, Meredyth didn't object. She didn't pull away or utter any token protest but felt, rather, a rock-solid comfort and steadiness beneath his attentions.

Somehow, quite naturally, Devin's lips moved to meet hers, a sweet and tentative kiss. And chaste. When he pulled back for a moment to look into her eyes, her name came to his lips and emerged on a sigh. "Meredyth . . ."

"I . . . I must leave here," she whispered brokenly, like a bewildered child. "I've caused a terrible tragedy, and God is telling me to go home where I belong."

Caught off guard, Devin almost blurted, "Don't be absurd! God has naught to do with it." But he bit his tongue, realizing that it was his own reluctance, whatever he might try and convince the world, to permanently part company with Meredyth St. Andrews that was prompting him to say such things.

True, the Earl of Somerset would not be happy to learn of his daughter's behavior, especially any headlong pursuit of him that brought her into danger. That thought held a lot of weight, but it seemed that, of a sudden, so did the prospect of never seeing Meredyth again.

When had she become so important to him? he wondered with a mental grimace.

"Take me home to England?" she was asking him, her eyes so wide and full of expectation that his heart twisted within his breast. "On the *Lady Elysia?*"

He shook his head. "I've seen naught of cowardice in you, Meredyth St. Andrews," he told her in what he hoped was an acceptable tone. "Why would you want to run away? Don't you know you must face your troubles head-on? Running back to England won't solve anything."

The cynical side of him couldn't believe he'd said that. How many times had he wished her safely on a ship bound for London and out of his hair?

Yet as he heard himself utter the words, he realized it was

true. It was one of the things he admired about her, even if the motives for her behavior weren't always the most logical.

Meredyth pushed away from him, flinging her glossy chestnut hair out of her eyes. "I'm not running away," she said with a spurt of indignance, her green eyes flashing with sudden annoyance. "I belong in England, don't you see? I fled to Jamaica in the first place, but I'm not fleeing now. I just don't wish to create any more trouble."

Her chin dropped, and her beautiful green eyes closed against the pain of what she'd inadvertently done.

"Then think before you—" he began, and halted mid-sentence, snapping his mouth closed.

Instantly, the image flashed in his mind of Meredyth laboring up the mountain beside the donkey in the garish and constricting gown he'd procured for her. The sight of the purple silk, and all it represented, against her sweet and flawless flesh was akin to blasphemy.

Before she could even form a reply, he lifted one long, calloused finger to her jaw and traced it with a movement as light and gentle as the sweep of a moth's wing. "Fleeing again won't make anything right, love," he murmured, his eyes on her full, tempting lower lip. "No one doubts your importance to the mission," he added, his facility for lying his way out of tight spots causing the words to spring easily to his lips. "The children love and need you for more than merely reading lessons."

He leaned toward her, and Meredyth felt the potent pull of Devin Chandler the man so acutely that she swayed toward him slightly in answer. His finger glided over her chin and feathered down the silky length of her neck before coming to rest within the shallow depression in her breastbone, where a fragile but frentic pulse gave away his effect upon her senses. And, to his satisfaction, a light frisson shuddered through her.

If he could only persuade her to agree to stay, at least until he'd had his fill of her and was ready to let her go, mayhap

he could appeal, however shamelessly, to her noble side regarding the impropriety of going back on one's word.

"The ch-children?" she stuttered, the thought penetrating her
haze of misery.

"Indeed." His mouth was close to hers again, their lips a
heartbeat apart. "The children. Don't desert them now," he
entreated her with all the skill of a stage actor in a London
theater. "Show your mettle, Merry-mine, and your sincerity to
all concerned," he invited, like the spider to the fly. "You owe
it to them—Manuel's family, the children, Father Tomas. You
owe them some of yourself in reparation, don't you think?"

Meredyth pulled back, frowning, suddenly suspicious of the
man and his motives. "Why—" she began. "Why are you suddenly being so . . . kind?"

Devin turned an appropriately wounded look on her, thinking just how much she reminded him of her father and why
it would behoove him to send her back where she belonged.

She pushed away then and, with a straightening of her slender shoulders, lifted her lovely chin and looked directly into
his eyes. Surprising him again, she said, "I beg your pardon,
Captain Chandler. Here you are offering me comfort and encouragement, and I throw your courtesy right back in your
face." A shadow of this new distress crossed her tear-damp
face. "You're right. Running back to England won't change
anything." Unbelievably, she took one of his hands in hers.
"You helped me get safely out of that brothel and then Port
Royal. You were kind enough to give Dionisio and me shelter
and then escort us back to the mission with—" her voice gave
a queer little lurch, and the words died aborning. But he knew
exactly what she meant. Her fingers tightened around his larger
hand, which Devin found very pleasant but he remained silent.

"And now you've given me solid advice, advice like that
which my father or my brothers would have given me. I can't
thank you enough." Her gaze fell and enchanting color bathed
her fine cheekbones.

A bevy of contradictory emotions rushed through Devin in

the moments following her words. Triumph sought to gain the forefront, for he'd intended to convince her to stay longer, if only for his own selfish reasons.

After a brief but bitter inner battle, guilt won out, accompanied by a nagging sense of fair play in view of the fact that the Earl of Somerset had saved his life. The least Devin could do was keep to his part of a fairly simple and straightforward bargain.

And he belatedly decided (for the second time since meeting her) that he'd better get as far away from Meredyth St. Andrews as possible and as soon as possible. For his own good as well as hers.

Nine

"I've heard du Casse has an agent working in the area. In fact, the Frenchman himself may be in Port Royal."

Devin looked up at Woodrow Kingsley, his cup of rum half-way to his lips. "What do you mean 'agent'?" he asked. "He doubtless has agents all over the Caribbean and beyond."

Woody sighed and leaned back in his chair. They were in the sitting room of the town house and could hear the thud of Bakámu's steps on the second floor. The Arawak had made a swift recovery and insisted on accompanying Devin back to Port Royal, in spite of his awkward limp, a sennight after Manuel's burial.

Devin had lingered another day and night at the mission, in spite of his decision to do otherwise. He'd found himself doing something strange—not strange for him, but strange in his dealings with Meredyth St. Andrews: he'd worked very hard at making her smile, at chasing the shadows from her eyes, the pinched look from around her mouth when he suspected she was reflecting upon her precipitate actions and Manuel's resulting death.

It was like playing with fire. The more tentative smiles he coaxed from her, the more entangled he became in the feelings she unwittingly aroused within him.

"A snooper more than anything, from what I've heard, and right here in Port Royal." Woody's words pulled him from his pleasant, if slightly disquieting, musings. "I would be extremely careful around him, were I you," he cautioned.

"Has this mysterious agent a name?" Devin asked with a lift of one bleached eyebrow. "Like the rest of us mere mortals?"

"Pelton. Luke Pelton, I believe. Some displaced and disgruntled blue-blood, so I've heard. One of the most dangerous types in the Caribbean."

Devin leaned back his chair and crossed his legs on the corner of the table. "I'll take heed, Woody, because of your network of contacts, but I doubt he's any more dangerous than the next cutthroat. A blue-blood sunk to the dregs of piracy, no doubt. Or risen to the heights of it, depending upon one's point of view."

"Pirate!" croaked Henry Morgan. "Ugly pirate!" He whistled sharply.

Woody laughed aloud, while Devin merely threw the parrot a quelling look. But the plight of the pathetic-looking bird unexpectedly touched him. The exposed patches of flesh on the creature were sad enough, but that mangled leg. It was a small miracle the parrot had survived at all.

"Did I ever thank you for . . . him?" he asked, his eyes still on Henry Morgan.

"Not in so many words. Remember, he was a surprise and you haven't really had a chance . . ." Laughter lurked in Woody's voice. "But words aren't necessary, lad. I see the gratitude in your eyes."

Devin threw him a look. "Who rescued the creature?"

"One of my men . . . found it and took it home to his wife."

"He has the softest heart in the Caribbee Islands, poor fool." Devin studied Henry Morgan a bit longer. "His coloring's as drab as an overcast winter day in England." He shook his head, reached for his rum, and took another swallow. "At least compared to the colorful parrots and hummingbirds on the island. They put him to shame."

He turned back to Woody then. "Shouldn't we cover him with something? Mayhap he's cold, since he has only half his feathers. He looks more like a half-plucked hen than a parrot!"

Woody obviously fought to keep a straight face. "He's not quite that bald, and 'tis the end of May, lad, in Jamaica. The bird has no need of a coat."

"Then why is he hunched upon his perch like he's cold? Or mayhap he's afraid of something?"

"Henry Morgan ain't afeared!" bawled the parrot.

Woody shrugged and straightened the periwig he wore. "No doubt he feels inferior in such a sorry-looking state, but your insults can't be helping his self-image. Mayhap you're the wrong owner for him."

Devin threw him a speaking look and stood. He walked over to the parrot and put out one hand with an extended finger. "If you take a chunk from my finger, Henry Morgan," he warned gruffly, intrigued by the spunky bird, "I'll have Bakámu make you into an Arawak parrot stew. Dead parrots don't talk."

"Dead parrot! Squaaawk!"

Henry lurched forward on his perch, swung downward in a half-circle, and ended up upside down. For a moment, as the parrot hung suspended, Devin swallowed his laughter, for he saw immediately that the bird wasn't quite able to pull off the trick with only two claws on one foot. Instinctively, Devin reached out to catch the creature just as it lost its grip and plummeted toward the floor.

"Easy does it, Henry Morgan!" he cautioned the startled bird as he righted it and transferred it to his own finger. He stroked it a few times to calm it, then placed his other hand over the bird's talons, wrapped about his finger. "Let's try this again," he said, his voice low but full of laughter. "Dead bird," he said.

With his claws anchored, once again the intrepid Henry Morgan launched himself forward. He remained securely suspended, however, as he hung from Devin's finger. The African gray looked, for all the world, Devin thought, like a trussed fowl on its way to market, or a bat at rest.

"You did it, Henry!" Devin praised, hoping to make up for

any previous uncomplimentary comments, just in case the bird had understood him earlier. Henry Morgan was turning out to be a treasure trove of talent.

"One of a kind, just like his master," Woody managed between bouts of merriment. "And reckless, to boot."

"Good mate," Devin told the bird, ignoring his friend's comment, and coaxed it back upright. One wing fluttered as Henry Morgan straightened himself. "Looks like we won't have to sample parrot stew for dinner today," he said soberly, his attention still on the bird. Then, unable to keep a straight face for long, burst into laughter in unison with Woody.

A particularly loud thump sounded from upstairs, as if Bakámu had dropped his crutch.

"Man yer stations, mates! Pirates on board!" But it was the whistle so close to his ear that went right through Devin's head.

"If naught else," Woody observed, "he gives a good warning."

"Oh, aye!" Devin said, his ear still ringing. "Especially when the 'intruder' is already upstairs and happens to be my own servant." He sighed as if the world were on his shoulders, not merely an African gray, and moved toward the table. "What can he be doing up there that fair makes the walls tremble?"

"Did I tell you I think he's from a shipwrecked slaver?" Woody asked, ignoring Devin's question regarding Bakámu. "The *St. George*."

Devin shook his head. "If that be the case, a shipwreck was the merciful way out for those poor souls. Death is preferable to enslavement."

Woody nodded. "And so some believe. Mayhap you can learn something from Henry Morgan here."

Devin merely raised his eyebrows quizzically as he sat again, hoping Henry Morgan would behave, and changed the subject. "Du Casse's man, you said?"

"Aye. My suspicions keep going back to him for what happened to you."

Devin shook his head as he glanced at the stairs. "I'm no real threat to la Compagnie de Sénégal," he said in a low voice. "Neither du Casse nor any of the company's other shareholders are in any jeopardy due to my activities. For God's sake, Woody, I'm only one man! Rather like an ant attempting to raze a mountain, wouldn't you say?"

He shoved back his chair and stood again, causing Henry to flutter his wings slightly with the unexpectedness of the move. Devin was growing restless, eager to get out to see the progress on the *Lady Elysia*'s repairs and back to his own work.

"The men who back you are wealthy and powerful," Woody said, leaning forward, his voice soft but intense. His blue eyes flashed with the same fervor Devin felt. "There will come a time when we will make a difference, when your work begins to reap dividends. The cause is just! But anyone intelligent enough to have gained the influence and position du Casse has would also understand the danger a single man like yourself could present." He shook his head. "There is no other explanation for what happened to you, or Jimmy. Neither for the ransacking of your home nor Glasby's murder so soon after your own disappearance."

"Then consider me forewarned," Devin said. "And the sooner I meet this Pelton, the better. I like to see my enemy face to face—mayhap get to know him and better take his measure." He glanced at Woody. "I've been known to befriend the meanest of blackguards." A hint of a grin touched his mouth.

"Glad to see your sense of humor returning, lad," Woody said. "Thought you'd left it at Newgate . . . or up at the mission." His look was concerned however. "I suppose 'tis better to know your enemy. But, on the other hand, you knew Glasby. By God, the man worked for you, and yet he proved himself to be a viper waiting to strike beneath your very nose."

"Let's see how repairs are coming along on the *Lady*," Devin suggested, absently reaching to stroke the parrot. "I'm eager to see her again. She belongs on the ocean with the wind filling her canvas, not sitting injured and idle in Port Royal."

He was rewarded with another piercing whistle in his ear. Immediately his hand fell away and his eyes closed against the shrill reverberations chasing through his head.

"I don't think he's accustomed to such affection," Woody observed. "And speaking of affection, I thought you were occupied with another . . . lady."

Devin felt incriminating color stain his face. "She'll tire of Jamaica and go a-running back to England within weeks, mark my words," he answered with a valiant attempt at insouciance.

Woody leaned toward him and met his eyes. "There's no sin in falling in love, lad. 'Tis written on your face when you but speak of her. She must be quite lovely."

Devin's expression turned bleak. "Love? Hah! Surely you of all people understand what 'tis like to lose those you love, Woody. Why would you encourage me to become emotionally attached to anyone?"

Pain rose in Woodrow Kingsley's eyes. "Life itself is a risk. You know that, surely, in your line of work. There are no guarantees in anything."

"Aye, but you once told me that 'twas easier for a man to give up his own life than to lose a loved one."

Woody's gaze moved to the middle distance. He was contemplatively silent for a few moments. "Aye, lad. A dead man feels no pain. But I was younger when I said those words to you and have had time to ponder many things. I believe the truest loss is when a man—or woman—never gets the chance to feel love for another."

"I loved my m—"

Without warning, Bakámu came thudding awkwardly down the stairs just then. A cobweb hung from his hawklike nose, draped the front of his gleaming dark hair, but a smile lit his face, and Devin couldn't help but think of Meredyth St. Andrews and her fierce loyalty to the Arawak.

He wondered if he would think of her every time his eyes encountered the Indian.

"By the Mass! What were you about all this time?" Devin asked with exaggerated displeasure, glad to be able to steer the subject away from unsafe waters.

"Bakámu clean under bed, Chan-ler. Much work. Very dirty."

Devin felt the blood leave his face.

Henry Morgan chimed, "Dirty Chan-ler! Dirty!" and Devin wanted to wring the creature's scrawny neck. Or glue his beak shut.

Woody came to the rescue. "Found naught but dirt, did you?" he asked the Indian with what Devin recognized as an affected lightness.

"*Nada.* Only *arañas* and dust." His grin widened. "Chan-ler come see?"

Taking Woody's cue, Devin managed a ghost of a smile to match his slowly returning color. "Not just now, Bakámu. Master Kingsley and I are going to the docks to visit the *Lady Elysia.* I'll view your handiwork tonight." *Although I didn't bring you into my home to go nosing around beneath my bed!* he added silently.

He glanced down at the Arawak's leg, which he knew must still be swollen beneath the man's breeches. Bakámu was most uncooperative about Devin's attentions to his wound, as if he feared that Devin would send him back to the mission to recuperate further.

"Go boat now with Chan-ler?" Bakámu asked.

Devin stood and shook his head. He carefully replaced Henry Morgan upon his perch and turned back to the Indian. "You must rest now. Lie upon your own bed and prop up your bad leg, *comprende?*"

Bakámu's grin slid from his features like rain off a tar-slick surface. He looked crestfallen.

"Rest, *por favor,* before you make our dinner," Devin said in a lighter tone but with a definite ring of command to his voice. "When you're stronger, I'll take you to the docks," he added as a conciliatory gesture, suspecting he'd regret the promise. "But stay out from beneath my bed, won't you? Leave the dirt and—"

"No more dirt!" Bakámu said with a lift of his chin.

Devin nodded, deciding not to pursue it further.

"If that Indian finds the packet of notes, I'll throw him back to those crocodiles up the mountain," Devin threatened in a low voice as they walked across Thames Street. He had slowed his pace to accommodate Woodrow's limp, for the cobblestoned street was tricky even for a man with a normal gait. "He's the only man on the whole bloody island foolish enough to poke around under that behemoth of a bed."

Woody grunted and Devin slanted him a glance, for he thought he detected laughter edging the unintelligible sound. "Don't snicker, Kingsley," he warned. His gaze suddenly scanned the cloud-blotted sky. Rain was on the way. "I've had more invitations than you'd know what to do with since word of that bed got around Port Royal. Here I could be entertaining all manner of females, instead of leading the life of a monk just to protect those precious papers!"

Woody fit his cane into a crack between two rounded stones, tested it, and put his weight on it. "Damned slippery things," he grumbled. It had rained earlier and some of the stones were still slick. He followed Devin's glance at the sky and frowned. "And looks like 'twill get worse before it gets better. I feel it in my bones."

"To say naught of seeing it in the sky," Devin said dryly.

Woody ignored the statement. "And speaking of getting worse, m'boy, your temper is the foulest I've ever seen it. Mayhap you have been leading too monkish a life of late." He dodged a black youth, who hurried past them, weaving erratically to guide a gaggle of geese through the busy street.

"Foul, I?" Devin began, then closed his mouth. He hadn't

been the same since meeting Meredyth St. Andrews, but he couldn't admit that. "No doubt my stay in Newgate soured my temperament. A while in the Caribbean sun and all will be set to rights." *Providing I get my hands on the men responsible for Jimmy's death and remove little Sister Meredyth from my hair.*

At that moment, the swollen clouds overhead split open, wetting them almost instantaneously. "You need to have some fun, Devin," Woody panted, as Devin took his elbow and guided him into the lee of a warehouse wall.

As they huddled against the building, Devin glanced up again, suspecting that the shower would be of brief duration. He looked at Woodrow. "Would you care to clarify that?"

Woody nodded. "Acting Governor White is giving a ball in a little more than a fortnight. I informed him of your return, just to make sure, of course, that you would be invited."

"But I've work to—"

"Just when was the last time you were in the company of a decent female? Besides Meredyth St. Andrews, of course," he quickly amended.

Devin saw something flicker behind the older man's eyes but couldn't identify it. He paused momentarily, feeling as if his reaction to the question was more important than his companion was letting on. He was hard-pressed to keep his expression neutral at the mention of Meredyth's name.

But he knew the perfect way to allay all of his friend's suspicions. He threw back his head and laughed heartily. "Why, you old rake!" he exclaimed, amusement softening his words. "Will you never have done with your matchmaking efforts?" He laughed again. "I'll let you in on a secret," he said when he'd sobered enough to speak. "Nelly of Newgate awaits my return to London, after I make my fortune, of course, plundering Spanish galleons. I'm to fetch her straightaway, pay her debts, marry her, and—"

"And you've a nimble tongue to match the best of them, or

the worst." Woody cleared his throat and peered through the spring shower. "Nelly of Newgate, indeed."

Devin chuckled, but unexpectedly Woody's fist thumped against his arm. "Look," he said in an urgent undertone, his eyes narrowed at something in the street, his double chin pointed like the nose of a bloodhound scenting its quarry.

Devin's gaze followed his. As quickly as the clouds had gathered and the rain had begun to fall, a sliver of sun peeped through those very rainclouds to bathe the street before them in an errant, brilliant beam. The lingering smile disappeared from Devin's features, and the infinitely unwelcome nausea that hit him like a fist in the gut every time he saw one man enslaved to another assaulted him at the sight before them.

A score of African males, shackled and obviously cowed, shuffled along the wet cobblestones in pathetic rows, taking up much of the width of Thames Street. As the sun shone down upon the scene, it turned their skins to burnished ebony, save for the brief interruption of loincloths that loosely girded each man's hips and the unmistakable blight of open sores.

They were bareheaded, barefooted, and many of them squinted against the bright light of day, which told Devin they'd been detained in the dark and dank depths of some slaver's hold until very recently.

"Don't stare," Woody warned him *sotto voce*.

Devin's eyes narrowed. "And why can't I look over what's being offered on the market?" His voice was deceptively dulcet as the breeze brought traces of the stench of a slaver hold to his nostrils. "Mayhap I have need of a few slaves myself," he added, his words honed with a fine edge of menace. "There's the possibility I'll be making changes in the *Lady Elysia* to accommodate that most lucrative cargo—human beings."

Kingsley didn't answer, for now and again Devin would "purchase" a few slaves and secretly deliver them to freedom, either taking them to the mission and putting them in the hands of some trusted merchant or plantation owner who felt the same way he did or giving them to kinder masters, who paid them wages and treated them like human beings.

The work was time-consuming, tricky, and extremely dangerous. It wasn't always easy to find sympathetic souls, let alone to deliver human cargo into their hands with no one the wiser. And Devin knew if he decided to venture into the slave trade itself for an even better foothold, the decision was his, no matter how risky. Woody might not approve, but he could do no more than voice token protests. And now was hardly the time.

"Who's that behind them?" Devin asked. "I don't recog—"

A shout interrupted his query, and his gaze was drawn to a brassy-haired woman, a prostitute, being shoved into the midst of the moving slaves by another angry female. The latter promptly slipped into the shadows between two warehouses behind them, while the first woman had to fight to maintain her balance and extricate herself from the dark forms that closed in around her.

"Sweet Christ," Devin muttered, " 'tis Arabella!" He started forward, for no one appeared to be intervening on the woman's behalf. And the more she struggled, the more havoc she caused.

"Don't," Woody said, one hand squeezing Devin's arm. "She isn't worth the trouble—"

But Devin was already dodging bodies and ducking chains among the restive black men, toward the beleaguered Arabella. "Halt!" he called over his shoulder at the tall, dark-haired man who appeared to be in charge. He looked like Jon Treacher, Captain of the *Bristol*, but Devin didn't know him personally. "By the Mass! Halt, I say!" he repeated in his most authoritative ship captain's voice.

A stranger stepped forward from the perimeter of the street and moved toward Arabella as the group finally came to a stumbling stop. Chains clanked and a babble of voices shouted in a foreign tongue, punctuating the air as Devin disentangled Arabella from one particularly tall and gangly African, who seemed more confused than anything, yet too weak to represent a threat. Another was growling ominously, if unintelligibly, at both her and Devin.

"Did ye see them attack me?" Arabella demanded indignantly of Devin, then turned to bestow an openly inviting smile on the merchant who'd also come to her aid. "And I thank ye very much, Master . . . ?"

The face of Arabella's would-be rescuer turned beet red as he obviously realized the woman's occupation. He bobbed his bewigged head and backed away, avoiding the tangle of men around him. "Nay matter, mistress," he said in so hurried and timid a manner that Devin wondered what had propelled him to go to Arabella's aid in the first place. He was a skinny fellow, with protruding teeth, but obviously well intentioned. At least at first.

"And what of me, fair damsel?" Devin inquired with a lopsided grin as he helped to his feet the African, who seemed especially weak. He then steered Arabella out of the melée and noted her staring after the retreating merchant as if deciding whether to engage in pursuit or not.

"Thank ye, Devil Chandler," she mumbled half to herself, her attention still on the retreating stranger. She knew that he wasn't interested in her charms, but she was maddeningly slow getting clear of the slaves, he thought as the smell of unwashed bodies came to him once again. He had to practically haul her to the side.

"Ain't 'e the new merchant from the Colonies?" she asked no one in particular. Before Devin could speak, two men appeared to his right, unnoticed by him in his efforts to extract Arabella from her predicament. Too late, one of them grabbed the prostitute by the back of her gown and jerked her out of Devin's grip. "Since when do whores dare interfere with commerce?" the man growled, shoving her backward.

With a cry of surprise, she landed painfully on her backside on the wet street. Arabella squinted against the fickle sunshine at the intruder, obviously at a loss for words.

"Get out of the way," said the other man. He returned

Devin's look, his eyes narrowing with outright hostility. "And you as well. Take your whore and crawl back into your hole, zealot."

Devin stiffened instantly at the insult but reined in his outrage and fell back on the deceptively good nature that had helped him foil his enemies on more than one occasion. "Now see here, my good man," he drawled, forcing an easy smile to his lips. "There's no need for antagonism here. The lady—"

"She's no lady," the other said in a way that revealed to Devin he was more than likely a haughty aristocrat. "And she has no business darting out into the street like a—"

"I was pushed," Arabella defended herself, obviously having found her tongue. Devin turned to the newcomer and suddenly remembered Woody's words about Luke Pelton. He would be involved in trading or selling slaves; he would be a nobleman turned renegade.

Nobody paid any particular attention to Arabella in those tense moments as the two men took each other's measure and she struggled to her feet. Brushing herself off, she made a face at the slave, who was still growling in her direction, before briefly turning her frown upon the two newcomers. She then proceeded to flounce away.

"Don't you want an apology?" Devin called to her retreating form and noted that the back of her blinding pink satin gown was stained now, as well as disheveled.

A dismissive wave of one hand was her answer, and one of the two returned to his place on either side of the captives.

Devin's gaze was drawn back to the remaining man. "How dare you presume to speak for me?" the latter said, his eyes darkening with ire.

Ignoring the man's question, Devin unexpectedly held out his hand. "Let's begin again, shall we?" he asked amiably. "Devil Chandler," he introduced himself with a slight bow. "And you are?"

Disregarding Devin's outstretched hand, the man said shortly, "Pelton. Luke Pelton."

He made to swing away, but Devin put a hand on his arm to stop him. He felt the muscles beneath his fingers tense rigidly. Pelton's jaw stiffened as he looked back at him.

"What now?"

"How much are you asking for these . . . men?"

"What use would you have for slaves?" came the derisive question. "A defender of whores, a man who—"

Devin's brows shot upward, revealing none of his inner anger or the intuition that told him this man was all the more dangerous for some obviously personal agenda. He affably interrupted Pelton's tirade. "What kind of tone is that to use on a fellow Englishman, eh? By the Mass, Pelton, you don't even know me. And you're damned lucky that I choose not to be offended. This time." He placed his hands on his hips and canted his head speculatively at Pelton, the expression on his features taking the sting out of the last two words.

"Twenty-two pounds a head."

Devin glanced over his shoulder at the slaves chained to one another in mutual misery and said, "You're absolutely right."

Pelton's eyes widened slightly, briefly, in surprise. "Meaning?"

"Many of these blacks are sporting open wounds or so weak they can barely walk. Why, nearly the entire row was felled when Arabella was pushed into their midst." Devin shook his head with a moue. "You ask too much for specimens such as these."

He watched Pelton's reaction, thinking the man mouthed insults much more easily than he could take them, for his lips thinned beneath his moustache and one hand moved smoothly to the hilt of his sword.

"Do you want to settle the matter right here?" Pelton asked with soft menace.

Just then, as perfectly timed as divine intervention, the awkward movements of a swarthy-skinned man lurching toward them down Thames Street with the aid of a single crutch caught Devin's eye over Pelton's shoulder. A bird was perched upon his shoulder as he made his ungainly way toward them.

Devin groaned inwardly.

The Arawak paused to call through his cupped hands. *"Chan-ler!"*

Henry Morgan whistled piercingly, and Bakámu veered unexpectedly to the left in response to the assault on his eardrum.

In spite of Pelton's challenge, Devin had to quell a laugh. What a choice, he thought with rue, to either be run through by Luke Pelton or be made a laughingstock by the bumbling Arawak.

"Another time, perhaps?" he said glibly to Pelton, pointing over the latter's shoulder. "Alas, my servant calls." Let the man think him either a coward or too obtuse to have grasped the meaning of "settling the matter." It would be more in keeping with the impression he wanted to make upon the Englishman, anyway.

Just then the signal was given for the slaves to move on, and out of the corner of his eye Devin saw Woody veer sharply to alter his course from the shadows of the warehouse and toward Bakámu.

"Chan-ler!" he heard the Indian shout and bit down on his lower lip. "Go boat! Big water, *sí?"*

"Squaaawk! Go boat!" bawled Henry Morgan.

Fighting his laughter, Devin vowed to give the Arawak a thrashing he'd never forget. After a hearty hug of gratitude, of course.

He took a step back from Pelton, shrugging as he raised his palms; and noted the brief bemusement in the latter's eyes, as if the Englishman didn't quite know what to make of Devin and his behavior. Or didn't quite believe it.

Then it was gone, his hand fell away from his sword, and without another word he swung about in obvious disgust.

Ten

Meredyth stepped down from the hackney, one hand resting upon the footman's proffered arm, and stared at the two-story, half-timbered governor's house before her. The pale plaster of its outer walls offered refuge from the tropical heat and sunshine, while the blue-green shutters that bracketed its front windows reminded her of the aquamarine waters around Jamaica, cool and inviting in the somnolent Caribbean twilight.

Her traveling companions, Jackie and Ellen Greaves, looked totally in awe of the impressive edifice, and Meredyth wondered if they had ever been inside it before.

The footman relinquished her arm to Greaves, and with the women flanking him on either side, he proceeded up the short walkway to the front entrance.

"Do close your mouth, Ellie," Meredyth murmured, a distinct hint of mischief underlying her words, "else you catch a fly and choke on it."

Ellen's mouth snapped shut, and she threw Meredyth a grateful glance.

"Never thought I'd see the day Ellie lost control o' her mouth," Jackie said with a grin and was rewarded with a poke to the ribs.

"They'll never let you in the door if you can't act more ladylike 'an that," he warned lightly as they moved forward within the queue of couples and small groups headed toward the brightly lit entrance.

Easy chatter was carried back to the trio on the balmy sea

breeze, and Meredyth wondered for the hundredth time why she'd allowed Father Tomas to persuade her to return to Port Royal for something so frivolous as a ball.

"I'm in mourning," she'd protested. "And I have no escort. And I don't wish to return there—*ever.*" To her mortification, her eyes had filled with tears and she'd swung away from the priest to hide them.

He'd come up behind her then and put an arm about her shoulders. "You're not in official mourning. You're not blood family, *niña,*" he'd reminded her gently. "You can quietly mourn Manuel's passing for as long as you need, but I will not allow you to hide away here and remove yourself from all that life has to offer until your spirit withers. You're young and full of life. You deserve to participate in suitable activities for a young woman of your age and station." Then he'd added more firmly, "I'm in part to blame for emphasizing . . . er . . . unduly the importance of Bakámu's vision quest. This is a much better reason to go to Port Royal, Meredyth, is it not?"

The point was well-taken, if rather blunt, she had to admit. "But I didn't come to Jamaica to socialize," she'd told him, yet the Jesuit had countered that and every other objection, insisting that the governor would be offended if she didn't attend, especially since he'd obviously been apprised of her presence.

"Aye," she'd blurted. "The notorious Lady Meredyth, who rushes off into Port Royal in hot pursuit of a man she hardly knows!"

If she hadn't known better, Meredyth would have suspected Father Tomas of deliberately meddling in her life, of deliberately nudging her toward mingling with Port Royal society.

But it wasn't her way to indulge in self-pity. She'd bowed to Father Tomas's wishes, in spite of the fact that she'd had no desire to attend a ball. Not least of all in her considerations was the enthusiasm and outright encouragement by many of those living at the mission. It was as if there were a conspiracy to make sure she attended the function. The children even made her a garland of flowers to wear in her hair when she attended the ball.

Concepción, Carla's mother, requested Father Tomas's permission to accompany Meredyth to the earl's small town house as her personal attendant. And, of course, Carla wanted to come, too, so at the proper time she could help her mother create for Meredyth a fresh garland exactly like the original, which would surely wilt long before the ball.

And so it was a rather odd little procession that wended its way down the mountain to the earl's sugar plantation near where the sand spit leading to Port Royal joined the island proper.

Meredyth had already met Jackie and Ellen Greaves and got along well with the short and bubbly Ellie, who was in her mid-thirties. She'd stayed with the Greaveses upon first arriving in Jamaica and before being escorted up to the mission and had found the lively Ellie as warm and friendly as any older sister. And with an unmistakably mischievous sense of humor.

Now, with an obvious attempt at calm sophistication, Ellie lifted her chin and lengthened her short strides to keep up with her tall husband and Meredyth.

All the windows had been thrown open wide, and lamplight shone beckoningly from within. A footman flanked either side of the open door, and Meredyth could see the reception line within the foyer area. The deep drone of the servant announcing each arrival drifted back to her, and she evinced very mixed feelings regarding this public introduction after weeks of relative peace and anonymity.

As they ascended the few steps to the entrance, an unexpected tickle of anticipation moved within Meredyth, for she was by nature a gregarious person and under normal circumstances enjoyed being with others in a festive atmosphere. It had been her own decision to isolate herself in a mountaintop mission in the Caribbean, and the thought of what had driven her so far from home seemed frivolous now, in light of what had happened a few weeks before in Port Royal.

She felt a sudden rise of the guilt that had been an almost constant companion lately, and to counter it, she forced a smile to her lips as the announcement was made, "Lady Meredyth St. Andrews of London and Master and Mistress Jack Greaves."

She felt the flush of heat in her cheeks, for many turned to stare, the women from behind fluttering fans, the men more boldly. Acting Governor John White and his wife greeted them, and suddenly Meredyth was being introduced to an older gentleman with a silver fringe of hair and merry blue eyes.

"Your most eager escort for the evening, Lady Meredyth," the governor introduced. "Master Woodrow Kingsley of Jamaica."

"Aye," added the governor's wife, "and beware, my dear," she cautioned Meredyth with light exaggeration, "for Master Kingsley is a most eligible widower."

Kingsley answered his hostess, "I cannot do much pursuing, Clara, with my walking stick," and sketched a gallant bow, a bit awkward because of one stiff leg Meredyth couldn't help but notice. "Although my lady Meredyth makes me lament anew the loss of my former, vigorous gait. You do honor to a backwater like Jamaica," he said with a warm smile and raised her hand to his lips.

"And you are very kind," she murmured in reply. As she returned his smile, Meredyth noticed that after he placed her hand upon his arm, he paused for a fraction of an instant before leading her into the throng of people within the huge room before them. Almost as if savoring the moment . . . or showing her off like a proud father.

But her genteel upbringing took over, and in spite of her inner awkwardness, Meredyth handled herself with perfect poise as she was guided, head held high, into the perfume- and candle-scented air of the ballroom. She smiled into myriad faces, took in fleeting impressions of colors and fabrics of all kinds shimmering and rustling in the kaleidoscope of figures all around her, and a riot of vividly hued tropical flowers set in large vases everywhere. Their scent perfumed the air and blended with the other smells permeating the great room. The collective babble of scores of voices rose as one, a laugh, a phrase, or single word jumping out briefly from the blended cacophony of sound, before receding once again into anonymity.

The soft, sweet strains of music reminded her poignantly of home. Meredyth canted her head toward the sound, her eyes seeking out the musicians and taking on the glow of anticipation.

She felt her spirits being lifted by the tide of excitement.

"Good God! What is she doing here?" asked a voice, its owner obviously stunned.

"Quite a little surprise, *n'est-ce pas?*" came the reply. "But, on the other hand, *mon ami,* you'd heard she might be here. Isn't that why you are? Will you seek to win her back?"

Pelton drained the goblet of rum and reached for another in visible agitation. His hand was shaking. "I knew her father had interests in the Caribbean, but Meredyth is here in Jamaica?"

"Do you tremble from anger," his companion asked smoothly. "Or anticipation?"

The look Pelton shot him was frigid.

"Mayhap you can partner her for a dance later, and, as we say, *un tête-à-tête,* hmmmm?" His tone was sly, unctuous.

"How?" Pelton demanded. "After I explain why I left her high and dry?"

"You were tricked, were you not? Then blackmailed. Tell her the truth."

Pelton slashed one hand through the air. "That doesn't matter! Even if she believed me, she would never choose me over the earl, my word over his."

Du Casse shook his head, the long dark curls of his periwig hardly moving, so tightly were they coiled. "Then you may

have to resort to . . . ah, more drastic measures if you still
want her."

Pelton raised his drink to his lips and watched as Meredyth
St. Andrews was led across the ballroom. She looked much
the same, only even younger, as when he'd first set eyes upon
her and had had the audacity to fall in love with her.

"Who's that with her?" he asked tersely, wanting to run the
man through for no other reason save that he was with
Meredyth, and Pelton would forever be denied that privilege.

"Woodrow Kingsley, a man close to your new friend, *le
capitaine.*"

"The man's an imbecile," Pelton mumbled, hardly aware of
what emerged from his lips, so preoccupied was he with catching glimpses of Meredyth. "And of a certainty no friend of
mine, especially after tonight."

Du Casse slanted him a subtle look of warning. "Don't ever
make the mistake, *mon ami,* of underestimating Devil Chandler. He's as superb an actor as any you'll see on a theater
stage."

"May I introduce my friend, Captain Devin Chandler?"
Woodrow Kingsley was asking Meredyth as she sipped from
a glass of punch and watched the dancers move to the music.

Shock made her beautiful eyes widen as her gaze met
Devin's. He appeared as if conjured up by a skillful magician,
and while she'd secretly hoped that he might be present, she
hadn't known exactly what kind of men and women would be
invited into the governor's home and wouldn't have been surprised to see the likes of Mad Dog Davies or Maddy of the
Seaman's Folly, or even Arabella.

He smiled into her eyes, outwardly the epitome of the perfect gentleman—a far cry from the character she'd met at the
waterfall and then encountered at the Seaman's Folly.

Devin got the impression of new buds in springtime and
the color of the ocean on certain days and a riot of emeralds

reflected in the watered green silk of her gown that was perfect for the warm Jamaican night—a confection of exquisite silk, fine linen, and lace as frothy as seafoam and as pristine in hue. Trained in the back and demurely cut at the neckline, it was a gown worthy of a queen.

A virgin queen, sneered a voice. *She's not for you Chandler.* Trying to ignore the voice, he bowed deeply, his burnished, shoulder-length hair more impressive than any periwig in the room.

Careful of the drink she held, Meredyth curtseyed as far as possible, affording Devin a view of the mass of gleaming umber ringlets atop her head, woven through with a simple and delicate garland of small flowers, and a teasing glimpse of the top of the velvet valley between her breasts. A rose blossom of green silk was strategically positioned in the center of her off-the-shoulder and delicately dipping décolletage.

Meredyth felt even more heat seep into her cheeks. She tried to focus instead on Chandler's handsomely turned ankles and leanly muscled calves in their black hose. She was accustomed to him in his usual bucket boots or barefoot, she thought wryly as her gaze briefly touched his low-heeled black leather shoes with their silver buckles.

She straightened smoothly, realizing that her very physical thoughts were doing little to calm her hectic heart. She offered him her hand, feeling silly in light of the variety of emotions he'd managed to elicit from her in any situation thus far.

Devin bent over her fingers after cutting her a glance through his lashes. Enchanting color lit her cheeks and threatened to temporarily wash away the dusting of freckles he so loved.

Loved? one part of him thought in an unexpected spurt of perplexity.

"Forgive me, Captain Chandler," she said, distracting him from his wayward thought. "I didn't expect you to be here." The color highlighting her cheeks heightened yet again as she realized what she'd implied. Even though this was Port Royal,

Jamaica, Meredyth knew well that good manners always prevailed in public. "Rather," she quickly corrected herself, "I didn't know exactly who would be here."

"There's no need to apologize, Lady Meredyth," he said lightly after a glance at Kingsley. "We're more informal here in Jamaica, and even Woodrow will agree that I don't make a habit of appearing so . . . ah . . ."

"Respectable," Woody supplied without missing a beat.

A rather seedy-looking female sashayed past them in a lemon yellow gown dripping with black lace, a gown that brought the Seaman's Folly to Meredyth's mind with a pang. She watched as the woman gave Devin an openly come-hither look. He didn't acknowledge her any further than with the briefest of glances, his attention immediately returning to Meredyth. "Woody is always so complimentary," he said. "It comes from living alone too long. He's turning sour on me."

"Oh, aye, Lady Meredyth," Woody said. "Ask him when it was that he last wore a *justaucorps* and waistcoat or left his boots and cutlass behind."

"I don't remember," Devin said with a shrug that emphasized the breadth of his shoulders beneath his tapered, deep blue outer coat. It came to just above his knees, several silver buttons and silver-embroidered buttonholes open at the chest to reveal the pure white of the neckcloth above and below his waist to reveal a dove-gray waistcoat hugging his lean middle. Meredyth's gaze lowered to his knees, where snug, black breeches were secured by silver buttons. She wished she could see beneath the *justaucorps,* glimpse the outline of what she knew to be his firm thighs.

And even further, came an impish and errant thought.

Devin Chandler had no need for high heels, she forced herself to acknowledge in an effort to change the course of her very lusty thoughts as she brought her gaze up to meet his again. He was easily one of the tallest men in the room.

"Even pirates can be respectable when necessary," he said,

his crystalline-blue eyes glinting, and gave her a lopsided grin that sent her pulse racing madly.

His efforts to smooth over all differences, at least for now, touched her profoundly. She thought back to his words of comfort the day they'd returned Manuel's body to the mission, his obvious efforts to lighten her heart, and cast about in her mind for a way to make up for having called him a pirate. "Some so-called pirates are capable of putting gentlemen to shame." A soft and genuine smile curved her mouth, leaving no room for doubt as to her sincerity.

"You are too generous, Lady Meredyth," he murmured. "I'm afraid 'tis really no more than the trappings of civilization all about us. I would be more comfortable, as Master Kingsley said, in boots and cutlass and I'm loath to wear a wig, although I did bring one with me." He winked naughtily. "And while I see that you fit in as perfectly as a crowning jewel tonight, I can't help but remember the charming picture you made with your hair tumbling down your back, a large straw bonnet shading your fair face, and a chameleon peeking from your cupped hands."

"You'll excuse me, won't you?" Woody murmured and slipped away, and Devin wondered if his friend knew what he was up to. How could he not? he conceded. Woody knew him better than anyone.

But neither Devin nor Meredyth did more than nod as Kingsley discreetly withdrew.

"We got off to a rather bad beginning," Devin heard himself saying, thinking back to the resentment he'd carried to the mission upon his return from London. "I was inexcusably rude to you that first day and on subsequent meetings . . ."

Meredyth felt her breath catch in her throat at his honest admissions, at the sincerity in his voice and in his very fine eyes.

He's not much better than a pirate, warned a tiny voice. She pushed it aside.

"But my behavior wasn't exactly courteous, either," she said, as he reached to take her empty goblet from her hand.

He smiled at her and said, "May I? Brandywine or punch?" He handed it to a passing servant as she colored prettily at the mention of brandywine and answered, "Punch." He nodded at the man, and the latter promptly moved away.

"And just how is Bakámu?" Meredyth asked after drawing in a calming breath.

She held one hand at her waist, against the snug bodice with its tiny rows of cream-colored ribbon bows, which came to a point just below where her fingers rested, a closed fan suspended from her wrist, and emphasized the sweet curves of her body beneath the gown. Devin found himself staring at those slender fingers with their manicured nails and wondering how they would feel touching him, cool and gentle as they smoothed over his heated flesh, driving him to new heights of passion.

Stop it! one part of him admonished sternly. *Are you addled?*

"Did I tell you of Henry Morgan's newest feat?" he asked without warning, knowing he hadn't had a chance but desperately attempting to pull his mind from its carnal musings.

"Henry Morgan?" she said, her face lighting up. "Nay! Do tell me what he can do besides move you to mayhem." A beguiling dimple appeared on one side of her mouth, and she lowered her gaze for a moment, as if to rein in her obvious amusement.

He wanted her suddenly, more than anything, to laugh freely. He wanted to chase the last, lingering shadows from her lovely eyes. "Evidently the parrot was taught to play dead," he informed her.

Totally surprised, Meredyth lifted her questioning gaze to his just as the servant returned with two drinks. A smile hovered about her mouth, waiting, he thought, for a reason to dawn. "Indeed," he said, taking them and handing her one. "He heard me say 'dead parrot' in a dialogue with Woody and promptly did a dive from my finger toward the floor."

Her expression immediately changed to a look of concern.

She was so soft-hearted, whether it came to another human being or a bird, he thought. And easy to distress, which made one part of him want to protect her from the myriad cruelties of the world.

Rather than revealing his thoughts, however, Devin merely laughed softly. "Nay, 'twasn't what you think, Merry-mine. He kept hold of my finger, although he needed an extra bit of anchoring from me. I think at one time, before his foot was injured, he did the trick quite well without any aid."

"Clever bird," she said, breaking into a brilliant smile and neglecting to correct his audacious and oft-repeated endearment. "And has Bakámu taught him any Arawak?" Laughter laced her words.

"Nay. Only broken English . . . like his infernal 'Go boat, Chan-ler?' " His gaze sought the ceiling and he briefly touched his fingertips to his forehead in feigned despair.

Meredyth was moved to laughter again and tried not to dwell on the striking contrast between the snow-white fall of Venetian lace at his wrist and the teak tone of his sun-browned hand. Save for his outrageous boldness, he could have just stepped from Whitehall itself. His wit, charm, and elegance were without fault.

"Where exactly in England are you from?" she asked him before taking a sip of punch. She studied him carefully over the rim of her goblet and made a mental note not to drink the potent concoction too quickly. His mere presence made her strangely breathless, and she'd already had one glass. And her escort seemed to have disappeared. Who would protect her from Devil Chandler? Governor White himself? Or his wife?

No one can protect you from Devin James Chandler, an imp prompted. *That was already proven in a room at the Seaman's Folly . . .*

His expression altered slightly, the smile fading somewhat from his eyes as he said, "I hail from Ireland, not England, although my father was English."

Sensing she'd hit a sore spot, Meredyth said quickly, "Ah,

yes . . . your lady mother was Elysia, after whom your ship was named. A schooner, I believe?"

His eyes warmed at her attempt to steer clear of conversational shoals, although she couldn't know that his mother was of common stock. "A schooner, aye. And a beauty she is, just like her namesake."

"I should like to have known her," she said unexpectedly, her look thoughtful as she held his eyes. "I suspect she had the most wonderful sense of humor. 'Tis an enviable Irish trait."

In a world where the English, noble and otherwise, looked down their noses at the Irish, here was something rare: Lady Meredyth St. Andrews, daughter of an English earl, complimenting his mother, who'd borne him out of wedlock and gone to her grave loving the blue blooded rake who'd ruined her.

"And you were wrong, you know, Captain Chandler, when you said I had no sense of humor." She flipped open her fan, as if to emphasize her words, and casually plied it to her face. Her eyes shone with pure deviltry, which he did not miss. He was utterly enchanted by it and by her lack of snobbery. He found himself mentally preparing to engage in a matching of wits with this delightful daughter of Keir St. Andrews.

He smiled lazily, commanding his leaping heart to be still. "Indeed? Not very courteous of me and it was an incorrect observation, I might add."

"But you hardly knew me then, so I suppose I cannot blame you," she began sweetly.

"Lady Meredyth?" came a voice from directly behind Devin.

Meredyth looked over at Ellen Greaves, who was making her way toward them, Jackie in tow. He looked entirely intimidated by the whole affair, while Ellie was aglow with excitement. Her cheeks were splashed with high color, and wisps of her naturally curly hair had pulled free from Concepción's simple but pretty arrangement.

As they reached Meredyth and Devin, without warning, a

man passing by leaned toward Meredyth and struck out with one hand toward the layers of petticoat ruffles in the open V of her full skirt. She didn't have time to wonder why he looked familiar.

Diverted by the approach of the Greaveses, Meredyth caught only Devin's arm as it slashed downward toward her skirt and the stranger's arm. She heard a grunt, then a low-spoken curse and the soft bump of flesh against flesh.

"Scorpion!" Ellie mouthed the single word with revulsion.

Meredyth bit back a soft cry as she looked down and saw the creature skittering up her petticoats and Woodrow Kingsley appearing out of the surrounding crowd and batting the scorpion from among the ruffles with his cane.

It dropped to the floor, where Devin's shoe came down on it with swift finality, and Meredyth briefly averted her gaze. When she looked up at him again, it was to see another face beside his—an even-featured face with blue eyes and a sandy Vandyke beard and moustache, a face framed by a curling periwig and full of fury, a face she would have known anywhere.

"I would have rid you of the scorpion myself, Meredyth, but this court jester and his cohort would take the credit," Lucien Pendwell said in a voice icy with anger.

Eleven

Meredyth stared, stunned. Time was suspended.

But it was Devin Chandler who rescued the moment. "So we meet again, Pelton," he said, moving closer to Meredyth, sensing something was wrong. "And your manners haven't improved since first we met. You've a real penchant for name-calling, haven't you? Surely a less tolerant man than myself would have taken extreme offense—to say naught of my friend Master Kingsley here." He shook his head with a moue, in spite of the fact that he was fighting inwardly to keep his calm and wanted to smash in Pelton's face.

"We don't wish to seem ungrateful," Meredyth said, marshaling her wits and noticing the instant antagonism that materialized between the two men. Lucien looked harder than she remembered, his lips thinner, his eyes colder, and there was an almost savage aura about him. She couldn't help but compare the two, in spite of her chagrin at seeing the man who'd deserted her. "Thank you, Lu—"

She halted mid-word. Luke Pelton?

"Luke, now," he said unsmilingly. "A new name, a new beginning."

Meredyth frowned in bemusement. A new beginning? That was like rubbing salt into an open wound since it had been his decision to leave, not hers. And he was angry. Not awkward or apologetic in any way, but angry as she'd never seen him!

Yet, surprisingly, Meredyth was not nearly so unsettled or distraught at seeing him as she would have expected. The overwhelming emotion at first was surprise, then a cleansing anger began to spurt through her. It was just her luck that she'd traveled halfway around the world to get away from the man and the memories, only to find herself practically in his lap.

But even her sprouting anger was diluted; diluted by her experience in a humble mission in the wilds of the Blue Mountains of Jamaica; diluted by her having met and interacted with a man named Devin Chandler, who, with the force of his irresistible nature, had pushed aside much of the darkness that had enshrouded her heart and soul in the first place; and diluted by her part in the unnecessary death of a man, thus altering her outlook forever about what was truly important and what was of lesser consequence.

Somehow, during the past weeks, Lucien Pendwell's desertion had diminished in importance.

Then, too, Meredyth derived much comfort from the fact that she was surrounded by friends, most especially Devin Chandler himself, who seemed to sense Luke's fury and gave off his own reciprocal, though more subtle, hostility.

They'd evidently met before.

"Well, then, Lucien or Luke, whichever you are" she said, forcing a smile to her stiff lips, "I thank you for coming to my rescue." She held out her hand to him and felt Devin go rigid beside her as her former fiancé lifted the back of her hand to his mouth with an irritating slowness and pressed his lips to her flesh for what seemed an eternity.

Woodrow cleared his throat loudly, and Devin was sorely tempted to snatch Woody's cane and lay it across Pelton's neck. Instead, however, he coiled his fingers around Pelton's wrist, viselike, and said softly through set teeth, "You insult the lady Meredyth and make a spectacle with your lack of manners."

Devin's words brought Pelton upright, while his iron grip caused the Englishman to relinquish Meredyth's hand. He looked Devin straight in the eye. "And you, of course, being a peer of the realm, if born on the wrong side of the blanket, and a paragon of courtesy, have contributed naught to this spectacle." His eyes darted meaningfully to Devin's white-knuckled hand still attached to his wrist, and Devin finally released it. "This is the second time you've interfered with my actions this night, Chandler, and Jamaica's too small an island for the both of us." His eyes narrowed. "You'll not get away with ignoring my demand for satisfaction again, and to the death. Choose your weapons!"

Horror rose in Meredyth as she grasped his meaning. Her breath stuck in her throat, and fear suddenly burst through her chest like a battering ram.

"Lucien, how could you call a man out for so slight a thing?" she heard herself say in a thin voice.

"I don't consider our betrothal a slight thing, Meredyth." Luke's eyes glittered as they met hers. "Whatever you may think, I left you under duress, not by choice."

Her eyes registered disbelief at his revelation, while at the same time she half-expected Chandler to choke the life from him for his grave insult. But the latter said only, "What possible 'duress' could have caused you to jilt such a jewel?"

No one noticed Woodrow's gaze seek the ceiling before he sighed and leaned on his cane with a resigned shake of his head. Meredyth momentarily forgot her fear of Devin's reaction and shot him a quizzical look over his sudden flair for pretty prose.

"You're not responsible for my honor now," she insisted, her desperation beginning to impede her thoughts and actions like a nightmare from which she couldn't waken.

"I still have a copy of our betrothal contract," Pelton answered her.

"A mere technicality," Devin said evenly, "although most romantic of you. But I'm still interested in the duress that caused—"

" 'Tis none of your business," Pelton growled. "Now, name your weapons, your second, and we'll have done with this once and for all when the sun rises on the morrow."

"It seems rather that my honor has been impugned," Devin

informed him, "but I'll take cutlasses," he said as easily as if he were choosing a wine, "and Woodrow here can be—"

"Bakámu, of course, would serve you better," Woody cut in with a carefully schooled look of innocence. "He's younger and faster."

Faster, my arse, Devin thought. He's still using a crutch!

He could have felled his best friend on the spot. He was under enough pressure as it was. He met the latter's solemn gaze and caught the barely suppressed humor in it. Kingsley knew he wouldn't have trusted the Arawak to clean his cutlass, let alone act as his second in a duel.

"Why are you doing this?" Meredyth cried softly in distress, putting one hand lightly over her mouth. She held out the other to Pelton beseechingly, willing him to retract his challenge.

"Why, indeed?" asked another voice. "And whatever are you going to do to cause *la demoiselle* such distress?" It was Jean-Baptiste du Casse, with Governor White beside him. Now things were going to get complicated, Devin thought with an inner grimace.

He quickly took in the tall, thin du Casse with his great gray periwig and the impressive billowing sash at his waist that denoted his rank as a flag officer in the French Navy. From slave trader to naval officer to governor of the buccaneer-dominated St. Domingue, du Casse had made a name for himself around the Spanish Main and was one of the most powerful and influential men in the entire Caribbean. And not least of all because he was a much-respected buccaneer leader.

Devin wasn't the only one who secretly detested him. He watched the Frenchman sketch a perfect bow to Meredyth.

Governor White introduced du Casse to Meredyth, who was the only one of the group who had never met, or even heard of him.

Du Casse smiled into her eyes with Gallic intensity and asked, "Just what actions, if I may be so bold, Lady Meredyth, are *ces coquins* contemplating that brings a frown to your beautiful brow?" He slanted a glance at Pelton, as if in warning.

"A duel, sir," she said in a rush, grabbing at anything that might bring this madness to a halt. "Master Pelton demands satisfaction for a trifle—a complete misunderstanding, I assure you."

The guileless appeal in her vivid green eyes could have melted a rock, Devin thought as he watched her expressive features. "Making a meal of my lady's hand is hardly a trifle," he pronounced with a straight face. " 'Tis cowardly to back out of a duel now that 'tis arranged. Naught can be done but see it through."

He was suddenly and perversely bent upon further stirring the soup. Especially now that he knew Pelton was the man who'd caused Meredyth to flee England in humiliation, though there were now several reasons he'd like to dispatch the obnoxious Englishman.

"Mais c'est barbare—barbaric!—*n'est-ce pas, Monsieur le Gouverneur?"* he asked John White. "Especially if 'tis over the interpretation of, I take it, a man's kissing of a lady's hand."

A flush crept up Pelton's cheeks, but Devin managed to keep his expression bland.

"Indeed 'tis, if I may interject," Woodrow Kingsley said. "It was a misunderstanding, and we have become more civilized here in Jamaica than to revert to such primitive behavior, have we not?" he asked the governor.

Well done, Devin thought. How could the acting governor deny such a claim without demeaning the Jamaican colony and his own temporary authority?

John White appeared momentarily uncertain, then smoothed his expression and exhibited admirable diplomacy in the face of the "wisdom" of the infamous du Casse and one of the pillars of what "society" existed in Port Royal, Woodrow Kingsley. "We truly don't need to encourage such behavior on the island, unless your demand for satisfaction is, say, a mere drawing of the blood."

"An excellent way of putting it into a civilized perspective," du Casse said with a brief but meaningful look at Pelton. "If you meant no harm to the *demoiselle,* then let the matter drop, *n'est-ce pas?*"

Devin knew du Casse was considered by some to be a paragon of drawing-room virtues in addition to his reputation as an ambitious fighting man. He could be an effective mediator and, as governor of St. Domingue, had proven he could bring even buccaneers to heel.

If anyone could convince Pelton to withdraw his challenge, it was Jean-Baptiste du Casse.

The Frenchman's gaze switched to Devin then, the calm expectancy in his expression unmistakable. Devin quickly took in the appeal in Meredyth's eyes and felt his resolve to stir up Pelton's anger melt like warm candle wax.

He raised his eyebrows at Pelton with a slight exaggeration.

"Luc?" du Casse prompted.

Pelton was obviously at a disadvantage and furious. After a curt nod at Meredyth, then John White, he mumbled "As you wish" to du Casse, completely ignoring Devin and Woodrow, and backed away. Meredyth watched him turn and disappear into the crowd, a host of emotions whirling through her.

Meredyth heard little of what was said after Lucien—*Luke,* she silently corrected herself—disappeared. She was very much aware of Devin Chandler, in spite of her rather dazed state; but Kingsley, du Casse, and Governor White might just as well have not been there.

Lucien was there in Jamaica. How could she have known? And now that she did know, what was she to do?

Nothing, reason told her. *Would you flee from him again like a hare from the hounds?*

Of course not! she thought, with a hike of her chin. In that moment Devin Chandler's gaze captured hers. All thought of Lucien fled as easily as smoke dispersed on the wind. This man was an entirely different matter, she realized. He affected her enough to put all thought of her former fiancé to rout, and as the conversation buzzed around her Meredyth also realized that she'd wasted precious time, energy, and emotion on a man who literally paled by comparison to the outrageous and unpredictable Devin Chandler.

But why would you want to become involved with a scoundrel and a privateer? A man with questionable antecedents, at the least, and an even more questionable past?

". . . so Master Greaves tells me, milady," Chandler was saying, one blond eyebrow cocking.

Meredyth started slightly at his direct address and noticed that Jackie and Ellen had at last extricated themselves from the other group to join them.

Before she could comment, however, Devin, seeing her predicament, repeated, "The earl—in his privateer days, that is—abducted your lady mother?"

"That he did, an' a sweeter woman never lived," Jackie added with staunch loyalty to the countess.

"Nay, Captain Chandler," Meredyth corrected, willing her mind to clear. "My father's *crew* kidnapped my mother and presented her to Father as a surprise."

Color teased her fair cheeks, Devin noted, but she didn't shy away from the implications of such an action.

"The important part," she continued, holding Devin's gaze with her own, "is that Father fell in love with her then married her and made her his countess."

"A true fairy tale," Governor White observed.

"Hardly that, Your Excellency," Meredyth said with a wry movement of her lips. "Only the ending."

"Love conquers all, as they say," du Casse commented with a negligent shrug of one shoulder. "And if *la comtesse* was half as lovely as her daughter, one cannot fault your father's actions, however unorthodox, hmmm?"

"Only from a Frenchman," Woodrow said in an undertone

with a roll of his eyes. Devin caught it, however, and gave his friend a hint of a smile.

Violins, woodwinds, and a harpsichord sent the stately strains of a minuet drifting across the ballroom, and Devin said, "Will you do me the honor, Lady Meredyth, of this dance?"

She dipped her chin in acceptance, smiled at the others, and said "Pray excuse us, won't you?"

Ellen took her goblet and Meredyth held one hand out to Devin. He offered his arm and instantly felt himself floating over the floor as they moved to position themselves. He felt as though he'd just imbibed an entire case of brandywine.

But he was clear-thinking enough to wish to keep Meredyth's thoughts from the egregious Luke Pelton as he turned to her and could only wonder what had ever made Pelton jilt a woman like Meredyth St. Andrews. It was obvious they weren't of equal station, not that Devin was anywhere near her on the social scale either, even if one counted his natural father's title.

"If you must know," he said with a lopsided grin, "I'm obliged to dance this deuced scorpion off the bottom of my shoe."

The soft tinkle of her laughter threatened his very reason. "Tell me more, Lady Meredyth," he said, as they glided into the first of a series of figures, "about your mother and father, if you think it appropriate, of course. I'm intrigued by their history." His hand joined with hers, sending an unexpected jolt through her flesh.

At the powerful sensation, Meredyth thought of lightning racing, with stunning consequences, down a tree, while Devin was also reminded of a fork of lightning doing an erratic and brilliant dance across a ship's spar during a storm.

"My mother," she said rather breathlessly, "was ruthlessly abducted from her home in London, The Hawk and Hound, by several crew members from my father's brigantine."

They parted and postured, both with unconscious grace, both

obviously absorbed in each other. Meredyth's train swept the floor with a whisper that blended in with scores of other rustling trains, as light as the susurration of the waves from a rolling comber and barely discernable above the music.

"The Hawk and Hound in London?" he asked, wondering why a tavern had been her lady mother's home. Hadn't she perfect bloodlines on both sides? Not that he cared one whit.

"Aye, Captain Chandler," she said, an impudent dimple winking up at him. "Owned and run by her stepparents, the Daltons."

"Ah," he replied, courtesy preventing him from pursuing the matter further than that. "And I believe they still own the inn. Their son—Jonathon is it?—is the present proprietor."

"Mother's stepbrother, Uncle Jon."

"But your father's crew . . . ! How outrageously bold to do such a thing," he persisted.

She sidestepped one way, he the other, and he caught sight of one beribboned, cream slipper as it briefly peeked out from the hem of her dress. "My father was out of sorts, so Peter Stubbs, his former quartermaster, told me. Jackie Greaves will concur."

"They sought to improve his mood, mayhap?" He smiled guilelessly. "Quite a loyal group of individuals, your father's crew, going to lengths above and beyond the call of duty."

"My father is one of those few with the natural ability to command the loyalty of men."

"An excellent trait for a ship captain," he said. "And then he . . ." He trailed off, realizing that once again he was venturing into private realms.

"My father sailed for Jamaica with Mother on board, against her will," she finished for him as they slowly circled one another. Her last words were spoken over her shoulder, her lashes demurely lowered. He caught a fleeting glimpse of the tiny, jumping pulse in the hollow at the base of her slender throat and wondered if it was the story or his nearness that affected her.

He was determined, in whatever way he could achieve it, to wipe Luke Pelton from her mind and her heart. He would also be delighted, he acknowledged, to wipe the man off the face of the earth. He wanted to be the one who mattered to Meredyth St. Andrews, God help him. He was headed for certain disaster, probably heartbreak and betrayal, but he couldn't seem to help himself.

". . . should like very much to see the *Lady Elysia*," she was saying as they reached their original positions once again.

His heart lurched, and his gaze delved into her emerald eyes. Did she wish to leave Jamaica?

As if reading his thoughts, she said, "My father owns several ships, and I've always been fascinated by the sea and sailing. How are the repairs coming along on the *Lady Elysia?*"

They performed another figure, and Devin couldn't help but think of the way the earl had taken Meredyth's mother against her will, then somehow won her love. The very thought appealed to his recklessness, his sense of adventure.

And his growing desire for Meredyth St. Andrews.

You're supposed to be protecting her, not thinking of seducing her, came the voice from inside.

Their hands touched, linked, and Devin watched her eyelids lower slightly as if savoring the feeling. The sweep of her sable lashes shielded her gem-green eyes from him. He was reluctant to let go, but, of course, it would be unseemly in the middle of the minuet to cling to her in any way.

They finished the dance in silence, each steeped in wondrous sensations created by the presence, the brief but enticing touch, of the other.

"Would you like to see the *Lady?*" he asked her suddenly.

He watched her eyes widen slightly at the unexpectedness of his question. "Now? Tonight?" Meredyth asked, feeling a thrill of anticipation, and something more, skitter through her. Suddenly more light of heart than she had been since arriving in Jamaica, Meredyth could think of nothing more appealing than standing on a moonlit dock or the deck of a ship in the somnolent Jamaican night with Captain Devin Chandler.

Hadn't she literally thrown away her reputation when she'd chased him down from the mountains and into Port Royal and ended up in bed with him before witnesses at the Seaman's Folly?

And England, with all its social strictures, was virtually on the other side of the world.

"Don't think about it, Meredyth, just say you'll come with me," he said low, in her ear.

Luke sidled around the front of the building that housed Smythe Brothers, Ltd., careful to keep within its shadows. Port Royal was alive tonight, as always, and Luke realized he didn't have to be quite as cautious during daylight hours. Men still caroused the street before him, some with prostitutes, others with cohorts. A discordant symphony of laughter, raucous voices, and off-key singing drifted upward from the tippling houses and brothels that lined Thames Street, filling the night.

He could have been just one more miscreant skulking about the town and up to no good.

But his mission was too important to him to be caught and foiled. In his present mood, he'd kill anyone who dared to interfere.

He realized he'd made a poor decision once he reached the front door, considering the activity in the street before him, and, cursing under his breath, moved back around the side of the building to a door near the back. The shadows were even deeper here, a four-storied warehouse directly next door completely blotting out the moon and leaving only a narrow, pitch-dark alley between the two structures.

Luke Pelton was glad he'd chosen to wear black to the governor's gala: it served his purposes well now as he fumbled about the ground for a good-sized rock, intending to smash the padlock on the door. Under the cover of an especially boisterous trio of singing seamen lurching down the street just past the building, he attacked the door. The hasp dislodged more easily from the timber wall beside the panel, and Luke pried it from the wood rather than fight with the metal lock.

He didn't care how easily detectable his illegal entry would be the next morn, for there was no way anyone could prove he was the culprit and he had no plans for theft. He just needed confirmation of what he already suspected: that the Earl of Somerset, Meredyth's father, was behind Chandler's release and the refurbishing of the *Lady Elysia*.

If he felt too strongly about Meredyth to harm her, he could still get to Somerset through Devin Chandler, and what both Luke and du Casse suspected was Chandler's interest in ultimately destroying the lucrative slave trade.

Once inside, Luke tried to envision the layout of the first floor office, for he'd been there earlier in the day accompanying du Casse, who'd pretended to have business there, for that express purpose.

He felt around the oil lamp on the large desk in one corner of the room and found steel and flint. He lit the lamp on the second attempt in the dimness of the office and turned it down as low as it would go.

He looked through a stack of work orders dated over the past two months and came across the order for the *Lady Elysia*. To his deep disappointment, but not his surprise, the order was anonymous, originating in London and for hundreds of pounds. It was paid in advance, and directions on an attached piece of paper were to transfer any remaining funds, when the repairs were finished, to Captain Devin Chandler.

Pelton's hands ached to shred the order in angry frustration, but he merely replaced it on the top of the pile. Almost as an afterthought, he removed the most recent ledger, which sat neatly in place beside several others toward the front of the desk, and flipped through the pages for the corresponding accounts receivable.

He stilled briefly, raising his head at the sounds coming

from outside the front wall. Laughter filtered in to him, as well as a thump against the wall. He couldn't make out the words, but it sounded like some drunken sailor had plowed into the front of Smythe Brothers, Ltd., either by his own clumsy efforts or by the rough antics of his cronies.

The sounds faded as they continued on their way and Luke bent back to his task, turning up the lamp the slightest bit to aid him as he pored over the last few pages. As he suspected, there was no further information concerning the individual or individuals who ordered the repairs on the ledger sheet, either. But then, he knew that it would more likely be found on the order itself.

"A pox on him!" he declared softly. He closed the ledger with a snap and replaced it. There was only one thing left to do, unless he wanted to go directly to England and do some investigating on his own. And the latter action held little appeal for him, while the former appealed to him in every way possible.

"What're ye doin' snoopin' around here?" snarled a voice from the side door.

Twelve

Luke spun toward the sound. A burly seaman with dark hair and a bushy beard stood framed in the doorway, cutlass drawn, his expression menacing. The red kerchief he wore on his head brought to mind a red flag and a charging bull, only the bull was in possession of the flag.

Belatedly Luke remembered du Casse's words about never going anywhere in Port Royal without a sword or pistol. But he'd just come from the ball.

His mind went blank for a few moments, and he considered tackling the newcomer. Only briefly, however, because any seaman worth his salt could wield a cutlass with some skill, and they were too far apart for his plan to work. The seething anger that had driven him earlier had dissipated somewhat, making him think twice about killing anyone, especially in light of his failure to learn the identity of Chandler's backer.

What he wouldn't have given for a weapon!

"And just who are you?" he countered.

The man advanced on him, his cutlass a dangerous extension of his arm. "Davies. Some call me Aaron, some call me Mad Dog." His eyes narrowed speculatively. "Say there, I saw you with du Casse th' other morn, didn't I?" Some of the menace was replaced by curiosity and a tinge of awe. Du Casse was respected by some of the most unsavory characters on the Main.

"Aye. As a matter of fact, I'm here on his orders," Luke

lied. "And he won't like hearing of your intrusion or your threatening manner toward one of his agents."

Davies frowned, as if debating the wisdom of Pelton's words, and Luke's confidence grew.

"I got every right to be threatenin'. Gordon and Isaiah Smythe're my cousins."

Luke felt himself relax slightly. His chances of leaving the place unscathed were improving in direct proportion to his use of du Casse's name, or so it seemed.

Davies gestured with his cutlass. "Move away from that desk."

Pelton obliged, and the seaman edged forward, his eyes darting from Luke to the stack of work orders. He glanced down at the top one, the one for the *Lady Elysia,* his sword still pointed straight at Luke's elegantly clad form. He squinted in the low light but for naught. Luke guessed, with the buccaneer's next words, that he couldn't read in any light.

The intruder's dark eyes clashed with Pelton's. "Ye were riflin' through this stack o' papers, I'll wager," he growled. "Tell me what ye're lookin' for in my cousins' office fer du Casse an' I'll say naught about our meetin'."

Pelton hesitated. "Du Casse wouldn't like his private business revealed. If he'd wanted to make his intentions public, he'd have announced them to the entire town of Port Royal."

Davies didn't budge. His stance and expression remained obstinate. " 'Tis the only way ye'll get out o' here in one piece, Englishman."

Luke tensed. He had little choice.

"Don't." The cutlass homed in ever so slightly toward Luke's upper chest.

"Du Casse's business isn't yours!"

"It is when I find one o' his men sneakin' about my cousins' shippin' business!"

Luke felt like gnashing his teeth together in frustration. "You'll reveal naught about our meeting?" he growled. "On your word?"

The word of a ruffian like this means nothing, instinct warned.

Davies looked as if he would laugh aloud but did not. "I told ye once, Englishman, and 'tis all ye'll get."

Silence collected about them, stretched and tautened with growing tension, save for the muted sounds from Thames Street. Much of his loyalty for du Casse had literally disintegrated during those first stinging moments when the Frenchman had all but forced him to back down from the duel. Luke truly had no business breaking into the Smythe Brothers, Ltd. offices in the first place, especially without du Casse's knowledge.

But the Frenchman was moving too slowly for Pelton, especially now that Luke had discovered that Meredyth was in Jamaica and was obviously enthralled by Devin Chandler, who represented to Luke the man whose very name was anathema: Keir St. Andrews, Earl of Somerset, the man who'd turned his hopes and dreams upside down.

And hadn't du Casse mentioned asking Chandler himself? Surely the man could somehow be forced to reveal what he knew.

If he couldn't get to St. Andrews personally, he would take what revenge he could on Devin Chandler. For now.

"If you must know," Luke finally said, feeling the lift of satisfaction from what he was about to reveal, "I was looking for the order of repair for a certain ship."

"What ship?"

"The *Lady Elysia.*" The words came without hesitation now.

Davies's eyebrows snapped upward in surprise. "Devil Chandler's ship?"

Luke nodded. "Now, lower your weapon."

"Why?" Davies continued, ignoring Luke's command.

"I wanted to know who financed the refurbishment of the schooner . . . for personal reasons."

Unbidden, the image of Keir St. Andrews bursting through the door of the inn in London, of Somerset's feigning outrage at catching his daughter's betrothed tumbling another wench, came to Luke.

"Ye lied te me 'bout du Casse," Davies broke into his black thoughts.

Pelton shrugged. "I don't like to give in without at least token resistance."

Mad Dog's thick, dark brows drew together over his eyes. "Who's behind the pricklouse?"

Pelton shook his head, the bitter disappointment in his expression leaving no doubt he spoke the truth. " 'Tis anonymous."

Davies's craggy countenance darkened further. "Ye mean there's no name?"

Luke shook his head. "I'll leave now."

The cutlass lowered. Davies stuck out his lower lip thoughtfully. "Bet the same one who's payin' fer the repairs, rescued 'im from jail, too."

Luke didn't answer and began to walk toward the door. Immediately, the cutlass was raised again, blocking his exit. He cut Davies a narrow-eyed look, his hands fisting in anger.

"Not so fast, Englishman. My cousin keeps a spare bottle o' fine Madeira yonder," he jerked his bearded chin over one shoulder toward a small wooden cabinet near the broken door. "I think we've something in common when it comes to Devil Chandler and 'twould be worth yer while to listen to Mad Dog Davies when 'e offers 'is services."

He lowered his cutlass again.

"Services?" Pelton asked, feeling suddenly intrigued in spite of the fact that the man looked about as trustworthy as a ship without a helm.

Evidently satisfied that he'd snagged Luke's attention, Davies sheathed his weapon and turned toward the cabinet he'd just indicated. "Join me in a draught, at least," he invited over his shoulder. "If ye don't want to join me in a venture as well, 'tis yer loss." He rummaged through the contents of one shelf, then turned back toward Pelton after he'd found the dark, onion-shaped bottle, its cork secured with a twist of brass wire. He held it up in a kind of salute. "But I've a score to settle with that cullion Chandler myself, an' ye might want to hear me out afore ye go disappearin' off into the night."

His smile was so devoid of humor it gave Pelton serious pause, even as it further aroused his curiosity and lured him toward the man and his diabolical intentions.

"Just for a while," Devin had said.

The words chased round and round in Meredyth's mind as the hackney carried them toward the docks. Woody sat in the back, like a proper chaperon, Meredyth thought wryly, or as proper as one could be in the buccaneer capital of the world. His soft snores came to them as they neared Thames Street.

Exhilaration filled her in spite of Woodrow Kingsley's presence, the shadow of Manuel's untimely death, and Lucien Pendwell's unexpected and unwelcome appearance.

Just being in Devin Chandler's presence, she was fast learning, was exhilarating. Dangerous, no doubt, foolhardy, but titillating and exciting as well. He eclipsed every other male she'd ever met.

He was a devil, indeed, for he tempted her openly and shamelessly and obviously brought out the wantonness within her, for she did his bidding as willingly as if she were his handmaiden.

And, in spite of previous denials and her less than courteous behavior toward him, Meredyth admitted to herself that Devin Chandler had lightened her heavy heart, for his outrageous humor appealed to her own appreciation of the absurd.

Devin alighted after they came to a halt and tossed the coachman a coin. It glinted in the moonlight as it arced through the air. "Wait for us, my good man," he bade the driver, then extended one hand to Meredyth. "Come, Merry-mine," he invited dulcetly "and see my *Lady Elysia.*"

She looked over uncertainly at Woodrow Kingsley, who was

now awake. "Go . . . go, child!" he said with an emphatic wave of one hand. "I'm too old to go climbing about ships. I'll be right here should Devin fail to conduct himself like the perfect gentleman." He gave her a wink and slanted Devin a subtle look of warning before settling himself back against the squabs. He yawned behind one hand, and his eyelids began to droop again. "My hearing's still as good as ever, though, should you need me."

Years of etiquette made Meredyth hesitate.

Youth, however, with its innate zest for life, reminded her that this was Port Royal and that things were different here.

Devin leaned toward the carriage and placed his hands on her waist during her momentary hesitation. He lifted her and set her to the ground, his eyes shining silver in the moonlight, and full of wicked promise.

Just looking into his eyes made her breathless, in spite of the fact that Woodrow and the coachman still sat in close proximity behind them. She felt infused with his energy, as if he'd passed it on to her through his touch. Borne on the benign sea breeze, his clean, masculine scent mingled with the citrus-like essence of his cologne and mounted a sweet invasion of her senses. Recklessness trickled through her, increasing to a surge as he took her hand and led her toward the towering ship. It rocked in a quiet rhythm, the creaking of its planks and spars music to Meredyth's ears. Like her father, she loved the sea and was fascinated by the ships that sailed it.

Lucien Pendwell faded from memory, sounds from Thames Street behind them receded, and her misgivings melted away in the face of her secret excitement and anticipation. She tried to push away images of her and Devin Chandler, half-undressed and lying intimately together upon a bed.

Devin whistled softly, helping to dispel those provocative images. Sounds issued from below decks, then an answering whistle.

"All hands on deck! Pirates! Squaaaawk!"

A grinning Bakámu appeared with a dark silhouette perched

on his shoulder that could only have been Henry Morgan. The Arawak's teeth flashed in his shadowed face. "Come boat, *si?*" He tossed a rope ladder over the freeboard. So exuberant was the throw, not only did Henry Morgan flap his wings to keep from losing his purchase, but Devin had to duck to avoid being hit by the heavy cabling.

Christ, he thought darkly, he'll kill me yet. The thought crossed his mind to send the Indian into the deepest part of the hold before he could do any damage to the ship or anyone on it. And the parrot as well, since they deserved each other. If luck was on his side, they'd never find their way out.

Meredyth's soft laugh distracted him from his dark thoughts. "Are you hurt?" she asked.

He turned his most charming smile on her. "Nay, love. 'Twould take more than a bumbling Arawak to take off my head." He reached for the ladder, tested it, then held it steady for her. "You're not exactly dressed for climbing," he said wryly.

Meredyth cast him a look through her lashes, an impudent dimple appearing. "If you'll remain the gentleman, Captain Chandler, and keep your gaze averted while I ascend, I'll show you I'm not inexperienced at this."

"Then how will I know if you're having difficulty?" he asked innocently. But laughter hovered about his mouth.

"If it comes to that, you'll definitely know—"

"Land ho!"

Out of the corner of his eye, Devin saw the long, dark shape of the boarding plank suddenly descending toward them. He just had time to hook an arm around Meredyth's waist and jerk her aside before the heavy board crashed to the wharf. Grit and dust particles from both the dock and plank shot upward into the air, and Devin had to turn aside his head to cough. "What the hell are you *doing,* Indian?" he shouted at Bakámu, his features suddenly taut with anger.

"God save us!" cried the startled coachman.

"By the Mass, what's going *on,* Chandler?" called Woodrow Kingsley from the coach.

Devin felt Meredyth trembling in his embrace.

"Help *la señorita,*" Bakámu answered, his grin fading as he obviously realized he could have killed them both.

In the wake of the thunderous crash, Henry Morgan had scrambled away with a mad rush of wings to perch tentatively on the freeboard railing. He eyed the Arawak warily, for once seemingly speechless. But not for long.

"Kill the Spanish swine!" he shrilled suddenly.

"Arawak swine," Devin said under his breath as he looked at Meredyth to see how she'd fared. But Meredyth had one hand over her mouth, seized obviously by uncontrollable laughter. She hadn't been trembling with fear or relief but rather a fit of amusement.

He was suddenly grateful to Bakámu, even if just a little, for the chance to hold her in his arms. A grin found its way to his mouth. "I suppose we have no choice but to make light of it," he said.

"He . . . he meant well," she stammered between giggles.

How could he ever have thought this woman had no sense of humor? he wondered belatedly and let out a chuckle himself in spite of everything. Most females would have fainted from fright, humor the furthest thing from their minds.

Lady Meredyth St. Andrews, however, was obviously made of sterner stuff than that.

"Do you suppose he'll let us on board now?" he asked her lightly. "There's yet an arsenal of weapons he can use in his eagerness to be helpful."

Meredyth looked up at Bakámu, whose expression was downright contrite now. "I think he needs his captain's assurance that no harm was done."

Reluctantly, Devin dropped his arms from about Meredyth and called up to Bakámu, "We're coming up now. Just rest a moment, won't you? No harm done."

Bakámu immediately broke into a smile. *"Sí, Capitán,"* he

said and extended a finger to Henry Morgan, who was still sitting atop the rail. "Bakámu not tired," he said over his shoulder to them. "Watch boat for Chan-ler, *sí?*" He was already moving toward the main hatch before Devin could answer.

"I'll say one thing for him," Devin said in a low voice to Meredyth as he gestured her toward the boarding plank, "he's got strength, though not necessarily between his ears." He winked at her, hoping to hear her sweet laughter again. "Freed of his crutch, he's ready to put out to sea."

She gifted him with a smile, instead, that was just as much appreciated. "Let him feel useful," she urged. "He wishes only to please you, you know."

Devin was doubtful. "By guarding the ship for the night?" He chuckled softly. "I should be so lucky to have found another use for him."

"She's beautiful," Meredyth said for at least the tenth time. "You're so very fortunate you didn't lose her, or your life," she added, distress darkening her eyes. Until now, she'd never really thought about how close Devin Chandler had come to being killed. By lantern light, she'd viewed the areas of the schooner that had sustained damage, but the ship was nearly seaworthy once again, and except for painting and varnishing, you could never tell where she'd been hit by cannon fire.

"Thank you again," Devin replied from the doorway of his cabin. He leaned his shoulder against the doorframe, arms crossed, and studied her as she admired the interior of the small room with its two windows.

She frowned thoughtfully. "You'd said up at the mission that a peer of the realm obtained your release from Newgate?"

He lowered his gaze, his lashes hiding his expression for an instant as he said, "A man who, modestly, wishes to remain unnamed."

He met her gaze then, his own guileless in spite of the fact that he was lying to her.

He watched the color that blossomed in her cheeks at his direct perusal. "I'm glad, whoever he is, and whatever his reasons," she admitted with childlike candor. "Else I'd never have met you."

He watched her run her fingers over the polished teak desk beneath one window. "I think, in spite of his clumsiness, Bakámu is more a manservant type than a sailor. This room was an absolute disaster only a few short weeks ago." He walked toward one teak-paneled wall. "Look, not a scratch or gouge to be seen. And 'twas filthy."

Meredyth looked at him in disbelief. "They defiled this lovely cabin?" she asked, her appreciation of fine things violated by the thought of vandalism to Devin Chandler's haven while at sea.

He nodded. "But it could have been much worse. Bakámu is unexpectedly handy at woodworking—God knows how—for I wouldn't trust him with anything larger than a wood-carving knife. But he did most of the restoration of anything teak or mahogany himself."

The door closed. Meredyth ignored the sound—and its implications—and stepped closer to one wall to examine a small, unobtrusive carving of a face, cut directly into the teakwood. Simple but boldly stroked and accurately done, it looked very much like Devin Chandler's face. She reached out one hand and lightly smoothed her fingertips over the carving, the light from the great hanging ship's lantern across from it burnishing it to golden bronze. "Bakámu?" she murmured.

"Aye." He'd moved up behind her, his breath now caressing the exposed nape of her neck as he spoke. " 'Twas the image that came to him in his vision some years ago, so he said," Devin told her. Irony weighted his words.

Meredyth turned about, forcing him to retreat a step to maintain a proper distance between them. "So he wasn't lying after all!" she exclaimed. "You were meant to be part of his life, just like he believed."

Devin held up one palm toward her. "Now just a moment,

Merry-mine. Why couldn't he just have carved my face on the panel after having seen me in the flesh? After all, the man had ample opportunity to observe me while we were at the mission. And he's been living with me for—"

"He was ill," she interrupted him, "although he has been living with you for a few weeks . . ." She glanced again at the carving. "This is so accurate. It captures you perfectly. 'Tis as if he's known you for many years."

Devin blew out his breath with exaggerated resignation. "I feel like he's been dogging my every step for as long as I can remember! And that image is too sober, communicates too much . . . ahh, boldness and aggression."

Meredyth looked up into his eyes, but he was shaking his head with a moue, making light of the entire conversation.

"I think rather, Captain," she added with blunt candor, "the man in the teak is the real you, at least one important side of you that you would hide from the world for whatever reason."

She watched him lower his lashes for a moment, a ruse she was beginning to recognize for what it was—an infinitesimal dot of time in which he collected himself or thought of a new tack.

Even as she thought it, in a swift and unexpected move, he bent and lifted one of her hands to his lips. What a wonderful diversion, she had the presence of mind to think before tiny shocks went scampering up her arm.

When he raised his eyes to hers, there was only a trace of laughter left in their silver-blue depths. "You are most generous, Lady Meredyth, in your opinion of me. Especially when you were witness to how easily I agreed to withdraw from defending your honor."

With a lift of her chin, she answered, "Lucien's lingering over my hand is hardly reason to put a man's life in jeopardy, no matter what you men and your—"

"This," he said, taking hold of her hand once again and lifting it toward his mouth, "is the proper way to kiss a lady's hand." He lowered his head, his lips grazing her sweetly scented flesh as lightly as the imagined touch of a shadow. She tasted incredibly delicious, he thought as his blood began to play a tune through his veins.

"Quite a difference," she said breathlessly, her eyes clinging to his lips with utter fascination and anticipation.

Devin surprised her with a fleeting frown as he said, "If he touches you again in such a manner, I'll have no choice but to kill him."

Her mouth fell open, the spell suddenly broken. "Nay! There's no reason to be so offended!"

"Can't you see, Merry-mine, that if he really loved you, he would never have done such a thing in public?" His hand, which hadn't relinquished hers, tightened. "Or does he still hold your heart?"

Without thinking, Meredyth shook her head. How could Lucien Pendwell hold her heart after what he'd done to her and now, after she'd met the intriguing and unpredictable Devil Chandler, a man who'd made her run the gamut of emotions since she'd first encountered him beside a waterfall in a remote mountain mission?

"But I was offended," he said softly as he lowered his mouth toward hers.

Meredyth drooped her gaze to his mouth, before closing her eyes. When his lips touched hers, she allowed the kiss to go unprotested, even welcomed it as his warm lips grazed hers sweetly and lightly. It was reminiscent of his kisses at the Seaman's Folly and of his startling effect upon her in those first moments they'd met at the waterfall. Beneath his elegant attire, Devin Chandler was the same man she'd known for the past weeks, but something more as well.

Not unlike the anole, she had the presence of mind to think, capable of changing with lightning swiftness. But she guessed that his mood and demeanor changes were usually at his whim and for a reason, an important observation if she'd been thinking clearly.

But she wasn't, and that conclusion did not particularly interest her at that moment. How could it when her insides were beginning to melt as his mouth played over hers and the kiss deepened? He braced one arm beside her head, his palm against the teak wall behind her. The knuckles of his other hand traced the outline of her ear, her cheek, her jaw, with infinite tenderness.

Her mouth blossomed beneath his. She felt her whisper-light fichu slide from her bare shoulders and sigh to the floor and suddenly wished her hampering gown and petticoats would go the same way.

She froze, her heart drumming against her ribs and sounding magnified in her ears. What was she wishing? That he take her then and there like some woman from one of the nearby brothels?

It isn't like that, whispered the part of her that would throw caution to the winds and give in to her desire for Devin Chandler.

Aye, but 'tis! replied the faint voice of reason. *Has he said he loved you? Has he promised you aught but a tumble in his cabin?*

But do you want anything more? insisted the first voice. *It will only lead to more misery if you give away your heart again. Why not just live for the moment? For now?*

"Meredyth?" Devin's voice was dulcet as a whispering angel's in her ear and sent a volley of shivers dancing down her spine.

She pulled back and looked up at him, essaying to gauge the depth of his sincerity. The light from the lantern behind him formed a nimbus about his hair, turning the fine ends to spun gold, as if he were, indeed, a divine presence descended from the heavens.

Or the beautiful Lucifer ascended from Hell to rob her of her soul, came the thought out of somewhere, perhaps from the part of her that had been injured by Lucien Pendwell and was still wary, if not wounded.

"Have I hurt you?" he asked, his eyebrows meeting in a frown.

She shook her head, trying to clear it. Words failed her for a moment as she fought against the current of lust that still rivered through her. Potent stuff, Devin Chandler, she thought woozily. All the more reason to beware.

"N-nay. But I . . . I never thanked you," she began, then felt her voice strengthen as she grabbed at a handhold in the quicksand of overpowering emotions, "for what you did for me after we returned up the mountain."

"Oh, but you did," he murmured. "Have you forgotten already? 'I can't thank you enough,' you said."

"Uhh . . . such a kindness needs more than one . . . thank you," she finished lamely.

He studied her consideringly, but she could have sworn, even though his face was in shadow, that his expression held a hint of mirth.

"There is something for which you haven't thanked me properly, however," he told her without a qualm.

She brightened instantly.

"For the reversal of my stand regarding the duel . . ." He trailed off at the look on her face. "I helped avert disaster, wouldn't you say?"

She nodded, thinking back. "But at first you—"

"The end result is what counts, is it not?" he asked tipping up her chin with the fingers of one hand. His sweet breath sighed over her face and Meredyth automatically closed her eyes in anticipation of another kiss.

His hand left her upturned face as his mouth met hers, then joined the other hand, fingers gently burrowing beneath her luxurious hair and caressing her scalp, holding her fast.

As he joined his mouth to hers and wildfire set his very blood aflame, it hit him with the force of a thunderbolt that he was falling in love with Meredyth St. Andrews. That was the reason for his reluctance to see her leave Jamaica and, therefore, moved beyond his reach.

You're a fool a thousand times over if you think she's within your reach socially, came the voice. *Even as you hold her in your arms. Her father would tie your balls to the tallest mast in the Caribbean if you attempted to win her love.*

But if the earl had thought enough of him to entrust him with the watching of his daughter, he must have been willing to take his chances with Devin and Meredyth becoming involved romantically.

A second thunderbolt ripped through him so powerfully that his lips stilled for a moment against Meredyth's. It was very possible that the Earl of Somerset was one of the men who anonymously sponsored Devin and his work, and that was the real reason he'd gotten Devin released from Newgate. Also, very possibly, Woodrow Kingsley knew it.

He pushed aside his provoking thoughts, especially the latter, and reveled in the former by deepening his kiss. He dragged his lips over her cheeks, her exquisite brow, her saucy nose, murmuring, "Meredyth, Meredyth . . ." like a paean expressing what was in his heart.

He wrapped his arms about her shoulders and pulled her to him, the feel of her body against his driving his desire to fever pitch. The silken feel of her skin beneath his lips and the wildflower fragrance of her hair combined to cast the most heady of spells over him.

For once in his life, Devin Chandler, who'd always prided himself on maintaining a certain emotional distance from the woman with whom he was making love, felt his control slipping.

Thirteen

Almost immediately Devin felt the acquiescence of the woman he held. Her mouth opened to accept his searching tongue until it became one warm and silken cocoon with his.

Woodrow Kingsley was in a hackney beside the pier. Bakámu was roaming somewhere about the ship, Devin hoped getting lost in the deepest part of the hold, because he was intent upon one thing: making love to Meredyth St. Andrews and, in the process, wiping away all the hurt caused by Luke Pelton.

He bent to lift her high against his chest, their mouths still joined. She weighed next to nothing, or so it seemed to him, and he swung her around toward his bunk. But he was loath to let her go, so he sat down with her in his lap and proceeded to kiss her senseless.

Meredyth didn't seem to mind, from the answering intensity of her kiss, and holding her shoulders with one arm, he brushed the back of his other hand across her velvet neck and down and over the gentle swell of her breasts. He managed (with some subtle and expert maneuvering) to begin unfastening her bodice at the same time.

Meredyth gasped softly at the sudden feel of air on her naked bosom, but his lips wouldn't let her object as his fingers teased her nipples to firmness, first one, then the other. Lances of fire arced through her body, and a new, tugging feeling deep within her was so exquisite it was almost painful as Devin's mouth replaced his exploring fingers.

They were lying upon the bunk now, and Meredyth grasped the thick silk of his golden hair in reaction and pulled his head more firmly against her breasts. That most secret of places, the very essence of her womanhood, began weeping for him, anticipating, wanting him with an intensity that robbed her of her breath and her senses.

Somehow, as rationality fled, Meredyth acknowledged that nothing mattered save this man and these moments with him. She made a movement indicating she wished to rid herself of her garments, and Devin obliged, deftly working around rows of ribbon bows.

He carefully laid her green dress over the table, then turned and regarded her with a crooked smile. A vulnerable smile, she thought, and oh so sweet. She returned it with a tentative one of her own, although she felt her entire body heat with embarrassment and snatched at the single, light cover at the foot of the narrow bunk.

She was poised on the threshold of something she couldn't stop and didn't care to, either, as recklessness swept through her, making her impatient and shy at the same time.

Devin shrugged out of his blue coat and waistcoat, and came to stand before her in dazzling white shirt and breeches. His skin was a beautiful and healthy contrast against the fine lawn shirt, and so absorbed was Meredyth in her thoughts that she almost missed another smile.

He stood before her, tall and strong. His fingers moved to unfasten his shirt, his eyes locked with hers. It slid over his powerful shoulders and down his arms, which gleamed light bronze in the lantern light. He slipped out of his shoes and leaned over her.

Placing one knee between her thighs, Devin gently nudged them open, and braced on his arms above her for a moment. "Are you quite certain, Merry-mine?" he asked softly, his hair curtaining his cheeks. "I'll wager my ship and crew that you're yet a virgin."

Cease your babbling and take her! commanded a voice within him.

Don't! Or there'll be hell to pay! warned another.

"And I'm naught but a scoundrel in the eyes of many."

He couldn't ignore his conscience this time, for this was different—an earl's daughter, an untouched maiden, the woman he loved.

And would probably lose.

Her answer was to hold up her arms and reach for him. "Love me, Devin," she whispered. This is right, she added silently, whether aught comes of it or not. Whether I remain in Jamaica or sail back to England and never see you again . . .

And that had to be enough. For now.

The coachman's chin hit his chest, wakening him. He straightened, cleared his throat gruffly, and looked at the *Lady Elysia.* All was quiet, eerily so. No sound, no movement.

He glanced over his shoulder at the older gentleman in the back seat. He was sleeping, soft snores emanating from him and drifting off into the serenity of the night. Surely the man had imbibed more than his share of spirits at the governor's ball and was already sleeping it off.

The coachman shrugged to himself. He'd been told to wait, so wait he would, and meanwhile join his lone passenger in a nap.

"I'd never hurt you, Meredyth, you know that, don't you?" Devin whispered as he nuzzled her ear.

She nodded, but tears welled up in her eyes, for his words brought to mind memories of another hurt.

No person could keep such a promise to another. And she didn't expect Devin Chandler to even try.

Her head canted to one side as Devin worshipped the other with his mouth. A tear slipped from beneath her lashes, trickled down the other side of her face into her hair, and the force of her emotions dimmed her desire for a moment.

Until Devin took her chin and turned it toward him. "What's this?" he asked. "Meredyth? Look at me, love." The genuine concern in his words forced her to open her eyes to look into his. He was frowning.

Before she could open her mouth to answer, he gathered her in his arms and pulled her head against her chest. His lips in her hair, he murmured sweet words of assurance to her and rocked her ever so gently. "Trust me, Merry-mine. Trust me."

The lantern light spilled over their entwined bodies; the air was close and warm, scented from new wood and fresh hemp, from lantern oil, from man and woman and passion.

After a few moments, Meredyth reached out one hand to trace the outline of the musculature of his chest, renewed desire racing through her at the feel of his surprisingly smooth skin sheathing solid muscle beneath. A dusting of golden hairs provided a tactile contrast with his skin, and she dared to touch one of his paps. It budded in response and she heard him draw in his breath.

Intrigued by her power over him physically, Meredyth boldly reached lower, stroking the cleft between his ribs, then teasing his navel, and finally daring to brush her fingertips over the downy line of hair that lured her hand lower.

He groaned softly, and she stilled. "Oh, Meredyth, don't stop now," he rasped, sending a new rush of pleasure through her.

Her fingers tiptoed lower, lower still, until she encountered the engorged root of his masculinity. And she paused, suddenly feeling an unexpected tickle of apprehension. Surely she couldn't, no matter how much she might want to, accommodate him?

All she could picture suddenly was one of her father's stallions mounting a mare.

Her pause was agonizing for Devin, like hovering on the brink of a precipice of untold pleasure, then being halted from falling into its beckoning depths. "Ahh, Merry, my love," he breathed against her mouth, the rise and fall of his chest more pronounced now against hers, as if his heart would burst from its prison.

He pulled back, opened his eyes and looked into hers. He saw trepidation there and something more.

Innocence.

How could you even think to take her virtue? demanded the remnants of his conscience. *The daughter of the man who dragged your hide from the bowels of Newgate?*

He felt some of his raging desire begin to ebb.

If it weren't for St. Andrews, you might not even have met her! And here you are now . . .

"I'm s-sorry," Meredyth whispered, ashamed of her hesitation. Obviously she'd disappointed him.

" 'Tis all right, love," he said softly and sighed as if the weight of the world were on his shoulders.

"Devin—" she began, but was instantly silenced by one of his hands stroking the inside of her thigh. She swallowed the rest of her sentence as lusty urges sprouted anew deep within her and tingles skittered over her flawless flesh and toward the cleft that began to ache for something she couldn't name.

She opened her mouth to try again, but only a soft gasp emerged as his fingers found the core of her sexuality and mounted an exquisite invasion.

He watched undiluted surprise light her features, a moment of hesitation from innate modesty, then the ecstasy, full-blown, as her body responded naturally to his stroking fingers.

Devin's own desire began to rise once again as he watched Meredyth's sweet striving for fulfillment. Perspiration sheened her face, her lashes fluttered gently as her eyes closed, and as she moved against his hand, her thrusts became more urgent, faster.

His fingers aided her by increasing their magic, until Meredyth was catapulted beyond the realm of thought, reaching a quivering peak of ecstasy that made her momentarily immortal, bonded to this man in a way she was bonded to no other.

It was with supreme satisfaction that Devin watched her reach a shuddering climax.

"Devin!" she cried softly, a thousand tiny pulses throbbing through her body with her ultimate physical rapture.

His own response was instantly overwhelming in the wake of her release, and his own rapture began to peak, momentarily threatening to rob him of his very sanity. He crushed her to him, closing his eyes and envisioning, through a passion-induced euphoria, the melded lengths of their bodies, the smoothly powerful heaves of his own hips sealing his hand between them and his finger within her. Joined at chest, hips, and thighs, they were as one in every sense of the word except the final and most intimate coupling.

Rhythmic contractions of her hot and liquid core spasmed around his finger, sending the final wave of wildfire racing through his blood. He went rigid, calling her name in return, before his seed burst forth, bathing her lower abdomen, bonding them together in sensual joy.

Luke Pelton searched the ballroom with his gaze, his anger building with every passing moment, looking for Chandler and, more importantly, Meredyth. He'd evidently lost track of time, for his single drink with Davies and the birth of their tentative plan had taken longer than he'd intended.

He glanced at his brass pocket watch. It was after ten o'clock. His fingers tightened around the object momentarily.

He moved about the periphery of the room, a silent shadow in black, his blue eyes glowing with increasing frustration and ire.

The tall figure sporting a great, gray periwig moved into his line of vision. "I wondered where you were," du Casse said, halting Luke's perusal of the guests. "I hope you did not do anything foolish." He raised a thin, pale eyebrow, obviously expecting an answer.

Ignoring his question, Luke demanded, "Where's the lady Meredyth?"

"The last I saw, she was with Chandler." Du Casse frowned slightly. "I have had other business to attend to, Pelton, and trusted you would keep abreast of Chandler and his antics. You cannot allow your feelings for *la femme* to interfere with our work."

Luke met his frowning gaze. "If they're not here, then where are they?"

Although reason warned against it, Luke couldn't quash the hostility that emanated from him and, in the process, reached out to singe du Casse, as well.

Outwardly, at least, du Casse graciously backed down. "We are allies, are we not, *mon ami?* And look," he added placatingly, "Monsieur and Madame Greaves are leaving. I believe *la demoiselle* accompanied them here. Let me inquire." He motioned a liveried servant over and spoke into the man's ear.

Pelton looked sharply at the Frenchman, who shrugged. "We'll get to the bottom of this now, I believe, *n'est-ce pas?*"

Luke said nothing but watched as the servant appeared at the door to the ballroom and addressed Jack Greaves. The former motioned over toward where Luke and du Casse were standing apart from the revelers, near one wide-flung window.

Greaves said something to the servant, the latter bowed briefly, then returned to du Casse. "Master Kingsley escorted Captain Chandler and Lady Meredyth to the docks," the man related.

"The docks?" Luke said with a mixture of perplexity and irritation.

"Merci," du Casse said to the servant and slipped him a coin. He turned to Luke. "Of course, my friend. No doubt to show off his refurbished schooner and, *peut-être,* steal a few pleasurable moments from the lady when Kingsley's back is turned?" One corner of his mouth quirked ever so briefly.

"Are you goading me, du Casse?" Luke asked baldly.

The Frenchman put a hand on Luke's arm. *"Pas vraiment . . .* not really. What man in his right mind wouldn't try to sample the charms of such a beauty, though he cannot do much in the presence of a chaperon."

"That depends on the chaperon!" the younger man gritted.

"Calme-toi, mon ami," Jean-Baptiste soothed, "for there is no reason you cannot follow them discreetly, just to let him know you are not to be discounted as a rival, hmmmm?"

Luke opened his mouth to answer, then hesitated. His behavior this night hadn't been exactly admirable, not even the least bit courteous. And he was possibly slitting his own throat by antagonizing du Casse. The Frenchman had myriad connections and, therefore, a vast network of willing men from whom to choose.

Luke had already begun to make a lucrative living and, under du Casse's aegis, was in a more favorable position to wreak retribution upon the Earl of Somerset, particularly now, through Chandler. He'd tried to ignore the possibility of regaining Meredyth's affections, but her laughing image continued to haunt him, especially now that they were on the same island.

In spite of everything, the possibility of reuniting with Meredyth St. Andrews persisted in dangling before his tattered pride like the proverbial carrot before a donkey. And suddenly, the prospect of having her without her father's blessing didn't seem as formidable an obstacle as earlier. Certainly not an impossibility.

In fact, Meredyth's willingness itself began to lose its importance to him as well.

"Luc?"

"My apologies, Jean-Baptiste," he said, drawing his thoughts back to du Casse and the wisdom of remaining in the Frenchman's favor. "You're right. I'll rein in my temper and see if I can find our runaway jester and . . . Meredyth."

Du Casse nodded with a meaningful smile but cautioned softly, "However, do not do anything rash, *n'est-ce pas?* The time is not yet right and, as they say, *Tout vient à point à qui sait attendre.* Everything comes to him who waits."

But Luke Pelton didn't have the patience of Jean-Baptiste du Casse. And when he saw the hackney leave the dock beside the *Lady Elysia,* from his position in the shadows of a nearby slaver, he went straight to the tippling house Mad Dog Davies had been headed for after their little talk.

The stench of unbathed sailors, sour spirits, and pipe tobacco was almost overpowering after the clean air outside, but Luke swallowed his distaste and squinted through the smoky haze in search of Davies. When he spotted him, he strode over, ignoring the other clientele. "The ship appears deserted. I want to search it. Now," he told Mad Dog, who was getting bleary-eyed, but not flat out drunk yet, as far as Luke could tell. "The sooner I find what I'm looking for, the sooner you can have Chandler. Are you still with me?"

Davies looked at him warily for a moment, opened his mouth as if he would speak, then nodded. He finished his drink in one long swig and shoved himself up from the table at which he'd been sitting with several other nasty-looking seamen. Luke felt their eyes on him, full of suspicion and hostility. He was dressed like an aristocrat and aristocrats usually avoided places like this.

He gave them one cold, dismissive look, however, before turning his back to accompany Davies to the door, and there was no trouble.

"What changed yer mind?" Davies asked him with a sidelong glance as they moved toward the docks. "Ye n'er said nothin' 'bout searchin' the schooner."

" 'Tisn't important now. What matters is that we take advantage of the situation."

"What if Chandler comes back? Or the man on watch?"

Luke gave him a humorless smile. "Cold feet, Davies? And who said there was a man on watch?"

Wish You Were Here?

You can be, every month, with Zebra Historical Romance Novels.

YOU'RE GOING TO LOVE GETTING

4 FREE BOOKS

These books worth almost $20, are yours without cost or obligation
when you fill out and mail this certificate.

*(If the certificate is missing below, write to: Zebra Home Subscription Service, Inc.,
120 Brighton Road, P.O. Box 5214, Clifton, New Jersey 07015-5214*

4 FREE BOOKS!

Yes! Please send me 4 Zebra Historical Romances without cost or obligation. I understand that each month thereafter I will be able to preview 4 new Zebra Historical Romances FREE for 10 days. Then, if I should decide to keep them, I will pay the money-saving preferred publisher's price of just $4.00 each...a total of $16. That's almost $4 less than the publisher's price, and there is no additional charge for shipping and handling. I may return any shipment within 10 days and owe nothing, and I may cancel this subscription at any time. The 4 FREE books will be mine to keep in any case.

Name _____

Address _____ Apt. _____

City _____ State _____ Zip _____

Telephone ( ) _____

Signature _____ LF1095
(If under 18, parent or guardian must sign.)

Terms, offer and prices subject to change without notice. Subscription subject to acceptance by Zebra Books.
Zebra Books reserves the right to reject any order or cancel any subscription.

"Only a fool 'ud leave a schooner like this unwatched!" the buccaneer growled, obviously irritated at Luke's suggestion that he was having second thoughts.

"You may not realize it, Davies," he said, "but we are dealing with a fool. And if we encounter Chandler, we'll turn it to our advantage."

They approached the *Lady Elysia* and paused at the end of the boarding plank. "If you run into anyone, silence him," Luke said in an emotionless voice, his gaze going meaningfully to the buccaneer's cutlass. "We don't need witnesses."

"Pistol 'ud be easier."

Luke shook his head and started up the plank. "The noise would alert someone," he said under his breath.

"This here's Port Royal!" Davies insisted a little too loudly and a little too carelessly for Luke. "Pistols is always explodin' and cutlasses always a-clashin'!" He belched, as if for emphasis. "An' men learn real quick to mind their business."

Luke turned on him instantly, wanting to stuff the man's red kerchief in his mouth. *"Will* you shut up? If you become a liability to me, we go our separate ways, I swear!" he hissed.

Without waiting for Davies's reply, Luke boarded the *Lady Elysia* and stood listening for a moment. Davies swore under his breath as he lurched onto the deck like a dancing bear, and Luke began to regret ever including the man in his plans. He'd obviously miscalculated the extent of Mad Dog's inebriation since they'd parted company earlier.

"Chandler's cabin?" Mad Dog asked with a semblance of sobriety.

Pelton nodded. "Can you keep watch?"

"O' course." He took up a position behind the main mast, blending in with the shadows, his sensible suggestion mollifying Luke for the moment and giving him the confidence to leave the buccaneer where he was and cautiously approach the aft hatchway. Unbeknownst to Davies, Luke wanted to find any kind of written records that might exist, lists that purportedly named the worst of the slavers—ships and captains—and possibly described the living conditions in the holds. Even though those who opposed slavery were outnumbered, du Casse believed and had half convinced Luke that insidious forces could one day begin to undermine the operations.

Luke carefully descended the dark stairs, thinking sourly that Chandler had fancied up his ship with a stairway rather than using a simple ladder to descend into the bowels of the schooner. No doubt, he thought acerbically, to entertain the ladies when the *Lady Elysia* was in port.

That very thought was still in his mind when he swung toward the bow of the ship and froze. The door to what appeared to be the captain's cabin was partially open, and a wedge of light painted the wooden floor of the passageway. A muffled voice came to him—or was it more than one?—the sounds audible but not understandable.

One part of him told him to leave. The other urged him at least to sneak up to the door and see who was still aboard. Mayhap he'd made a gross miscalculation, and Chandler had left someone aboard to watch the ship.

But why would the man, or men, be in the captain's cabin?

Luke inched closer, wondering if he were being recklessly bold, but he was already aboard Chandler's ship—so close and now, possibly, foiled.

"Diablo socarrón, Enrique, sí?" said a heavily accented voice. The owner of the voice sounded highly amused.

Pelton peered through the slit along the hinged side of the half-open door. A man with his back to the panel was straightening the bedclothes on the single bunk. "Tsk, tsk, tsk," he mumbled, shaking his head. His long, blue-black hair caught the lantern light, and Luke guessed he was a native Carib or Arawak Indian. No doubt a cabin boy, though he looked like a grown man.

As the Indian straightened, Luke got a clear shot of the parrot perched rather precariously upon his shoulder. One clawed foot slid forward over the Indian's shoulder, and with a flutter of its wing, it righted itself. From where he stood, Luke strained to scan the small cabin from his hiding place. Evidently, the Indian was talking to the parrot.

The Indian chuckled and said to the parrot, "Bakámu not fool. Bakámu know. Señorita Meredyth and Chan-ler, hmmmm? On bed, *sí?*" He turned toward the door, his eyebrows tenting suggestively before they sought the cabin ceiling. A huge grin split his face from ear to ear before he drew in a slow and savoring breath. *"Mujer.* Scent of woman. Perfume."

Luke instantly flattened himself against the bulkhead as the Indian's words rang through his mind like clarions in the wake of the man's knowing, lascivious expression. Anger boiled up from within Luke, and it was all he could do to remain where he was.

Bakámu bent to retrieve some object from the floor at the foot of the bunk. "Aha!" he exclaimed triumphantly, holding up what looked like a hair bodkin. *"Por el puelo de la señorita,"* he said with a knowing nod of his head. "For hair!"

Luke remained where he was, fighting to gain control over his raging emotions. That bastard Chandler had compromised Meredyth aboard his own ship.

What better place? came the taunting thought.

Luke closed his eyes, trying to marshal his wits and save his anger for Chandler, not the savage on the other side of the door.

". . . *es muy masculino."* He chuckled again as he moved toward the desk, then placed the bodkin upon the closed ship's log. When Luke heard his steps, he was unprepared for the Indian's departure. Unthinkingly and with a strength suddenly born of outrage and jealousy, he shoved himself away from the wall and threw his body against the door with all his might.

The slamming door caught Bakámu completely off guard and set Henry Morgan a-flapping as the bird was knocked backward. *"Pirates!"* he bawled as the wood panel smashed against the stunned Indian's face. The Arawak slowly slid to the floor, dazed. Blood trickled from his nose.

Luke Pelton derived a deep satisfaction from injuring the man who obviously served Devin Chandler. A sudden, malicious grin skipped across his features as he savored the fleeting moment, then cautiously pulled open the door to see his handiwork.

He had to duck to avoid the feathered missile, which, with a loud squawk and a mad flapping of wings, swooped by him and sailed up and out the hatchway.

Fourteen

Meredyth gingerly touched her fingers to her lips, her gaze trained upon the looking-glass she held with her other hand. Her eyes were huge, their expression sated; her lips were rosy and full from Devin's lovemaking.

She watched helplessly as color flooded her features and desire bloomed anew deep within her at the memories of what she'd shared with Devin Chandler. Never in a hundred years would she have expected such tenderness and concern from a man like him.

Then Meredyth remembered that he'd saved Bakámu's life without even having set eyes upon him previously, and at great peril to his own. And despite the Arawak's declarations that indicated otherwise, Meredyth suspected the Indian had been instantly won over by Devin's selfless courage.

Surely, she acknowledged, his oft-outrageous behavior was a cover for a soft heart. And more than enough courage.

Making a meal of my lady's hand is hardly a trifle.

Meredyth stifled a laugh behind her hand as she remembered his straight face and the tiny twitch at one corner of his handsome mouth. The hand mirror slowly lowered as she reminisced.

Yet he'd obviously been ready to meet Lucien on the field of honor; his next words had proved that. And what had he said at the Seaman's Folly? She frowned slightly in concentration. *Did you think I'd risk tangling with the likes of Mad Dog Davies?*

Again, a giggle bubbled up her throat. If she hadn't been so outraged, she would have realized it had taken some quick thinking to set up her rescue himself, and his way had led to less violence and potential bloodshed.

Marry come up, but she felt as if she'd drunk an entire bottle of brandywine, and all because of Devin Chandler! She doubted if she would be able to sleep the tiniest bit this night, for her thoughts wouldn't leave Devin and their shared intimacy.

"Lie still, Merry-mine," he'd said quietly when their love-play had ended, and he'd stood and walked over to a wash basin sitting on a bolted down washstand between the bed and the desk. He'd then proceeded to bathe her belly with a soft wet cloth he'd dipped into the basin. The tender movements were soothing and oddly arousing at the same time, and Meredyth let her lids drift downward so her eyes wouldn't be forced to meet his warm blue gaze.

"Here, love," he'd said then as she'd put her hands to her hair in an attempt to straighten it after he had helped her into her gown. His fingers had lingered over the bodice, and he'd slanted her a sweet and naughty grin before he'd attacked her curls.

With Meredyth seated between his legs, he'd begun to repair her coiffure. It had been relatively undisturbed, save for a few lost bodkins, most of which they'd found—two on the bed, another on the cabin floor. His fingers felt less clumsy than she would have imagined, and Meredyth was secretly amused at his attempts. The results hadn't been half bad, as she'd noted upon arriving at her father's town house and retiring to an upstairs bedchamber. Mayhap Devin Chandler would have made a better lady's maid than a privateer, she'd thought with a smile.

Meredyth felt little guilt about what they'd shared. Devin had managed to keep her maidenhead intact, or so he'd assured her. At the same time, he'd also gifted her with undreamed-of pleasure. The same solid sense of loyalty and love that had bound her mother to the earl all those years ago, even after he'd taken her halfway around the world against her wishes, now rose in Meredyth, and she realized with a sense of wonder that she loved this man called Devil Chandler, loved him in a way she'd never loved Lucien Pendwell, for the very thought of Devin made her giddy, made her spirits soar. She wondered if her prolonged hurt and outraged sense of betrayal by Pendwell had been more the result of having her affection and loyalty thrown back at her, rather than a broken heart, more a matter of pride, which she'd inherited from the St. Andrews side, than bitter disappointment in love.

Master Kingsley had been half asleep when they'd returned to the hackney, and Bakámu was nowhere to be seen. After the coach lurched to a start again, Kingsley had mumbled an apology and immediately slipped back into slumber. Meredyth could still picture several sparse silver hairs that lay across his forehead drifting upward as he snored softly, though at the time her thoughts were not on Woodrow Kingsley.

"May I see you on the morrow, Merry-mine?" Devin had asked softly after they'd alighted before the Somerset town house. Woody was still sleeping, and the coachman seemed unconcerned with them. They'd stood at the door, her hand remaining in his long after he'd pressed her fingers to his lips. The light from a single brass lantern beside the doorway had illuminated half his face, giving him a mysterious look, save for the warmth and sincerity in his silver-blue eyes.

"Aye, Devil Chandler," she'd replied with a saucy tilt of her head as she pretended to consider him and his request. "I would imagine the *Lady Elysia* looks much different by day than by night. And I should like to meet your crew."

He nodded, his eyes on her mouth. "What crew I've managed to gather since my return," he'd said with a rueful smile. "My boatswain's been doing a slow but thorough job of gathering those of my former crew who were loyal and rounding up new men. But there's no real hurry." One eyebrow cocked. "That is, my lady, unless you wish to return to England on my ship."

Meredyth had caught the teasing glint in his eyes and something much more profound. Her face had warmed. "Nay, Captain. I have no wish to leave Jamaica just yet."

"I'm glad," he'd said. "And I promise to be respectable, during the day at least." He'd frowned then. "Mayhap 'tis a good thing you'll be going back to the mission in two days. I'll be more inclined to act the gentleman than if . . ."

He'd swallowed visibly, and his brows drew together. "Meredyth," he'd begun huskily, searching for words. " 'Tisn't my wont to deflower innocents."

Her fingers upon his lips had silenced him. "Don't apologize," she'd murmured. "There was no real harm done, was there? Who will know but us? And I'll never regret one moment of it."

He'd smiled—a shy smile, Meredyth had thought, if Devin Chandler were capable of such a thing. He'd looked suddenly very young to her and very vulnerable. "You must return to Father Tomas the day after tomorrow?" he'd asked.

She'd nodded, her heart—and her trust—in her incredible emerald eyes. "But you'll visit us, won't you?" Now it was her turn to feel shy.

"Indeed, love," he'd answered, one knuckle brushing the velvet flesh of her flushed cheek. "Naught could keep me away . . . ever." His voice had dropped almost to a whisper with the last word. "We'll dine at the new Oyster House in Port Royal on the morrow. Would you like that?"

Meredyth had nodded with girlish eagerness.

"And I'll make certain Woody doesn't drink before we start out. My behavior will be above reproach." He'd raised her hand to his lips. When he'd broken away, Meredyth had been ready to melt into a puddle at his feet. "Until eleven of the clock on the morrow then."

The sound of activity downstairs roused Meredyth from her sweet thoughts. She replaced the hand mirror and stood resolutely, determined to begin anew with Devin Chandler. In spite of her encounter with Lucien Pendwell—she had to think of him as Luke Pelton now, she reminded herself—and in spite of the unpleasant beginning she and Devin had had, she felt herself aglow and happy beyond description with what had blossomed between herself and the privateer captain.

Meredyth strongly suspected that she was falling in love.

She cared not one whit that she knew little of Chandler's background, save that he was of Irish descent, at least partially. And the fact that her father, too, had once been a successful privateer endeared Devin to her even more, for Meredyth greatly admired and loved her sire.

It was in no small part Chandler's doing that she felt like laughing again, a direct result of his stimulating combination of outrageousness and tenderness. She suspected much of his earlier brusqueness and impatience with her had been a defense. Much as she would have had it otherwise, Meredyth guessed that Devin had tried to hold himself aloof from her from the very beginning, acutely conscious of the fact that she was the daughter of an earl.

But she would convince him that it didn't really matter, that a person's worth was not to be judged by his or her station in life. The countess's mother had been unwed when she'd conceived Meredyth's mother; the identity of the father had never been discovered, and it hadn't mattered to Keir St. Andrews when he'd asked for her hand.

"Meredyth?" Ellie called from the bottom of the stairs, sending her thoughts scattering once again. "Are you here?"

"Aye, Ellie." She straightened her shoulders and with buoyant steps, moved toward the door.

Devin strode up the boarding plank, the night wind skidding across his skin like a premonition. He was still a-tingle from his time with Meredyth, full of new and wonderful feelings. A tender half-smile curved his mouth even as some deep-seated instinct clenched within him as he stepped up toward the deck.

He paused, pushing thoughts of Meredyth aside for a moment as he listened intently, his head canted away from the ceaseless susurration of the sea lapping at the hulls of the ships and the wharf around him.

Nothing. Nothing save the distant rise and fall of voices of those who would continue their carousing until they were unable to utter an intelligible word or demand coordinated movement from a limb.

The breeze teased his hair, blowing strands of it across his cheek, and his eyes narrowed suddenly as he heard what sounded like the faint sound of a bird.

A parrot? Nay, it couldn't be. There'd been no sign of Bakámu or the bird when he and Meredyth had emerged from his cabin, and although he hadn't given it much thought at the time—preoccupied with his tumultuous thoughts and feelings about the woman at his side—he wondered now why Bakámu had disappeared before he and Meredyth had left the *Lady Elysia*.

As he stepped on deck, out of the shadows a flapping form came swooping toward him, and Devin's first instinct was to throw up an arm and duck. Damn the fancy garments he wore! They were restraining in the extreme compared to his everyday attire.

But although he automatically bent his knees slightly and stiffened in an attitude of unthinking self-defense, he raised his left arm rather than his right and allowed the apparition to land on his hand. Devin transferred the parrot to his shoulder with a soft sigh of relief.

He placed two fingers over the bird's beak. "Quiet, mate." he said under his breath, hoping the parrot wouldn't start up his normal barrage of remarks. The bird seemed to wax outrageously eloquent in Devin's presence.

Almost simultaneously, Devin caught a thump from below decks, the second such sound he'd heard since he'd set foot on the boarding plank.

Unease shimmied through him.

He slipped his dagger from beneath his coat and crept toward the forecastle, his right hand remaining lightly over Henry Morgan's beak.

The parrot, as if in direct defiance, dodged his head from beneath Devin's restraining fingers and nipped one of them.

"Ouch!" Devin growled softly, a heartbeat away from throttling the bird. "Damn you!" He briefly touched the injured finger to his lips. "Stick to your nuts and berries!" He glared at the parrot sideways, his teeth bared in anger, then clapped his hand over the creature's beak once again and threatened softly, "I swear to God, I'll pluck and roast you if you so much as peep."

He paused then, listening for more sounds from below, but all was silent. The hatch was open, and Devin stealthily lowered himself into the opening, his dagger blade now clenched between his teeth. With both hands on the side rails of the ladder, he could only pray the parrot would remain silent.

As he descended into the Stygian blackness, Devin depended upon his familiarity with every inch of the schooner for guidance. Had he been blind, he still would have known exactly where he was by memory, touch, and smell—just like with a well-remembered lover, he thought wryly, forcing Meredyth's distracting image from his mind's eye.

He stepped off the last rung and swung about, pausing to study the passageway that bisected the ship. The pungent scent of newly cut pine, the more astringent smell of tar, and the faintest hint of oil came to him, masking the smell of the tight living quarters of fifty-odd crew members. All was dark, except for a slim blade of light that glimmered beneath the door leading to the upper section of the hold, where munitions were stored and which doubled as ballast.

What would the Arawak be doing there? And why would he have allowed himself to be separated from Henry Morgan? Devin wondered uneasily as he quietly moved forward.

Instinct told him Bakámu wouldn't have disappeared down there of his own free will for so long a time, despite his curiosity and obvious fascination with the ship. Surely he'd explored enough on his own to know his way about and could have no logical reason for remaining in the dark and damp hold of the ship for any longer than necessary. Yet the light coming from under the door indicated that the Arawak evidently was down there, and probably up to mischief.

Or—a much more sobering thought—someone else was because the light was definitely coming from the powder locker.

Devin flattened himself against the wall, heedless of Henry Morgan's possible reaction to such close quarters, though one part of his mind now wished fervently that the bird and he had parted company before they'd descended the hatch. He sidled silently toward the door, registering the parrot's awkward slip-slide dance upon his shoulder in obvious response to the protruding struts in the bulkhead bumping them from behind.

He drew in slow, deep breaths, forcing calmness in spite of the suddenly accelerated beat of his heart, and reached out toward the door. His fingers touched the wooden panel, and he gave it a push. It creaked in response, as if reluctant to reveal the secrets within the room behind it, and Devin inwardly flinched at the unwelcome noise.

He straightened briefly, wondering if he should just go barreling in there with what surprise he could still muster, for surely his presence had been announced by the damned door hinges, or continue his stealthy exploration. A few seconds crawled by before Devin decided to continue. He moved closer, put his flattened palm against the panel, and slowly eased it open.

He slipped around the doorjamb and flattened himself against the inner wall, his eyes seeking the weak source of light. When he spotted it, his heart lurched, for it was coming from a lone, unshielded candle on the floor, a certain invitation for fire had the schooner been at sea. That single candle posed an even greater threat when one considered it was only an arm's length away from several powder kegs.

And the missing Bakámu, trussed and gagged like a Christmas goose, was propped up against one of those very powder kegs. His nose was bloodied and his eyes were huge with fear.

Knowing someone had probably set this up as a trap, Devin nonetheless couldn't help his concern for the Indian sitting between fire and fuel, nor his fear for the *Lady Elysia*. His eyes narrowed consideringly for a moment, then the choice was made. With his dagger in his right hand and pointed toward the partially open door, he sprang at the candle, his first intention to put it out and, thus, douse the room with darkness. If there were any miscreants about, they would be just as inconvenienced by the absence of light as he. And if they were already gone, he'd have no trouble freeing the Indian and leading him above decks.

His fingers were mere inches away from the candle when he realized it wasn't fear in Bakámu's eyes but a warning.

It was too late to change his course, and the room was plunged into total darkness as Devin hit his mark. Chaos ensued. Henry Morgan shrieked shrilly and flew off as someone grabbed Devin's ankle and held fast. He jerked around and thrust the blade at his attacker before going down on his backside in a jarring loss of balance, his dagger swishing through the empty air.

Dropping the weapon, Devin kicked savagely to free his leg, but just as he felt the fingers about his ankle break away, something as hard as a cannonball crashed into the side of his head and pitched him into blackness.

His eyes still wide as two dinner plates, Bakámu watched helplessly as Devin was lifted and dragged roughly toward the open portal. A sickening thump told the Arawak that his master's lolling head had struck the doorframe. Frustration made him growl from deep within his throat. He struggled against his bonds but in vain. His mouth worked against the tight gag, also in vain.

A hand reached out from seemingly nowhere and righted the

candle, for the flame was still alive. The owner of the hand then tipped over an opened keg, sending the wooden cover clattering and spewing a cloud of acrid-smelling dust over the floor.

The man nudged the candle closer to the black powder spilled onto the wooden floor, then gave a soft, sinister laugh as he swung about and retreated toward the door.

The sound of oars dipping into the sea slowly came to Devin through the pain in his head. He tried to remember what happened, and as the memory flashed back, pain exploded in his mid-section. "Stay still," snarled a low voice in his ear, "else we'll feed ye to the sharks!"

He hadn't been aware that he'd moved, but he concentrated on remaining stock still, wishing to avoid additional pain. The night wind reached him in fitful puffs as he lay on the bottom of what was evidently a small boat. Where was the cullion taking him?

"Don't kill him just yet, Davies," said another voice in an undertone. "He's useless to me dead at this point."

Davies? Devin groaned inwardly. Sweet Christ, he was in deep now! And a second miscreant was aboard as well. No doubt one of Davies's men. 'Twas a miracle he'd survived the blow to his head, for Manuel hadn't been so fortunate outside the Seaman's Folly.

Before he could ponder events much longer, Devin was awkwardly heaved from the boat and slung over a brawny shoulder. He briefly considered attempting to throw his captor off balance with some serious wriggling and bucking, but red-hot pain lanced through his skull with every movement. And even if he succeeded, what chance would he have in the sea with his hands and feet bound and with a rag stuffed into his mouth and secured so tightly that his jaw was numb? He'd sink to the bottom like a block of granite.

So he remained unmoving, feigning unconsciousness as he

was hoisted up a rope ladder, obviously aboard a ship anchored somewhere in the harbor.

"Who goes there?" called a voice, no doubt the anchor watch.

"Davies," answered Devin's captor, sounding a bit winded, which immediately made Devin wish he weighed a hundred stone. "Got a man whose tongue needs loosenin' up, Denby. And don't need no ruckus from ye or anyone else."

The name "Denby" didn't ring a bell, and Devin's thoughts flashed back briefly to Bakámu and the powder kegs. But there wasn't anything he could do to save the man or the schooner in his present predicament. He had to find a way to gain his freedom first. And the effort involved in even that much thinking made his aching head throb as painfully as a living piece of iron caught between a blacksmith's hammer and the anvil.

As he was roughly jounced around, he went in and out of a fog of pain, and the next thing Devin was aware of was being dropped into a hard wooden chair and bound to its straight and rigid back at his waist and shoulders. They surely couldn't bind him any further, he thought with a mental grimace, for it felt like every part of his body was covered with hemp and the blindfold seemed to tighten around his head with every moment that passed.

Nausea assailed him then, as the sour stench of vomit, urine, and excrement, human suffering and death, came to him along with the dankness of a ship's hold. It was all Devin could do not to heave up the contents of his stomach and choke behind his gag.

He was on a slaver or else a ship that carried both slaves and other cargo. And it didn't bode well that he was in the hold instead of a cabin, for there would be no concern about making a mess in what was obviously already a cesspit. Davies often worked aboard slavers, as Devin recalled.

The gag was jerked from between his teeth, and hard on its heels came the frigid deluge of a bucket of water. While the coldness was welcome in that it helped restore his senses somewhat, when he ran his dry tongue over his lips he tasted brine. Seawater, which would only make him thirsty.

He withdrew his tongue quickly, for he suspected his captors wouldn't offer him one drop of fresh water before they tortured him either to unconsciousness or death. Woody had been right—his activities had been found out, and this time he'd get a hell of a lot more than a warning.

"Now, Chandler," said a vaguely familiar voice in his ear, "tell us exactly who freed you from Newgate and provided the funds to refurbish the *Lady Elysia*. Then, and only then, will you be freed."

The second voice sounded like it belonged to Luke Pelton. Outrage spewed through him. Davies was bad enough—a cutthroat with a grudge to settle—but Pelton was a different story. He worked for Jean-Baptiste du Casse, which meant he was involved in the slave trade, and he'd hurt Meredyth enough to send her halfway around the world from all that she knew and loved. Now he was demanding information that, revealed to the wrong persons, would possibly implicate the Earl of Somerset in Devin's work.

It hit him like a blow from an iron fist. For the second time, and with growing certainty, he suspected the Earl of Somerset might belong to the group of men who anonymously employed him. Could the bargain to keep a watch over Meredyth St. Andrews have been only a screen? That would surely explain Pelton's interest—and, ultimately, du Casse's—in the identity of Devin's rescuer and benefactor.

What Davies's involvement was didn't concern him, for the buccaneer wasn't intelligent or influential enough to be in on such important and highly covert dealings.

A fist crashed into Devin's jaw, sending his mind reeling as his head snapped back on his neck. Pain splintered anew through his cranium. But before he could even catch his breath, a sopping cloth was thrown over his face, and when he was able to draw in a breath, he sucked in the heavy, saturated cloth instead and began to choke.

Someone grabbed his hair and yanked back his head. "Who was it, Chandler?" growled a voice in his ear. Pelton. Or so it seemed in the roiling chaos that had taken over his thought processes.

Couldn't say. Never tell . . . who . . .

"Maybe this'll help," said the other voice with undisguised malice. And just as Devin was pulling a puff of precious air into his lungs, another wave of water washed over his head and shoulders. It trickled into his throat, cutting off his breath as the sodden material seemed to fill his mouth. He tried to cough it up, but, unable to draw a decent breath, Devin found his efforts futile.

"Spit it out!" snarled Pelton. "Who plucked you from Newgate and sent you back to Jamaica?"

The world began to go black behind the blindfold. Spots like shooting stars speared through his mind's eye, and he felt himself going into a faint. Unexpectedly his head was released, and as his chin hit his chest, Devin gulped in some air. "Go to—hell!" he gasped in a parody of speech, then coughed again.

"Why you—"

"He's lyin'," growled Davies, and someone backhanded him. Lights flashed inside Devin's skull, his ears rang. He tried to conjure up images of Meredyth, Bakámu, Woody—anything to bolster his resolve, and he came up with deep, clear green. Eyes . . . her eyes . . . the earl's eyes, too. He could never betray anyone in that family.

No. His mouth silently formed the word, but he couldn't speak for the pain in his head.

A fist plowed into his stomach, knocking out what little breath he'd managed to pull into his lungs and ramming his chin into his chest once more; and because his shoulders were anchored to the chairback, he couldn't double forward in a natural reaction or shield his middle from another punishing blow.

"Don't be stubborn, Chandler." Pelton's voice scraped across his eardrum. " 'Tisn't worth dying for now, is it?" A hand shoved back his chin again and the cloth, which had begun to peel away from his face, was pushed back in place.

A wave of brine washed over him again, and he tried to hold his breath. Impossible. His lungs were starving for air. Water . . . saltwater trickling down his throat like acid, burning . . . cloth filling his mouth, blocking precious air, choking him. . . . Unconsciousness beckoned.

"A name, Chandler," someone rasped in his ear. The voice sounded distant, unreal, and unrecognizable now. "A name and you're free . . ."

"Then *I* get 'im," another voice said. "We got some unfinished business—"

"Shut up!"

Noooooooo! Devin cried silently, then sank into a beckoning chasm of nothingness.

"Ye killed 'im!" Davies accused Luke with a menacing scowl. "I wanted a turn with 'im—got a score to settle."

Luke ignored the buccaneer as he made certain every knot with which Chandler was tied remained firm.

"He took a woman from me at the Folly," Davies continued, like a whining child. "Thought she was a boy, but them green eyes an' fine dark hair. . . . She weren't no whore. A virgin, I'd wager, an' he stole 'er right from under me nose."

Luke cut Mad Dog a freezing look. No, it couldn't be. What would Meredyth ever be doing in a brothel? Yet he was reminded of what the Indian in Chandler's cabin had said. "You'll get your turn later. He's not dead, just unconscious. Gag him tightly, and we'll come back in the morn."

Fifteen

Bakámu stared at the black powder that tainted the floor, for as the unique stench of it filled his nostrils, it occurred to him what it was—the powder for the white men's weapons. And when the candle burned down, the powder would probably ignite, sending Chandler's beloved ship up in flames and him right along with it.

But he wasn't important in the scheme of things. If Wishemenetoo decreed that Bakámu should die while serving the man who'd saved his life, so be it. It surely would be a more noble death than one between the jaws of a hungry crocodile. He only hoped that he could accomplish this one task and that Chandler was still alive and would, ultimately, save his own skin.

He tested his bonds yet another time, and the keg behind him shifted slightly. Bakámu was humiliated by his predicament. Not only had he been used to lure Chandler into a trap, but his earlier carelessness—and now his inability to free himself—could lead to the destruction of the vessel.

He tried to scoot forward, a possible plan forming in his mind. Maybe he could move the barrel with his body, then roll onto the candle, thus extinguishing it. He scooted again, with more force and whacked his head against the keg.

He saw stars for a few moments. Maybe he should roll sideways instead of trying to dislodge it by throwing himself forward. He bent his knees and pulled his feet to him, struggling for purchase against the floor, then threw himself sideways.

The keg rocked, leaned temptingly, then righted itself. He tried again, belatedly realizing that if he wound up beneath the heavy keg, he could be injured.

Bakámu was undeterred by the thought. He flung himself to the side a second time, pushing with his bare feet against the floor. The third time he was successful, except that he momentarily ended up with the keg beneath him—feeling like a turtle flipped helplessly onto its back, a most ignoble position for an Arawak warrior.

From the corner of his eye, the seemingly innocuous flame from the candle reminded him of the seriousness of the situation and he renewed his struggle to budge the barrel. He succeeded in rolling downward and onto the floor, coming to rest with the keg lodged against his back and side.

By the Great Spirit, he thought in frustration, he had to get to the candle! It was so near, yet so far as he lay pinned to the floor only an arm's length away. He tried to jerk his body toward it, thus dragging the barrel with it, but it was almost impossible.

Almost.

Pure desperation drove him now, and Bakámu lunged sideways, willing the heavy barrel to move with him. It budged the smallest bit. He smiled inwardly with triumph and tried again. And again. Each time he managed to scrape the keg a fraction closer to the candle and, in the process, loosening the bonds that held him to it.

Then he rested for several moments, gathering his strength for one last herculean effort and thinking of what would happen if somehow the candle ignited beneath him once he was over it.

He dismissed the thought. Had Chandler thought twice about plunging into the river to save him? He didn't think so. He owed Chandler his life.

The flame danced tauntingly. Bakámu could feel its heat on one cheek as it burned lower. Or was it the warmth of his body, for he was sweating profusely in the close confines of the room. He set his teeth, tensed every muscle in preparation, and heaved with all his strength like a mammoth inchworm. Just as he was about to roll over onto the candle, just as he felt triumph begin to blossom within him, his head slammed back against the keg and knocked him out cold.

"Chandler!"

As he hung suspended somewhere between sleep and unconsciousness, Devin heard his name. Through the fog of pain and exhaustion, he also recognized it as female, although he couldn't think past that.

"Is 'e alive?" asked another voice.

A hand gently took hold of his chin and raised his head. The blindfold was removed.

"By the Pope's balls! Who did this to ye, Devil?"

Devin tried to open his eyes, but one was swollen shut and the other wouldn't cooperate. The glare from a lantern was blinding as sunlight. "Doesn't . . . matter now . . ." he managed to rasp, momentarily finding it easier to make his voice work than his eyes. "Get . . . me . . . out of here. Hurry."

He felt a knife sawing at his bonds, and relief began to filter through him. "Who?" he muttered.

"Why, we're pirates, o' course," said a second feminine voice. He knew that voice. "Sweet Jesus but it stinks in here!" she muttered with audible disgust.

"Aye, but we be the good pirates," said the other with a snicker. "We come to free all the slaves in this here hold, 'cept ye're all we found. An' a sorry specimen ye be."

"Only fer the moment," said the familiar voice. Maddy.

"Maddy?" he mouthed, the name a husk of sound.

"Aye, but 'twas Arabella who had me fetched and asked me to help 'er."

Devin's good eye was open now. It focused on the brass-bright hair of the woman butchering his bonds. He hoped she didn't slit his wrists. "How did you—?"

"I was walkin' past the docks with a faithful customer," Arabella offered. She gave him a broad wink, which was barely discernible by the meager light in the gloomy hold. As she spoke, she began cutting the rope at his waist. "I figured," she continued, "the least I could do was help ye, since ye came to my aid that day in Thames Street, even though I gave credit to the merchant." Her words turned sheepish as she mumbled, "Never did thank ye proper."

She attacked the rope about his shoulders, then his ankles, obviously concentrating as she fell silent for a moment.

"She sent 'im to fetch me at the Folly. We may be whores," Maddy said from the side, holding up the lantern as she scrutinized his face with narrowed eyes, "but we ain't indecent. We feel things like loyalty, same as anybody."

Devin took Arabella's offered hand as he slowly stood, willing away the dizziness. His midsection felt like one huge bruise, his head and face throbbed. He hoped his wobbly legs would hold him up, for he didn't need to be carried out of the hold of a stinking slaver by two females.

He took a tentative step.

"Who did this to ye?" Arabella asked.

"You don't know?" he asked in answer.

"I saw a red kerchief waving like a banner, had to be Davies. But I didn't know t' other one. He weren't a buccaneer, though. That much I can tell ye."

Maddy lifted a handkerchief to her mouth and nose. "Never smelled a slaver from the inside," she said, swinging the lantern in an arc to get a better glimpse of their surroundings before they departed.

"Take a good look, Maddy," Devin told her. "Even animals don't suffer the same fate on an ocean voyage." As soon as the words were out of his mouth, he regretted them. Their eyes met briefly before she looked back at the evidence of the inhuman treatment given anyone unfortunate enough to end up in a slaver's hold. There was no hiding the tiers of narrow wooden shelves that lined the walls and the stink of vomit, excrement, and disease that had become part of the ship and that nothing but purging flames could ever cleanse.

Yet there was something about Maddy that inspired trust, and in spite of his second thoughts about revealing his very strong, albeit secret, anti-slavery stand, Devin's instincts told him she wouldn't ever betray him. Deliberately, anyway. Devin glanced around quickly, his ribs aching with every breath, his vision blurred, but he was determined to burn into his brain, once again, the images of man's bestiality toward his fellow man, lest he ever falter in his belief in his work.

Arabella seemed unaffected, however, by both his comment—if she'd heard it—and what their surroundings represented and was already taking the lead up the ladder of the lower main hatch, her full skirts swishing with her movements.

"How did you manage to find exactly where I was?" Devin asked Maddy as she handed the lantern up to Arabella and began the ascent.

"Why, Arabella's customer's a crew member o' this ship," the woman said over her shoulder. She grinned conspiratorially. "An' he knew jest by watchin' an' listenin' to the boat's oars a-splashin' in the dark, exactly which ship they was goin' to. He's waitin' fer us."

"An' if he ain't there," Arabella said from above them, "I'll have to turn a trick er two fer the crew to ensure our leave-takin'." She paused, then added darkly, "An' when I catch up with 'im, I'll have 'is manhood!"

As Devin took his turn at the ladder, a host of hurts vied for his attention, but he set his teeth and made his body move. He covered his pain with a lopsided grin, tried unsuccessfully to wink, and said to his rescuer through bruised lips, "But I'm worth it, sweetheart, aren't I?"

What he was really thinking, however, was how welcome a drink of cool, fresh water would be just now.

It was quiet as they made their way out of the depths of the ship's hold, and once on deck, the men on anchor watch were not in sight. Whether it was deliberate or otherwise, Devin didn't know. The night air caressed his bruised face, refreshing after the sweltering confinement of the hold.

He insisted on Maddy and Arabella going first, while he stood at the rail with the lantern. A sailor waiting in a small boat below helped the women with a minimum of commotion, then looked up expectantly at Devin.

"Much obliged to you," Devin said as he lowered himself into the boat, "for rowing the ladies out to me."

"Jest hurry, mate—er, Cap'n," the sailor told him, his gaze going briefly to the deck of the ship above them, "afore Denby decides I didn't give 'im enough coin."

"I'll repay whatever you gave him," Devin said, then added, "You wouldn't happen to have a pistol would you . . . uh, Master . . . ?" Devin asked, suddenly apprehensive of a reappearance by Pelton and Davies.

"Call me Goldy. Andrew Golden o' the *Bristol*." He inclined his head toward the slaver and attacked the oars. "An' nay. A dagger . . . but no pistol. Expectin' more trouble?"

"Could be." But Devin's mind was unclouding with the rush of the sea breeze, the familiar, welcome sound of open water around them. And concern for Bakámu and the *Lady Elysia* awakened in him. Jonathon Treacher was captain of the *Bristol* and worked for la Compagnie de Sénégal, he knew. Undoubtedly, the captain had close ties to du Casse.

"A man by the name of Davies on the crew by any chance?" he asked as another thought struck. Davies went from crew to crew, known as a hard worker but undependable because of his heavy drinking.

"Mad Dog Davies. Aye." He rolled his eyes.

That explained the choice of the *Bristol*.

Devin understood the need to keep track of his enemies, and they were growing in number by the day, or so it seemed. He either had to get serious about carrying slaves on the *Lady Elysia,* change the base of his operations, or, like Woody had told him earlier, get out of the business completely.

"Yer face needs tendin'," Maddy said, breaking into Devin's thoughts. "We'll take ye home and—"

Devin shook his head and was immediately sorry. "My face will heal. I need to get back to the schooner," he said grimly. "They ambushed me and left one of my men beaten and bound on board with an unattended candle in the middle of the powder locker. No one will find him before dawn . . . if the schooner isn't blown to bits before then."

"Damn that pricklouse Davies!" Maddy muttered beneath her breath.

"Did you recognize the other culprit?" Devin asked Arabella, even though he already knew who it was.

Arabella shook her head. "Nay. 'Twas hard enough to see Davies, but, like I said before, 'is kerchief gave 'im away. As fer the other, he weren't dressed like no pirate. More like gentry. Fair-haired, too."

As they neared the docks, Devin scanned the dark sea about them for any other small boats headed for the *Bristol.* Surely he hadn't seen the last of his two abductors, but once he was armed with a pistol, he'd be better equipped to fend them off, or send them to their Maker.

When they boarded the schooner, Henry Morgan dove toward them from the rigging, shrieking like a banshee, "Pirates! Man yer stations, mates!" Everyone's nerves were on edge, and even the unflappable Maddy let out a startled squeak as the African gray careened downward, made a pass, then returned and landed on Devin's outstretched arm. They found Bakámu unconscious, lying in the middle of the small munitions locker and on top of the culprit candle.

In spite of his concern, Devin guessed what had happened to knock the Arawak senseless, and he grinned to himself. Goldy helped him carry the Indian to the captain's quarters, and after thanking the man and giving each of the women a dramatically loud kiss of gratitude on the cheek, Devin told them he was certain they had more important things to do with their evening and watched them troop from the cabin, a knowing grin on his face.

Before he turned to Bakámu, however, he retrieved a pistol he kept hidden in the cabin and tucked it in his belt. "Hey matey," he said, leaning over the Arawak, "are you awake?"

The Arawak didn't move.

Well, he thought, a few words of gratitude wouldn't hurt. "You're one brave warrior," he said, thinking of all the bumbling things the Arawak had done and that it was only by the sheerest luck that he hadn't blown both himself and the schooner to smithereens. Devin placed one cool, wet cloth on the Indian's forehead and with another blotted the blood on his face. "You saved the *Lady* and I'm grateful for that."

Bakámu's one eye popped open, then the other. "Bakámu save Chan-ler's boat, ehhh?" A grin of triumph split his face from ear to ear, then, as if it pained him, the smile quickly faded.

"Save Chan-ler's boat. Squaaawk!" echoed Henry Morgan from where he perched upon the bunk post. "Where's the bawds?"

A knock sounded at the cabin door. "Cap'n?"

Devin had the pistol drawn and leveled at the portal in a blink. "That you, Flaherty?" he asked, recognizing the muffled voice.

"Aye, Cap'n."

Devin released a pent-up breath as his boatswain entered. "Jesus, Cap'n!" the short but powerfully built man exclaimed, his brown eyes widening. "Guess I shouldn't've allowed the Indian to stand watch over the *Lady,* but ye don't have to shoot me as punishment, do ye?"

Devin shook his head, gave Flaherty a half-grin, and replaced the pistol. "Of course not. Good boatswains are hard to come by these days, even those who make mistakes in judgment," he added, sobering. He swung back toward Bakámu. "A couple of ruffians left him bound and gagged in the powder locker with a lit candle." He bent to feel the bump on the back of the Arawak's head.

"Poor bastard," Flaherty muttered.

"Bakámu have father," the victim said with a scowl that would have done any outraged Arawak warrior proud.

Flaherty waved a hand in dismissal. "Didn't mean nothin', my friend. Glad ye're in one piece." He stared for a moment at the Arawak's scorched shirt with its powder stains.

But Bakámu's expression had brightened considerably with the boatswain's words, and Devin had to suppress a smile, though the urge was fleeting. "From now on, three crew members, minimum, anchor watch," he told Red Flaherty over his shoulder. "No one, aside from the crew, is allowed aboard the *Lady* without clearance from me directly." He stood and turned to face Flaherty, tossing the cloth toward the basin from which it came.

"Aye, Cap'n. Consider it done. But do ye know who attacked Bakámu here, an' why they threatened the schooner? Looks like you took a beatin' yerself." Frowning, he scratched his red-stubbled head, then shook it, sending the thin, tarred braid that hung down his back snapping across his shoulders.

"I believe they were looking for me," Devin began, glancing into a small, square looking-glass mounted on the wall over the washstand. He winced at his image. "They used Bakámu as a lure and jumped me from behind as I was about to go to his aid. I suspect they acted on orders from the same people who were in league with Giles Glasby."

Flaherty bristled visibly. His large hands clenched to fearsome fists at his sides. "Leave it to me, Cap'n. The ship'll be guarded like the crown jewels from now on, ye can count on it! In fact," his look turned sly, one eyebrow curling suggestively, "if ye can describe them sea snakes, me an' a few of the crew can mayhap do some snoopin' an'—"

"No." He cut Flaherty's sentence short. "I value your loyalty and your willingness to take my side, but I'm not certain of their identities and these are dangerous people. Let me handle it my way, Red, and if I need help, you have my word that I'll enlist your aid."

The boatswain nodded, folded his arms across his chest, and regarded Bakámu with a thoughtful frown.

"Help me get him up," Devin directed Flaherty. "Are you ready to go home?" he asked the Arawak.

Bakámu moved his head slowly from side to side, and an obstinate expression planted itself upon his copper-tinted features. "Bakámu guard boat. Do better this time, *sí?*"

Devin shook his head. "Not tonight, my friend."

The Arawak pushed himself to his elbows, his expression brightening. "Chan-ler give Bakámu pistol, *sí?* Guard boat."

"Squaaawk! Give 'im a pistol! Where's the bawds?"

A piercing whistle bounced off the walls of the cabin, and Devin thought his head would burst. The image of Bakámu brandishing a pistol, however, helped him focus his thoughts. "Shut up, Henry Morgan, or you're a dead b—" he gritted, then belatedly remembered the bird's trick and pictured him crashing headfirst to the cabin floor.

Indeed, the African gray appeared to be eyeing the floor, as if assessing his chances for survival should he perform on command. But his bowed white head came up abruptly, and he merely crowed, "Henry Morgan ain't afeared, ye greasy riff-raff!" and stared at Devin with his basilisk eyes.

"Sorriest lookin' bird I ever seen," Flaherty commented. "If ye don't mind my sayin' so," he added quickly when Devin threw him a look.

Then the captain burst out laughing. "I agree, but he can be quite entertaining when he isn't sharpening his rapier tongue on some unsuspecting fool."

He bent to help Bakámu sit up. "Home with you," he said lightly. "The *Lady* will be fine for the rest of the night. Flaherty here will stand watch until dawn. 'Tisn't so far away now," he added with a twist of his lips.

"Bakámu—"

"Is going to bed at the town house," Devin finished for the

Indian and straightened as the Arawak stood without any help. The latter peered at Devin closely now.

"Chan-ler hurt. Bakámu tend."

Devin nodded his head to placate him. "At the town house. If you're up to it, you can see to my bruises, though I'm capable of seeing to them myself."

Flaherty moved into the passageway to let them through. "Aye, Cap'n, an' both o' you could use a tot o' brandywine to ease yer hurts before ye go to sleep."

Devin nodded, wondering if the wine would put Bakámu safely to sleep or have him hanging from the ceiling beams. But his thoughts moved on to more serious matters, like the outrageous actions of his abductors.

And Meredyth. Would Pelton decide to take out his frustrations on her? Or would his tactic be to try and win her back, hiding his true motivation? Was she still vulnerable where the blackguard was concerned? She was young and gullible, although, he acknowledged, certainly intelligent enough not to take any bait Pelton might throw out again.

He hoped. Pelton was older, more experienced, and certainly devious enough for two.

Bakámu said something in Arawak, and Henry Morgan hopped from the bunk post and flapped over to his shoulder before they exited. The short flight of the parrot caused a minor turbulence in the close cabin air and lifted strands of Devin's hair. He blew out his breath in resignation, further disturbing a few more untidy wisps, and followed Bakámu and the bird.

"Henry Morgan's me name. Huntin' treasure's me game! Squaaawk! Where's the bawds?"

Devin chafed beneath Bakámu's ministrations, but he knew the better he looked, the less he would have to explain to Meredyth. The cold, wet compress did feel good against his swollen eye, and he'd swigged down almost half a bucket of water. But he needed at least a few hours of sleep before he'd be ready to face the world.

"Will you feed that bird so he'll cease his caterwauling?"

"Parrot likes Chan-ler. Show off talents, *sí?*" Bakámu said with a crooked grin.

Devin removed the Arawak's hand from the cloth on his eye and replaced it with his own. "I'm a grown man and I can tend myself. You need some rest and so do I, so quiet him down and go to bed." He drained his cup of brandywine. "First, drink your brandywine, then to bed with you, Indian. Do you hear?"

"*Sí.*"

Devin thought he saw a wounded look pass through the Arawak's dark eyes, but he might have imagined it. A twinge of conscience made Devin add, "The sooner you're fit, the sooner you can go back and help watch the ship." He stood then and strode toward the stairs, ignoring his protesting ribs.

"Chan-ler! Squaaawk! Chan-ler's desertin' ship!"

He needed sleep. Then he would be better able to decide a course of action. As he stripped off his clothing, Devin admitted to himself that he needed to be much more cautious. He had to carry a pistol at all times, especially when he was alone. He had to maintain a watch—an armed watch—around the clock on the *Lady Elysia*. And possibly on the town house in his absence, for he doubted, even if Bakámu agreed to remain there rather than on board the *Lady,* that he would be much of a deterrent to anyone serious about exposing Devin's activities.

And besides, the Indian was exhibiting a most disconcerting desire to become a crew member of the *Lady Elysia* rather than remain a house servant.

Not least of all was his appearing before Meredyth looking, as sorry as he did. Aside from alleviating her concern, he feared he would have a hard time lying to her. Especially now. And to even imply that Pelton was involved. . . . Well, he just couldn't come out and tell her the truth, and for more reasons than merely revealing Luke Pelton was a blackguard of an even baser kind than she probably already believed him. Devin would have to resort to lying, something that had never been difficult for him before. But could he lie to Meredyth?

Surely he must, for he couldn't bear the thought of missing their outing together in the afternoon, of not seeing her or touching her or laughing with her.

He lay down upon the bed, sinking into the mattress's embrace with a sigh of pleasure and resignation. He would have to lie to her with utmost skill, or he would lose any ground he'd gained with her. And Devin Chandler, scoundrel, privateer, and spy, couldn't bear the thought of that. He would have to remind himself sternly of the consequences of revealing the truth while engaged in his fabrication.

On the other hand, he acknowledged, lying convincingly to Meredyth St. Andrews might backfire and cast him not only out of her affections but out of her life anyway, for Devin also knew that the more involved the lie, the greater the chances of tripping up and getting caught within its web. With his luck obviously having taken a turn for the worse, by the time he'd finished his explanation, he'd end up the frog prince waiting to be kissed by a beautiful maiden to transform him.

And so, he could put her life in jeopardy by telling her the truth. Or he could tell her a lie that could very well make him out to be a villain and permanently end their budding relationship.

He rolled over and buried his head in the crook of one arm, a low and muffled groan of frustration escaping his lips. Now how was he supposed to sleep with *those* thoughts blasting through his mind like a barrage of cannon shot?

Easy does it, Chandler, calmed a voice. *You've been in stickier situations before. You'll do what needs to be done and get the woman, too. Haven't you always?*

But there was so very much at stake here—his fight against the slave trade. And Meredyth St. Andrews, whom he wanted like no other woman before.

And even the proverbial cat had only nine lives.

Sixteen

"What in God's name happened to you?"

At the sound of Woody's voice, Devin looked up from replacing a broken belaying pin in the pinrail.

"What happened to you? Squaawk!" Henry Morgan mimicked. "Kingsley's a bloody gimp. Henry Morgan ain't afeared!"

Devin hid a smile at the parrot's greeting and watched Woody answer Bakámu's wave. The Arawak's nose looked like it spread over half his face, but he wouldn't tolerate a plaster on it. "Look like Spanish thief," he'd said. "Bakámu not hide face. Need air."

Devin hadn't realized his own bruises were so readily apparent from the side, let alone from the far end of a boarding plank. Mayhap he needed to borrow a straw hat from the good *padre*. That thought brought Meredyth to mind and sent a flash of anticipation through him.

"That bad, eh?" he said with typical insouciance as he twisted a line about the new wooden pin in a double figure eight.

Woody hobbled up the plank, his eyes narrowing against the sparkling morning light. When he reached Devin, who was brushing off his hands with nonchalance, he reached out and took the younger man's chin between his thumb and forefinger, which made Devin wince, then proceeded to examine Devin's battered visage in the uncompromising daylight.

"A black eye, swollen cheek beneath," he ticked off, "cut lip, bruised jaw—"

"Which you're hurting," Devin cut in, pulling away with another wince.

"I'm sorry," Woody apologized, but there was no softening in his eyes. He moved closer so that they were almost nose to nose and said in a low voice, "What happened to you, lad? They're after you again, aren't they?"

The sounds of men refurbishing and making the schooner seaworthy rang in the air, their voices piercing the morning stillness along with a growing number of others along the docks. The morning mist was being burned away by the hot Jamaican sun, and seagulls dipped and dove through the skies, their screeches adding to the meld of background noises. New wood and fresh pitch, rotting fish, exotic cargo, and the tang of saltwater perfumed the air. Devin considered taking Woody below decks, but it was too glorious a morn to waste a single moment in the bowels of the ship.

"Come with me," he said, then turned and moved up to the relative privacy of the quarterdeck. When they'd reached the aft rail, Devin leaned back and crossed his arms over his chest. He lifted his gaze to the towering masts, outwardly contemplating their furled canvas. "She's beautiful again, Woody, and almost ready for a trial run."

"Huumph," Woody grunted, crossing his own arms but keeping his eyes on Devin's upturned face. "She was always beautiful, even injured. We've said the same before." His expression hardened. "Now, instead of trying to distract me, tell me just what happened. If you lie, I swear I'll write to Somerset and tell him you've neglected your part of the bargain concerning his daughter and—"

Devin's eyes clashed with his. "I wouldn't be so quick to threaten. 'Tis like the pot calling the kettle black, wouldn't you say? Especially after your dereliction of chaperon duty last eve."

Woody poked Devin in the chest with a finger. "You took advantage of the situation, boy! I trusted you to behave like a gentleman."

"Never trust me, Woody, and least of all to act the gentleman. You should know that by now. And naught happened but a few stolen kisses, in spite of your guttersnipe thoughts."

Woody's face turned beet red before he countered, "Or did someone—like Jackie Greaves or even Luke Pelton—take exception to your whisking Lady Meredyth down into your cabin. If that's the case, then I—"

"I wish it were."

The somberness of his voice obviously alerted the older man that the problem was worse than the defending of Meredyth St. Andrews's virtue. He stepped up beside Devin, shaded his eyes with one hand, and joined the captain in seeming absorption with the sails for the benefit of any observers. "I knew it!" he exclaimed in a low voice. "Tell me who battered your face," he hissed through set teeth.

Devin swung toward the sea behind them and stared at the outline of the *Bristol* in the near distance. "They caught me off guard," he said over his shoulder in a low voice. Woody joined him at the rail. "In fact, they caught Bakámu first, after we left the ship last night. They roughed him up a bit and tied him to a full keg in the powder locker with only a candle for company."

Some of the blood drained from Woody's flushed face as Devin gave him a sidelong glance. "That's better, my friend. You'll arouse suspicions if you look like our conversation's giving you apoplexy." He grinned, which hurt his stiff and sore face. His head still ached like the devil, but he never liked to worry Woodrow Kingsley unduly and the grin was for the older man's benefit.

He looked back to the water, enjoying the cool kiss of the sea breeze on his abused flesh. He heard Henry Morgan's whistle and a few garbled words in the background, which prompted a spirited but indecipherable answer from one of the crew members. "They used him to get me down there, then took me to the *Bristol* for . . . questioning."

"Who, lad?

"Luke Pelton and Aaron Davies. They wanted information and weren't the least bit subtle about it, as you can see."

"Why those—" Woody began, then asked, "By the Mass, how did those two ever hook up?" Without waiting for an answer, he lowered his voice and leaned closer to Devin. "What exactly did they want to know? As if I needed to ask," he added darkly.

Devin hung his head for a few moments, contemplating the water directly beneath them. "Merely who had me released from Newgate and who's responsible for the refurbishing of the *Lady.*"

Woody made a strangled sound, and Devin's eyes met and held his for a brief but intense moment. "But I'll not let a pricklouse like Davies or a snake like Pelton succeed in moving me from my course of action." His words were little more than a husk of sound, but there was no mistaking the underlying steely determination.

Woodrow returned his gaze to the sun scintillating like a molten copper coating off the sea, cleared his throat, and squinted against the glare. "There's something you should know, lad, even if I'm the only one who thinks so."

Devin grinned again but returned his gaze to the water. "Mayhap that my benefactor is also one of my employers? I've suspected as much for a while."

Woody's sharp intake of breath was his answer. "The less you know, the better."

"An admirable strategy . . . for everyone but the benighted fool who's shielded from such vital information." Devin paused, then added, "The only thing that puzzles me is why the earl set me to keeping track of his lovely daughter. 'Tis rather like . . ." he glanced at Woodrow through his lashes, one side of his mouth crescenting, "setting the wolf to guard the sheep, isn't it?"

But Woodrow was obviously too upset to move away from the original subject. "The point, Devin, is that you must give this up before you get yourself killed. You—"

Devin started to shake his head, then stilled. "Nay," he said softly. "I'll take more care—forewarned, forearmed." He pointedly planted his foot on a lower rail and drew Woody's gaze. The shiny butt of a small pistol was barely discernible above the rim of the boot. "There's another just inside my shirt," he said, "lest you still think me ill-prepared. I've also tightened anchor watch and have two men watching the town house night and day. I'd hate to be trapped within my own home with only the Arawak for help, and it would be even worse to walk into a trap upon returning home late one night."

"Henry Morgan ain't afeared!" mimicked Woody. "No one gets past him unannounced, you know."

"True," Devin mused aloud, his lips twisting with amusement. "But I'd just as soon not put my safety in the claws of a parrot. Yet, if I see either Pelton or Davies face to face, I'll challenge them directly. And I'll need you to act as second."

Woodrow turned troubled blue eyes on his friend, an objection obviously on the tip of his tongue.

"That is, if I run into either of them before I can carry out my own . . . er, *appropriate* retaliation."

"Which could be even more dangerous than demanding satisfaction," Woody said on a profound sigh. "How did you get away?"

Devin put an arm across his friend's shoulders. "You'll never believe it even when I tell you, Kingsley." He turned the older man away from the rail. "Come to my cabin for a tot of juice or, better yet, rum, why don't you? You look as if you could use some." He laughed softly, though not without discomfort. "Then I'll tell you how it pays to have friends in high and *low* places. I'll tell you, that is, if you agree to play chaperon again later this morn."

He felt Woodrow's shoulders stiffen. "Now, now. 'Twill be aboveboard, I promise. I'll treat you to a meal at the Oyster House with the lady Meredyth and me."

"You're truly a scoundrel!" Woody sounded only mildly outraged, however, and his shoulders relaxed beneath Devin's arm.

"They don't call me Devil for naught," Devin replied lightly as one eyelid dropped in a wicked wink. "And a true scoundrel wouldn't even invite you to come along, my friend."

Woody thumped his cane emphatically on the deck. "And if the earl were here, he'd immediately see what a mistake he'd made by putting his trust in you and have the lady whisked back to England."

Devin's smile dimmed at the very thought. "Better he should clap me in chains," he muttered beneath his breath.

Morning brought an unexpected visitor to the Somerset town house. When Meredyth heard voices below, her pulse started racing as she set down her morning draught only half finished, for it could have been Devin. She glanced at the lantern clock. He was early and possibly unable to stay away from her for another two hours.

Silly chit, admonished her sensible side. But her pumping heart wouldn't ease until Ellen came running up the stairs and burst into her room, curly brown hair a-flying. "Meredyth—" she began breathlessly, then obviously realized her *faux pas.* "Oh, forgive me," she amended, her expression changing immediately to chagrin.

Meredyth, thinking how very unladylike she herself was behaving, put her hands on Ellie's plump shoulders and, with glowing eyes, exclaimed, "Devin?" Color flooded her cheeks, for she wasn't even near ready for company, just fresh from her bath.

Ellie's brow furrowed slightly as she said, "Nay. Rather the gentleman we met last eve. Pelton. Master Luke Pelton."

Pelton watched Meredyth descend the stairs, a host of emotions going through him. He was a fool to even have thought to pay her a visit, but it irked him in the extreme to know that

Chandler was after her. And, even more, that she appeared to reciprocate the interest.

He'd decided after meeting Chandler the night before that if he, Luke, couldn't have Meredyth St. Andrews, then neither would the cocky bastard who'd escaped from the hold of the *Bristol* in the early hours of the morn.

And if Meredyth refused to see him, he'd go find her himself and Greaves be damned!

That Meredyth would even look twice at such a man galled him to the point that he would have committed murder to prevent the blossoming friendship. Devil Chandler had a way of burrowing under Luke's skin and irritating him mercilessly.

Now, rekindled anger and a sense of vengeance drove him. Mayhap it was because he'd possibly underestimated Chandler, for the privateer captain had succeeded in disappearing from the *Bristol* like some mountebank magician, if one believed Jack Denby. And further manipulations of Luke's life by anyone even possibly linked to the Earl of Somerset or his family were unthinkable.

Meredyth looked flustered, as well she might. Her cheeks were pink, her hair damp and hanging down her back, as if she were fresh from her bath. Her eyes sought his, registering a mixture of disbelief and tentativeness, as if she were torn between his audacity and apprehension of the reason for his early and unexpected visit.

She opened her mouth to speak, but Jackie Greaves appeared behind Luke and said, "Since Lady Meredyth's come down to see ye, ye can talk in the sittin' room over there." He inclined his head toward the small salon as he came abreast of Pelton, with a look that conveyed suspicion and outright protectiveness toward Keir St. Andrews's youngest daughter.

Meredyth gave Greaves a half-smile, which lit up her face, animated her striking eyes enough to poignantly remind Luke all over again of what he'd been literally blackmailed into giving up. Her dowry was no small consideration, either. Once again, fate seemed to be laughing at him by placing her here in Jamaica like the most tempting of apples in the Garden of Eden.

Luke gave Greaves a nod of acknowledgment and placed his fingers beneath Meredyth's elbow. As he guided her through the doorway, he felt the tension in her arm, and she shook off his hand in a manner that was a scant breath away from discourtesy.

"What? No 'Good morrow,' Meredyth?" he began.

"I don't see that we have aught to say to—" she began as she faced him.

He held up one hand. "I know I'm the lowest of the low in your eyes, and I understand why you feel that way. But I've not come to justify my behavior all those months ago, only to warn you about Chandler, Meredyth."

"*Lady* Meredyth," she said coldly, obviously attempting to keep some distance between them.

It piqued his pride. She could associate herself with the dregs of Port Royal, yet speak thusly to her former fiancé. The fact that he had no antecedents to match hers meant little to him. His father was a minor noble who'd dwindled away his small fortune on women and wine, but at least Luke's parents had been wed. Not so with Chandler, he'd discovered. His mother was an Irish whore.

"My lady," he said through stiff lips, fighting to keep his temper, "I've come to tell you, for old friendship's sake, that Devil Chandler is a blackguard of the lowest sort. He—"

"And you, Lucien—or Luke or whoever you are—are a paragon of righteousness, someone in a favorable position to judge another and then spread malicious gossip?"

He caught the bitterness in her voice, something new. Her father had done this to her, not he. But she would never believe that.

"I'm not deserving of you, at least in the eyes of your father, but neither is Chandler. And the earl isn't here to protect you."

"Better that you had thought to warn me about your own deviousness, Lucien, rather than put me through such humiliation; and now you seek to return to my good graces by inventing stories about Captain Chandler?" She glowered at him, ire flashing in her eyes.

" 'Twasn't my own deviousness, as you put it, Meredyth, but rather your father's." He smiled nastily, feeling his jaw twitch, which set his moustache a-quiver. "I know, however, that you'd never have taken my word over his, so I'll tell you what I have to say and then be gone. Devil Chandler is a cutthroat and a pirate. And worse. He masquerades as a semi-respectable privateer, but in truth he's up to his neck in the slave trade."

Meredyth had no way of knowing whether he spoke the truth. She hadn't really asked Devin what cargo he carried aboard the *Lady Elysia,* and he hadn't volunteered the information. She was inclined, however, because of her feelings for Devin and her grudge against Lucien for the past betrayal—no matter how he might try to lay the blame at her father's feet—not to believe him.

"There are many who make a living by selling others into bondage, Lucien, but I doubt Devin Chandler is one of them." She folded her arms obstinately over her chest, her eyes narrowing as she prepared to protect Devin. Could she be so wrong about two men? one part of her mind asked, but she chose to ignore the implications for the moment. She didn't need new doubts arising now, particularly before the man who'd jilted her.

But the seed had been sown.

" 'Twas not my choice to leave you, Meredyth."

She fought back a wave of humiliation as memories assaulted her. "And, pray tell, whose choice was it?"

"I've already told you. Your father was behind my leaving, but I'll not go into details."

"How convenient to blame the earl when he's across the Atlantic and unable to defend himself, Master Pelton. Are you quite finished?" she asked brittlely, feeling outrage fuel her smoldering anger at him. How dare he come seeking her out to warn her of Devin Chandler and accuse her father of some kind of chicanery?

He sketched a rigid bow. "Quite, though I must say, Lady Meredyth, that we'd have suited well, you and I, had things been different. 'Tis no small compliment to me that you fled clear to Jamaica to escape your unhappiness."

She drew in her breath sharply. If he'd slapped her, he couldn't have insulted her more. Especially because it was the truth, as much as she might wish it otherwise.

"But I sought to do the same, and now here we are, a chasm still separating us. My lingering affection makes it all the more imperative that I warn you against making another mistake."

"You aren't fit to clean his boots, Lucien." Inwardly, she was appalled at her words, yet at the same time it felt wonderfully cleansing to vent some of her wrath on him at long last.

She felt him strip her with one last, encompassing look before he returned his gaze to her face. His eyes were arctic, his features drawn with fury. He reminded her of someone she wouldn't want to meet alone on a dark London street. A most sobering thought.

And she'd thought to wed this man? Had run away to Jamaica to try and escape the anguish of his loss?

As if sensing her unflattering thoughts, without warning he spun on his heel and strode to the doorway. He paused and looked over his shoulder at her, adding, "If I wasn't good enough for you, Chandler has absolutely no hope of winning Somerset's approval. Brace yourself for another heartbreak, sweeting, should you be foolish enough to give your affections to such a common pirate. 'He that lies with the dogs, riseth with fleas,' I believe 'tis said? And word has it that you've already lain with him."

Meredyth started forward, not quite certain what she would do when she reached him, but an answering anger and outrage were mirrored in her eyes.

Ignoring her, Pelton disappeared through the door before she could reach him.

"Meredyth?" Ellie called. They almost collided as Meredyth stalked angrily from the room. "What did that nasty man say to you?" she asked, her plump cheeks flushed with anger, her hazel eyes ignited.

The door closed soundly, and Jackie came striding toward them. "Should I have held him, Lady Meredyth?" he asked, a dark look on his boyish face. "Did he insult you?" He half turned as if to return to the door, when Meredyth's hand on his arm stopped him.

"Nay, Jackie. Let him go. We're well rid of him! And to think I thought I loved him!" she blurted, then felt her own cheeks pinken to match Ellie's. She closed her eyes and shook her head. "Let's go upstairs," she said quietly to Ellie when she opened her eyes again.

"But, Meredyth—" Ellie began.

"Nay, Ellie. He's gone and good riddance." She struggled a moment for composure, then managed a weak smile for both of them. "I never want to have to speak to him again, lest I run him through! Mayhap Captain Chandler will teach me to use a cutlass." But the corner of her mouth didn't curve with humor as it was wont to do when she said something absurd.

She turned toward the stairway, chagrined at how easily Devin Chandler's name had come to her lips, and confused, in spite of her desire to give him the benefit of the doubt and dismiss Luke Pelton's words. "Will you help me get ready, Ellie?" she asked distractedly as she mounted the first step.

"Of course, Meredyth." Ellen gave her husband a fleeting look of apology and hurried toward the stairs.

"And, Jackie?" Meredyth looked over her shoulder and flashed him a brighter smile. "I'll not keep you from your children one day longer, and Carla and her mother need to return to the mission, as well. The morrow will be a good time to go back to my father's plantation and the next morn I'll go back up the mountain."

Jackie bobbed his head. "Sure thing, milady. If you want, I'll make arrangements straightaway."

When they reached the bedchamber, Meredyth turned to Ellie. "You aren't to blame, either you or Jackie," she said. "You didn't know what had happened between us in England."

" 'Tisn't any of our business, anyway," Ellie answered as she glanced at the dress Concepción had laid across the bed earlier. "Not that we wouldn't do anything for you, Meredyth. Jackie works for the earl—we both do—and he'd lay down his life for any of your family."

Meredyth drew in a deep breath, then let it out slowly. "That isn't necessary, truly." Her look turned impish. "Who would support those little devils at the plantation, who no doubt pine for their parents even as we speak?"

Ellen dropped her hands onto her hips and rolled her eyes. "No doubt, they don't even know we're gone and have the place in an uproar."

Meredyth laughed aloud. "I can picture it, but their hours of freedom are numbered as of this moment."

She turned to the dress on the bed and watched Carla smooth imaginary wrinkles from it with a small, brown hand. The child looked up at Meredyth and smiled shyly. *"Bonita."*

" 'Tis lovely," echoed Ellen.

"Not too fancy for a drive through Port Royal?"

Ellie shook her head. " 'Tis perfect for a spring day in Port Royal. Concepción has a way with an iron. You'll dazzle Captain Chandler, but he'll be torn betwixt wantin' to show you off and hidin' you away from all the men—rowdy or nay—in Port Royal."

Meredyth cast Ellen a look through her lashes. "We will dazzle him, Ellie, and you flatter me overmuch. Concepción can perform miracles with my hair, and between the two of you, I'll do him proud."

Ellie blushed with obvious pleasure at the compliment. "You would do any man proud, Lady—er, Meredyth. Now, the dress first. Then we can decide what Concepción is to do with your hair."

Meredyth removed her wrapper and helped Ellie raise the pale, sprigged lawn gown over her head and settle it over her slender shoulders, then down to her waist and over her petticoats. The rich, apricot-hued underskirt of lightweight silk rustled softly as it settled along her hips and thighs and was shown off to advantage with the lawn overskirt drawn back on either side. Meredyth had particularly chosen this dress to take to Jamaica for any possible daytime outings if she ever left the haven of the mission. She was glad now that she had. She'd also packed the one ball gown she'd worn the night before, at her mother's insistence.

Ellie proceeded to treat Meredyth like royalty, in an obvious effort to erase any lingering unpleasantness from Luke Pelton's visit, which endeared her even more to Meredyth, who already liked immensely the good-natured and generous woman Jackie Greaves, her father's long-ago cabin boy, had married.

Once the dress was on, Concepción experimented with Meredyth's heavy chestnut tresses while Ellie and Carla watched. "I like the sides pinned up, but the back loose and curling across your shoulders," Ellie said matter-of-factly. " 'Tis a nice contrast, your dark hair against the gown."

"I'm going for an outing," Meredyth exclaimed when Carla handed her a string of seed pearls and a slim length of apricot ribbon, "not a ball! You wear the pearls, little one," she said with a laugh of pure happiness and draped them about Carla's thin neck.

But Meredyth's eyes were alight with approval and as round as Carla's as, with the hand mirror, she watched Concepción weave the ribbon through the curls spilling from her crown.

She refused to think about Luke Pelton's accusations and their consequences for her deepening relationship with Devin Chandler. Rather, beneath the attentions of Carla's mother, she deliberately guided her thoughts to safer territory—to the ball and her enchantment with Captain Devin Chandler, which had resulted in their interlude in his cabin on the *Lady Elysia*.

Roses bloomed anew in her cheeks, and the heat in her face abruptly called her back to reality—to the three others in the room, and what they would think if they could only read her thoughts.

She was ready at half past ten, and time suddenly seemed to come to a patience-testing halt. Only ten minutes crept by as her gaze returned repeatedly to the domed and filigreed brass lantern clock atop the armoire when a commotion downstairs heralded Devin's arrival.

Surely it was him this time.

She drifted down the stairs, knowing who it was before Jackie could even tell her, never hearing a voice call out from the bedchamber that she had forgotten perfume.

She stood, rooted to the spot, a frail, fledgling willow quivering from the colliding emotions that spoke to her, each voice more strident and demanding than the other, like the forces of nature tearing at that tender sapling, anticipation clashing with trepidation within her breast, delight vying with embarrassment as her pulse quickened and the blood churned through her veins. Simple caution cried out against the possibility of having her heart trampled again.

The clashing feelings suddenly coalesced, and Meredyth forgot the past, grew unmindful of anything that could happen in the future, focused on the immediate present. She stood immobilized in body and mind for one eternal yet ephemeral moment as her gaze went to the man standing in the small foyer before her.

He stepped forward, his tall, impressive frame blocking her vision of everything behind him, eclipsing everyone and everything around him. Then shock rode her features, jarred her insides, as she looked up into his face.

Seventeen

Devin bowed, lowering his eyes momentarily. "Good morning, Lady Meredyth. Mistress Greaves."

For a moment, silence reigned, courtesy preventing an immediate barrage of questions; but as Devin raised his eyes again, he couldn't bear the look on Meredyth's face. He wanted to erase it and reassure her.

He moved closer and held out a small, wrapped package, one side of his mouth curving a trifle stiffly. The gesture was to distract her—and Ellen as well—for only Jack Greaves had registered little surprise when he'd answered Devin's knock. The man had been a seaman, just like Devin. He understood the rough and tumble life, what went on among the docks and brothels of the waterfronts the world over, and had merely raised an eyebrow at the sight of Devin, his eyes communicating understanding.

"A small token for you," Devin said lightly, "to distract your thoughts from my battered face, which is nothing serious, I assure you." His smile widened and, hiding the hurt it caused, he looked at Ellen. "I hope I don't offend, mistress, but my man did the best he could with cleaning and patching." He managed a wink. "We don't call him bumbling Bakámu for naught."

"No need to explain," Jackie said with a chuckle that spoke volumes and came around to take Ellen by the hand. "Enjoy th'afternoon," he said, as he led his wife toward the kitchen. "An' give Master Kingsley our regards, Cap'n."

By this time Ellen had obviously recovered her wits. "Oh, aye," she echoed, then pulled back. "Meredyth?" she said brightly. "Why don't you open Captain Chandler's gift?"

"Never you mind," Jackie said. "Curiosity killed the cat."

Color flooded her face at the rebuke, and Devin said, "She's not the only one." He laughed softly as he glanced up the stairway at Concepción and Carla peeking down at them over the banister. "I should have brought four separate packets."

"Indeed, Captain," Meredyth said in a slightly strained voice, accepting the parcel. "What woman could resist taking a peek at a gift from a ship's captain, who's undoubtedly been to exotic ports all over the world?"

He watched her lower her gaze to the parcel and remove the string. It came away easily, and the wrapping paper even more so, to reveal a tiny bottle of perfume. The stopper on the vial was exquisitely blown, in the shape of a flower, and the contents of the transparent body tinted pale green.

"I hope I don't disappoint, ladies, but this treasure is from right here in Jamaica. I've never smelled the like, and I think the old Carib woman who created the perfume has captured the essence of her island with this particular fragrance. She's as good as any Parisian perfumer."

As Meredyth carefully unstoppered the bottle, a clean and delicate scent drifted into the air, bringing to mind cool and crystal clear waterfalls, and the fruited lushness of pristine white flowers indigenous to the Caribbean.

Meredyth closed her eyes for a moment, allowing the fragrance to envelop her, the heady scent to penetrate her olfactory senses like a living essence. Every time she used it, she realized, the beauty of Jamaica, Island of Springs, would come to mind.

And Devin Chandler . . .

" 'Tis beautiful!" breathed Ellen.

By now, Devin noticed that the two at the top of the stairs were all but hanging over the railing, eyes rounded, mother and daughter alike, and he truly wished he'd brought them each some small token for their own.

But this particular perfume was for Meredyth. It was Jamaica, created by a woman whose antecedents had been an integral part of the Caribbean for centuries and who knew what delicate combinations of elements would please a female. It was also meant to be worn by a woman like Meredyth St. Andrews, who complimented both the civilized and the untamed sides of the island.

Meredyth belonged in Jamaica, with him, came the sudden and unexpected thought, like a shooting star across the open expanse of his mind.

"Thank you," Meredyth murmured with a soft smile of gratitude that made his heart drop to his feet. She carefully touched the stopper to the delicate area beneath each ear, restoppered it securely and slipped it into an unobtrusive pocket in her full skirt.

He led her out into the perfect Caribbean morning, where a hackney, its top raised against the powerful rays of the sun, waited with the driver and single passenger, Woodrow Kingsley. The gentle breeze off the ocean was wonderfully refreshing as it caressed her face and teased her hair. "Good morning, Master Kingsley," Meredyth greeted with a smile as sunny as the morning itself, and felt her face grown warm, in spite of the fact that he couldn't possibly know of the intimacies that had transpired between Devin and herself the night before.

But the older man seemed preoccupied, in spite of his cordial greeting. Devin, however, claimed her gaze and her interest. He handed her up into the open coach, the contact of his hand every bit as sweetly shocking as the night before when they'd danced at the ball, then he stepped up behind her and joined them.

At first, Meredyth gazed shyly down at her matching apricot silk and kid shoes, with their embroidered sprigs like those in her overgown; she fingered the feathered fan that dangled from her wrist, hoping that Devin would think her shy rather than rude, for she found it disconcerting to meet his eyes—or, rather, the eye that was fully open. The cut on his lip, the swelling of his cheek beneath his battered eye, the purple bruise on the opposite side of his jaw—each injury cut her to the quick, for she was soft-hearted, like her mother, the Lady Juliana (or Brandy, as the earl was fond of calling her). The sheen of a touch of balm on the cut lip caught her eye in the sunlight, and Meredyth felt an almost irrepressible urge to touch her lips to his in a gesture of infinite tenderness.

"Does it pain you to be seen in public with me like this?" Devin asked her with a wry but stiff twist of his lips.

Her eyes met his. "Nay, Captain Chandler, not at all!" Indeed, he looked the gentleman, just as he'd looked at the ball, and still managed to take her breath away with the fine width of his shoulders beneath his broadcloth waistcoat. The sun gilded his long hair, which shone like a beacon, even in the daylight. "Rather, it pains me to see your hurts," she answered honestly. "We could have done this another day, perhaps, when your cuts and bruises are healed. Indeed," she narrowed her eyes slightly and took a quick inventory of his torso and legs, "are there other injuries that you hide even as you make light of those on your face?"

Devin instantly regretted his question, for obviously it had been concern for him and not embarrassment which had caused her eyes to avoid his so studiously at first.

"Indeed," mumbled Woodrow beneath his breath. "His brain has been so scrambled that he cannot think straight."

Both young people looked at him. "Woody's in a foul humor, I fear, from all the rum he downed at the governor's ball last eve. Men his age don't recover from overimbibing as quickly as in their youth."

"Hummph. I've seen you green around the gills as any untried youth from too much celebrating, Chandler," Woody retorted. "Now have some pity and cease baiting me." He smiled at Meredyth. "And mind your manners and pay the lady the attention she so richly deserves, lest I tell her that you're not really hurt at all, but rather had your Arawak accomplice paint your face and put a cork plumper in your cheek to puff it out."

This last was said with such obvious irony that both Meredyth and Devin burst out laughing. Devin was enchanted by her laughter and wondered if he would ever tire of it; he also knew that Woodrow Kingsley's unusually dour mood had been brought on by his concern for Devin and that eventually Devin himself could coax him out of it.

"Oh, Devin, now look what we've done!" she suddenly exclaimed, the merriment disappearing from her features like a shadow before the light. "Your lip is bleeding!"

"Serves him right," Woody muttered and folded his arms across his chest.

But Meredyth was already dabbing her linen handkerchief at his mouth. Were it not for the uneven cobblestones beneath the hackney wheels, her touch would have been as light as that of a butterfly, Devin thought.

He caught her wrist. "Don't bother," he said. "You'll stain your handkerchief, and 'tis just as easy for me to take care of it." With that, he flicked his tongue lightly over the cut and promptly made a face. "By the Mass, what did that Indian put in this balm? Tastes like gun powder." His upper lip curled with genuine distaste.

" 'Twouldn't surprise me," commented Woody, his gaze still on the sights about them, "considering he spent the night in the powder locker."

Devin gave him a long, considering look. Was his friend actually covertly threatening to draw Meredyth into the sordid little episode by appealing to her curiosity? And thus use his silent threat as leverage to get Devin to cease his work?

It was obvious that only good breeding prevented Meredyth from asking what had happened to him. He had to invent a story, and quickly, to meet Kingsley's challenge head-on and at the same time present Meredyth with a satisfactory explanation for his visible injuries.

He drew in a deep breath, which reminded him of the injuries hidden beneath his clothing, cut the breath a little short when his ribs protested, and looked Meredyth directly in the eye. "Of course, he probably has a point," he said, throwing a brief, bland look at his friend. "Henry Morgan flew off—frightened, no doubt—while Bakámu and I were in the hold. We had to hunt for him then, because the wretched bird wouldn't utter a peep, no matter how we called."

The appearance of a dimple heralded Meredyth's soft burst of laughter, and Devin thought how easy it was to make her laugh now, compared to when he'd first met her at the mission. She had transformed into a different person, it seemed, and he wasn't about to upset the applecart by mentioning Pelton's name or his part in the abduction.

"I made the mistake of splitting up with the Arawak—'tis always safer to have him under my nose to keep him out of mischief. But I thought I heard the parrot in the powder locker."

"Do I really want to hear this?" Woody asked no one in particular.

"Suffice it to say," Devin continued lightly, "I was ignorant of the fact that Bakámu was already in the locker, evidently crawling about behind some stacked powder kegs. Unfortunately, I moved so stealthily into the room that the Arawak didn't hear me." He rolled his eyes exaggeratedly, and Meredyth got the distinct impression that he was a master storyteller.

"But it seems the parrot did and shrieked some ungodly epithet, causing Bakámu to leap to his feet and overset one of the stacked powder casks nearby. More specifically, near me."

"You were hit in the face by a barrel?" Meredyth asked, her smile dissolving.

"We were both knocked silly, Lady Meredyth, and I'm not certain who's the worse for it." Not one of his more heroic tales, he thought. It made him sound as inept as the Arawak.

Meredyth covered her mouth with one hand but couldn't so easily hide the amusement in her vivid green eyes. " 'Twould seem you, indeed, have acquired a man who has devoted his life to you, at risk to your own."

Devin nodded. "Thanks, in great part, to your efforts, milady. 'Tisn't every day that a person like yourself braves the Blue Mountains of Jamaica and then the iniquitous Port Royal to right a perceived wrong."

Instantly, Devin knew he'd made a mistake as he watched her eyes darken with distress. She was thinking of Manuel, obviously, and he could have bitten off his tongue and tossed it to the gulls.

Without warning, the hackney lurched to avoid a horse-drawn dray loaded down with dozens of sacks of sugar. One of the coach horses reared up in the traces, jolting the vehicle and flinging Meredyth forward. Devin steadied her before he said over his shoulder to the driver, "Easy there. Attend to where you're going, man."

" 'E must be full o' drink," the coachman called back, obviously referring to the driver of the dray. "I make my livin' driving 'bout Port Royal," he said emphatically, "and I ain't caused any accidents yet."

"Well, just in case you're wondering," Woodrow said on a sour note, "your passengers are still in one piece."

"Drive past Fort Carlisle," Devin called to the coachman, "then on past St. Paul's and southwest along the periphery of the town."

"Aye, guv'na," the driver said and settled himself on his seat. "Where we endin' up, if ye don't mind my askin'?" he added over his shoulder.

"The Oyster House, at the end of Fisher's Row," Devin answered. The coachman nodded.

"If he doesn't pay attention, we'll end up in a collision with another dray," Woody grumbled.

Devin laughed aloud, glad for the distraction of the carelessly driven dray. It had obviously diverted Meredyth's thoughts from where he'd unwittingly pointed them. "He's just trying to get a glimpse of the most beautiful woman in all of

Jamaica." He winked at Meredyth with his good eye, and she smiled shyly.

"Silver-tongued Irishman," she teased, her eyes a-sparkle. There wasn't a trace of derision in her voice. "But if you insist on talking, your lip will never stop bleeding. However will you eat?"

He leaned forward and whispered conspiratorially, "I won't need to, Merry-mine. Just watching you will be enough for me." Woody threw him a look, but Devin ignored it, instead reaching into a pocket and taking out a black eye patch. "And I won't subject you to this eye any longer," he said. "Although I left my kerchief at home lest someone think me a pirate in the act of abducting you."

"You look striking, even with a stringed black eye-patch," Meredyth told him. "And where is your earring?" she asked with mock sternness, like a mother asking a child where he'd left his mittens.

He produced it from the same pocket with a grin. "Do you mind?" he asked.

Meredyth shook her head, her eyes suddenly shining with unshed tears, which he didn't notice at first as he bent his head to tie the string about it. As he put in the earring, however, he caught the glimmer of moisture along her lower lashes and stilled. "Merry-mine," he asked softly, "have I offended you?"

She lifted her chin and sniffed. "Nay, Captain 'Tis. . . . 'Tis just that you remind me of my father, who was a gentleman privateer." She lowered her lashes, then peeked up at him teasingly, "Of course he didn't wear a patch, he had no reason, but some among his men did . . . do."

Glad of her seeming recovery from her nostalgia, he said lightly, "I should someday like to meet the earl. He sounds like a fine man."

The eagerness in her expression, however, made him feel like a liar of the basest sort. Yet he couldn't tell her. And while he could understand her missing her home and family, not for the first time, the thought of Meredyth St. Andrews leaving Jamaica left him feeling oddly empty.

"Fort Carlisle!" the coachman called out, and both Devin and Meredyth were quickly distracted from their immediate thoughts, as he pointed out things of interest. They turned south to High Street and passed St. Paul's rectory and church. "And there's the exchange, a meeting place for the merchants," Devin told her, "similar to the 'Change in London, though on a much smaller scale." He pointed out the paved and covered walk along the north side of the church.

Devin showed her the herb and fruit market and the great market bell in the heart of High Street, the synagogue, the courthouse, a goldsmith's shop.

"I cannot believe how many buildings are on this narrow sand spit," Meredyth marveled aloud. "Surely one would think the city would sink beneath all the weight."

Devin nodded thoughtfully. "There are hundreds of two- to four-story structures, many of them brick and built upon hasty fills at the edge of the water to accommodate the rapid expansion."

Woody's mood seemed to improve, and he added, "No danger of sinking, I'd wager, but *sliding* off the sand could be another story. Foolish men give little thought to tall brick buildings resting on loose gravel."

Meredyth frowned thoughtfully as they continued along the southwest waterfront. Breakers came crashing in, spewing white foam into the somnolent tropical breeze. The air shimmered with heat waves, distorting the hazy silhouette of the Blue Mountains behind them. Sandpipers skittered across the sand, for this side of the town wasn't as heavily populated as the north side.

Devin watched the changing expressions flit across Meredyth's fine features and felt a rich and warm contentment settle deep within him from her obvious interest in her surroundings. And her seeming happiness at being with him.

Thoughts of Luke Pelton and Aaron Davies receded before

the sweet onslaught of her very presence, and other, equally important considerations faded. Even his aches and bruises seemed to subside in his growing elation. He caught himself picturing a little girl with rich, dark curls and sparkling green eyes like her mother's, or mayhap she'd be blonde, but her eyes would definitely be emerald. Perhaps she would have a naughty little brother or two to make her life a real challenge.

Love means loss, a voice warned unexpectedly. *Love means putting down roots . . . commitment . . .*

He frowned and caught Woody watching him as he watched Meredyth, a knowing look on the older man's face. It seemed to say, *Aye, settle down and have a family, lad, and get out of this sordid and perilous business.*

They were swinging west then, onto Fisher's Row, and the driver's voice rang out, "Yonder's Fort Charles!" His arm indicated the fortified structure at the southwest tip of the narrow, winding sand spit that ended in the city of Port Royal.

"And up ahead are the turtle crawls, or pens," Devin told Meredyth, "if you like turtle soup or mayhap beef and turtle stew. And a bit farther on, the meat and turtle market."

"And then The Oyster House," Woody threw in. "My stomach's a-rumbling."

Devin said, "We can hear it. If you continue to be pleasant, I'll see that it's soon filled."

"I shan't have turtle soup," Meredyth said to Devin, her eyes suddenly shadowed. "I prefer turtles for pets rather than my dinner." Her gaze returned to the approaching pens, and she quickly regretted admitting such a soft-hearted sentiment.

"I thought you favored anoles, milady," Devin said with a lift of one brow, making him look more rakish than ever. "You can have oysters, if you wish. Anything but turtles. Then . . ." His voice trailed off as he caught sight of a familiar figure at the side of the street, near the pens. Du Casse. There was no mistaking the tall, lithe form sporting the elegant periwig, in spite of Devin's hindering eye patch. And the Frenchman's companion was Luke Pelton.

Devin felt his body tense, and he fought the urge to halt the hackney, leap out of it, and challenge Pelton then and there. A muscle jumped along his jaw, and with an effort he directed his gaze away from the pair lest Meredyth notice them, too. His hand wandered downward to pat the reassuring bulge of the pistol in his boot cuff, and as he straightened, his eyes met Meredyth's. Her gaze briefly lowered to the almost hidden pistol butt, and as they returned to meet his, he read a keen intelligence in them. And a silent question.

"We're in Port Royal, Lady Meredyth, not London, though I know many who would also carry a concealed weapon in some parts of London." The statement sprang easily to his lips, but more and more Devin Chandler disliked lying to Meredyth St. Andrews. Even tiny fibs made his conscience point an accusing finger at his tongue.

"And, of course, I have a lady to protect."

Meredyth seemed to accept his last statement. "I don't question the wisdom of carrying a weapon, but you do have a cutlass at your waist, Captain. One could easily feel you are prepared for battle, and had you a cannon or two for good measure, my father would say you were about to order your crew to man their battle stations." She touched one finger to her lips while she regarded him consideringly (a mixed blessing for Devin because even though she might have put him on the spot, she couldn't get a glimpse of Pelton if her attention was on him).

"Devin hasn't lived to the ripe age of eight and twenty by being careless," Woody said lightly. "Privateers are often murdered for their caches of valuables—real or imagined—or the monies from such. A cutthroat could start handsomely with the takeover of a valuable ship like the *Lady Elysia,* milady. And Devin's town house was already ransacked while he was in England this past winter."

"Thank you, my friend," Devin said, *except for the part about the town house,* he added silently, for Woody could have told Meredyth the truth and raised all kinds of problems for him just to emphasize a fact that was becoming more and more a point of contention between them.

Pelton and Du Casse, still deep in conversation, were left behind as the driver picked up the pace of the horses. "That up ahead is Fort James," Devin told Meredyth, relaxing somewhat, "and around the corner at Lime and Queen's streets is our destination."

"So many forts," Meredyth commented with a shake of her dark head. She watched briefly through the open stockade gate as red-uniformed English soldiers went about their business. A British flag fluttered in the breeze from atop the outermost stone wall facing the ocean, and behind the fort, from the setting of the sapphire-domed Jamaican sky, the brilliant and blinding glare of the sun danced across a scintillating and shimmering sea. "To protect the harbor?"

Devin nodded. "Ours is one of the best natural harbors in the world. But the British, after wresting Jamaica from the Spanish, wanted to make it impregnable by heavily fortifying the reef that commands it and nearly encloses the entryway."

"Port Royal is now the greatest buccaneer stronghold in the Caribbean—larger and more strategic than Tortuga in Hispañiola," Woody added. He thumped his walking stick on the coach floor and leaned forward, quite animated now. "Many a Spaniard in his bed across the ocean has called upon God to destroy it and the men who use it as their base of operations."

"My father told me that buccaneers weren't welcome here after Henry Morgan became governor," she said.

Devin gave her an arch look. "Wouldn't you look the other way if the buccaneers preyed on Spanish towns and Spanish shipping?" he asked. "The governor encourages the presence of the brethren because they're unofficial allies of the English, unsavory marauders though they are."

A small group of ebony-skinned Africans were being herded along Fisher's Row and toward the docks. They looked miserable to Meredyth, stoop-shouldered and thin beneath their burdens—hogsheads and bundles of tobacco. It was obvious, for the moment anyway, their spirits had been brutally subdued. She cast Devin a look askance, but although his expression was unreadable, his jaw, for some reason, was set as firmly as sculpted rock. She couldn't tell how he felt about the scene being played out before them, yet the sight of those poor men laboring along the street beneath the hot sun brought back Luke Pelton's words.

Without warning, Devin's gaze met hers. He read the puzzlement in her expressive face—she wasn't good at hiding her emotions—and steeled himself for the question he hoped wouldn't come, ever.

"Such a sight is common in the Caribbean, Meredyth," he said in a voice devoid of emotion. "You'd best ignore it and look at the pleasanter side of life here."

The sound of his deep and normally expressive voice sounding like a cold stranger's sent a chill through her, but Meredyth told herself she was allowing Pelton to influence her and her opinions.

"Oyster House up ahead!" the driver called out.

And suddenly the cloud that had settled over her heart dispersed. Devin disembarked and extended a hand to her, his silvery-blue eyes warm and admiring. Woody followed.

"Want me to wait, guv'na?" the coachman asked, including Meredyth in the assessing look he gave his passengers.

Devin tossed him a coin, and Meredyth watched it glinting silver in the sunlight as it arced through the air. "Come back in an hour and a half or so," he told the man. "Wait if we're still inside. I'll make it worth your while." He held out one arm as he looked back at Meredyth, assuming an expression that made him look, she thought, like a handsome and wicked pirate with his patch and earring and long flowing hair. A buccaneer would have been an insult, for they were more often than not dirty and crude.

Eighteen

The interior of The Oyster House made it obvious that it did not cater to the rabble-rousers of Port Royal. It was a new, two-story brick building boasting glazed sash windows. One part of the first floor was for public dining; Meredyth caught a glimpse of bare wood trestle tables and benches. The other half was a private dining room, with cloth-covered tables and chairs and imported oaken wainscoting around the lower half of the walls. The room was brightly lit from its high sash windows facing west. As they were ushered into the private dining area, Meredyth saw that what looked like a billiard room opening off of it. The second floor, according to Devin, housed rooms for travelers.

The three of them were seated before a window, overlooking the open-air meat and turtle market and a small tiled building on the north side of the market.

When Devin noted their position, he said to Meredyth, "If you don't like this view, milady, we can sit elsewhere."

How considerate of him, she thought, and gifted him with a smile of gratitude that reminded him of emeralds and pearls shining beneath a benign sun. "The view is perfect." she told him. "We're far enough away from the market to avoid unpleasant sights, yet close enough to the street to be mightily entertained."

Devin placed one hand over his heart, his mouth forming a wounded moue (his lips were losing much of their stiffness, finally, though the cut still stung if his smile waxed too wide).

"My lady Meredyth, I intended to entertain you while we dined."

"On that note," Woody announced, getting to his feet with more agility than he'd exhibited in seating himself, "I'm off to visit with the Widow Timmons and her son across the way. If they'll do me the honor," he added, tilting his head in the direction of an occupied table at the other side the room.

"You old devil!" Devin said with a knowing look. "If you offer to pay for their meal, they'll surely invite you to join them."

"Would you rather I stayed?" Woody asked, his white eyebrows peaking innocently.

"Nay."

The answer came out so fast, Meredyth had to suppress a smile. Surely Master Kingsley was still subtly irking Devin for something that seemed to have been on his mind since they'd first arrived at her father's town house. And she had the distinct impression that it was somehow linked to Devin's mishap in the powder locker.

Woodrow was nodding at Meredyth and drew her from her musings. "I'll be close enough to keep an eye on our patch-eyed pirate here, yet far enough away to afford you a bit of privacy. But," he added, his look turning stern as his eyes met Devin's, "should he forget his gentleman's role and resort to boorish behavior, or worse—"

"Why, Kingsley, how could you even think such a thing?" Devin objected with a smile as guileless as that of a cherub in a Reubens painting. But for some reason he couldn't bring himself to say aloud that Meredyth St. Andrews had agreed to accompany Captain Chandler the privateer. The claim to gentleman had never been made to her, or anyone else.

An unexpected and totally uncharacteristic feeling of unworthiness ghosted over Devin, like the cold and formless fingers of a phantom. Fortunately, it was short-lived, and he suppressed a shiver. It wasn't that he'd ever considered himself worthy of wedding a noblewoman, but marriage had rarely come to mind in the past. And if it had, he'd dismissed the thought from his mind as readily as he'd fling away a piece of flotsam left on deck after a roiling sea.

"He's really being very considerate," Meredyth told Devin as Woodrow limped away.

"Kingsley?" he repeated in a shocked undertone as they sat. "I doubt it, Merry-mine. 'Tis more likely he's after a woman to look out for him in his old age. And about time, too."

Meredyth removed her bonnet, and he watched the light from the window catch the deep gold highlights that flashed here and there in her chestnut hair; he suddenly ached to run his fingers through its glossy length. He surreptitiously studied her pure profile as she looked through the window at the view of Fisher's Row, the market and the ocean beyond, then sat back and watched her openly.

"What's that small square building to the far side of the market?" she asked him without taking her gaze from the view.

As his eyes appreciatively traced every sweet contour of her face, he answered, " 'Tis referred to as the cage or lockup. Fort James is just beyond. They use it to discipline miscreants." He leaned forward and pointed toward a wharf just north of the lockup. "See that dock?"

"Aye," she leaned forward even more, peering through the glass, her movement emphasizing the creamy expanse of her neck and throat. He remembered the taste of her skin from the night before.

With an effort, Devin managed, "Just beyond that is the fort, and around the corner is Thames Street."

His words drew her attention away from the view and her eyes met his. Two points of color dotted her cheeks, and he knew exactly what she was thinking. He almost regretted reminding her. Almost, but not quite, for her reaction pleased him inordinately.

" 'Twas the most memorable encounter I've ever had on the *Lady*," he said softly, truthfully, losing himself in the clear, liquid depths of her eyes. "What are we going to do about it?" he added unthinkingly. He was suddenly and unexpectedly adrift in dangerous waters, yet couldn't seem to stop his wayward tongue, his impossibly euphoric expectations.

He felt as if someone else had taken over his very thoughts and speech. And dreams. He vaguely remembered that sweet and inexplicable madness that had overtaken him upon their first meeting. If he had thought it an unwelcome nuisance then, it hung over him now like a towering wave about to break. There was nowhere to run.

All depended on Meredyth St. Andrews' response.

Her lashes lowered, and the color in her cheeks deepened to an enchanting coral. It was all Devin could do not to reach over and take her into his arms and make her his in every sense of the word, declare her his before the other patrons of The Oyster House, before all of Port Royal, all of Jamaica, in the eyes of God.

Christ, I'm losing my mind, his sensible side thought, just like Woody had said. What if she expected the answer he really would never give, could never give?

No fear of that, Chandler, came the voice inside him. *You're just being decent about last night, trying to dissolve any guilt she might feel.*

"Naught for now, Captain Chandler," she said before his recreant tongue could come to his rescue. And she laughed softly, having the good manners and diplomacy to make light of the situation. "You cannot be gallant and offer to speak to my father, for he's halfway across the world. So we'll just have to . . . behave like a lady and gentleman, as Woody said."

The relief he told himself he should have felt turned to a ball of lead that sank to his feet, dragging his heart with it. "Or I could abduct you, like his lordship did the countess," his lips said in seeming defiance of common sense.

God evidently decided it was time to rescue Devin from himself and intervened in the form of a serving girl, who appeared just then at the captain's elbow. She placed a simple glass vase of orchids in the center of the table, gave Meredyth a half-smile, and turned her attention to Devin.

While Devin ordered for them, Meredyth took a peek at the girl, who was obviously of mixed blood. She was tall and slender, with lovely almond eyes and cocoa-colored skin. An intriguing combination, Meredyth decided. The girl's hair was concealed beneath a small lace cap, so Meredyth could tell nothing about its length, texture, or color save that it was dark.

"Oysters, milady?" Devin asked with a lift of one brow. "With fresh fruit and boiled vegetables, perhaps?"

Meredyth nodded. "Chocolate, too, if I may?"

Devin pretended shock. "What? No coffee? The Oyster House serves the best coffee in Port Royal!" He leaned toward her, peeled up the patch and peered at her with mock menace as he added, "Especially that brought in on the *Lady Elysia.*"

"Chocolate, please," Meredyth persisted prettily, meeting his look steadily from beneath the wealth of her dark lashes. "And coffee at the end of the meal."

"Touché," Devin commented, dropping the patch back into place.

She smiled, a smile as bright as the sun-drenched day. "Coffee is all the rage in London, but I still prefer chocolate."

He felt giddy with thoughts of her words concerning speaking to the earl. One did not speak to a young woman's father for anything less than courtship and marriage. Was she encouraging him, or being coy? Coyness didn't seem to be a part of her makeup, but Devin had learned that few women were ignorant of the art of coquetry when the situation called for it. And how well did he really know her?

Well enough, said his soft and smitten heart.

But he wanted to believe she felt something for him, something more than friendship, and surely her response to his lovemaking the night before indicated something more. Of a certainty, it had indicated trust.

He allowed his eye to wander toward the street, hoping to see something or someone—even Pelton—to distract him from his feelings, to prevent him from making an absolute fool of himself and drooling over Meredyth St. Andrews like a fawning St. Bernard. Years of holding himself aloof emotionally from people, especially the opposite sex, prevented him from giving her his trust in return. And, even more so, his love.

Or so he hoped. The very concept of such deep emotional commitment seemed to ceaselessly pop into his mind of late, and he knew it was because of the young woman beside him, looking at him and speaking animatedly.

Devin Chandler suddenly felt like a piece of driftwood, tossed to and fro on a churning sea of colliding emotions.

His self-doubt returned, even as he fought his impossibly high hopes. The Earl of Somerset might set him to keeping watch over his daughter, but marriage was another thing altogether.

". . . other cargo do you carry besides coffee?" she was asking him as the serving girl brought their coffee and chocolate.

The world suddenly grew dim, as if the sun had been covered by a cloud. The orchids in their dainty vase blurred into a kaleidoscope of color as he struggled to get hold of himself. His worst fears were going to be realized, it seemed, and there wasn't a thing he could do about it.

He took a sip of the aromatic hot coffee, scalded his sore lip, then set it down so quickly that the liquid sloshed over the rim and stained the clean tablecloth to one side of the cup and saucer.

He should have ordered Rhenish!

Meredyth, however, didn't appear to notice, for the moment after she'd asked the question, she'd once again presented him with her profile as she looked out the window. She raised her own drink slowly to her mouth, sipped, then replaced the cup with a soft clink, without even looking at the saucer. The tip of her tongue absently touched one corner of her mouth. Her eyes were slightly narrowed, as if she were viewing something puzzling or unpleasant.

"The usual cargo," he said when he'd collected himself and

could sound nonchalant. "It depends," he grinned his most charming grin (considering the state of his face), "on which way we're traveling."

Meredyth turned her head to meet his gaze and caught that very grin he fought so hard to feel. Her own mouth curved slightly in answer, but her eyes also held a suspended look.

The serving girl set a basket of fragrant, freshly baked bread before them and a small ramekin of creamy butter, thus interrupting the brief moment of expectation that had sprung up between them. "Bread?" he asked, offering her the basket.

As she buttered the crusty end she'd chosen, she remarked, "I was just curious, Captain, as my father still runs a shipping business."

He breathed a tiny sigh and smiled slightly, for exaggeration was one of his strong points. "The usual for a privateer—from the northern colonies and from across the Atlantic, the *Lady Elysia* carries aught anyone could need!" He waved a piece of bread in the air as he warmed to his subject. "Inexpensive clothing for the slaves and servants, wines from Madeira, the finest French brandywine, New England fish, pork, peas, and onions." He took a bite of the bread, washed it down with a sip of coffee, and continued. "We also bring in lumber." He thought a moment as he nestled his coffee cup into its dainty English saucer. "From Ireland, barrels of only the tastiest salted beef and firkins of the most luscious butter," he glanced meaningfully with his uncovered eye at the butter before them, "and the finest flour from the Chesapeake, New York, and Pennsylvania."

Meredyth's eyes took on their former sparkle as she listened to his melodramatic ramblings and allowed herself to be entertained by his antics. A good diversion, he hoped, and threw himself into it even more heartily. "But all that pales when compared to what we carry east across the Atlantic from the exotic Spanish Main—sugar, molasses and rum, tobacco, indigo, cocoa, cotton, and ginger."

Meredyth found herself suddenly gazing at the tanned flesh of his neck, the movement of his adam's apple as he spoke, a rich contrast to the alabaster of his neckcloth. She wanted to touch her lips to that strong, corded column, in the worst way. The very thought of kissing Devin Chandler anywhere sent a curling heat through her mid-section.

Stick to your purpose, a voice warned, interrupting her very physical thoughts. And then Luke Pelton's voice, *He masquerades as a semi-respectable privateer, but in truth he's up to his neck in the slave trade . . .*

"The *Lady Elysia* isn't a slaver, then?" she blurted as a wave of relief dissolved her dread of the answer.

He paused in mid-sentence, the warmth seeming to drain from his good eye. Very quietly, he asked, "Did she smell like a slaver, Meredyth? They say you can smell a slaver from five miles downwind."

She felt the blood leave her face at the memory of the stench of a slaver she'd seen upon her arrival in Port Royal. It was something she would carry with her forever.

"Who told you such a thing? Pelton?" he asked, startling her.

Something in his voice, however, the subtle shift in his demeanor, and the change in his eye, raised the hair on the back of her neck. "Do you always answer a question with a question?" she asked, trying to affect lightness.

"And is this the Inquisition?" he returned softly. One finger tapped the snowy tablecloth, for gentle emphasis. "I make a living from privateering, I don't apologize for that; but the *Lady Elysia* is not a slaver."

She lowered her gaze to the tablecloth as color touched her cheeks. "My apologies, Captain." Her eyes met his again. "I was merely curious and didn't mean to sound like a barrister."

The finger found its way over to the back of her hand, which she'd set down, loosely clenched, beside her plate. She felt the warm, callused skin stroke her own beneath; not a bold move, but rather the conciliatory gesture of a shy child who isn't quite certain what misdemeanor he's committed.

"Do you find the selling of one human being to another offensive?" he asked in a neutral voice.

"Aye!"

He waved a hand in the air expansively, seeming to have recovered from his brief but strange mood. "But a man has to make a living, sweeting, and the slave trade is the most lucrative business in the world! Except," he raised a finger, "of course, for the looting of Spanish galleons. Sometimes, as I said earlier, one has to . . . look the other way."

Meredyth had the distinct feeling he was testing her in some way. She knew it was dangerous to openly oppose slavery, especially when one was living in the very hub of Caribbean commerce, which included heavy slave traffic.

The oysters and vegetables arrived, and Meredyth took one look at the mound of shells before her and said, "I can't possibly eat all these!"

Devin laughed. "Whatever you don't finish, I'll take home to Bakámu. He'll love you forever if you feed him."

Meredyth raised her eyes to his, noted the teasing light, and said, "I don't know if that's a good thing or nay."

Devin looked surprised. "You don't enjoy almost being brained by falling boarding planks, milady?"

"No more than you enjoy walking into barrels."

Their laughter rang out, intermingled, his velvet bass, her sweet soprano, and several diners glanced their way, including Woodrow Kingsley.

"Andrew Timmons is looking at us," Devin said when he'd sobered. "More specifically, at you."

Meredyth bowed her head, trying to recapture a straight face. "I'm afraid I've made a spectacle of myself—of us."

"Nonsense," Devin assured her. "You have a sense of humor, and when you smile the whole dining room lights up. People are drawn to you like—" He snapped his mouth closed. And jarred his sore lip.

"Aye?" she pressed, meeting his look.

"Like I was."

Oh, what a mewling fool, Chandler, he thought. Dust off your heart and pin it to your sleeve, why don't you?

Meredyth extracted an oyster from its half-shell and popped it into her mouth. "How sweet of you to say such glowing things about me, but even were I the female version of the Pied Piper, I couldn't accept Master Timmons's attentions, or anyone else's."

Devin opened an oyster shell, then looked straight out the window past Meredyth. "Because of your humiliating experience with Pelton? Don't be absurd." He glanced at her askance. "He's lower than that scorpion at the ball, and it couldn't even dance." He chewed the oyster, then dropped the shell with a clatter.

"But, mayhap 'twasn't his—"

The doubt in her voice caught at Devin's heart. He suddenly set down his fork and leaned toward her. " 'Twas no one's fault but his own, Meredyth!" he said in an urgent undertone. "The man is . . ." He hesitated, uncertain of just what to tell her. The last thing he wanted or needed was Meredyth St. Andrews defending the knave who'd jilted her, then kidnapped and beat him senseless!

Anger and an alien jealousy made him careless. "Why don't you ask Pelton what he does for a living?"

"Why, he's in the shipping business and—"

"Aye. That he is!" He skewered another oyster from its shell, his eyes refusing to meet hers. "Tell me about your home," he added, obviously attempting to change the subject.

Meredyth, a bit bewildered by his sudden and uncharacteristic umbrage—although she thought mayhap she could understand how, after their tense meeting at the ball, the mention of Luke Pelton could irritate him—took a sip of chocolate and regarded him thoughtfully over the rim of her cup.

When his gaze met hers again, his eye seemed to hold a teasing light, as if he'd swiftly recovered his good humor. "Forgive me, Merry-mine," he apologized.

Eager to put the subject of Luke Pelton aside, Meredyth cast about in her mind for a safe and pleasant topic. "Your lady mother, Elysia, tell me about her. That is, if you don't mind my asking?"

He frowned slightly, then decided to be honest with her, as honest as he could be while revealing his mother had slept with a smooth-tongued Englishman and was subsequently left to live with the consequences of her actions alone and impoverished, until her early death.

"My mother was a sweet and gentle soul," he said, his voice softening with loving memories. "Her hair was dark as freshly turned loam, her eyes like indigo—at least 'tis how I remember her."

"An Irish beauty. But you don't take after her." She halted, appalled at what she'd said. "I mean, you're very pleasing to the eye," she amended, "but fair-haired. And your eyes are almost gray."

Devin laughed aloud. "Pleasing to the eye, am I?" he said, watching her blush enchantingly. "Thank you kindly, milady." He was glad of the chance to redirect the conversation, to avoid talking about his English father and Elysia's death. "But how about you? Where exactly in England do you live?"

"Somerset Chase, in Somerset." Meredyth realized he'd deliberately changed the subject and didn't press for more information. In fact, she felt her eyes mist without warning at the thought of home and family.

Somerset. Devin's heartbeat stuttered as if he'd received an unexpected and powerful blow. His father's family had lived in Somerset, England, and so had Devin for a while, before Southwycke's death and before he'd run off to Bristol to find a ship to take him back to Ireland, even though his mother was dead.

He'd never made it back to the land of his birth until he was a man grown.

"Of course," he found himself saying inanely. "I never associated your father's title with the county." The earl was one of the most powerful men in England.

An oyster stuck in his throat, and he took a drink of his

cooling coffee to wash it down. Why, just this one time in his life, couldn't the woman beside him have been common? Or the daughter of some minor noble whose title was hardly worth the paper upon which it was written?

"Aye," she said softly, her tear-filled gaze going to the street in an attempt to hide her distress. "Somerset Chase is the most beautiful place in all of England. Near enough to the sea to hear the murmur of the waves on a calm day and their roar in a high wind . . . Devin?" Her voice changed abruptly, and her hand blindly reached out for his arm.

"Aye, love, what is it?" he answered unthinkingly as her tense fingers dug into his coatsleeve.

"L—look . . ."

Look he did, with his one eye, and what he saw drove all other thought from his mind. Pelton and Du Casse walking toward the entrance of The Oyster House. He fought to rein in his temper. He couldn't just grab Meredyth and sneak out the back door like some puling coward, though it might have been feasible had he been alone. He had no wish to meet Pelton again until it was on his own terms and at the time of his choosing. He wanted every advantage, and he didn't want Meredyth involved in any way.

He felt like a rat trapped in swiftly rising bilge water, a sorry-looking rat, with a patch partially covering evidence of Pelton's perfidy and stinging memories threatening to blow reason to bits.

"You don't have to speak to him," he said, his mind racing. Then, with outward calm, he pushed back his chair and stood. "You'll excuse me, Lady Meredyth?" he asked, having decided to meet the storm head-on.

"Nay, Devin," she said, alarm rising in her splendid green eyes. "Don't—"

"You needn't be subjected to his egregious behavior again, nor need you fear I'll embarrass you in any way."

Meredyth caught a glimpse of another side of Captain Devin Chandler, the side that lurked just beneath his facade of near foppish disdain for all things serious, the side that had obviously made him a successful privateer captain. She knew that nothing she could say or do would prevent him from his course of action.

She helplessly watched him stride across the dining room, forboding crawling up her spine.

"Andreas?" Devin said to the Dutch-born proprietor who stood beaming at his customers from the doorway of the private dining room.

"Ja, Kapitein Chandler?" the short, bald man said.

"Is the billiard room occupied?"

"Nee, Kapitein."

"Good. There are two gentlemen entering your establishment," he said in a low voice and slipped a coin into Andreas Van Susteren's relaxed hand. The thought occurred to him briefly, and not without irony, that he'd always given Van Susteren an excellent deal on his coffee. "Please see that the one called Pelton goes directly to the billiard room, won't you?" He pressed the Dutchman's fingers closed around the coin. " 'Tis urgent—tell him that—but don't give him my name."

He turned and quickly disappeared into the billiard room, closing the door partially behind him. Whatever happened, he thought with a mental grimace, he didn't want to give Pelton the satisfaction of seeing what he and Davies had done to Devin's face.

Within moments, a sharp knock sounded at the panel, and it was pushed open. Cautiously, someone took a step forward. "Who wishes to speak to me?" a voice demanded. It was Pelton. "Identify yourself!"

Devin didn't answer, forcing the silence to stretch ominously. Pelton put a hand on his sword hilt and took another step forward. "I say, who—"

In a blink, Devin pounced on his nemesis from behind the door, one arm hooking around Pelton's neck and pulling him backward and off balance; the other hand gripped Pelton's sword hand and slammed it between his shoulders. He used the momentum to nudge the door shut behind him, tightening his hold until Pelton began to emit a choking sound.

With his other hand, he reached for the knife in his waistband and pressed its razor-honed tip against Pelton's cheek. "Now, you slimy pricklouse, let's see what you can do one on one, with the element of surprise on *my* side!"

Nineteen

"Identify myself like you did on board the *Bristol* last night?" Devin ground out in his ear. "I could easily kill you and consider myself within my rights, you know that, don't you, Pelton?" He eased up enough so his captive could speak.

Pelton let out a low growl, then a raspy, "Not . . . in . . . England!"

"We're a long way from England and civilization," Devin hissed right back. "You and Davies have already demonstrated that!"

Pelton struggled against Devin's hold. "Let . . . me . . . auuugh . . ." His command ended in a gasp as Devin tightened his forearm against his adversary's windpipe.

"Just shut up and listen, Pelton," he warned. "I don't care what excuse you give du Casse, just leave here! Do you understand? Don't even dare take yourself off to the public room. Just leave the premises. If you even go near the private dining room, I'll have you keelhauled on the *Elysia*'s trial run, after I break every bone in your body! You're not the only one who can employ cutthroats."

Pelton's labored attempts at breathing were the only sound in the room. Devin applied enough pressure on the blade to draw blood, eliciting a soft gasp of alarm from Pelton. "Just to let you know that I'm serious and that I have two pistols on my person, whatever you think, I'm willing to use them on you if you cause Lady Meredyth any distress or go crying to du Casse about this little encounter."

He jerked Pelton about so that they were facing the door. "Do you understand?"

Pelton grunted.

Devin eased his hold on the other man's throat, then quickly slid Pelton's sword from its sheath as he released his twisted arm. "You can come back for this another time," he said, as he flung the sword toward the wall. It slid to a clattering halt. "Now get out, and if you aren't gone from this establishment in three minutes, you'll learn the very last lesson of your miserable life: just how foolish it is to underestimate Devil Chandler."

With that, he gave Pelton a shove and immediately closed the door behind him. His lip was bleeding again and his head was aching from tension and his efforts, but he refused to be distracted.

He listened at the door for a few moments and could hear only the soft thud of Pelton's footsteps across the carpeted floor. Satisfied for the moment, he propped up the sword in the corner behind the door, then adjusted his waistcoat and sleeves. He pulled out his handkerchief and dabbed at the blood trickling from his lip, then folded it and wiped the dampness from his brow. He took a slow walk about the room, skirting the large billiard table, as he attempted to regain his breath and his composure, straightening his neckcloth as he went.

He glanced at his pocket watch, then tucked it back into his waistcoat, deciding that he'd give Pelton another minute before he returned to the dining room.

A thought struck him then, and he decided to go first to Van Susteren for one more favor.

Pelton was in a cold fury. He stalked along Fisher's Row, unmindful of the people around him. The only reason he'd left The Oyster House (after some lame excuse for giving his regrets to du Casse) was that he didn't want to be humiliated before the Frenchman. And Meredyth. With his sword sitting in the billiard room, blood on his neckcloth, rage boiled through his veins.

He held his handkerchief to his neck again, but this time it came away with only a faint smear of blood. He tucked it away and moved toward Thames Street, envisioning presenting Devin Chandler's head on a platter to—

"Master? Master Pelton?" a youthful voice called from behind him.

He whirled, ready to strike out at whoever was unlucky enough to seek him out at so inopportune a moment. A young lad in shirt and breeches, his feet bare, his mop of curling blond hair framing his cherub face, stopped dead, the look in his sky-blue eyes turning wary. His locks stuck to his sweat-damp brow.

"M—master . . . a message for ye." He thrust the missive toward Pelton.

"From whom?" Luke snarled.

The lad took a step backward, his arm still extended. From his hair and eye color and the myriad freckles and red blotches on his fair skin, Luke surmised he was Dutch.

"Don't know, master. 'Twas urgent though."

Luke snatched the note. "Where did you come from?"

But, nimble as a sandpiper, the boy was already scrambling away. "Oyster House," he called over his shoulder and ran off.

Luke's fingers froze. As he read the contents, the hand in which he held the note began to tremble. Then his fingers convulsed about the paper until his knuckles turned the color of bare bone:

Pelton:

    Choose your weapon and meet me on the field of honor near Gallows Point, two mornings hence. Bring your second, and I will provide the physician. I would challenge you on the morrow, but my ship has her trial run in the morn.

                                                           DJC

The last line was an open insult to Pelton and made him grit his teeth. Chandler was either a fool, as Luke had first thought, or a clever conniver. Whichever, he was infuriating, and Luke looked forward to killing him once and for all, damning Mad Dog and his interest in the accomplishment of the privateer captain's death. Davies had been foolishly trusting of Jack Denby, the man on watch aboard the *Bristol*, and hence they'd been foiled, affording Chandler this latest underhanded accosting of Pelton.

It was of no consequence to him that he'd done the same, and worse, to Chandler.

He dropped the crumpled note at his feet and turned back toward Thames Street, ignoring the hot noonday sun beating down on him with a vengeance. He had plans to make and carry out before meeting Chandler and killing him, whether honorably or nay.

Meredyth watched Devin approach their table, an anxious expression on her face. He looked calm enough outwardly, but his cheeks carried high color and there was a barely banked fire in his eyes when they met hers as he sat down.

"Devin, are you all right?" she asked.

He smiled, wincing as the cut on his lip pulled open again, and said, "My . . . business has been taken care of." He inclined his head toward the pile of oysters still before her. "And how is your meal?" He picked up a plate of fresh and beautifully arranged exotic fruit and extended it to her.

"I think when I leave Jamaica I shall miss the wonderful fruit and juice most of all," she said with a sigh as she speared a slice of succulent pineapple.

"What?" he said, outwardly wounded. "And here I thought 'twas me you'd miss first and foremost."

Meredyth set down her fork and leaned toward him. "Did you have a confrontation with Luke Pelton?" she asked, her lovely features taut with concern.

"Ahem. . . . Forgive the intrusion, *n'est-ce pas?*" It was Jean-Baptiste du Casse.

Devin slowly stood and acknowledged him with a nod.

"How good to see you again," Meredyth told him with a tight smile.

He bowed gallantly. "The pleasure is all mine, *mademoiselle.*" But Meredyth noted that the smile stopped short of his eyes.

"Were you looking for someone?" Devin asked with deceptive innocence as his eyes met du Casse's.

"*Pas vraiment.* Not really. I just thought mayhap you'd encountered Monsieur Pelton and were the cause of his abrupt and unexpected departure. As I'm leaving for Saint Domingue early on the morrow, I still have several things to discuss with him before I depart. He left here in a rush and with a rather vague explanation."

Devin held the Frenchman's eyes steadily. "Why would I ever cause his departure from anywhere, sir?" He felt Meredyth watching him.

Du Casse shrugged. "*Eh bien,* I'll just have to dine alone, then catch up with Luke later."

"How's the slave trade these days?" Devin asked with an unholy light in his eyes.

Du Casse narrowed his gaze at Devin almost imperceptibly before he said, "Lucrative as always, for the individual as for the French economy." He smiled suavely and bowed to Meredyth again, who appeared about to say something more to him. "*Alors, au revoir, mes enfants.*" She caught Devin's warning look and tightened her lips with mutiny, but remained silent.

As the Frenchman moved away, Devin reseated himself. "Thank you for not inviting him to sit with us, Meredyth. I do detest his kind."

"The French?"

"Nay," was all he would say.

Meredyth helped herself to more fruit, then passed the plate to Devin, a thoughtful frown chasing across her brow. "Monsieur du Casse is involved with la Compagnie de Sénégal, isn't he?"

Devin couldn't conceal his surprise at her knowledge of such matters when he looked up from his plate. "He is. Very involved."

The serving girl came over to refill Devin's cup, and she offered Meredyth a fresh one also for coffee. Meredyth sat back and watched the girl's quick, efficient movements. When the server left, she said, "As a lad of eight years or so, my father was impressed by a slaver captain. 'Tis a very painful thing for him to speak of, but Mamma told me it caused him great humiliation and nightmares for many years after. Once he escaped from that slaver and its captain's clutches, he never again sailed with any ship that dealt in slaves, nor did he ever allow his own ships to become involved in the business." She looked at Devin, a question in her eyes. "I can't help but feel the same—that is, I'm against one human being capturing and selling another. And I'm not afraid to admit it, even here in Port Royal."

"I respect your beliefs, Meredyth." He leaned toward her. "Just see that you don't launch any foolish campaigns while you are in the Caribbee Islands. 'Twould be foolhardy and downright dangerous, even for you." He smiled then. "Are you ready for something sweet to round out the meal?"

Her lashes lowered as she stared at the dark coffee in her cup.

"I certainly am," Woody said from behind them. He limped around to sit across from Meredyth. "I hope you don't mind if I join you again for a cup of coffee?"

Meredyth looked up, a greeting in her eyes. Devin's eye, however, held a very different message, but he merely sat back with a sigh.

"Did your friends leave?" Meredyth asked, glancing over her shoulder.

Devin's gaze followed hers, and, to his annoyance, Andrew Timmons nodded at Meredyth and smiled as he followed his mother from the dining room.

"He would have liked an introduction, Lady Meredyth," Woody told her benignly, "but Mistress Timmons—ever protective of her only chick—was appalled by the 'patch-eyed pirate' sitting at your table. She asked that I perform the introduction another time, when Devin isn't present."

Devin laughed dryly. "From what I hear, the widow Timmons doesn't want little Andrew introduced to any eligible female, no matter whose company she keeps." He made to stand. "Mayhap I should seek her out myself and—"

"Devin!"

Devin reseated himself with a hefty sigh and a seraphic smile.

Devil, indeed, Meredyth thought with an inward smile.

Woodrow shrugged and smiled at Meredyth. "But to return to the subject, Lady Meredyth's beauty and antecedents are more than enough to put to flight any objections a sensible mama might have. Except, evidently, for a borderline scoundrel."

"Then I'll just have to take it upon myself to become the lady Meredyth's constant companion—complete with cutlass and patch—if 'twill keep Andrew and his mama away."

Meredyth gave him a subtly assessing look, secretly pleased at his words. Devin Chandler's presence was comforting and titillating at the same time, and she was flattered by his stated, if unlikely, intentions. As she added sugar to her coffee, Meredyth acknowledged that, a few months ago, Chandler would have been the last person she would ever have considered appropriate as a suitor, even though she'd been taught that a man's worth came from within, not from a title or acquired wealth.

Quite unwittingly, images from the recent past flickered through her mind's eye, images of him as he'd looked during their first meeting high up on a mountain, near a waterfall, which held special memories for her mother and father: tall and splendid in face and form and a maddening combination of outrageous humor, arrogance, and menace.

Goose bumps skittered over her flesh at the thought, and liquid lightning spurted deep down where he'd touched her the night before. Languor sifted through her limbs like a warm spring shower.

". . . you just have an encounter with Pelton?" Woody was asking Devin.

"Briefly," Devin said tersely.

"I think 'tis high time you seriously considered shipping a substantially larger number of slaves," Woody continued, ignoring Devin's sudden irritation. "You might as well make it worth your while and take advantage of the demand around the Main."

Kingsley's words dispersed Meredyth's romantic musings like seafoam before a high wind. Her eyes went to Devin, but he was staring at Woody as if the older man had lost his mind. Only for a moment, however, for Meredyth noted how quickly his expression of bemusement changed to one of almost relaxed *ennui,* and he shrugged his shoulders. She was unwittingly reminded of his ability to act and, therefore no doubt, lie.

"We need not bore the lady Meredyth with such talk," he said with a vague smile of apology for Meredyth. But there was a barely concealed look of intensity in his eyes, as if he were gauging her reaction to Kingsley's revelation. "Especially when I have just convinced her that the *Lady Elysia* is not a slaver." His eyes cut to Woody, a stern warning in them.

Woody shrugged and took a gulp of coffee. "Devin dabbles in the slave trade, milady," he said lightly. "He'd be a fool to pass up such a potential for profit; but I've been trying to convince him either to get into it in earnest or get out."

There was no mistaking the emphasis on the last two words, and Meredyth frowned slightly, still possessing the presence of mind to wonder why, in spite of her shock.

But Devin knew exactly what his friend was alluding to and was sorely tempted to reach over and wring his neck. Obviously, Kingsley had decided that he could warn Devin to get out of the informant business to his heart's content in front of Meredyth St. Andrews. But he obviously didn't know of

Meredyth's aversion to the slave trade or, if he did, thought it less important than his self-imposed duty to protect Devin from his increasingly dangerous position.

Devin sighed and sat back, glancing momentarily out the window.

Meredyth, reeling from the revelation and the evidence that Devin had lied to her, stared at him, a kaleidoscope of feelings bursting through her.

He captured her gaze suddenly, carrying an indecipherable message.

"Are you ready to see the *Lady* by day? We're taking her for her trial run in the morn." His face lit up as he spoke of his refurbished schooner, his visible eye took on a glow of excitement.

She felt Woody's attention on her and was momentarily uncertain as to how she could gracefully refuse when visiting the ship today had been her suggestion.

"Surely you wouldn't want to miss the chance before you return to Father Tomas?" Devin prodded meaningfully.

"Of course not, Lady Meredyth," Woody added. "The *Lady Elysia* is one of the most beautiful schooners in the Caribbee Islands."

It was a conspiracy of males, she could tell, just like when her father and brothers had joined together to "persuade" Mamma or Kerra or herself of something about which they lacked proper enthusiasm. Well, she thought, what could it hurt? Especially when she need never see the captain again if she didn't so choose once she was back at the mission.

There was no possibility of Meredyth St. Andrews ever maintaining ties, especially of friendship or romance, with a man who bought and sold slaves, no matter how many or how few, and who lied to her. (Was he, in his own way, as bad as Luke Pelton? she wondered.) For now she would appease him and keep to the original plan for the day.

"Then, Master Kingsley," she said to Woody, "as a woman who appreciates beauty and the daughter of a former privateer captain, I would be remiss in not viewing the schooner by daylight."

But she didn't look at Devin. Rather, she finished her coffee and bestowed her sweetest smile upon the older man.

The *Lady Elysia* was a magnificent vessel, Meredyth acknowledged once again as the hackney came to a halt before the dock. The foresail and mainsail were unfurled, and a man perched halfway up the mainmast appeared to be testing the tarred stays that secured it. Watching him hurt her eyes, in spite of the hand that shaded them, for the bleached canvas was blinding-white beneath the coruscating Caribbean sun. The fine oak of the hull shone with new varnish and the polished brass fixtures vied for attention. The bowsprit, with its raven-haired siren as figurehead, had been carved with a loving and skilled hand. The woman looked almost real. Elysia, his mother, the mother he still loved enough to call a lady, was brought to vivid life through a woodcarver's mastery.

Meredyth felt Devin's gaze on her and, against her better judgment, lifted her face to his. He was watching her admire his ship. Had her expression softened with thoughts of his mother?

Not wanting him to interpret her sentimental bent as a softening of her umbrage with him, she was prompted to say, "The light of day flatters her, which is more than I can say for a woman exposed to the tropical sun." She reached down and donned her wide-brimmed apricot bonnet.

She tied the ribbons as Devin asked softly, "Would you do her the honor of rechristening her? I need all the luck I can gather while out at sea."

His words weren't soft enough.

"At this rate, you'll need all the luck you can gather anywhere you are," Woody mumbled acerbically as he alighted with the help of the coachman. He squinted up at them from the dock, as if daring Devin to explain his words to Meredyth.

Then, before either of them could react, he turned abruptly and limped toward the boarding plank.

Devin jumped down lightly and helped Meredyth from the coach. "Devin, I don't think I—"

"My friend is in a foul mood today, or haven't you noticed?" he asked her, deliberately brushing aside her halfhearted protest. "But don't let him unsettle you. There are a few business matters we disagree on . . ." He trailed off. At her bemused expression, he added, "He's not above prevarication or exaggeration, especially when others are present, to get his point across to me."

He put a hand to the small of her back and firmly guided her forward. Several men from the schooner acknowledged them with a wave, but Woodrow Kingsley's words stopped Meredyth cold. "Someday, if Devin lives long enough, ask him what really happened to him last night, milady . . ."

"Master Kingsley!" called a sailor from the *Lady Elysia's* deck, capturing their attention. "A message for ye." He came striding down the gangplank, and Meredyth was instantly reminded of her father's dear friend Peter Stubbs.

Devin introduced him as his boatswain, Red Flaherty, and Meredyth realized he was younger than Peter. But his build, his mannerisms, and his obvious confidence reminded her poignantly of the earl's former quartermaster . . . and home.

"I'm honored, milady," he said, executing a rough but adequate bow.

"I didn't know you could bend that far, Flaherty," Devin said with a straight face.

Red grinned. "At least I'm agile enough to keep my mug from bein' beaten to a pulp, Cap'n, though the patch is impressive, I'll say."

Meredyth caught the word "beaten" and wondered if the boatswain knew something she didn't.

Devin laughed. "Touché, you old rogue. What have you for Woody, here? A summons, mayhap, from the king? 'Twould delight me to no end if he were called away from Jamaica."

At Woodrow's look, he added, "Temporarily, of course."

"Yer man Standish said 'tis urgent that you return to the warehouse. He seemed mighty riled about somethin' er other an' made me promise to give ye the message prompt-like."

For a moment, Woodrow Kingsley's eyes narrowed consideringly at Flaherty. He glanced at Devin, then said, "Very well. But who'll take over as chaperon in my absence?"

"Why, Flaherty here," Devin said quickly. "Or any number of the men aboard the *Lady.*"

Woody cast his eyes toward the heavens. "God help us if I'm foolish enough to trust your crew with such delicate matters."

"What if we promise to stay on deck in plain view of all of Port Royal?" Devin asked with a wicked grin.

Woody's eyes narrowed again, as if he were gauging Devin's sincerity and the length of time he might be tied up at the warehouse with a problem.

"This is absurd, Kingsley. 'Tis broad daylight," Devin reminded him. "What can possibly be unseemly on the open deck before the world?"

"Nothing would surprise me," Woody said, "where you are involved." But he bowed to Meredyth and said. "I'll be back as quickly as I can, milady. Enjoy your tour." He arched a warning eyebrow at Devin before he swung back toward the hackney.

With a flourish, Devin offered Meredyth his arm, and they proceeded up the boarding plank, with Flaherty behind them. Once aboard, Devin introduced Meredyth to the crew members who were aboard at that time and proceeded to show off the schooner.

"I cannot tell you how disappointed I am that you were less than truthful with me, Captain Chandler," Meredyth said while admiring the view of the ocean from the stern of the ship.

"Is that why you're so quiet?" he asked, studying her profile at his leisure as he leaned against the rail.

"What do you think?"

"I know I didn't lie to you, Merry-mine. My ship is not a slaver."

"But you carry—"

A shrill whistle cut across her words. "Female aboard! Our goose is cooked! Squaaawk!"

Devin and Meredyth turned to see Bakámu making an unexpected appearance with Henry Morgan on his shoulder.

"I wondered where you were, Arawak," Devin said dryly, eyeing the bottle of brandywine and two goblets the Indian carried on a small, round tray.

Meredyth noted that Bakámu looked only a bit less battered than his master.

"Bakámu in cabin, brought re-feshmens for Chan-ler and lady." He executed what passed for a bow to Meredyth, no mean feat considering his burden and the fact that, doubtless, bowing wasn't an Arawak form of greeting.

Devin pictured the tray tilting and its contents sliding onto his clean deck, but he held his tongue. He didn't want to distract the Indian.

He looked at Meredyth, a question in the lift of one golden brow, amusement in his voice. "Would you like some brandywine, Lady Meredyth?" he asked with pure deviltry in his eye. "Remember, all of Port Royal could be watching."

Unwilling to risk hurting Bakámu's feelings, Meredyth said, "Then I think Port Royal would approve, given its reputation." And what harm could one glass do, she thought, having just eaten her fill at The Oyster House?

Devin studied her for a moment, looking absurdly wicked, and absurdly masculine, in his eye patch. Meredyth thought he was about to advise against it, but he reached for the bottle, uncorked it, and poured the rich, garnet-colored wine into the goblets. He handed her the first, took the second for himself, then motioned Bakámu to set down the tray.

The Indian backed away, wearing a sublimely silly grin, and Devin wondered what he was up to. Then he remembered Bakámu's surprise for Meredyth below decks. Well, it would be nigh on impossible to get her to his cabin now. Or would it?

"Female on board, mates! Bad luck!" bawled Henry Morgan.

"To your stay in Jamaica," Devin said as he lifted his goblet. "May it continue indefinitely and fulfill your fondest dreams, Lady Meredyth, as it has mine."

Meredyth found herself momentarily without words in the wake of his tender declaration. Or was it his facile tongue and penchant for exaggeration?

She smiled her appreciation of his toast, her gaze locked with his, and recklessly downed several swallows of the brandywine.

Twenty

He felt like he'd just leapt into an abyss blindfolded.

And he realized that he was in love with Meredyth St. Andrews—wholly, unconditionally, irrevocably. He, a bastard privateer captain, was head-over-heels in love with the daughter of the Earl of Somerset, the man who had entrusted her to his care. More fool he, Devin thought with an inward grimace.

Or had the earl had a secret agenda? Was Devin the fool, and not the clever earl? But why would an earl ever take the chance of sacrificing his daughter or her reputation?

He couldn't think. He was being drawn into the vivid and irresistible depths of Meredyth's eyes, like a man inadvertently floating too close to a whirlpool, and being helplessly swept into its dizzying vortex.

He downed the goblet, watching her over the rim. She raised her glass again and took another drink, as if in answer to his challenge. Then, nudging him from his trance, she said, "Why did you lie to me, Captain Chandler?"

"I didn't lie," he said, as he reached for the bottle of brandywine. He was going to need the whole bottle to find his way out of this one, he acknowledged. "The *Lady Elysia* is not a slaver. Never was, never will be."

"But you carry slaves, Master Kingsley said so. And you didn't deny it. So you lied by omission."

"I omitted nothing. You asked what cargo we carried. I named that which we carry most. There are other goods we carry, but I didn't name every single one."

Fire lit her eyes, reminding him once again, of the earl. "If you've ever carried *one* slave, 'tis too many!" she insisted and took another sip of wine before turning back to the view of the sea behind them.

He moved closer to her, until his lips were at her ear. "And you had better keep your voice down, Merry-mine, and your dangerous and unpopular opinions to yourself. You're in the Caribbee Islands, not some English drawing room far removed from the real, brutal world. You can get yourself killed if you make known your vehement opposition to the wrong people."

By the Mass, hadn't her father warned her of such things? he thought in exasperation. But it was fear for her that prompted his warning.

Sometimes the powers that be unfairly toyed with a man's life, much like a great cat batting about a confused and bewildered mouse. It was imperative he warn her about her radical views on the slave trade, views exactly the same as his own; yet it was equally imperative he hide his same feelings pertaining to slavery. In fact, he had no choice but to lie, for his own protection as well as hers.

It was obvious, by his words at The Oyster House and on the dock today, that Woody was willing to throw a wrench in the works by fair means or foul to get Devin to cease his activities. He supposed this latest altercation on board the *Bristol* had been the last straw for the older man, who had been like a father to him for as long as he could remember.

Woodrow Kingsley was obviously mellowing in his old age and becoming much too concerned with Devin's safety when there were more important issues at stake.

Meredyth was staring at him in disbelief. "Do you think, even though I'm a woman, that I would allow that thought to bully me into silence?"

His lips twisted with rue. "Probably not." He wanted nothing more in that moment than to make mad and passionate love to her, to transform that troubling frown into an expression of pure, sensual bliss.

"Señorita Mer-dyth!" came Bakámu's voice from the aft hatchway.

Devin sighed to himself at the interruption, then realized he should be grateful for the timing of the Indian's reappearance. The conversation had not been going well.

Meredyth turned away from the rail and mustered up a smile for the Arawak. "Aye?" she said.

"Need more wine, *sí?*" he said, pointing to her empty goblet.

"I think not," Devin answered for her.

An imp, a small but interesting legacy from the countess, leapt to life within her. It wasn't Devin Chandler's place to tell her when she'd had enough wine! And she glanced down at her glass before holding it out to Devin, who still held the bottle.

Bakámu eagerly snatched the bottle from his master and refilled her goblet. He smiled with obvious satisfaction at Meredyth and said, "Bakámu have surprise in cabin. Chan-ler's lady come see?"

Devin leaned back and crossed his arms, a moue of expectation shaping his mouth. He knew she liked Bakámu and would have wagered the schooner itself that she would never hurt the Arawak's feelings for aught; yet she also knew it was improper to be alone with any man belowdecks.

What would his Merry do? he wondered with a wicked glint in his eye.

"Henry Morgan ain't afeared!" the African gray bawled from the rail, and Devin had to smother a smile. For once the parrot's timing was on the mark.

"He's been working on this project all morn," he added helpfully. "Ever since I told him how much you admired his woodcarving skills."

Meredyth looked from Bakámu to Devin, then back to Bakámu, slightly at a loss. The wine didn't help, or mayhap it did for it was tasting better with every sip. "What if we await Master Kingsley's return?" she suggested, coloring at the implication that she couldn't be trusted with Devin Chandler.

Bakámu's expression fell. He hadn't been privy to the conversation earlier, and even if he were, Meredyth wondered if he was familiar with the concept of "chaperon." If he were, would he care about following decorum when the use of the custom implied mistrust of Devin Chandler, the man to whom he was absolutely committed?

"Oh come now, man," Devin said to the Indian. "Don't look so disappointed. Obviously, Lady Meredyth wishes to wait for Master Kingsley's return and 'twon't be so long, I wager."

But Meredyth caught the subtle challenge in his words, and when she looked at him, he held up his glass in a mocking salute. If there was one thing Meredyth St. Andrews couldn't resist, it was a challenge. Especially while drinking potent brandywine as if it were water.

She looked contemplatively at the goblet, as if seeking the answer there, then at Devin's Chandler's face. He'd thrown a gauntlet at her feet, as surely as if he were formally challenging her to a duel.

"Very well," she said to Bakámu and Bakámu only. "I'll go with you for a moment. Then we'll . . ." she gave Devin what she hoped was her best aristocratic, down-the-nose, look, "rejoin Captain Chandler on deck."

The Arawak's look brightened until she mentioned Captain Chandler. "No Chan-ler?"

Meredyth handed Devin her goblet, as she would a servant, lifted her lovely chin, and said, "No Chan-ler. Do you wish to show me or nay?"

The Indian's eyes narrowed slightly. Devin knew that look. He could smell the wood burning. Surely Bakámu was even more devious than himself, and soft-hearted, righteous Meredyth St. Andrews was his perfect dupe; she'd already demonstrated that.

He stifled a smile, gave Meredyth a half-bow, and watched

her follow the Arawak. "Enjoy, Merry-mine," he said very softly. "While you can."

Meredyth studied the half-finished relief in the teak paneling. Positioned just across and down a little from Devin's face was Meredyth's emerging face. Bakámu hadn't begun her hair yet, but it was definitely her face. She felt heat steal over her cheeks at the thought of her face so near Devin Chandler's in the intimacy of his private cabin, teakwood carvings or not.

There was something not quite proper about it, but exactly what it was eluded her wine-inhibited thoughts. " 'Tis lovely," she said to Bakámu, smiling blearily at him.

Marry come up! she thought with a vague sense of alarm, she suddenly needed to lie down or get back up on deck in the cool sea breeze and sunshine. The stuffiness of the cabin was only adding to the dizzying sensations sweeping through her.

She felt simultaneously invigorated (why, she could have been the Queen of England!), ready to take on the world, and languorously drowsy. She felt like indulging in a nice nap in the bunk behind them. Surely, after a refreshing nap, she could sail this beautiful ship all by herself!

She pictured Devin Chandler's hands over her own on the *Lady Elysia*'s wheel and yearned in some deep and secret part of her to feel his flesh against hers.

Face flaming, she looked up at Bakámu, who was studying his handiwork with an unmistakable look of pride imprinted upon his coppery features. His dark eyes met hers suddenly. *"La señorita Mer-dyth.* Chan-ler's woman." He fairly beamed.

"It's quite obvious, isn't it?" Devin said from the open doorway.

His voice sent a frisson through Meredyth and a minor prick of annoyance, the latter a sop to her dwindling sense of propriety. What was he doing here? she wondered, fighting her uninhibited physical response to his presence.

"Chan-ler's woman!" shrilled Henry Morgan from Devin's shoulder. "Squaaawk! Bad luck!"

She whirled, feeling the cabin move with her (or was it her imagination?), and affected irritation. "What?" she began as her eyes went to his face, her flawless brow furrowing.

"At least on the paneling, I should say," Devin corrected himself over her fledgling protest.

Was that a smirk on his bruised but beautiful mouth? she wondered, feeling growing anger at herself for having imbibed the wine and being lured into his cabin. Didn't she know he was a scoundrel? A devil?

She glanced at Bakámu, who was staring at the floor, a blush riding his cheeks. Without warning, his dark eyes encountered hers again, and the Arawak actually had the temerity to grin, inane though it was. He shrugged, obviously for once at a loss for words. "Bakámu take bird, *sí?*" he said, with the sudden enthusiasm of a man who'd just discovered a chest of Spanish treasure.

He hurried over to Devin, held out his finger to Henry Morgan, then transferred the parrot to his own shoulder as he slipped into the passageway. Meredyth started to follow him, her bonnet swinging by its ribbon from one hand, hoping the cool expression she tried to assume would discourage Devin from trying to dissuade her, or, worse, physically prevent her.

Devin's foot nudged the door closed behind him. Like an omen, the latch clicked into place, and Meredyth found herself staring in dismay at a solid oaken panel. Her fingers curled into fists at her sides.

Then he was saying in her ear, "We have some time together, Merry-mine, before you leave for the mission."

She started at the flutter of desire that tickled her insides as his warm breath caressed the tender flesh of her earlobe. "Flutter" was an understatement, she had the presence of mind to acknowledge, for the feeling was more like a swarm of butterflies. "You. . . . You're a knave, Devin Chandler," she accused and retreated a step.

"I never claimed to be aught else." He took a step toward her.

"I'll call for your men," she threatened, never dreaming he would really ravish her. "I'll pound on the door and someone will hear me!"

"My men are loyal to me and only to me. Coming to your aid would be tantamount to mutiny."

"We're not at sea!"

"Ah, ever the privateer's daughter, aren't we?" he said with a quirk of his sinfully seductive mouth.

She came up against the wood frame of the bunk. "Don't make me desperate," she blustered, suddenly the smallest bit afraid of what could happen.

"Why not, Merry-mine?" He narrowed the distance between them. "I've been a desperate man ever since I first set eyes on you and your splendid eyes, your perfect nose, and your come-hither mouth. That sprinkle of freckles that captivated me from the very first, that glossy wealth of hair that beckons a man's hand until it itches. You had 'do not touch' stamped all over you, but, fool that I was, I dared allow you to creep under my guard and into my heart. You, the daughter of an earl, who thought I was naught more than a cutlass-wielding pirate.

"You, a kind and generous soul who seemed to open your arms and heart to me, insisting I tread where I had no business going."

He shook his head in mock perplexity. "And now you say me nay? Now you become prudish—not at all like last night, I might add. I could have taken your maidenhead in a blink. We were that close!" He leaned toward her, beaming his single eye into hers. "And can this sudden reticence possibly be because of something Woodrow Kingsley said? Something I neglected to tell you when I was listing the cargo I carried?"

She shook her head, unexpectedly touched by his words. "Nay! 'Tis my reputation, think of that!"

"Did *you*, Meredyth?" he asked softly, inexorably. "Did you when you recklessly followed Bakámu down here?" The import of his words sobered her like a splash of icy water. "You're either wanton or a fool, milady. Or mayhap you're in love?" His voice lowered to a whisper with his last words.

He was dead serious, hoping against hope she would tell him with her lips what he thought he read in her eyes.

"Or will you let a common privateer tumble you but never stoop to consider sharing such profound feelings with the same man?" he pressed, needing to push her to some kind of admission.

But he didn't expect the admission he got.

"Nay!" she cried, her eyes filling, to her dismay. " 'Tis more than what Master Kingsley said! Luke Pelton told me the truth this morn. Kingsley only confirmed it."

His heart stumbled in its steady cadence. "Pelton? You spoke to Pelton this morn?"

Meredyth tried to move toward the door but was blocked by his right arm propped against the small bedpost. "Meredyth?" Her name on his lips was this time a captain's command to divulge all.

"Aye! He came to speak to me, to warn me about you. He said . . . that you were up to your neck in the slave trade." A tiny hiccup escaped her lips, to her chagrin, and she loftily lifted her chin in sweet defiance to collect her dignity. One of her dark curls dislodged and came sliding down from her crown to nestle impudently against her soft, flushed cheek.

Devin couldn't help but laugh, which did little to enlighten her. He threw back his head and indulged himself for a moment. "Up to my neck in the slave trade, love?" He gestured with his left arm to his cabin behind them. "See you any evidence of such a thing?"

"What, pray tell, would I see in your cabin to prove or disprove the claim?"

He lifted one shoulder. "I have no idea. I only thought to point out the absurdity of what Pelton told you when you told me yourself the *Lady* doesn't smell like a slaver. Even empty of cargo, the stench of human misery would be unmistakable."

"But. . . . But you do carry them and are considering . . ." His warm, wine-kissed breath sighed over her face, and she watched his lips, quite unexpectedly mesmerized by their shape and mobility, in spite of the slit that threatened to bleed when he smiled broadly.

"Carrying a handful of slaves can hardly be called 'being up to the neck in the slave trade.' "

"But . . ."

A thought struck him. He frowned, looking suddenly sinister with his black eye patch. "Did he touch you? Did he hurt you in any way?" His words were soft but full of menace.

Meredyth shook her head. "Nay, but he said—"

"Nay," he cut her off, "he merely filled your head with lies, the swine."

She stared at him, her lips parted innocently, but oh-so-temptingly, as if she wanted to believe him but was still tethered by Pelton's interference.

And so the renegade Englishman was obviously bent upon creating a rift between them first by his bold actions this morn, then by his having followed them to The Oyster House.

But Luke Pelton would die as he deserved in two days and wasn't worth Devin's time or the energy expended in anger.

Devin's hands went to her shoulders and his lips touched hers with infinite gentleness before he pulled briefly away to whisper, "What has all that to do with what is between us, Merry-mine? Will you be Merry-mine? For always? If your father doesn't keelhaul me for even thinking myself worthy of you?"

Their mouths joined, and Meredyth's half-hearted objections scattered like clouds before a dispersing wind. He tasted of sea breeze and wine and male, and a tincture of metallic to remind her he'd been hurt the night before. For some reason, that thought brought on a wave of tenderness and concern to combine with the warmth seeping through her like some insidious and powerful drug. Languor spread through her limbs, her trunk, and her most secret and sensitive of places began to weep for him, as nature began preparing her for what was to come.

She removed the patch that hid his one eye from her, and he didn't object as it dropped to the floor behind him. Then she was drawing his face toward her again and touching her lips to the bruised area with feather-light kisses.

"Meredyth," he murmured and began to remove the pins from her hair. He wanted to run his fingers through that wealth of dark and glossy mane. He would never tire of savoring its silken softness as gossamer strands caressed his callused fingers, entwining about them like a lover's arms.

He knew not how long they had been there, though Flaherty would no doubt go to his death in the name of following Devin's orders and Kingsley would be furious. But Devin wasn't about to give up this opportunity. He'd never told a woman he loved her, had never loved a woman more than physically. Meredyth St. Andrews was different and the intensity of his feelings frightened him, for there were so many things that could go against him. Probably would, if he would allow himself to be realistic. But he wanted to bind her to him, praying that between what he suspected Meredyth felt for him (if it weren't only his pitiful hope), and what the earl would be forced to do to salvage his daughter's reputation (if he didn't kill Devin first) somehow he would have her for his own.

He was a foolish Irish bastard, with a pocketful of dreams that was even more foolish.

He didn't—couldn't—think of the consequences of his plans going awry.

In seeming answer to his thoughts, Meredyth was impatient, thunder pounding along her veins as the wine dissolved her inhibitions and her heart was claimed beyond redemption by this scoundrel called Devil Chandler. Suddenly, her lips were at his throat, where his neckcloth was open to reveal that fine bronzed column she'd often secretly admired. Her tongue tickled his adam's apple before tracing a slick path down to the hollow of his throat. The feel of his strong and steady pulse was erotically stimulating against her seeking tongue, and Meredyth made no protest as she felt his fingers slide from her hair to the fastenings at the back of her gown.

She wanted to give herself to Devin Chandler, more than anything she'd ever wanted in her life. It felt natural and good and right. There was an almost mystical connection between their souls, and Meredyth wanted to explore this and discover exactly why she was willing to give him what she'd given to no other.

But he all but admitted he carries slaves, warned a faint voice. Her blood was singing through her body, however, pounding in her ears, and desire dissolved that warning voice in an instant.

She allowed him to undress her and lay her upon the bunk, then he stood before her. She watched him, as tremors rippled through her awakened body, in the wedge of sunlight that bathed his form as he swiftly shed his clothing. He was magnificent, she thought as her gaze moved from his solid and lightly hair-sprinkled chest down to his narrow waist and the flat planes of his belly and the downy golden arrow that drew her eyes to the shadowed nest of his masculinity.

She drew in her breath, her face flaming and her core suddenly flooded with liquid fire, bathing her anew in heated moisture and causing her thighs to part in a natural reaction to his coming.

"You're breathtaking, Merry-mine," he said in an awe-tinged voice as he moved onto the bunk beside her. One finger traced the slope of her pert nose. "From the crown of your head to the tips of your sweet little toes. And I want you more than I've ever wanted anything in my life. Say you want me, too, my love." He waited expectantly, feeling balanced on the tip of a swordpoint at the mercy of a whimsical wind. Only the sound of her sweet voice reciting the right words could gently nudge him to the haven of her genuine love or impale him upon the rejection he feared.

Unaware of Devin's inner turmoil, Meredyth felt the fever within her grow apace with his nearness and his wondrous words that were music to her ears and balm to her half-healed pride. She felt like she was flying under the influence of the brandywine and, even more, the reverent look in his eyes, the gentle sound of his voice. Meredyth felt she was approaching the pinnacle of something she couldn't quite name, nor did she really think about it or attempt to define it.

He was watching her, a smile curving the corners of his mobile mouth and, she realized, waiting for her to speak.

"Aye," she murmured, feeling utterly wanton and reveling in the sensation beneath the tender heat of his gaze. She felt like a fledgling green shoot, opening herself to the warmth and benevolence of a bright spring sun. And she wanted that same sun to nourish and sustain her, to bring her to full maturity and blossoming.

She smiled into his eyes, feeling like she was floating in a sea of pleasure, and she wanted the man beside her to join her. Her arms twined about his neck and she didn't have to exert much pull to bring his mouth down to hers.

As they kissed, their tongues entwining and retreating in the clash and play of that primal ritual, he stroked the velvet skin of the side of her breast, then traced down to the sweetly curving cay of her waist. Meredyth moaned a soft protest as he withdrew his mouth and slid slightly down her body, leaning over so the ends of his blond hair tickled her belly. He brushed his lips against the pink striations from her corset lacings at the side of her waist that crisscrossed her otherwise flawless flesh. "No need for these," he murmured, his breath sighing over her ribs like a zephyr. "You've no need for those torturous underthings."

His tongue then dipped down to her navel, circling teasingly, before it lowered and turned her blood molten. Meredyth felt the heat threaten reason—her very sanity—as that most exquisite tension gathered within her, just like the night before, promising her everything and more.

His questing tongue parted the hair of her pubis and touched that most sensitive of places, opening her cleft and stroking it, making Meredyth writhe beneath him. When he found the small, silken bud he sought, he gently nipped it with his teeth, and she stiffened, her fingers digging like claws into the mattress beneath her.

"Devin," she murmured, " 'tis wicked, this thing we do . . ."

"Shall I stop?" he asked, raising his head and watching the passion suffusing her features.

Her hands in his hair were all the answer he needed, as she pulled him toward her again. He worked his magic with his tongue until he could hold himself back no longer.

"Ah, Merry, my love," he crooned softly as he straightened above her. "I cannot wait any longer to make you mine. Do you understand, sweet?"

She opened her eyes, deep and luminous as twin pools in an enchanted forest, and looked into his. "Aye, Devin. Take me to heaven again," she whispered. "Please."

Their mouths met once again, and Devin positioned himself over her for a suspended moment, then, with a graceful twist of his hips, he entered her. She stiffened slightly when he encountered the barrier proclaiming her innocence, and in one last moment of swiftly fleeing sanity, he hesitated.

She groaned again at his hesitation and wrapped her legs about his waist in an effort to continue their loveplay.

Devin pulled his lips from hers long enough to reassure her, "The pain will be quick, then 'twill disappear, love, never to return again. Trust me."

Their eyes met and held as he thrust through her maidenhead then, watched her eyes widen in surprise, then her features tauten with pain. He stilled again, resting within her. "Forgive me, Merry-mine," he whispered. "I'd never hurt—"

But Meredyth had raised her head just enough to touch her lips to his, and she began to move her hips beneath him, establishing her own rhythm of rapture. Devin kissed her deeply, swabbing the honeyed recess of her mouth with his tongue as he sheathed his pulsing manhood within the hot, wet silk of her, joining in the age-old tempo of love and procreation in the corresponding recess between her thighs.

He felt her contractions and pulled his mouth away to look into her eyes. They were glazed with passion as they stared back, reflecting his own tumultuous emotions as, with unspoken words and the language of his body, he pledged himself to her forever.

They delighted in watching each other as they increased the tempo of their intense and erotically choreographed mating, until the room silently exploded around them, setting them free, free of mortal constraints and cares, raising them above all the petty and paltry human concerns, as for a single, blissful moment they became one.

Twenty-one

As Meredyth lay in his arms, she felt warm and secure, like she belonged there. Sleep drifted over her. She dozed.

"Merry?" he said softly. His gaze caressed her relaxed features.

"Ummmm?" she murmured, only half-awakened at the sound of his voice. She snuggled closer to him, and her hair tickled his nose.

It was lovely, he thought, spread out like a rich, umber shadow about her head, over one shoulder, and down to her breast. His breath caught for a moment. Just like the rest of her.

Oh God, he thought, the threat of heartbreak looming over his head like the sword of Damacles. There wasn't one part of or one thing about Meredyth St. Andrews that he didn't love. All the more fool, he.

"Merry!" he said with more emphasis as he attempted to interrupt his rogue thoughts. "Wake up, love. I've decided to try and restore your reputation."

And ruin my life in the process, as any deserving lovesick fool, he added silently.

The laughter in his voice brought her back from Morpheus' embrace. Her lashes lifted and her green gaze met his, just in time to accept the token kiss he lightly brushed across her half-parted mouth.

He smiled into her eyes. "Did you hear me, Merry-mine?

How do wedding bells sound to you? Mayhap I can even send for Father Tomas?"

He surely was mad, but it was unexpectedly of tantamount importance that he salvage her reputation. If she wanted a marriage in name only, then later an annulment, he would go along with it. Surely, he thought with an inward grimace, it was the least he could do after deliberately luring her down to his cabin and into his very bed.

Devin's sudden attack of conscience even included deciding that, as much as he would have had it otherwise, Meredyth St. Andrews could never love him and surely wouldn't hesitate to accept his offer to save her name and then toss him aside as soon as legally possible.

His words penetrated her fog of confusion, and as she gazed into his eyes, she caught a suspended moment of unguarded hope and something more. Or was it her imagination and the aftereffects of potent brandywine?

Then, as quickly as it had appeared, that glimpse into his heart was gone, and the light in his crystal-blue eyes turned teasing, irreverent, as if the entire matter of her deflowering and his offer of marriage were no more than one of his outrageous jests.

Meredyth suddenly remembered she was lying naked in his bed, in his arms. He was as naked as she was, although obviously as unconcerned about it as if it happened every day. Of course, nothing was beneath Devin Chandler. Why she'd allowed herself to be charmed and seduced by him surely had more than a little to do with the brandywine, though her sense of fair play told her she couldn't blame her reckless drinking on him.

She grabbed the sheet and pulled it over her body, at the same time pushing away from him, and coming against the solid wooden wall. Her head still buzzed from brandywine and sensation tingled through her, but in the aftermath and in the face of that wicked grin he now wore she felt the beginnings of shame and humiliation. This was different from the night before. She was no virgin now, and it didn't take a Sir Isaac Newton to realize it!

And to make matters worse, he'd actually had the gall to add insult to injury by mouthing a most unromantic and, obviously, insincere proposal of marriage!

He didn't force you to come down to the cabin, reminded a voice.

Nay, but he'd certainly prevented her leaving it once she was there!

Devin read the emotions skipping across her face like ripples in a pond and evinced another wave of regret that he hadn't proposed in a very convincing fashion, yet he couldn't bring himself to let down his carefully erected guard for longer than a few moments.

Neither would he ever regret what they'd shared this day.

"Well?" His eyebrows tented in exaggerated expectation. "Shall I make an honest woman of you?" He reached out and put a hand on her knee beneath the sheet and squeezed lightly.

"Just like that? Marry a scoundrel who not only seduces me in broad daylight with half his crew aboard, but—"

"I didn't force you down to this cabin, Meredyth."

Acknowledging how gullible she'd been to follow Bakámu below decks, Meredyth began to search desperately for excuses. "The brandywine. . . . It clouded my judgment, Captain, and I can assure you that—"

"That you had no business accepting Bakámu's offer to drink. You'll remember, 'twas his suggestion?" He sat up fully and crossed his legs, Indian style. Meredyth tried to ignore how disarming and dangerous he looked at the same time with his tangled blond mane and guileless blue eyes, and his facial bruises and iron-muscled torso attesting to the fact that he was a man first and foremost, capable of lying, brawling, seducing a woman, and worse. "In fact, no one twisted your arm to get you to follow him, as I recall." He sighed heavily, made a moue as one would with a naughty child. "You shouldn't allow your soft heart to interfere with your sense of propriety, Lady

Meredyth." He winked at her. "And especially when in the company of a scoundrel in the wickedest city in all the world."

Meredyth edged over past him and modestly swung her legs over the side of the bunk. "Aye, and the wickedest scoundrel, as well," she said darkly, "who should have been more concerned with decorum than tricking me!"

He leaned toward her and nuzzled her ear. "Admittedly so, but I meant what I said, Merry-mine, about wedding you." She looked directly into his eyes as he added softly, "And this wickedest of scoundrels would never jilt you."

That was his mistake, for he suddenly heard Meredyth defending Luke Pelton and his actions. "There's more to the story than we know," she snapped at him. "But I've yet to get to the bottom of it—"

He took her chin between his thumb and forefinger. "You'll not get to the bottom of anything!" he said sharply. "Whatever it was Pelton told you, 'twas untrue. He was trying to save face. What more would you expect from a man like him?"

So now he was criticizing her taste in men.

"At least he makes an honest living," she shot back. "He hasn't dirtied his hands with the slave trade like some, who then claim that a slave here and there as cargo isn't even worth considering!"

"Then why is your precious Luke so thick with Jean-Baptiste du Casse? Did you ever wonder about that, Merry-mine?"

Her eyes widened as she stared at him, obviously given pause.

"Aye, sweet. You hadn't thought about that."

And you had no business pointing it out to her, an inner voice chided.

He released her chin. "I'll ask it once more, then never again, Meredyth. Pelton leaves you high and dry, causes you to flee to the Caribbee Islands to heal your broken heart, and yet you would believe such a man over me?"

She began donning her drawers beneath the cover of the sheet, glad of something to claim her attention with him so close to her. As she reached for her stockings, she said, "And exactly what kind of man are you, pray tell?"

"Mayhap the man for you." The words were soft but intense, and the cabin was as still as death for a fleeting space of time.

"My father doesn't believe in slavery, I told you," she said into the heavy silence, ignoring his implication. "He would never have allowed me to wed Luke Pelton if he were involved in the trade."

He couldn't tell her. He was now in a position where he had to lie about his own involvement in the slave trade, for her own safety. Nor could he tell her how he really felt about her, for in her remorse over her actions, she'd grab at anything she could to use as a weapon against him. And especially his professed love. It was only natural that a decent woman would grab at something with which to defend her impulsive behavior, and if it were too painful to blame her unspoken attraction to him, she would convince herself that because of the few slaves he supposedly imported to the Main, he was the lowest of the low and that would be reason enough to hate him.

And in the process, she would hide what he suspected were her real feelings from him and, more importantly, from herself.

"Meredyth," he said more gently. "There are any number of ship captains in Port Royal who'd be happy to wed us, and quickly. If for naught else but appearances! You can always get an annulment later." He snapped his fingers, the gesture meaning to convey a nonchalance he was far from feeling. "Just like that!"

He forced his features into an unconcerned half-grin before he saw her apricot slipper flying toward his face. Ducking a split second too late, he caught it in the ear. "Have pity, milady," he exhorted with a twist of his lips, "I'm an injured man."

"Not injured enough," she gritted, retrieving the slipper from his lap with an angry jerk. How she wished that barrel had hit him in the groin! She felt instantly contrite at her very unkind thought. Dismay filled her, too, at the thought of such serious injury to Devin Chandler . . . and the part of him that had brought her such pleasure.

She felt her face glow with embarrassment at the lusty thought and doubled her efforts to ignore him and dress herself as quickly as possible. It was outside of enough that he'd actually had the nerve to speak of marriage and then, in the next breath, annulment. He was no better than Luke Pelton.

What was wrong with her, she wondered bitterly, that she'd allowed herself to become entangled with one scoundrel, only to flee him and his rejection to seek solace in the shelter of the arms of another?

Devin Chandler brought out the absolute worst in her. And here she was, deflowered, to prove it. He certainly was no gentleman! To allow her to drink her fill of brandywine, then subtly challenge her to follow the Arawak below decks. *Oh come now, man. Don't look so disappointed. Obviously, Lady Meredyth wishes to wait for Master Kingsley's return.* The echo of his words mocked her, and she felt the hot moisture of tears burning the backs of her eyes. But she wouldn't weep in front of him! She'd return to England, where no one would know of their episodes in the cabin of the *Lady Elysia,* or if word did get out, she wouldn't care, for she'd never allow another man near her for the rest of her life!

As much as she would have preferred it otherwise, Meredyth was obliged to let him help her with the fastenings at the back of her gown. Even beneath her clothing, the feel of his fingers made her skin tingle, and she wondered if Devin Chandler were, indeed, the Devil that he could wreak such havoc on her senses. She was enthralled by him, she had to admit, even though she knew him to be a knave and a seller of slaves.

Somehow, he produced the bottle of perfume he'd given her (was he a pickpocket, too?) and dabbed the stopper beneath each ear, the base of her throat, then at her wrists. "Whenever you wear this, love, think of Jamaica, won't you? Think of me." The words carried an undertone of regret and a poorly concealed wistfulness.

Meredyth peeked at him through her lashes and caught an unexpected glimpse of a different facet of Devin Chandler. But the moment he raised his gaze to her face, it was gone.

He stood and retrieved his shirt and breeches. He donned them quickly and with an economy of motion, then strode to the door. "Bakámu?" he said in a low voice.

"Sí, Capitán." the Indian's voice came through the panel. "More brandywine?"

The sly devil! Meredyth thought. He surely had been standing guard at the door all this time!

'Tis no more than you deserve! said her conscience.

"Fetch Flaherty for me. Quickly."

Devin turned and leaned against the door, his gaze steady but unreadable. "This is no time to balk, Meredyth. What if you've conceived a child?"

His words hit her with the force of a physical blow. Child? Of course there was that possibility, but she hadn't even had time to think of it.

Devin watched the look of defeat that came over her face. "A child . . ." she whispered.

Of course, he thought with unaccustomed bitterness. Why would the daughter of the Earl of Somerset ever want his child?

"Cap'n?"

Devin turned and lifted the latch. He slipped outside the door and closed it behind him. Meredyth was too miserable to care in those moments. She'd run away to Jamaica only to get involved with a blackguard privateer. She'd thrown away her virginity like it was some tawdry and worthless favor and was now left to face the possible consequences of her behavior an ocean away from her family.

Self-pity ill becomes a St. Andrews! snapped her pride.

Indeed, she had to face her troubles, not give in to despair as she'd done once already.

The door opened again, and Devin stepped in. He watched as her chin unconsciously lifted in defense; she wasn't going to make this easy, he guessed.

"You may wish to wash your face and arrange your hair, milady." He inclined his head toward the washstand. "We are to receive company shortly."

Footsteps sounded overhead, and unintelligible male voices. What sounded like a shouting match ensued near the general area of the boarding ramp. Could Master Kingsley have returned?

"And what company is that?" she said, rising and moving toward the washstand.

"Captain Marteen of the *Gisela* is a friend of mine. I've sent Flaherty to fetch him to perform the ceremony. You'll not leave this ship a disgraced woman. You'll not leave my cabin as aught but my wife, like it or not."

To his surprise, although her back stiffened as she lifted the cloth to dip it in the basin, she voiced no objection.

In fact, she said nothing more to him until the ceremony.

Woodrow Kingsley, who looked positively apoplectic, and Red Flaherty were the witnesses as Captain Rhys Marteen performed the brief ceremony in heavily accented Dutch. He was a big, burly blond, with a broad smile and kindly blue eyes. If he suspected the reason for the hastily arranged marriage, he was circumspect enough to keep it to himself.

The cabin had been neatened by Bakámu, upon whom Meredyth now wished she'd never set eyes. He had been the one who'd set this whole chain of events in motion, she thought with uncharacteristic bitterness, and he had caused her to go chasing after Devin Chandler into Port Royal when Manuel had wound up the victim of her rash actions. And on this very day the Arawak had deliberately manipulated her into entering Devin Chandler's cabin.

Of course, Devin had even managed to round up Maddy from the Seaman's Folly and Arabella so that, Meredyth supposed, she would have some female company among the gaggle of men aboard the *Lady Elysia*. He didn't seem to care that they were whores, and Meredyth told herself it didn't really matter as Maddy placed a garland of exotic flowers over her freshly combed hair.

The floral scent blended beautifully with the fragrance Devin had applied to her pulse points and perfumed the close confines of the cabin and its occupants.

She went through the motions of the ceremony—if that was what the hasty little travesty could be called—and pledged her troth in as strong a voice as she could muster. Devin's words had been calm and rich, and his eyes had locked meaningfully with hers, as if he would impart something he could not say aloud. Meredyth sounded as steady as she could command her voice, for she was doing this willingly and for the child that might have been conceived, even though she suspected that Devin spoke truly when he said she wouldn't leave the schooner as anything but his wife.

Then there was the added surprise of the exquisitely etched gold band that Devin slipped on her finger. It was a perfect fit, and Meredyth couldn't help but wonder if it had been pilfered from some now dead Aztec or Mayan princess from the jungles of the Yucatán Peninsula or even an Incan emperor from the mountainous Andes region farther south.

When they were pronounced man and wife, Meredyth accepted his chaste kiss, but it served as a vivid reminder of what they'd shared and could continue to share if she so chose. Turning her thoughts away from dangerous territory, Meredyth suffered the congratulations of the crew members above deck, which appeared genuine, and from the two prostitutes.

"Devin's a good man," Maddy told her. "And I've known many. He'll do well by ye."

And Arabella whispered, "He saved me life not long ago, milady. He'll never desert ye."

Well, she assumed the two women knew him as well as any other females and were giving her their sincere opinions. Her gaze went to Devin, who was toasting with Flaherty and Captain Marteen, and, as if feeling her attention, he looked straight at her. He smiled as easily as if it were the most natural thing in the world for him to do, and her heart flipped over in her chest like a beached fish.

That was the problem. All he had to do was flash her one of his sinfully beautiful smiles or recite some ridiculous piece of bombast, and she slid beneath his spell, even with his bruised visage. Whether he was half-dressed, like the first day she'd met him, or the picture of sartorial splendor acting the part of the perfect peer of the realm at the governor's ball, Devin Chandler possessed the power to make her blood sizzle through her veins.

Or mayhap it was the way the sun gilded his hair like a blessing from the gods or the way he could charm anyone, man or woman, to do his bidding when he so chose.

Marry come up, but she had to get away from him!

Meredyth averted her gaze and, to her relief, found herself immediately included in the small talk between Maddy and Arabella. She listened half-heartedly, wondering how to leave this entire farcical scene, when a hand on her arm snagged her attention. She looked up into the kind azure eyes of Woodrow Kingsley.

"I know I've failed you miserably, m'dear, and I'm prepared to do anything in my power to help you extricate yourself from this predicament, including removing you from the presence of these two . . . er, ladies." He cleared his throat and took her arm.

"Oh, nay, Master Kingsley," Meredyth protested softly, good manners automatically taking over. What did it matter now if she were in the company of two whores, when she'd just relinquished her virtue without a qualm to a rogue like Devin Chandler and then consented to wed him? And besides, Maddy had come to her rescue at the Seaman's Folly. How ungrateful to treat the woman with anything other than kindness.

"The ladies are most refreshing in the company of so many males," Meredyth told Woody. She managed a smile to accompany her words, thinking how appalled a proper London matron would have been to hear such words for two prostitutes from the daughter of the Earl of Somerset.

"Why, how kind o' you to say so," Maddy said, her surprise obvious. Meredyth noticed for the first time that the woman looked as if someone had dragged her from bed in mid-afternoon—her bright titian hair half-heartedly fixed, her normally heavy make-up looking faded.

Meredyth wondered if it were as obvious that she'd just been with a man, then blushed furiously at the comparison. Lord, but she had to get away from this ship, its captain, and all the people around her—colorful as they were and entertaining, under normal circumstances, no doubt.

"I trust your business matter was taken care of?" she said to Woody in an effort to divert her unhappy thoughts.

He looked as if she'd struck him, so pronounced was the guilt in his eyes. A flush stole over his features and up into his balding pate. " 'Twasn't so important after all, milady, but Flaherty got it wrong, or else 'twas a conspiracy, I vow! Flaherty, Devin—"

"And Bakámu," she added darkly. "Please, Master Kingsley, if you would be so kind? Help me take my leave as soon as courteously possible. I want to return to the town house, then go straight to my father's plantation."

From there, she thought, she would continue on to the mission and, hopefully, find solace there. She would refuse to see Devin Chandler until she'd sorted out her thoughts and feelings. Maybe.

One thing she would not do, however, was run back to England after making so monumental a mistake. She'd run once, and look where it had landed her! She would make her plans when she was safely away from Port Royal and Devin Chandler and think about the possibility of a child later.

Somehow the thought of carrying Devin Chandler's child was unexpectedly soothing, for it would be an extension of him, without all the complications of the man himself involved. And he wouldn't even have to know.

"A penny for your thoughts," the man himself murmured into her ear, taking her by the elbow and guiding her away from Kingsley and the other two women.

She looked up at him from beneath her wide-brimmed bonnet, more like a cornered doe, he thought with rue, than a blushing bride. The sea breeze teased tendrils of her dark hair, making it dance about her lovely, pale face, but her jewel-bright eyes carried the sheen of tears, he noted. His normally imperturbable conscience shifted unbearably.

" 'Twas the only thing to do, under the circumstances, Merry-mine," he said softly, his eyes telling her things he didn't dare utter with his lips. Not now, surely not ever. "For your sake and the . . . child's if there should be one." His lashes lowered, for he didn't want her to see the pain he knew he couldn't hide completely. "I'll write the earl a letter when you're ready to leave Jamaica, explaining the situation, taking the blame, and offering no contest should you wish to obtain an annulment. I'll swear I never touched you after we were wed."

"How noble of you," she said through a tight-lipped smile, strangely disappointed because he was so willing suddenly to let her go. But she knew he wasn't noble. What had she expected?

An image of her father carrying off the countess years ago flashed in her mind's eye, a romantic and intriguing thought, a picture that had always stirred her imagination even though she knew it had initially caused her mother much pain and humiliation. But then the countess had fallen in love with her captor and been prepared to follow him anywhere.

Devin Chandler, however, wasn't about to carry her off, and although that might mean that he wanted her so much he would defy the world, it wasn't necessarily the answer to her problem. It didn't mean he loved her, only that he lusted after her and, obviously, she after him. Her daydreaming was merely a romantic flight of fancy that an inexperienced school girl might dream up, certainly not a woman grown.

And she would have jumped overboard before ever sailing on a ship that might be carrying slaves, however few.

"The lady Meredyth wishes to leave, Devin," Woody said, intruding into their few moments of private dialogue. The voices and laughter around them covered the animosity in his low voice but not the anger and censure in his eyes. "I've promised to take her back to the town house, with or without your permission."

Devin traced her delicate jawline with a finger. "You look peaked, love. 'Tis a good idea, if 'tis what you wish. But you are my wife presently, and I'll accompany you in the morn to the plan—"

"Nay!" she said much too quickly for Devin. Something shriveled within him at her determination to be rid of him.

"I'm your wife in name only," she said in a low, anguished voice, "remember that! I'll be safe enough with the Greaveses. And Father Tomas promised to send several men from the mission to escort me back."

Devin nodded, not trusting his voice, and took her elbow to guide her across the deck. She quickly said goodbye to Maddy, Arabella, and several of Devin's crew standing with Captain Marteen. She thanked him, also, though she perceived a subtle question in his eyes that made her want to disappear.

Devin didn't give Woodrow a second glance, feeling, as they descended the boarding plank, his own anger with, and an unreasonable sense of betrayal by, the man who was like a father to him. "If you need aught, Meredyth, send a message."

They reached the dock, and Meredyth looked up at him one last time. "You've done quite enough for one lifetime, Captain Chandler," she said, then swung away to wait for Woodrow Kingsley.

From across Thames Street, a man watched the goings on aboard the *Lady Elysia*. When the two prostitutes finally left, he fell into step beside them as they headed away from the schooner toward the Seaman's Folly.

"Arabella, luv," he said to the younger woman, "I've an itch only ye can scratch."

Arabella looked up at him. "Why, Henry Sykes, ye bloody rascal! Where've ye been these last weeks?"

"Doin' some work fer du Casse. Just got back, and I've a sudden and ragin' appetite fer me Arabella." He put an arm about her shoulders and squeezed.

Maddy looked askance at him. He was of medium build, with thick, dark hair and eyes to match and walked with a decided hitch. Good-looking devil, if you liked the type, for there was something about him.

Hadn't she seen him with Mad Dog Davies the other day? Which meant he was lying to Arabella and had been in Port Royal at least several days. Maddy hated a lying man, and snitches, too. She'd never liked Sykes. From what she'd heard, he was a snake in the grass, a tattler to the highest bidder, because he was too lazy to do any physical labor. And the Spanish Main was, among other things, a hotbed of intrigue.

Well, she thought as she moved ahead of the bargaining couple, Arabella's clients were her own business, especially regulars, and she'd certainly seemed glad to see him.

Maddy moved on ahead, catching only ". . . a weddin' aboard that fancy schooner the *Lady Elysia?*" before she was out of earshot.

Twenty-two

7 June, 1692

They left at 10:30 the next morning for the St. Andrews plantation. Meredyth's headache upon waking had been so debilitating that Jackie Greaves had decided to postpone their departure until she felt better. Meredyth was too ashamed to tell them she wasn't really ill but had merely imbibed too much brandywine. Nor, after her return to the town house, did she divulge anything about what had happened beyond dining at The Oyster House and visiting the *Lady Elysia*.

How could she bring herself to tell these good and simple people that she'd behaved little better than a woman working at any one of the brothels that abounded in Port Royal?

To her surprise, Woodrow Kingsley showed up and then waited patiently in the parlor until Meredyth felt well enough to leave. " 'Tis the least I can do," he told her, his eyes sending the added message, *now that the damage is done.* No one objected to his presence; in fact, Jackie seemed glad to have another male for company and eager to talk to him about anything to do with ships as soon as they left Port Royal.

Meredyth couldn't help but feel grateful to the older man, for it was obvious that riding a horse was extremely uncomfortable for him. She wondered if it helped expiate his evident guilt as failed chaperon by taking the physical abuse of a jouncing ride in the hot sun.

Of course, she thought acerbically as roses bloomed in her

already warm cheeks, it wasn't his fault neither she nor Devin couldn't be trusted not to sneak off like two animals in heat.

She was glad for the shielding bonnet she wore.

Ellen Greaves had a dislike for riding as well, Meredyth had learned on the earlier trip to Port Royal, though it was more mental than physical. She'd ridden before, she'd explained to Meredyth, but after she'd been unexpectedly thrown from a normally dependable horse, preferred the smaller, if less cooperative, donkeys ("Not so far to the ground!" she'd said laughingly to Meredyth.). A wheeled conveyance would have suited both women better than horses in the tropical sun, though the former would have been the poorest way to traverse the winding sandspit to the island proper.

Unfortunately for Meredyth, even the simplest walk was jarring to her aching head, in spite of the concoction Concepción had given her (which had tasted like something Bakámu would have come up with, she'd thought at the time), though the drink had dulled the pain considerably. Also, with each step taken by the animal beneath her, Meredyth was reminded anew of what had happened the day before, and soreness between her thighs wasn't the only sensation she felt, to her acute embarrassment.

Devin Chandler was constantly intruding into her thoughts.

It was an unusually quiet group, even when they paused to rest, because, it seemed, everyone was aware that something wasn't right with Meredyth, but no one was bold enough to ask nor to inquire why Meredyth had been escorted back to the town house by Master Kingsley rather than Devin Chandler. And Woody didn't offer any explanations.

Embroiled in her own troubling introspection, crushed beneath a cumbersome mantle of somberness, Meredyth was too preoccupied to attempt to put the others at their ease. She was relieved that they had little inclination to talk as they skirted the ocean toward the main body of the island. Carla hobbled about the sandy beach chasing sandpipers and gulls, like a normal child, with seemingly not a care in the world. It lifted

Meredyth's spirits to watch the little girl engage in normal childish activities with such innocent abandon.

They were forced to a halt shortly after an hour. "The horses are actin' queer," Jackie said and dismounted.

Meredyth roused herself from her miserable musings enough to watch as Jackie took time to point out things of interest along the beach to Carla, and she suddenly wondered if she would be doing the same thing one day with Devin's child.

Would she have the patience to sort through the shells the child would inevitably wish to gather with innocent wonderment at the world of the sea and the sand? Would she laugh with her son or daughter as the lacy foam from receding breakers tickled their bare feet, then slid away and disappeared back into the bosom of the sea? It would have to be, of course, the sea off the western English coast, for surely she couldn't remain in Jamaica.

"Señorita Meredyth?" Meredyth looked up from beside her mount, where she'd been lost in her own world. Carla was standing before her and Jackie behind the child, a slight frown between his eyes. "The birds are gone."

Meredyth's eyes met Jackie's as, at first, the child's words didn't quite sink in. Jackie looked vaguely troubled.

"What is it?" she asked him, and reached out to Carla, who, releasing her crutch, eagerly came into her embrace.

"Somethin' ain't right, m'lady," he said in a quiet voice. "Look." He pointed to the beach behind him, which was suddenly deserted. No sandpipers. Meredyth raised her eyes to the sky. The seagulls were suddenly gone, too, which accounted for the sudden and eerie silence, broken only by the soft susurration of the sea.

"Even the horses are acting oddly," Woody said as he limped up to them. Ellen and Concepción were engaged in a quiet conversation nearby, in the shade of several mango trees. "Haven't you noticed?" he asked Meredyth, then looked at Jackie.

Meredyth felt foolish because she hadn't noticed in her preoccupation, and she was a good rider, skillful enough to allow her attention to wander in spite of her mount's sudden skittishness. She frowned at the animal's flattened ears and its wide and wary eyes. It stomped restlessly, tossed its great head, wild-eyed, then quieted for a time.

Unease tracked up her spine as she watched Ellen try to remount her own uncooperative mare.

"I've never seen anything like it," Woody said in a low voice. He pulled out his pocket watch, which Meredyth thought a strange thing to do, though the mundane movement was also somehow reassuring. "Twenty minutes to twelve," he said to no one in particular.

"Weigh anchor!" Devin called through his captain's horn. He knew it was late in the morning for a trial run—almost half past eleven—but little things here and there had kept him and the crew busy until now. Near midday or nay, the *Lady Elysia* was going for a short trial run. Mayhap it would help him get his mind off his new wife, and mayhap not. But he would give it a good try. Maybe if he wore himself out with physical labor at sea, the wind and sun beating at him like it did only in the Caribbean, he'd be exhausted enough to sleep that night, something that had eluded him in his empty bed the night before.

The schooner eased away from the dock area without a hitch, her sails unfurled to catch any errant breeze that might come up on this somnolent and still late morning. He glanced toward the mountains. The air shimmered with heat, and he wondered about Meredyth out in the Jamaican sun, heading toward the St. Andrews plantation, then up into the Blue Mountains to a primitive and lonely Jesuit mission.

Christ, he must have been pickled with brandywine to have allowed her to leave him! She belonged at his side. Hadn't she admitted she loved ships and the sea? It was in her blood. Her father had been a privateer like Devin and passed down the love of the sea to his daughter.

Your work is too dangerous to involve Meredyth St. Andrews a voice reminded him, *whether for a trial run or forever. What kind of life could you offer her, even if she consented to be your wife in more than name? Even, if by some miracle, the earl gave his blessing to the union?*

And, of course, first and foremost, at least in Devin's mind: She didn't love him. She had obviously enjoyed what they'd shared physically, mayhap even enjoyed his company somewhat, but not love. He'd been a fool to ever entertain the hope or the imaginings. It had to be the Irish blood running through his veins from his whimsical, romantic mother, whose life had ended up a tragedy, with only remnants of her unrequited love for a cold and selfish Englishman and a bastard son.

A knot formed in his chest, in spite of the beautiful day and the restored ship beneath his feet, a knot which grew so large and painful that it threatened his very breath, and for a moment he felt dizzy. There seemed to be no room for his heart or his lungs to function.

He coughed, drew in a fresh drag of tangy ocean air, and felt the knot suddenly melt into a liquid anguish that sluiced through his blood like the most potent of poisons. Tears sprang unbidden to his eyes, and as he lurched toward the rail, he thanked the powers that be for the excuse of sun and wind on the water.

"Cap'n? Somethin' amiss?" Emil Rogers, his quartermaster, asked.

With a lopsided grin, Devin waved him off. "Got a faceful o' water, Rogers. Forgot what it's like to be on the high seas again."

The man laughed and shook his head, then answered the call of another sailor behind him.

Devin drew in deep, slow breaths, then released them. He had to get hold of himself and his runaway emotions. He was living his worst nightmare; everything he feared, should he have ever allowed himself to fall in love, was manifesting itself tenfold, like a premonition of disaster come true by some gypsy seer.

The horrors and deep despair of Newgate had been child's play compared to accepting the fact that he could never really have Meredyth for his own—to love, to cherish, to share the joys of children.

"Chan-ler?"

Devin raised his head from contemplating the aquamarine water that moved by the ship like the flash of jewels beneath the sun. Bakámu stood at his elbow, with Henry Morgan in his usual place. But the Indian said nothing for a moment.

"Aye?" Devin prompted the Arawak, who wasn't normally at a loss for words in any language. The parrot was silent as well.

Bakámu cast his gaze about the ocean, then the skies, then back to the retreating island.

Devin followed the Indian's eyes, at first thinking it some kind of game or Arawak ritual or some exaggerated behavior designed to impress him.

Devin held his silence then, following the Indian's look back to the bright, cerulean vault of the sky, and noticed there were no seagulls about, or any other birds for that matter.

As if reading his thoughts, Bakámu said, "No birds." He pointed to the sky.

Devin narrowed his eyes at him, then glanced at Henry Morgan. "Aye, and so there aren't. And what's *his* problem?"

"Bird know. Wishemenetoo angry with Chan-ler. Not want him to leave Señorita Mer-dyth. Your woman now."

Devin rolled his eyes as he turned his face toward the open sea. "Don't tell me, Bakámu, you're a shaman now? From a long line of shamans, I suppose?"

The Arawak said nothing. Henry Morgan said nothing.

"We are returning, you know. This is just a short jaunt to see if the ship is seaworthy."

"If ship not sea-worthy, sink. We die. You never see Merdyth again."

"Now that's a clever piece of reasoning, Indian. You're surely descended from a line of wise and intuitive shamans."

Bakámu obviously had no idea what "intuitive" meant, nor did he seem to care. The frown between his eyes did not abate.

"Henry Morgan!" Devin exclaimed to the African gray. "Where's the bawds?"

The parrot returned his look like a miniature basilisk and remained silent.

Canting his head slightly, Devin considered the bird. "Play dead parrot, Henry?" he coaxed.

Henry Morgan lifted a wing and preened, ignoring Devin as if he hadn't spoken.

"I wager if I go for his throat, I'll wring a squawk out of him," Devin mumbled.

"Look," Bakámu said, pointing off to the larboard side of the schooner.

A small formation of dolphins—five to be exact—were swimming close to the *Lady,* which struck Devin as odd. They were too close to the island, normally swimming playfully beside a ship when it was farther out at sea. And these dolphins were going around the moving ship, or seemed to be, their gray dorsal fins glistening in the sunlight.

Devin stared, fascinated. "Master Dobbins!" he called out to his first officer, who was at the ship's wheel. "Can you see those dolphins?"

Richard "Rink" Dobbins, a sandy-haired man of medium height and wiry build, craned his neck. "Aye. Bit queer, ain't it, so close to the island, I mean?"

Devin stroked his jaw thoughtfully but said nothing. If something were wrong, something cataclysmic in nature, the first to sense it would be the animals.

He glanced over at the gray parrot, who was silent as a stone as he sat on Bakámu's shoulder. Then there was the absence of any birds overhead—the entire sky was empty, in fact as far as he could see. The erratic behavior of the dolphins added to the puzzle. And, of course, Bakámu sensed something, though Devin was more inclined to trust the creatures of the air and sea than the Arawak. But what did he really know about Bakámu and his previous experiences?

He glanced over his shoulder. Most of the crew on deck seemed more interested in the smooth operation of the newly launched schooner than in what signals nature might be giving them.

Then, suddenly, the dolphins were gone, disappearing as if they had never been. And Bakámu was saying in an agitated voice, "Back! Go back to island, Chan-ler!"

Emil Rogers was at the rail, with the second officer, Tobias Galbraithe.

The sea was dead calm, the sails beginning to luff indolently in the wake of the disappearing breeze. Devin didn't know whether to turn back or continue out to sea.

"Go back!" Bakámu whispered so softly, Devin thought he was imagining it, until he looked at the Arawak's face. It was decidedly pale for his normally light copper complexion. His dark eyes suddenly held the wisdom of generations of Arawaks before him, reaching back through the mists of time.

Devin's hackles raised, and a chill that had nothing to do with any sea breeze wafted over him.

Devin looked at Dobbins at the wheel and made his decision. "Bring her about!" he ordered the first officer, his commanding voice traveling over the deck. Then, through his captain's trumpet, "Trim the sails! The wind's a-dyin' and we're returning to port with any bit of breeze we can catch. If we must, we'll ride the tide!"

Shouts of "Bring her about!" echoed along the deck, and men scurried to follow orders. Devin hoped he wasn't overreacting and being fooled by a handful of demented dolphins . . . and a crackbrained Arawak.

* * *

Luke Pelton watched with narrowed eyes as Mad Dog Davies disappeared beneath Devin Chandler's huge bed.

"Tight squeeze, Pelton," Davies said in a muffled voice from the shadows. "Care to join me?" The sarcasm was unmistakable.

"Just tap the floorboards," Pelton told him tersely, "and if aught sounds hollow, see if you can pry up the wood. You're not being paid to make jests." He wondered how wise it had been to give Davies a small crowbar, something to use as a weapon if he decided he didn't need Luke anymore, though it was a bit late for second thoughts.

They'd paid an urchin to distract the man watching the town house (if it hadn't worked, Davies would have had no qualms about killing him), then had slipped inside. Not trusting the buccaneer behind his back, yet needing a willing partner, Luke had persuaded Mad Dog to search beneath the bed, claiming that du Casse had insisted the papers were somewhere in the town house and most likely beneath the ridiculously huge and heavy bed that took up most of Chandler's bedchamber. The agent who'd searched the town house for du Casse while Chandler had been in England had come to the conclusion that the papers were either cleverly concealed beneath the great bed or somewhere else entirely.

Du Casse had offered to send the same man with Pelton, then changed his mind just before his ship had left for St. Domingue and taken the agent with him for another assignment.

"You are on your own, *monsieur*," du Casse had told Pelton, obviously perturbed by what he perceived as Luke's crude and premature dealing with Chandler on the *Bristol*. "But do not spoil months of work in the name of vengeance, *n'est-ce pas?*"

Luke was irritated with himself for allowing Chandler to get under his skin and thus gain the upper hand, especially during yesterday's run-in. He should have killed him two nights before, while he had the chance, and shipped his putrefying corpse to the Earl of Somerset. Then, he should have persuaded

Meredyth to forgive him, told her whatever lies necessary, and in the event that that failed, taken her off by force.

A double stroke against Keir St. Andrews. He was getting desperate, Luke realized, when he was thinking of ignoring Meredyth's safety. But trampled pride and outrage could drive a man to desperate measures. And it surely wasn't his fault the earl had delivered his delectable daughter practically into his arms.

Davies's thumping broke into his turbulent thoughts. "Have you found something?" Luke called out in a low voice, suddenly impatient to prove that Chandler's activities in the past had been contrary to the interests of la Compagnie de Sénégal and to lend credence to his suspicion that Chandler worked for the Earl of Somerset, and possibly others.

"By the Pope's balls!" exclaimed Davies, and Luke heard the scrape of the crowbar and then what sounded like a loose board being overturned. It was all he could do not to dive under the bed himself and see what had caused Davies's exclamation. "I need light," the buccaneer said. "Gimme a candle!"

"Just bring out what you've found, Davies. You can't read anyway," he said impatiently, then realized the ill-tempered buccaneer might take offense and reluctantly amended, "I . . . er, rather, 'tis too tight a space to do aught. Just bring it out into the light."

A board clattered back in place, and the scrape of the crowbar across the floor indicated that Davies was following his instructions. But the thought of a crowbar in the other man's hands was suddenly menacing, considering the kind of cutthroat Aaron Davies was, a man who'd turn on his partner like a rabid dog on its master.

Luke got to his knees and rested his right hand on the butt of a pistol tucked in his waistband beneath his loose, unbuttoned coat. Davies's head appeared, his red kerchief askew over his craggy forehead.

And then Luke felt the town house shudder beneath him.

His stomach protested the alien motion and flip-flopped within him as Davies cried, "Englishman! What the . . ." and clumsily tried to scramble out from beneath the bed.

The entire building heaved. The heavy bed crashed to the floor, pinning Aaron Davies from the shoulders on down, an expression of stunned disbelief stamped across his features. His chin slammed onto the floor, but he made no sound, his blankly staring eyes revealing that he was already beyond help.

Pelton threw himself toward the window, sensing it was his only chance to escape the crumbling building as the walls cracked and the ceiling wavered above him. He heard the chest of drawers behind him do a dance on its wooden legs before he plunged through the window, certain of the nasty fall to come, but even more certain of perishing in the deathtrap behind him.

Devin consulted his watch as they crawled toward Port Royal. Twenty minutes of twelve. By now, the entire crew was uneasy, most of them watching the approaching sandspit or scanning the sea around them. With every available piece of canvas opened to the wind, there was little to do save maintain their course.

Suddenly, the schooner's speed increased slightly, but as Devin studied the sails above him with a critical eye, he realized it was not because of an increase in wind velocity. Rather the thrust seemed to come from beneath the ship.

Beneath the ship? he thought in consternation. Mayhap those deranged dolphins were carrying the ship back to port. Hadn't stranger things happened according to sailors' tales? Ludicrous an idea as it was, the question remained: Why back to Port Royal?

Several of his men glanced at him, trepidation and outright fear written across their countenances. He looked at Bakámu. The Indian was sitting cross-legged at the aft-most point of the rail, his face tilted toward the heavens, palms raised, and the tattered excuse for a parrot on his shoulder.

Devin glanced at several of the crew closest to him. Some of them were now watching Bakámu with strange expressions.

The Arawak was frightening his men, that's what he was doing! Devin made to turn about. He'd haul the fool below decks if he had to, for the last thing he needed now was a panicky crew.

A hand on his shoulder stopped him in mid-motion. It was Rink Dobbins. He handed Devin the speaking trumpet. "Say something to them. Reassure them, Cap'n."

Devin shot a look at the helm. Galbraithe had assumed Rink's place. He looked back at Rink and wanted to laugh but he knew better. He was the leader, ultimately in charge and responsible for the life of every man aboard. No matter his own thoughts and feelings, he had to keep his men calm, they had to remain prepared. He raised the horn to his lips. "Stand by, steady as she goes," he said levelly.

"Seems we're ridin' one devil of a wave," Dobbins said in a thin voice. "A tidal wave."

Their eyes met and locked. "Earthquake?" Devin said.

"I'd say, Cap'n. Just as well we're at sea." The *Lady Elysia's* speed increased noticeably. "God help us," Rink said and moved off to help Galbraithe manage the wheel.

Devin could feel the tremendous power propelling them toward Port Royal, and he fought down his alarm as they approached the town. He watched in disbelief as Fort James crumbled like a kicked sand castle and slid into the sea. The air was filled with a roaring sound, and the entire waterfront before them teetered, collapsed, and was swallowed by the sea. Other blocks behind began to disintegrate and disappear.

Sweet Jesus . . . his town house . . . the documents!

Meredyth! She was somewhere between Port Royal and the plantation. Please, God, he prayed for the first time in memory, keep her safely out of Port Royal.

Devin was frozen to the deck, one hand white-knuckled as

it still clutched the speaking trumpet. He glanced to the east, toward the other end of the sandspit, and in the direction Meredyth and her party had gone, but could discern nothing. The Blue Mountains were lost in the dull, reddish sky that was spreading across the narrow strip of land like a glowing oven.

The noise was now beyond thunderous, as if the mountains themselves were falling, and Devin devoted another precious few moments to silently beseeching God to spare his Meredyth, as he braced himself for the ship's uncontrolled entry into sinking Port Royal, a puny projectile heading straight into the jaws of the behemoth of destruction.

For a few frightening moments, all was madness.

The horses reared and shrilled in terror as the ground beneath them rolled like an earthen breaker and the waves slapped madly at one another in the sea.

"Get down!" Jackie yelled, pulling down Carla and covering her small body with his own.

Out of the corner of her eye, Meredyth saw Ellen fall from her frightened horse and cover her head with her arms to protect herself from the mare's flaying hooves. As Meredyth slammed against the sand, the thought flashed through her mind that Ellen would never again set foot in a stirrup after this second fall, if she survived. If any of them survived.

Woody was already down, apparently having lost his balance immediately, and he reached out for Meredyth's hand. "Earthquake," he shouted to her, and she closed her eyes and clung to him like a lifeline; for here was Devin's friend, her only link to him at this moment and during this catastrophe.

If she survived, would he? Would she ever see him again?

The roaring around them sounded like a battle in the sky, and Meredyth could imagine how much worse it would be in the crowded city of Port Royal, with three- and four-story buildings built upon fill, precarious to begin with and surely not able to withstand this.

Gritty sand filtered into her mouth as the earth rumbled beneath her; she inadvertently inhaled some and began to choke. Was she to suffer so ignominious a death as choking on a mouthful of sand during an earthquake?

In the midst of her frustration and despair she thought of Devin. Dear God, where was Devin? She now shared a bond with him that could never be completely severed, child or no child, and the thought of his death was frightening enough to make her push herself to her knees, even though common sense told her she couldn't help anybody for the moment.

I have to go back to Port Royal! she screamed silently. *Devin's there, Deviiinnn . . .*

The ground shuddered beneath them, the sun dimmed above. A huge wave came rushing ashore, towered over them like a living entity, then crashed downward, slamming Meredyth back onto her stomach and knocking the breath from her body. Briny sea water burned her eyes and spurted up her nose and into her partially open mouth.

Twenty-three

Meredyth waited, the fingers of her right hand dug into the sand at the side of her head, her left hand still clutching Woodrow Kingsley's, as the water receded. The wedding band she'd transferred to her right hand winked in the dimmed sunlight and suddenly felt foreign and heavy on her finger, reminding her of the man who was now her husband, if he were yet alive.

She raised her head slightly and spat out sand and seawater, coughing until her lungs ached from her efforts to clear her air passages. Tears mingled with the saltwater that stung her eyes and burned the back of her throat, but she was finally able to draw in deep gulps of fresh, life-giving air.

She dared to lift her head higher, but her soaked bonnet rim flopped into her face, obscuring her view. She fumbled with its soggy ribbons and flung the hat away. Beside her, Woody was coughing, too, but to her relief, Jackie Greaves was holding and soothing little Carla, even as the child's mother was bent over a prostrate Ellen, a short stone's throw away.

Meredyth released her death grip on Woody's hand, sat up and stretched out her arms. "Here, Carla," she said. As the child crawled to her, her eyes wide with fright, Meredyth said to Jackie, "Go to Ellen. She was struck, I think." But he was already getting to his feet.

She gave Carla a reassuring hug and a tender kiss on the forehead, then set her down beside her. "I'm right here," she reassured the child, then moved onto her knees and crawled to Kingsley. "Master Kingsley?" she asked in a raspy voice. "Are you hurt?"

Woody was facing away from her. At the sound of her voice, he brought up his head, turned onto his left cheek, and opened his eyes. His lashes fluttered, and Meredyth feared he might faint. " 'Tis . . . just . . ." He coughed. "Just a bit . . . of seawater." Meredyth helped him sit up and thumped him on the back.

"Your heart . . ." she began, then let her words trail off in dismay at her blunt and very personal question.

" 'Tis my leg that pains me, child. My heart is fine."

The ground trembled again, and with a whimper of terror, Carla flung herself to Meredyth's side. Everyone froze for a moment.

"We're as safe here as anywhere," Woody said after another bout of coughing. "We'll be all right, little one," he said, his watering eyes on Carla. "Although this was the worst I've witnessed in all my years in the Caribbee Islands."

His eyes then met Meredyth's, their thoughts obviously along the same vein, for he added, " 'Tis those in Port Royal who'll suffer most."

Meredyth's expression mirrored his concern. "Aye. We— I've got to go back. They'll surely need help."

Before Woody could answer, she stood and held out a hand to Carla. "Come, we must see to Mistress Greaves. She's hurt."

The child obeyed, straightening and hopping onto one foot. She pointed to her fallen crutch, a few feet away, and Meredyth retrieved it. She looked at Woody, a question in her eyes.

"I'll be fine, milady," he said with a ghost of a smile. "Just winded. I can get to my feet on my own. You help Master Greaves."

As it turned out, Ellen had sustained a gash on the skull from a flying hoof, but the bleeding was subsiding under Concepción's attentions. Ellen was sitting up now, looking pale and soaked, but still perky enough. "Go find those wretched animals," she told her husband, pointing with one arm to nowhere in particular. "And after my children almost became motherless because of a horse during an earthquake, don't ever tell me again that a horse is safer than a donkey!"

"You can ride with me," Jackie said with a smile, obviously relieved that she wasn't seriously hurt. "I'll keep ye safe." He stood and looked about. The sky was still reddish, the air heavy, the sea churning.

"I must go back!" Meredyth said. She lifted a hand to shade her eyes, scanning up and down the beach for the horses. They were all in sight, though not together.

Her new ring felt like a cool weight on her finger, a silent, damning reminder.

"You can't go back there," Ellen objected immediately. " 'Tis too dangerous! Come to the plantation—"

"Devin is there!" Meredyth insisted, wringing out a section of her sopping skirts and feeling like she weighed as much as one of the horses. "And others. The entire town might need help, and I cannot go anywhere until I've at least gone back to see what happened."

Jackie whistled, and two of the horses came trotting toward them. One of them was Jackie's gelding, the other was the mare Meredyth had been riding. She grabbed its reins.

"What if there's another quake?" Jackie asked her.

"I'd not be any safer elsewhere," she said. "You and Ellen take the others to the plantation and I'll go back to Port Royal. I promise if I can't help—if the situation is hopeless or if there's naught I can do—I'll return to the plantation as soon as I can."

Woody was standing by now, moving around as if to loosen his stiff legs. He was still pale, his thinning silvery hair plastered to his forehead already starting to dry. "I'll go with you, milady. You cannot just hie yourself off to Port Royal unescorted." The first signs of color tinged his cheeks, an obvious reminder of how he'd already failed her as a proper escort. "And I doubt you'd ever find a dependable escort for your trip back if Port Royal has suffered serious damage."

That was the least of her worries now, but Meredyth bit her tongue.

Devin had uttered similar words weeks ago, and he'd been right. "But your leg . . . and you've lost your cane."

The cane was nowhere to be seen, evidently a casualty of the wall of water that had washed over them. "I'll be fine, as long as I don't have to do much walking." He looked at Jackie. "I don't suppose we could coax another horse over here?"

"You can have mine," Jackie said, grabbing his gelding's reins and smoothing one hand over its glossy neck. "But I don't think either of you should be goin' back yet."

Woody shook his head. "I agree with Lady Meredyth. We may be needed in Port Royal." His expression turned grim. "Devin is back there, for starts, and my friends, my business. 'Tis right that you and the mistress return to your own family and the plantation, but my sense of duty calls me back to Port Royal." He looked at Meredyth. "And it seems the lady now has obligations in the town, as well.

Meredyth caught his meaning, though the others couldn't possibly know yet. She was Devin's wife. Under normal circumstances, her first concern should be her husband. Bitter laughter echoed through the passages of her mind. There had been nothing "normal" about any aspect of her life since she'd met Luke Pelton and suffered a crushing blow to her pride. Aye, she acknowledged, not a broken heart, she knew now, for she'd never really loved him.

And the man she did love, whether it was wise or not, whether he was the worst scoundrel in all the Caribbee Islands or not, could be lying injured or even dead in Port Royal.

A frigid draught swept up her spine, and a sense of unbearable loss mushroomed in her chest, tightening it until it hurt.

Resolutely, she turned to the mare and put her foot in the stirrup. She didn't care how ladylike she looked or acted, time was of the essence, and this was not the time or place to worry about niceties. As Meredyth dragged her weighted gown over the saddle, she noted out of the corner of her eye that Jackie had led the gelding over to Woody and was helping the older man up into the saddle.

"Have a care now," Jackie told them both. "As soon as I get the others to the plantation and make sure all is well there, I'll return to Port Royal with help."

Woody nodded as his horse tossed its head, obviously still unsettled. "I only hope there's someone left to help," he said in a low, grim voice. But Meredyth caught his words to Jackie and, once again, felt a coldness touch her skin, leaving goose bumps in its wake.

"Godspeed you all," she said to the others as she turned the mare toward Port Royal.

"I still don't like this," Jackie said with a shake of his head. " 'Tis against my better judgment."

"Señorita Meredyth!" Carla cried and clung to an obviously disapproving Concepción.

"I'll see you at the mission, sweet," Meredyth said over her shoulder with a wave and a half-smile. She kicked the mare into a trot and was satisfied to hear Woody's horse close behind.

The last thing Luke Pelton remembered was hitting water, unexpectedly caught up in a monstrous wave that carried him along like a piece of driftwood. He knew how to swim—a rare thing among seagoing men—and had always felt the safer for it. But there was no swimming against the mountain of water that swept over Port Royal, swallowing the town as it went like a hungry sea serpent. He didn't fight it, couldn't even dodge the obstacles that came his way, striking him and causing him to ricochet off other objects until he felt like a human cannonball.

Any injuries his landing in the water may have saved him, he suffered now as he was bombarded with debris. He stubbornly cleaved to the surface, however, using all his strength and agility to stay afloat as he was swept along.

Other victims floated around him, some flailing their arms in pathetic attempts to swim, others clinging to floating objects, but many of them lifeless.

He didn't want to become one more corpse.

Then, seemingly out of nowhere, a rope hit the water before his nose, and he grabbed it, not knowing what it was attached to, but hoping, nevertheless, that it was something buoyant.

Suddenly, looming off to the side was a vessel. A schooner! He pulled himself hand over hand along the line until he'd gathered up the slack, then felt himself being hauled toward it by one of several men at the vessel's rail. He couldn't believe it. A bloody miracle. A goddamn, bloody miracle!

Almost two-thirds of the town had literally disappeared before Devin's eyes, leaving him with a sick feeling of helplessness. If they were lucky, the *Lady Elysia* wouldn't be smashed to smithereens when this monstrous wave finally spent itself on what was left of Port Royal. He didn't know whether to curse the fates or thank them for having put them on the schooner and away from the town when the earthquake hit.

There was little they could do save hang on and ride the wave, but as they neared what had only moments before been the waterfront, the schooner somehow began to ease back from the crest and their mad rush toward disaster slowed. Maybe it was because the huge wave was beginning to spend itself in the shallower waters of the port, Devin thought, but he wasn't a scientist and he certainly hadn't enough time to ponder the phenomenon.

In those endless moments just before they sailed over what had been the docks and Thames Street, Devin began to hope. As they moved into the sunken part of the town, which was littered with debris and drowning townspeople, Devin knew they had been singled out for a purpose: to rescue anyone they could from the hungry ocean that sought to swallow the sandspit.

"Throw out the rescue lines and all the blackjacks you can find!" he called through the speaking trumpet, which had remained clenched in his rigid fingers, "Use anything we've got to fish these poor souls from the water!" He looked at Rink Dobbins at the wheel, Galbraithe stalwartly beside him. "Steady as she goes!" he encouraged his officers, suddenly feeling less helpless as determination moved through him.

They moved into the town, and many of his crew members began tossing ropes and the lifesaving blackjacks over the rail of the *Lady Elysia*. Out of the corner of his eye Devin caught sight of another vessel and did a double take. Most of the vessels anchored in the harbor had been overturned, moored to the sea bottom by their heavy anchors. Several were already half-sunken. But a frigate Devin recognized as the *Swan* had miraculously survived the earthquake and was now riding the encroaching sea, its crew plucking victims from the water.

Devin took over the wheel and devoted himself to guiding the schooner through the sunken blocks of the northeastern side of Port Royal, thus freeing Dobbins and Galbraithe to direct the rescue efforts. As badly as he wanted to help, he dared not risk his schooner after having come so close to losing her and trusted only himself to bring her through this, especially when lives depended on the ship's survival. And, if it sustained damages or sank, he would only have himself to blame. Or the Fates, who seemed to delight in throwing obstacles in his path.

Devin noticed that Bakámu had finally roused himself from his trancelike state and pitched in to help pull victims out of the water. He didn't have time, however, to pay much attention to the rescue attempts, for trying to navigate over the ruins of Port Royal required all his attention.

"Men overboard! Squaaawk! Toss the blackjacks!"

He knew the worst had passed. Henry Morgan had broken his unnerving silence and was now giving orders to the crew.

One by one, people were pulled to the safety of the *Lady Elysia*'s deck, and Devin was relieved to be able to be involved in their rescue. He saw scores of victims who were beyond anyone's help now and had to fight to hold down his gorge at the sight of women and children floating face down around them. Pets, beasts of burden, timber, and furniture from homes, the contents of now sunken warehouses . . .

God in heaven, he prayed, let Meredyth be safe! Why hadn't he sent her back to the mission earlier? He knew the answer to that, and it was selfish beyond measure when he considered the consequences of his behavior. He'd deflowered her with the calculating cunning of that matchmaking Arawak, forced her to wed him so that, ostensibly, he could spare her reputation, and now she might be dead.

Scarifying pain knifed through his chest. He couldn't bear the thought, and his hands tightened on the polished mahogany wheel. For the second time that morning he felt the heavy weight of despair threaten to sap his energy and determination.

Nay! She wasn't dead, couldn't be! Somehow he knew it!

You're a prophet now? whispered a scathing voice. *'Tis a bit beyond your abilities, don't you think, Chandler?* Harsh, mocking laughter sounded in his head.

He concentrated on finding a suitable place to ground the schooner, thankful for its shallow five-foot draft; closing his ears to the pitiful sounds of those huddled on deck and the shouts of his men mingling with the survivors who'd joined them in their rescue efforts, he focused himself.

He felt a small hand on his thigh and glanced down. A little girl, dripping wet and pale as ashes was staring up at him beseechingly.

"Will ye find my papa?" she asked softly, tears sheening her great hazel eyes. She seemed oblivious to the chaos around her, and the gash on her small, smooth cheek. Somehow, in some way, she reminded him of Meredyth.

He could barely hear her above the noise all around them, but he could read her lips and there was no mistaking the anguish in her eyes that could only indicate a child suddenly alone in the world.

"Flaherty!" he called as he caught sight of the boatswain bending over a man collapsed against the rail. Red turned immediately at the sound of his captain's voice.

Devin glanced down again at the child at his side, then looked briefly back at Red. Returning his gaze once again to the water before him, Devin said as soothingly as he could manage, "Go with Master Flaherty there, child. Mayhap he can help you find your papa."

The child put her hand trustingly in Flaherty's and moved with him to the rail. "Send someone to fetch more blackjacks from beneath the bunk in my cabin," Devin called, suddenly remembering an extra stash of the life preservers he'd added as part of the refurbishment of the *Lady Elysia*.

Just then Bakámu walked by Flaherty and the child. The boatswain spoke briefly to the Arawak and left them. "I'll get the blackjacks, Cap'n," he said, moving across the now chaotic deck.

Devin barely had time to notice how the Arawak squatted down beside the child and began introducing her to Henry Morgan, blessedly distracting her for the moment. He returned his attention to his task, noting that the invading sea seemed to stop on the south side of High Street, the small, surviving section of the thoroughfare barely recognizable. He narrowed his eyes against the light. If he could set the schooner down on that strip of High Street, they could debark and make their way up Horne's Alley to New Street, then beyond to Cannon and Yorke Streets, for these appeared to be, for the most part, above water. Mayhap they could use the courthouse or even the synagogue as temporary havens for the lost and injured. Or a place to lay out the dead.

"Brace yourselves," he cried, not daring to release the wheel to use his horn, and the ship plowed onto the higher sand of High Street where it intersected the narrower Horne's Alley. A great, grating sound came from the keel below as it scraped across the sand, and people who were unable to grab hold of the rails or masts and unsecured objects that were scattered about the deck were thrown forward.

Although he'd braced himself, Devin came up hard against the helm. The *Lady Elysia* ground to a jolting halt.

He let out his breath and briefly touched his forehead to the cool wood of the wheel.

"Chandler!"

The snarl rose above the suddenly silent deck. It came from behind him, and the savage note in it was chilling.

Devin slowly turned about, acknowledging something familiar about that snarl. There, behind the aft hatchway, stood Luke Pelton, the flintlock pistol in his hand pointed right at Red Flaherty's head. The latter's wrists were trussed behind him as he stumbled from the hatch, the end of the rope leading from his bound hands to Pelton's free hand.

A babble of panicked voices rose up, and crew members instantly quieted the passengers as Devin held up a hand for silence, a hand trembling from outrage at what Pelton had managed to do. Not only had he taken Flaherty captive while the boatswain had been fetching the blackjacks, but he'd also injured the man. A bleeding slash cut across Flaherty's cheek from jawline to cheekbone.

The pistol looked suspiciously like one Devin kept in his cabin, which meant that the man had been rummaging through it when Flaherty stumbled upon him.

"Let him go, you miserable coward," Devin said in a taut, controlled voice as he stepped away from the wheel. He had to try to get Pelton to let down his guard. Mayhap he could get the Englishman to somehow underestimate him again, in spite of their encounter at The Oyster House.

A crewman stepped toward Devin, cutlass drawn. "Stay your hand, Sanders," Devin ordered quietly. "I'll not risk Flaherty's life, do you understand?"

"Aye, Cap'n," answered Sanders, *sotto voce*. "He's only got two shots wi' that flintlock. With a little luck, th' only sure death'll be Flaherty—"

"Nay." The single, emphatic word was as good as a direct order to the entire crew.

Sanders signed audibly as he retreated and lowered his cutlass. Devin heard him say, "Surely taken leave of your senses, Cap'n."

"Nay, lad, just moving up a meeting on the field of honor." To Luke, he said, "Let him go, Pelton," as he took several steps toward him and Flaherty. "Do you hear me? This is between you and me."

"We do it my way, Chandler, or he's dead."

Devin halted, an idea forming in his mind. He crossed his arms over his chest and gave the Englishman a disdainful look. "'Tis a hell of a way to show your gratitude for my men having fished you out of the sea, wouldn't you say, Pelton?" His eyebrows peaked and he made an exaggerated moue as he shook his golden head. "But then, I seem to have forgotten 'tis your wont to sneak up behind your adversary rather than face him man to man."

A few gasps went up here and there from the rescuees. His crew, however, remained tense and silent.

"Your tactics at The Oyster House were naught to brag of, either!" Pelton's face looked like a thundercloud, his voice raspy with rage. "And now I seek to settle things between us and make the lady Meredyth a widow."

Devin casually moved two more steps toward the hatch. "Then I'll consider us even, Pelton, and demand that you let my boatswain go. We'll settle this man to man. Obviously, you couldn't wait until the morn." Scorn edged his words. It was deliberate and exaggerated. "Or is a duel too fair a contest for you, as well?"

Another man gasped softly at the insult.

But Pelton angrily shoved Flaherty forward. " 'Tis just that I cannot wait to rescue the lady Meredyth from your scurvy attentions. I would make her a widow this day, for she can do far better than you."

Red stumbled and landed on his hands and knees a few feet

from his captain. "But you threw away your chances with her, Pelton," Devin said as, without taking his eyes off Luke, he moved toward the fallen crewman.

"Don't!" Luke warned sharply. "You've more important business with me. Let someone else attend him." His eyes darted about the deck. "I need a sword, since you took mine. Unless you want pistols."

Devin shook his head. "Swords are more dependable," he said as conversationally as if they were discussing the weather. Over his shoulder, he called, "Sanders! Will you loan Master Pelton your cutlass? If it ends up in the drink, I'll buy you another!"

The answer was Sanders's sword sliding across the smooth deck and coming to rest near Pelton's feet. He tucked Devin's pistol in his waistband, which made Devin frown inwardly. But he didn't know that Devin had a weapon beneath his shirt, as well.

" 'Twould be wise to clear the decks," Devin advised. "Let everyone debark so no one gets—"

"Nay," Luke cut across his words coldly. "That takes time, and time means opportunity for tricks." He picked up Sanders's cutlass, his eyes on Devin all the while, and straightened. "Time is of the essence and tricks unacceptable." He turned sideways and held up the cutlass in invitation.

Devin raised a gilt eyebrow. "You have no concern for the injured?" But he knew the answer to that even as he feigned a casualness he was far from feeling.

"Take your position, Chandler, before I run you through where you stand!"

Devin responded, thinking of the advantage he had in dry clothing over Pelton's wet garments and the latter's probable fatigue from having survived the earthquake and the churning waters that had swallowed half of Port Royal.

He could always resort to his favorite ploy to ensure a victory, and that might save some time, as well. He had victims to see to and a wife to find.

With all the flourish and grace of a dancing master he sprang toward Luke Pelton. Luke jumped to meet him, and sparks flew as steel met steel.

Meredyth and Woody made it back to Port Royal, or what was left of it, in less than half the time it had taken them to travel toward the plantation. The skittish horses seemed to have extra energy and to be eager to release that nervousness in a distance-eating canter.

Woody never complained, though Meredyth glanced behind her several times to make certain he was with her. Certain he was ignoring the pain their reckless ride was causing him, Meredyth decided she could continue to ignore the remnants of the headache that still plagued her.

The sights that greeted them, however, were grimmer than Meredyth had imagined, never having seen the results of an earthquake before in her life.

Much of Port Royal was gone, disappeared into the sea, and the section of town that remained was badly damaged. Woody estimated that roughly one-third of the town had survived.

Meredyth fought her horror and helplessness at the sight of the wounded and dead, for fear she would topple off her mare in a dead faint. That would be completely useless and absurd when it appeared that every able man and woman was needed to help the victims of the catastrophe.

People half-buried beneath rubble were being extricated by their fellow survivors, and many were walking the flooded streets in a daze. Where the water had receded enough to bare the ground, people were actually trapped in fissures that had rent the earth, then evidently just as quickly closed up again, crushing them. Heads here and there stared lifelessly ahead, while others cried out piteously for help. Some were fortunate enough to have only sunk to their shoulders and were struggling to pull themselves and other living victims free.

"Mother of God!" she muttered aloud and slid from th[e] mare, intending to pitch in and help these poor souls.

She looked over at Kingsley, a question in her eyes. H[e] awkwardly dismounted and gathered up the reins of bot[h] horses before moving toward her. "We need these animals,[" he said, then, obviously reading the desperate query in he[r] expression, he said, "The *Lady Elysia* was scheduled to tak[e] a trial run. If she's out at sea, Devin is safe. But if she returne[d] to port before the quake hit . . ."

Meredyth whirled around, her hands clamped over he[r] mouth at the grim pictures that flashed through her mind's eye[.]

"Help," cried a weak voice from a short stone's throw awa[y.] "Help us, mistress . . . please . . ."

Meredyth's chaotic thoughts were rudely pulled back to th[e] situation as Woody moved up behind her. "Mayhap we ca[n] use the horses to drag some of these people free," he said an[d] limped toward the woman who had called to Meredyth.

She was still unable to move for a moment, anchored b[y] private anguish and the horrible reality all around them. The[n] she heard the cries of a child not far from the woman wh[o] was calling to her. The child's arms and shoulders were movin[g] weakly to pry himself from the narrow fissure that was a dea[th] trap for some. "Mamma!" he cried, and in that momen[t] Meredyth pushed all else from her mind as she stumbled ove[r] her wet skirts to reach him.

Twenty-four

Devin suspected that he had more energy and strength than Luke Pelton, but nonetheless he proceeded with his oft-used technique to tire his opponent while acting like the fight itself were a game to him. If not carefully and believably executed, the plan would be for naught because Pelton would realize what was happening.

Devin met and countered Pelton's first several slashes like an instructor showing off his elegant parries, before dodging and dancing out of reach of the deadly blade. Both men were of similar height and weight and light on their feet, and their boot heels clicked and shuffled over the otherwise silent deck.

"Are you afraid of being struck?" Luke asked with heavy irony.

"Hardly, my friend," Devin answered lightly. "Half the match is agility and lightness on one's feet, the lethal blow to be anticipated only as the *finale*."

Luke's eyes slitted as he contemplated his opponent, and Devin wondered if he'd yet persuaded Pelton that he was dealing with a man more interested in appearances than reality. Pelton may have been unscrupulous, but he wasn't stupid, though he seemed to have a habit of letting his emotions rule his head. Because of his own outburst of temper in the billiard room, Devin now had to work twice as hard to make Pelton wonder if he was really dealing with a fool or not.

The Englishman's answer was an indisputable snort of contempt and impatience, which told Devin exactly what he

thought of that view, and an increase in the ferocity of hi
strokes.

Devin had hoped to confine the fight to the quarterdeck
for most of the rescuees were on the lower deck. But Pelton
obviously had other ideas, for he quickly advanced with deadl
thrusts, forcing Devin down the two steps and off the quarter
deck. The main mast came up solidly behind him, and he at
tacked Pelton with a flurry of beautifully executed strokes bu
deliberately and, he hoped, deceptively lighter than he woul
use in an all-out struggle.

But it seemed Pelton wasn't taking the bait and wasn't tiring
as quickly as Devin had anticipated. Luke's counterattack drove
Devin toward the larboard rail.

When Pelton had him almost backed up to the rail, in
reckless risk—the likes of which had earned him the sobrique
"Devil"—Devin leapt to the smooth top of the barrier, praying
he wouldn't fall and break his neck. He'd occasionally indulge
in such horseplay with a few of his crew on calm seas an
had fallen overboard a number of times, to the delight of hi
men, before he'd improved his balance.

Several sounds of surprise came from the onlookers, and
Devin allowed his mouth to curve into a triumphant grin. He
even advanced a few steps, on the attack—a rather awkward
attack, with bent back and careful parries—to keep Pelton from
driving him backward on the rail that seemed to narrow be
neath his feet with every step he took.

"Jesus Christ, Cap'n, get down!" implored one of his men
from somewhere behind him. It registered dimly, and Devin
couldn't help but picture Woodrow Kingsley rolling his eyes
to the heavens at Devin's fancy but foolhardy footwork.

That break in his concentration cost him his balance, and
he whirled into the air to cover his fall, double-handedly
swinging his cutlass about him in an arc for security, and
landed an arm's length from the rail. The devil's own luck, he
thought ruefully, having just missed the little girl in Bakámu's
charge.

And then all hell broke loose.

"Squaaawk! Kill the greasy riff-raff!" bawled a certain pain-in-the-arse parrot.

The bird distracted Devin enough to give Pelton a chance to deliver him a nasty upswing. knocking the cutlass from his hand. Devin froze for a moment in feigned disbelief, and Luke took advantage by slicing sideways at his midsection.

Devin came to his senses in an instant and ducked for his life.

Without warning, an object came whistling through the air and pinned Pelton securely to the rail by the sleeve of his left arm. It was a dagger, and another gasp went up. Who in the hell had disobeyed his orders? Devin wondered briefly but thankfully.

He should have known.

"Fight fair—like warrior," Bakámu admonished Pelton in stentorian strains, his brow furrowed with ire. He pushed Devin's cutlass toward him with one foot, and Devin had just enough time to bend and snatch it up before Pelton tore his sleeve away from the rail and advanced, his expression full of fury now.

"You wouldn't be so generous, Indian," Devin threw over his shoulder, "if you knew this villain was responsible for your beating the other night."

Pelton lunged at Devin, his wicked sword point slitting the latter's pale lawn shirt and drawing a ribbon of blood across his midsection.

Devin didn't dare glance down but felt the needlelike pain and consequent trickle of blood just above his navel and decided it was time to get serious.

He jumped back, his concentration focusing on Pelton and Pelton alone. No one else existed for the moment as he marshaled every bit of his expertise and experience to direct at his opponent.

"Getting worried?" Pelton sneered and lunged again with surprising speed for a man who should have been at least slightly affected physically by his recent brush with death. But Devin was ready. He turned aside Pelton's blade with a skillful twist of his wrist and a resounding echo of metal on metal.

A child started to cry, at first barely registering on the periphery of Devin's concentration; yet the urgency of the situation suddenly recommunicated itself to him. The lives of some of the people aboard his own vessel were possibly hanging in the balance and others in the stricken town were dying.

He feinted to the right, then brought the cutlass arcing back over Pelton's head and toward the man's right shoulder. Pelton unexpectedly caught the strategy, swiping upward to his right to counter the blow before Devin could slash his upper arm.

But the Englishman's swing suddenly seemed to lack the power of his earlier blows and, as if he sensed that Devin may have noticed, Pelton immediately went for Devin's midsection again.

Devin nimbly danced aside, spun, and brought his blade straight across where Pelton's thighs should have been. But Pelton had jumped the wicked blow, landing heavily. He lunged upward, his sword tip pointed at Devin's throat, and Devin turned aside, feeling the passage of air as the blade whistled harmlessly by. Swinging back in a lightning move before Pelton could withdraw, Devin knocked the latter's cutlass up and out of his hand.

A cry of triumph from several of his crew went up as the weapon sailed over the rail and into the shallow water.

"Toss him another," Devin ordered, taking advantage of the moment by inhaling a few deep breaths and retreating a step.

"Never mind!" Luke panted, removing the pistol from his waistband. It was a clumsy move, and Devin desperately dove toward the firearm with his cutlass, hoping to knock it from Pelton's fingers. But it discharged into the sails above their heads.

As Devin dropped the sword and threw himself toward Pelton, the latter tried to grab him with his free hand. But Devin wasn't about to become a hostage, and he flung his arms about the other man's middle, butting his head into his belly and knocking him down onto the deck. At such close range, Pelton couldn't aim the clumsy flintlock and hit Devin with his second and last shot. Nor could he hold Devin hostage.

But he did hit Devin in the side of the head with the pistol butt before Devin could wrestle it away from him. Stars erupted before his eyes, as his hand groped desperately for Pelton's wrist. The blow reminded him of the blows he'd suffered while bound like an animal in the *Bristol*'s hold. A fresh volley of anger exploded through him.

"You'll never have Meredyth, you bloody pirate!" Luke rasped in his ear, further fueling Devin's fury. "You'll have to kill me first!"

"Gladly!" Devin gritted back and rammed his sore head upward into Pelton's chin. Before the latter could recover, Devin brought his knee up into his opponent's groin with a resurgence of energy, momentarily paralyzing Pelton.

He groaned beneath Devin and tried to shove him away, but Devin's hands were now around his throat, his body temporarily pinning down the stunned Englishman.

"Pistol!" someone shouted from what sounded like a great distance, but Devin was too intent on choking the life from his adversary to heed.

He lifted and slammed Pelton's head against the deck. "Will—you—give—up?" he rasped.

Pelton bared his teeth in anger. "Nay, Irish whoreson!"

Devin formed a fist and smashed him in the jaw, saw his eyes roll, and hoped the bastard had given up, for when all was said and done, he derived no pleasure from killing, even a man like Luke Pelton.

The figure beneath him started to go limp, or so Devin thought as he fought the red haze of anger veiling his vision and clouding his common sense. Then he realized it was an attempt to throw him off guard, for he felt Luke's arm tense.

He heard a banshee shriek cut through the air and was suddenly pushed aside by the Indian. As he tumbled sideways, unaware that Bakámu was pushing him out of the line of fire, there was a tremendous roar in his ear and what felt like a cannonball seared across his side.

That pricklouse Pelton had shot him! he thought through a mist of pain, and in reaction dragged his body toward the downed Pelton, intending to shove away the interfering Indian and crush Pelton's windpipe.

If he was going to Hell, he wasn't leaving Pelton behind.

His eyes registered a dagger, then spurting blood as the Arawak slashed Pelton's throat.

Dark spots peppered the inside of his eyelids and the world receded.

They weren't far from the courthouse, which had survived the quake, and Emil Rogers temporarily took over while Devin was unconscious. Most of the rescuees, fortunately, were able to be moved, or moved on their own, up Horne's Alley and over to New Street and the courthouse. Luke Pelton's body and two others who had died after being fished out of the water were taken to the courthouse to be laid out, as well.

Rogers, however, deferred to the ship's surgeon, Daniel Eames, who recommended that Devin not be moved.

"But the word is they're setting up a temporary hospital there," Flaherty insisted with obvious concern. One weathered cheek sported a white plaster.

"I can handle this," answered Eames with a slight smile of assurance. He was the ship's newest crew member, recommended by Emil Rogers himself, and had just met his captain the day before. The son of a physician in the Colonies, he'd run away to sea at the ripe age of eighteen, after the honorable Doctor Eames had became the dishonorable Doctor Eames and disgraced himself and his family. But Daniel had been fascinated with his father's vocation and had committed to memory everything his father had taught him.

Eames was a small, wiry man of about thirty, with a ready

smile and a warm handshake. His sandy hair was long and lank and therefore always tied back from his face. His good-naturedness, the sparkle of amusement lurking in his golden-brown eyes, made him seem like little more than a youth.

" 'Tain't serious then?" Galbraithe asked.

Eames shook his head, setting his large gold hood earring a-dangle.

"Nay, not really. A lot o' blood, but no ribs broken as far as I can tell. The shot didn't penetrate deep enough t' reach any organs luckily. But he can rest here until the bleedin' stops."

Rink Dobbins scratched his head. "Mayhap you oughta bleed 'im, Doc. Ye know, give 'im a phle-phle . . ."

Eames shook his head. "No phlebotomy. He's lost enough blood."

"But don't ye need to get rid o' the bad blood?"

For the first time, Bakámu spoke up, his normally good-natured expression replaced with anger. "Warrior needs all blood Wishemenetoo give him. Only white man stupid enough to take more blood from wounded man!" His voice was full of contempt.

All eyes went to the Arawak.

"Look here, Indian," Dobbins said with a frown. "Don't know where the cap'n found ye, but phlebotomy's a proper medical *per-ceedure!*"

"For fools!"

Dobbins took a step toward Bakámu, his expression suddenly threatening.

Rogers grabbed Rink's arm. "Hold on, fer God's sake, man! He saved the cap'n's life when none o' the rest of us lifted a finger."

Rink turned on Rogers. "We were obeyin' orders! He . . ." he cut Bakámu a scathing look, "don't follow nobody's orders! 'Sides, the cap'n coulda saved 'imself, even that stupid parrot coulda seen *that.*"

"Squaaawk! Stupid! Stupid parrot! Stupid matey!"

Flaherty broke out in a grin and had to turn his head as Rink threw Henry Morgan a suspicious look. The gray's words broke the tension. Devin mumbled something, and Daniel Eames said, "Help me get 'im to his cabin." He looked at Bakámu, who appeared ready to pounce on anyone who would deliberately rob Devin Chandler of any more blood.

"Too warm in cabin. Better here. Bakámu make shelter from sun and—"

"Don't push yer luck, Arawak," Dobbins said, thrusting his jaw out belligerently. "Ye won one battle, but Doc here says the cap'n goes below decks, and below decks he goes!"

"Meredyth. Got to . . . find . . . Merry . . ." Devin mumbled from some unknown place of pain.

"Then Bakámu stay with Chan-ler." It was a statement, but no one seemed to have any objection to it as they lifted their fallen leader and carried him toward the hatchway.

It was rough going. Meredyth had a woman on the mare and was leading it. Woody was astride the gelding, with a small boy and girl before him in the saddle. Only at Meredyth's insistence would he ride himself. "You surely cannot negotiate this rubble!" she'd said in exasperation.

Evidently, even Woodrow Kingsley had reservations about crossing her when those eyes ignited with emerald fire.

It had been all they could do to continue on after exhausting themselves rescuing those who'd fallen victim to the shrinking and swelling earth. Most of those who had been swallowed by fissures and were still visible were dead, or close to it. Stray dogs barked as they circled dying victims, then moved closer to sniff the half-exposed corpses, making Meredyth's stomach turn. She looked away, unable to help those wretched souls who'd mercifully already passed from this world.

The woman, who turned out to be the Widow Timmons from The Oyster House, swayed in the saddle. "Andrew . . . Andrew . . ." she murmured with dull despair.

Meredyth put out a hand to steady her. "Easy now. Just a bit farther, I think." She looked back at Woody. "How far now?" she asked, hoping the courthouse was close. She was hot and tired, with the sun beating on her bare head, her steps careful and laborious through the rubble-strewn town: the air was thick with the stench of death and destruction.

Her shoes offered little protection from the bricks and timbers over which they were forced to trudge when they couldn't avoid the debris. It didn't take long for those pretty and dainty leather slippers to shred to ribbons. But Meredyth ignored her injuries, more concerned about one of the horses breaking a leg.

Woody looked around. "The town's almost unrecognizable," he said wearily. They'd just met a merchant who'd told them all of Thames Street had disappeared into the sea, along with several blocks immediately behind it, and Woody's spirits had wilted considerably. "But we're on Cannon Street, and the next one over is New Street. The courthouse is there, and mayhap they'll have fresh water and physicians. And someone who can tell us the fate of the *Lady Elysia.*"

Meredyth thought she detected a break in his voice, but she didn't acknowledge it, for her own heart was leaden. She was anxious to reach the courthouse and other people—anyone who could give her information. Yet she was also apprehensive about receiving bad news upon their arrival, and she couldn't find the motivation to comfort Woody when, as time passed, she herself believed there was less and less hope of Devin having survived the catastrophe.

She directed her gaze toward the St. Andrews town house. The buildings in that part of town seemed, for the most part, intact. Maybe they could find Devin and take him there.

At least they could spend the night there, she thought, if the building was still stable. The thought heartened her a little and she turned to look at Woody. He was looking in the same direction. Their eyes met, and he nodded. "We can mayhap go to the town house after we safely deliver these people."

His voice strengthened as he said with more determination, "And after we find Devin. If one ship can make it, so can others."

They'd passed one marketplace, onto which a French vessel—evidently a captured prize, for England and France were at war—by some miracle had been deposited by the sea.

Meredyth's mood lightened just by hearing Woody make such a positive statement, even though they saw no other vessels in the immediate area. Soon they were approaching the red brick building that Woody identified as the courthouse. People milled about it, and Meredyth's hold tightened on the reins of the mare.

As they moved closer, Meredyth could see many of the survivors were lying upon the ground, injured or exhausted. Others were moving between them to tend them. To one side, lay what appeared to be a row of corpses, some of them shrouded, some not.

"Don't look at the dead, milady," Woody said, "nor you, Widow Timmons," he added. Widow Timmons, however, was obviously still dazed and didn't respond.

"Mayhap Mamma and Papa are there," said the little boy, finally summoning the courage to speak up. He was about ten years old, his sister six or seven, and both children's cheeks were smudged with dirt and streaked with half-dried tears. One of the lad's arms lay limply across his lap, having been broken, and Meredyth admired his stoicism; he'd emitted little more than soft, sporadic moans as they'd plodded through wrecked Port Royal.

Meredyth reached up to Widow Timmons when they came to a halt before the courthouse. It was, miraculously, still standing. "Let me help you," said a voice from behind her. Then almost immediately, "Oh my God . . . Mother!"

Meredyth looked up at an attractive man she recognized as Andrew Timmons. She blinked, unable at first to comprehend such luck. He was pale and covered with dirt and blood, but he appeared hale enough.

He glanced at Meredyth over his mother's shoulder as he gently helped the latter down off the mare and into his arms. Meredyth must have looked shocked at his disheveled and blood-smeared appearance, for he gave her a vague smile and said, " 'Tisn't as bad as it looks. I've been helping tend the injured, milady."

". . . saved my life . . . Andrew," the Widow Timmons blurted. "She . . . saved me . . ." She released her son and turned back on unsteady legs to Meredyth.

Meredyth was about to brush off the woman's seemingly sincere gratitude when Woodrow Kingsley came up beside them, the children still astride the gelding. "Lady Meredyth, this is Arabella Timmons and her son, Andrew. I regret the circumstances of this introduction." He limped forward and put a hand on the matron's arm. "Are you feeling a bit better now, Arabella?"

Arabella Timmons nodded, her expression indicating that she was not quite herself, though she could now speak coherently. "My Andrew is safe." Her fingers tightened visibly about her son's arm as her eyes searched his face. Her features were wan and drawn, lank wisps of her salt-and-pepper hair hanging about her face. Her gown was torn and filthy.

"To the courthouse with you all!" ordered a familiar voice. It was Governor White. His face and voice were grave, but aside from being disheveled, he appeared unharmed. He nodded at the ladies. "We've got to get organized, and the courthouse is a good place to use as temporary headquarters." He applied gentle pressure to Meredyth's arm. "Take the mare and the children and go."

Andrew guided his mother away, while Meredyth took the gelding's reins and Woodrow fell behind with her mare to speak in low tones to the governor.

"Have you heard of any ships surviving the quake?" she heard Woody ask John White. "We saw a French vessel back a ways, sitting squarely in the center of one of the marketplaces and . . ." He let his words trail off.

"Aye," the governor answered in his grave voice. "We've seen the frigate *Swan* rescuing victims from the floodwaters and heard that Captain Chandler's schooner did the same before it was beached not far from here."

The *Lady Elysia* had survived. Meredyth was afraid she'd imagined the words. That meant that Devin had survived, too, and had even helped rescue victims of the earthquake. Relief showered over Meredyth like a welcome summer rain over parched earth.

Her limbs went weak with the most profound unburdening of fear she'd ever evinced, and she almost went down on her knees. She quickly straightened like a drunkard giddy with glee. Fortunately, nobody noticed her misstep beneath her long skirts.

He's alive . . . he's alive . . . he's alive . . .

Her heart thrummed to the rhythm of the words: her abused feet were suddenly insensitive to what they encountered beneath her, carrying her over the broken earth and debris like wings skimming an air current. She tugged at the gelding's reins, causing the horse to whinny and jerk up its head at the renewed and rougher pull on its soft mouth, all sound of the men's voices dimming before the joyous thoughts cascading through her mind.

Then the smell of blood—of death—invaded her nostrils, and her attention was unexpectedly snagged by the row of bodies to one side of the damaged red brick building.

Meredyth couldn't help herself. In spite of Woodrow Kingsley's warning, in spite of her own reluctance, she slowly walked toward where the dead lay.

The children they'd rescued had been reunited with their father, though their mother was still missing. Andrew Timmons and his mother, who'd seemed to have recovered enough to want to be useful, were helping others with the injured and the distraught. Governor White supervised and encouraged, consulted and consoled.

"Milady?" As if thoughts could produce flesh and blood, Woody called from behind her.

She turned and drew in a sustaining breath. "I must. . . . We don't really know if Devin survived just because the ship did."

"Then let me look," he said gently and moved up to her using a piece of driftwood someone had given him as a walking stick. He leaned heavily on it, as if the weight of the world were on his shoulders now. " 'Tisn't a sight for a woman."

Every instinct that had propelled women from the dawn of time to battlefields and catastrophes to aid or search for their loved ones came rushing to the fore. "He's my husband!" she said with sudden fervor, her spine straightening with resolve. "And why should I be cosseted when others are suffering?" Her eyes lit with that spark of green flame that signaled St. Andrews's ire.

Woodrow Kingsley sighed audibly.

"Mayhap there are others I know here and can . . . identify." Her voice grew husky with emotion as she said the last word before she added quietly but firmly, "I'm unharmed—others are not so fortunate."

"Then let me accompany you." He took her elbow without waiting for permission, and they swung back toward the grisly business.

Even though it was approaching twilight, the dying sun briefly caught and reflected the golden tones of a corpse's hair just before one of the volunteers pulled a covering of some kind over the body's head and shoulders. It appeared, from where Meredyth stood, to be a man, and she was drawn toward it.

She didn't know if Woody had seen what she had, but the hair color was achingly familiar and her heartbeat slowed to a sluggish churning beneath her breast.

"Milady?" Woody asked quietly.

"A man over there, a blond man . . ."

Several men were swiftly shrouding the victims already lying there, for others were bringing in dozens of the deceased.

Woody opened his mouth to speak, but in her rising agitation Meredyth was quicker. "My good sir," she addressed the
one closest to them. Her voice sounded hollow and ineffective
to her, but she obviously caught his attention.

He looked up, his face a study in despair.

She pointed toward the body with the blond hair. From the
length of the corpse, the man had been tall and lean, and a
seaman she guessed from his breeches and boots. She raised
a shaking finger. "May we see this man?" she asked, her voice
quaking.

The man stared at her, but she wasn't quite sure why.

"Did you hear the lady?" Woody snapped. "Raise the coat
and be done with it!

The man scrambled to do as he was bidden. In his haste,
delicacy was thrown to the winds, and he flung the coat aside
so exuberantly that the entire corpse was exposed to their
gazes—the tangled, blood-matted blond hair, the gore-soaked
shirt, and the gaping slash below his chin that resembled a
second mouth with obscenely pouting lips.

It was Luke Pelton.

Meredyth felt her gorge rise and lifted a hand to cover her
mouth. She grasped Woody's arm with the sudden strength of
Hercules, unable to tear her eyes from the body.

"Enough!" Woody told the man, and tried to pull Meredyth
away. "Cover him, for God's sake!"

Meredyth, however, was rooted to the ground and wouldn't
budge. When she finally turned tormented eyes to his, she
couldn't speak.

"At least, child, 'tisn't Devin."

She shook her head, fighting to find her tongue. "N-nay,
but . . . but he was murdered!" Horror infused her words.

Woody frowned. "It happens all the time on the waterfront
here, any waterfront." He looked over at the man who was
recovering the remains. "Know you how this man died?"

"Any fool can see 'is throat was slit."

Meredyth felt Woody's body tighten with anger. "Know you aught more?"

The man squinted up at him, still squatting. "What's it worth to ye, guvna'?" he asked slyly, looking from Woody to Meredyth and back again.

Woody's mouth fell open, as if he couldn't comprehend the man's greed in the midst of such tragedy. Meredyth, however, reached purposefully into her skirts and produced a coin.

"Don't give him—" Woody began, his voice full of contempt.

The coin flashed dully in the dying daylight before the man caught it, bit on it, then tightly fisted his fingers around it. "Man who brought this one to me was from the *Lady Elysia*. 'E said the bloke was killed by Cap'n Devil Chandler hisself."

Twenty-five

His side was on fire.

Devin lifted heavy eyelids and was greeted by a familiar face in the light of a single lantern. Bakámu. He closed his eyes with alacrity. Were they in Hell together? Nay, it wasn't hot enough.

"Chan-ler feel better?"

"Better than what?" Devin croaked. "I hurt like hell, and where . . ." He opened his eyes again and recognized the inside of his cabin aboard the *Lady Elysia*. Suddenly, the floodgates of memory burst open: the earthquake, his duel with Pelton, Meredyth.

Meredyth.

He thrust himself up onto his elbows and gasped softly at the pain. Bakámu put one fingertip on his chest and commanded, "Chan-ler stay bed."

Devin looked down at the restraining finger and the plaster that appeared to cover his entire torso. The bands of linen wrapped about him constricted his breathing when he tried to inhale deeply.

Then he remembered. Pelton had used one of his own pistols on him and evidently had hit him in the side. The image of a knife-wielding Bakámu and the accompanying fountain of ruby-red blood in the sunlight came to him then, and the last moments before he'd fainted turned crystal clear. In an attempt to save Devin's life, the well-meaning but interfering Arawak had robbed Devin of the chance to kill Pelton.

Devin doubted Pelton could have hit him had Devin been left atop the Englishman and allowed to strangle him, the bore of the pistol too long, the weapon too cumbersome at such close range.

The Arawak had almost caused his death in his clumsy attempt to "save" him! The thought was almost enough to make Devin collapse again onto his back, but he had to find Meredyth.

He sat up, closing his eyes against the fiery agony in his right side, and swung his legs over the side of the bunk. The Arawak's finger went rigid and Devin was unable to make any further progress.

He tried to knock Bakámu's hand away, at great cost physically. The finger was momentarily dislodged, then returned. Devin glared up at him with bloodshot eyes. "If you don't take your hand away, Indian, I swear I'll have you trussed and taken back to wherever you came from before I pulled you from that crocodile's jaws!" He was hissing, teeth clenched, he realized, and his furious mien must have given the Arawak pause for his hand fell away and he backed up a step.

"By the Mass, get back here and help me!" he barked, acute discomfort making him irritable. Beneath the pain, his profound fear for Meredyth grew, like a living thing, with every moment that passed. He'd already wasted the entire night.

"What time is it?" he demanded as he grasped Bakámu's forearm.

"Not like that," the Arawak said and locked his arms beneath Devin's left shoulder. As he eased Devin from the bunk, the Indian answered his query. "Sunrise."

A knock on the cabin door sounded. Now, who in the devil had sneaked up on silent feet while he was struggling to stand? he wondered with a flash of annoyance.

"Rogers and Eames," Emil answered.

"Come in."

When they'd complied, Emil Rogers exclaimed, "Cap'n! What're ye doin' out o' bed?"

Devin grimaced and motioned Bakámu toward his brass-bound wooden chest of clean clothing. " 'Tis morning, is it not?" he asked gruffly.

"But—" Eames began.

Devin held up his left hand sharply. "I'll not be coddled like a sick babe when there's been an earthquake and people need help!" He glanced at Bakámu. "Clean shirt and breeches and be quick about it."

"Cap'n, as the ship's surgeon, I can't let you leave—"

"Show me your credentials, Eames," Devin said shortly. "If you're not governor of Jamaica or captain of this ship, you can't forbid me anything." With Bakámu's help, he struggled into the clean shirt. "Where's Flaherty?"

"Here, Cap 'n," the boatswain said from the doorway. Gritting his teeth, Devin began unbuttoning his breeches. "Check for any supplies we might have on board. Surely, we can spare them for the survivors."

"We delivered our passengers to the courthouse yesterday. "They're settin' up a sort o' headquarters fer the town there.""

Devin nodded and allowed Bakámu to peel down his breeches because it hurt so to bend. "What's the status of my injury?" he asked Eames as sweat beaded his forehead and upper lip.

Eames ran a hand over his face in obvious defeat. "Flesh wound to the right side—"

"Broken ribs?" Devin demanded, trying not to think about the length of healing time that would require.

"Nay. Mayhap bruised but none fractured."

"Good. I'm going first to the courthouse. You can accompany me with any supplies and any remaining crew members to help out. Eames, your services will be much needed. And leave a few men on board as anchor watch."

The look on Rink Dobbins's face was comical. Devin could read his mind: *Anchor watch for a stranded ship?* But the first officer did not object nor did any of the others. Plundering and looting would increase in the stricken city long before it got better.

"Orders understood?"

Mumbles to the affirmative.

Devin looked at Daniel Eames. "How about a good belt of brandywine before we leave?"

Meredyth was up before the sun. She had decided, on Woody's advice, to remain where she was for the night, though she'd insisted she be allowed to help with the injured. He reluctantly agreed to the latter, for Meredyth deliberately gave the impression that that was the only reason she would agree to stay. Safety in numbers, they both had agreed, for the soldiers from the surviving Fort Charles were continually trickling in and, Woody hoped, providing help and protection under the governor's direction.

More and more small patrols of men ventured into the ruins of Port Royal in search of survivors.

"As soon as 'tis considered safe," he'd told her in no uncertain terms, "I'll accompany you back to the plantation. You can look in on the town house first, but you don't belong here, milady."

"Where exactly do I belong?" she'd asked sharply, exasperated. "Don't we all have an obligation under the circumstances?"

He'd looked away, obviously torn.

Immediately, she'd felt contrite. "Forgive me, Woody."

He'd shaken his balding head. "Nay, child. Forgive me. You're much more noble-minded than I."

Meredyth was filthy, her mouth gritty, her hair a mass of tangles, and her pretty lawn gown didn't bear thinking about. Nor was it important now. She pitched in wholeheartedly, comforting children and parents alike, as well as stanching bleeding wounds as best she could, while the two physicians at the scene attended to the more serious injuries.

An hour after sunrise, stains of blood had been added t
the marks left by sea water, dust, and grit on her gown. Sh
was holding the hand of a dying woman known to her onl
as Deborah and offering what pitiful comfort she could in th
absence of the woman's family. The young woman was suffer
ing severe internal injuries, according to one of the physicians
and there was nothing they could do. She was also only a few
years older than Meredyth, she guessed, which brought th
chill brush of death even closer.

Despair and helplessness washed over her as she felt Debo
rah's life slipping away like sand through a sieve, when i
dearly familiar voice came to her.

"Meredyth?"

She forced her thoughts away from the woman beside he
and slowly raised her head. Her fingers clenched Deborah'
limp hand like a vise.

Devin.

Meredyth remained where she was, sitting on her heels
clutching the departed woman's hand. Her gaze hungrily rovee
over him, taking in everything from the visible bruises on hi
beloved face to the stiff manner in which he held himself, one
arm protectively across his torso. He'd been hurt.

He moved forward awkwardly, one of his crew members
and Bakámu, who'd been close behind him, discreetly dropping
back.

Meredyth released Deborah's hand and straightened slowly
afraid she'd fall on her face if she moved any faster. She'd hac
precious little to eat or drink, preferring to give it to the
wounded, and the dizziness that assaulted her was the resul
of her own selflessness. She stood for a moment fighting the
tendency to sway.

Devin couldn't believe his eyes. She was alive, though the
only thing recognizable about her was her dark hair and those
magnificent green eyes. She'd been through hell, obviously
having been caught in Port Royal when the quake hit rather
than having made it to her father's plantation.

Suddenly she was in his arms, great tears sliding down her cheeks. He crushed her to him unthinkingly, then sucked in his breath sharply as his wounded side protested with a vengeance. He shifted her slightly to his left and buried his face in her hair, swearing never to let her out of his sight again, even if it meant abducting her and taking her to an isolated island somewhere in the lesser Antilles to live out their lives.

"I prayed you would be at the plantation before this hit," he said quietly, "and that was bad enough. Had I known otherwise, I would have gone mad with worry." His eyes glistened with emotion.

She tightened her arms about his neck and unthinkingly tried to bury herself in his body, his strength, unwittingly causing him more discomfit. He would have endured anything, however, in those moments, just to keep her securely in his arms.

When she lifted her face to his, his lips touched hers gently, tentatively at first, as if he were afraid she would disappear or crumble in his arms. Then his trembling hands touched her face. He sifted his fingers through her silky hair, encountering snarls and tiny pieces of debris, reminding him how close to death she'd come.

He closed his eyes, rested his chin atop her head, and tried to control his raging emotions. "We were at sea when the quake hit, Merry-mine," he told her in a soothing voice. "We sensed something seriously amiss, and I think 'twas Bakámu's Wishemenetoo who called us back." He chuckled softly, then grimaced.

Meredyth continued to cling to him, though with a more relaxed grip, soothed by the steady cadence of his heartbeat beneath her ear.

He massaged one hand up and down her back comfortingly and spoke like a parent reassuring a frightened child. "We ended up rescuing many who were caught in the tidal wave that washed over Port Royal and lost none of the crew."

She was quiet a few moments in the wake of his words. "I

didn't know if you were safely out at sea or—" She shuddered and buried her face in the pillow of his chest.

"It's over, love," he murmured. "You don't have to worry about me now." He pressed his lips to a tangled skein of her hair. "The worst is over, and I'll take you back to Father Tomas where you can heal and forget this ever happened."

They stood alone, a tiny island of security in the midst of the chaos and anguish all around them, and reveled in the feel of each other. Warm living flesh, and steadily beating hearts.

"Devin?" she asked without warning.

"Aye?"

"How . . . How did you come to meet up with Luke?" she asked in a muffled voice, and he immediately stiffened at the unexpected utterance of the name of his nemesis.

"Pelton? For the love of God, Meredyth, why would you even bring him up now?" he asked, thrown off guard.

She tried to pull away but only half-heartedly for fear of hurting him and a reluctance to break the contact. He was just as reluctant and held her firmly.

"It. . . . It's important to me, Devin," she said with quiet insistence. "Tell me how you met up with him."

He toyed briefly with the idea of lying to her. Lying had always been easy. But not with Meredyth. And the consequences might come back to hurt him more than the simple ugly truth.

"One of my men pulled him from the floodwaters," he said in a flat voice. "He was fortunate it wasn't me, or I'd have let him drown," he added darkly in the face of the memories of Luke's challenge and subsequent determination to kill him. He paused a moment, oblivious of his verbal blunder, and frowned. "How did you know about him?"

Meredyth finally pulled away from him and met his eyes. Hers were troubled, and Devin had the frightening feeling that this was the beginning of the end.

Ignoring his question, Meredyth asked, "Did you kill him, Devin? Did you have to end his life by slashing his throat?"

His hands tightened on her arms, and for a fleeting fragment of time he almost forgot the burning pain in his side. "In one question you ask if I killed him, then before I can answer you jump to the assumption that I did and question my supposed method! Which is it, Meredyth?"

She frowned. "You're taking advantage of the circumstances and trying to confuse the issue, Devin Chandler!" she said heatedly, then lowered her voice. "Did you slash his throat?"

"Does it matter?" He couldn't believe what was coming out of her mouth. Why didn't she ask who'd shot *him?* Or was she afraid the answer would, indeed, reveal her precious Luke Pelton to be twice a traitor?

"Why don't you ask if he shot me?" he asked in spite of better intentions. "A handspan to one side and he'd have taken out my black heart. Would *that* have been more acceptable to you?"

The stricken look on her face made him sick inside. He reached for her once again. "Merry," he said softly, "this is absurd! We've found each other, we've both survived, and—"

She held her ground, remaining where she stood. "I'm sorry you were hurt, Devin. But to rescue Luke only to—"

"I told you I didn't rescue him!"

"—slash his throat," she finished as if he hadn't spoken.

"She saw the body, lad," Woodrow Kingsley said from behind Devin.

He slowly turned around, the familiarity of the voice penetrating rather than the words. "Woody!" he exclaimed, gingerly placing his left arm about the older man's shoulders and giving him a squeeze. "Thank God!"

"I'll drink to that!" Woody said with a suspicious sniff. He looked exhausted and hurting. He glanced at Meredyth, who'd bent over Deborah and was pulling the woman's tattered fichu over her face. He lowered his voice, "But you must realize that Lady Meredyth saw Pelton's corpse over yonder," he motioned toward the makeshift mortuary with his chin, "where the men from the ship left it."

Devin was dismayed. "You let her see that gruesome piece of work?"

Woody leaned heavily on his driftwood stick and dropped his gaze. "There was no help for it. She's a woman grown lad, and she insisted. Said that as your wife, she had every right to look for you."

For some reason, Woody's revelation only angered Devin further. "She does pretty much whatever the hell she pleases, doesn't she?" he said in a low, harsh tone, frustrated beyond measure at her reaction to Pelton's death. "Whether it's running after me into Port Royal because of some Arawak's fertile imagination or inspecting a row of corpses like a commanding officer from Fort Charles inspecting his troops!"

"Fort Charles is no more," Woody reminded him soberly, obviously to divert his thoughts and defuse some of his anger.

Devin cut him an accusing look. "So you side with her now?"

Woody put one hand on the younger man's forearm. "Devin, I'm not siding with anyone! We're standing here in the after math of an earthquake! 'Tis absurd to be anything but happy to have found each other alive! To *be* alive! Why must you allow a dead man to come between you now?"

Devin watched Meredyth through his sandy lashes as she bowed her head over the dead woman. "She accused me of slashing his throat, when I did no such thing! My honor's at stake here, Kingsley, and she cannot give me the benefit of the doubt."

Woody raised his eyebrows and lowered his voice. "And when have you ever been concerned about your honor? You name yourself a scoundrel, 'Devil' is your sobriquet, if you'll remember!"

Meredyth straightened then and faced the two men. "Forgive me, Captain Chandler," she said in a strained voice. "I've no wish to argue over, or compare, the qualities of a dead man with yours." Life was so fragile, so precious, she'd learned that in the wake of Manuel's death, and it was being reem

hasized all around her moment by moment. And now Debo-
ah. In the face of all this, what acceptable reason could Devin
ave possibly had to kill Luke Pelton? Whatever it was, it
urely was petty and insignificant.

What reason can any man have for killing another?

Self-defense. The words tiptoed through her mind. Too
oftly. Unheeded.

"Pray excuse us," he said over his shoulder to Woodrow as
e took Meredyth by the arm. He firmly guided her a short
istance from the others and then turned her back to face him.
His blue eyes were icy. "After what he did to you, how can
ou be concerned about *Pelton?*" he asked tersely, an alien
ealousy threatening to overwhelm reason. "Either you were
till in love with him and you jumped in my bed to have your
evenge and you care not one whit for me, or you're an un-
eeling little coquette, charming and luring men into your web
nly to turn your back on them when something better comes
long!"

Ire flashed in her eyes. "You traffic in slaves! What does
hat say about *you?*" she returned. "About what kind of man
ou really are? And now you've done murder!"

So this was how it was going to be, he thought, one part
f his mind struggling to cling to his sanity in the face of
oming catastrophe, personal catastrophe. But this time he
vouldn't play the fool or give in gracefully. "I've done no less
han Pelton ever did! Do you understand, Meredyth? Whatever
ou lay at my head, 'tis no more than *he* ever did! You accept
is word over mine because you met him in some London
lrawing room?"

His face was pale, and Meredyth remembered he'd been
vounded and was possibly bleeding again, for his shirt was
tained with fresh blood from the binding he obviously wore
eneath. How had he been wounded? she suddenly wondered.

His hand upon her forearm tightened. "Answer me,
Meredyth!"

And why don't you ask if he shot me?

In confusion, Meredyth put her hands over her ears to bloc out his earlier query, a childishly protective gesture, and a unconsciously defiant move.

He misinterpreted it and turned livid in a rare show of Iris temper. When he trusted his voice enough to speak, he sai "So you won't answer me now? Nor even listen?"

He could have accepted the fact that she regretted their ma riage, that she'd ever shared intimacies with him, because l was a privateer, a bastard born with no roots, no antecede to speak of. But even his well-practiced self-control deserte him in the face of coming out second, in her eyes, to a blac guard like Luke Pelton.

And now she wouldn't even listen to him.

Devin grabbed her hands and pulled them away. Her long lashed lids flew open, misery and uncertainty muddying th normally clear, fresh hue of her eyes.

She shook her head. *Answer him!* cried her reasonable side *Tell him you'll listen at least!* But she sensed it was too lat He was too angry, and any feeble denial she could offer woul be just that—feeble, ineffective, and certainly unbelievable.

In self-defense, she threw up a shield: her own anger. "No is not the time, nor this the place to discuss anything," sh said through stiff lips. "There's so much real misery here, s much to be done, and. . . . I promised Luke that I would se to his burial."

Real misery? Devin thought, stunned. And she'd promise Pelton—or, obviously, his corpse!—to see to his burial?

It was all he could do not to raise his face to the heaven and howl in frustration.

What about *his* misery? Evidently it wasn't important t her. Their future together wasn't important to her. Becaus there wasn't any future. That was clear as a starry Jamaica night sky. There never had been any future, and he'd finall fallen hopelessly, irretrievably, in love like every starstruck foo he'd ever scorned. It had been his worst fear. He'd opene himself to her, allowed the arrow of profound affection t pierce his defenses, thereby making him vulnerable. He'd dared to believe she cared.

And, like an expert marksman, she'd aimed her arrow with practiced precision, loosed it, and struck him straight through the heart. If she'd ripped out that still-beating organ and nailed it to the mainmast of the *Lady Elysia,* the act couldn't have been more shattering to his hopes and dreams, the substance of his life itself. She was a part of him, and without her he would forever be like a man reft of a precious, irreplaceable limb.

This woman he loved beyond all reason had evidently never stopped caring for another. A dead man, now, whose death she laid at his feet as if he were some common criminal.

She was looking away from him, as if she yearned to leave him and get back to helping where she was needed. She looked pale and tired, and he wondered if she'd eaten since before the earthquake, if she'd slept at all in the hours before dawn.

But she would have enough strength to bury Luke Pelton, the man who'd jilted her, the man who worked for Jean-Baptiste du Casse and la Compagnie de Sénégal, the man who'd joined forces with a cutthroat like Aaron Mad Dog Davies, then abducted and beaten himself and Bakámu, with the intention of killing him and winning back Meredyth's affections.

Devin didn't know whether to laugh at the absurdity of it or cry at the tragic irony.

The task before him would prove to be no easy one, he knew. He couldn't just kill his love for Meredyth St. Andrews on the spot. He would have to bury it slowly, day by day, week by week, month by month, on and on until he breathed his last.

He tried to calm himself, to accept his fate with grace and employ the cool, clear thinking that had served him so well before he'd met Meredyth St. Andrews.

A sudden, disturbing thought struck him. As long as he was a part of the tiny group of informants intent on breaking up

the slave trade, Meredyth would be as much in danger as h
was if she remained connected to him in any way.

He should be thanking his lucky stars that she had mad
the decision for him, for he obviously hadn't been the lea
bit objective about anything that concerned the two of then
He'd been rash and desperate enough to marry her not onl
to salvage her reputation but, more importantly to him, hopin
that she might somehow return his feelings.

He forced his mind to more practical matters. His paper
had been lost with his town house, but he had much of th
valuable information committed to memory. He still had muc
to do on behalf of his employers and the thousands of victim
they would ultimately serve.

"Where did you sleep?" he asked suddenly, fighting to hid
the emotional turmoil seething inside him.

"Right here, though none of us slept much." She put th
heels of her hands to her eyes and tried to massage away th
burning, too tired to even attempt to guess what he was up t
now. He'd gone from fury to an almost unnatural calm. Sh
was emotionally and physically exhausted, but she wasn't s
numb inside as she was torn by colliding feelings: an absur
happiness at seeing him alive, tempered by the shockin
knowledge of what he'd done, relief that he was there to lea
on, to take over and help direct them in their work, yet als
irritation at his unwarranted anger, and now puzzlement at hi
sudden distance.

She summoned a tired half-smile. "Master Kingsley slep
close to my feet, like a hound guarding a bone. And h
snores—"

"I want you to return to the mission," he cut her off, hi
face stony, his words spoken with the same imperturbability.

Bemusement skipped across her features. Before she coul
question his command, however, he continued implacably
"Your intentions and efforts are noble, no one doubts that, bu
you're genteel and a lady born. I will not have you endangering

your health or your life by remaining here a moment longer. I'll arrange an escort back to the plantation."

He looked as if he were going to add something more but, instead, he swung away. Her hand on his arm made him hesitate.

He slowly turned back and met her angry green eyes. "You cannot tell me what to do!" she said. "Especially in a situation like this, where every person is needed and—"

"And you forget, Meredyth, that you are my wife!"

Her lips tightened with mutiny. She had, indeed, forgotten that fact. If it was legal—if Rhys Marteen had really been a ship captain possessing the authority to perform a marriage ceremony, if the well-wishers aboard the *Lady Elysia* were really that or just friends and crew members performing a service for Devin Chandler and, in the process, taking advantage of the plentiful rum and brandywine produced seemingly out of thin air.

Or had it all been a dream?

"In name only," she heard herself say calmly enough. "I will ask for an—" the word stuck in her throat like a fish bone "annulment when I return to England, but for now no one will send me away from where I'm desperately needed!" Her eyes warned him to keep his distance, and he was reminded of her tendency toward zealotry. But if it was to be a battle of wills, Lady Meredyth St. Andrews wouldn't triumph this time. He was responsible for her well-being, married or not, in light of his bargain with the earl, and he'd be damned if he would allow her to work here like some slave, subjected to death and disease and God knew what else with the town and its institutions in shambles.

But she'd made the decision for him. By severing herself from him, she'd made things easier as far as forcing him to make a choice regarding his work. He would go his way and she hers, and both would be the better for it, or so he told himself. Jamaica was his home, not hers, and of a certainty she didn't belong in Port Royal, in spite of her altruistic mo-

tives. She hadn't before the earthquake and certainly didn
now.

She was like a swan in a mud puddle. And he, born on th
periphery of that puddle, had dared to try and capture he
attention and then her affections.

As he motioned to Red Flaherty and Toby Galbraithe (th
escorts one part of his mind had already chosen), Devin ac
knowledged that he would surely be punished in some way b
the Earl of Somerset for what he'd done, but now the direction
of the rest of his life seemed clear to him, miserably clea
Empty of love and fraught with heart-wrenching memories
that was what Fate had intended for a cocky Irish bastard nick
named "Devil," who'd dared to overstep his bounds.

And whether Meredyth was willing or not, sending his re
bellious wife back to the haven of Father Tomas's mission wa
the last decent thing he could, and would, do for her.

Twenty-six

The last thing Devin ever expected was the unannounced arrival of the Earl of Somerset himself, in the wake of Meredyth having remained at the mission without a word of communication between them for six weeks. It had been sheer hell, and Devin had almost taken the *Lady Elysia* for a nice, long voyage. As it turned out, he was doubly responsible for Meredyth St. Andrews now, and until she decided to return to England, his hands were tied. But he refused to go crawling back up that mountain to give her an ultimatum or force a decision from her.

For weeks he'd lingered around Port Royal, alternating between helping to rebuild the city and taking short two or three day commercial jaunts about the Main to keep himself busy, his crew happy, and his ship providing them all with a livelihood.

You did what . . . what . . . what?

The Earl of Somerset's words bounced off the walls of his memory, like drumbeats keeping time with the swinging of Devin's machete as it slashed through the undergrowth. Surely, the foliage here renewed itself by the hour! And the furious earl had decided part of Devin's punishment (or so it seemed to Devin) was to single-handedly widen the constantly overgrown path all the way up to the mission.

I wed her to salvage her reputation, Devin had reluctantly

explained. *I had a deep affection for her, your lordship, thoug*
we've since . . . parted ways. And I gave my word to coopera
fully in the procurement of an annulment.

Devin swiped a forearm across his dripping brow, h
flushed face heating even more at the memory of that admi
sion. His side ached, even though it had been six weeks sin
the earthquake and he'd had time to heal. His body, at least

*I see you've had a grand time here in Jamaica since I re.
cued your hide from Newgate!* Somerset had declared with so
menace. *And at my daughter's expense, whom you'd given you
word to keep watch over.*

Devin had held his emerald gaze. *You never told me sh
was lovely and captivating, with a mind of her own, and adep
at burrowing her way beneath a man's defenses until he can
even remember his name!*

*Ah, yes, I'd forgotten. You said you had . . . what was it? . .
deep affection for her?* Somerset had pronounced slowly, h
eyes narrowed consideringly at Devin. They were of a lik
height, but the earl as dark-haired as Devin was fair, his thatc
of chestnut hair peppered with silver. *So you deflowere
Meredyth in your cabin—out of this deep affection, c
course—then arranged a hasty wedding to save her name?*

Devin had met his accusing glare with outward calm, think
ing how it had been more than the earl had offered Meredyth
mother after he'd abducted her and taken her to his bed. O
course, Devin hadn't known for certain, he'd not presse
Meredyth for such intimate details at the governor's ball tha
night. But he'd suspected as much, and the long silence tha
followed the earl's accusation obviously forced the man t
color faintly across his cheekbones.

A direct hit, Devin had thought with satisfaction. *I will re
pay the funds used to refurbish the schooner,* he'd said then
*and have no wish to accept your ten thousand pounds since
I did not uphold my end of the bargain. Beyond that, I car
do nothing more but offer my sincerest apologies, which I'n*

*certain seem insignificant to you, and pray you don't clap me
back into gaol.*

The earl had drilled him with his enamel gaze. *I should
have let you rot in Newgate, you rakehell! If you have such
deep affection for my daughter, why are you here and she
there?*

Devin whacked an overgrown, bushy croton with a vengeance as he thought back to his answer. Beautifully hued leaves
went flying as did several screeching macaws in a brilliant
flash of scarlet and blue.

*The last time I saw Meredyth she was still in love with Luke
Pelton, accused me of murdering him, and then appeared more
concerned about burying him than the fact that I was bleeding
to death before her eyes. Bleeding to death because the bastard
had shot me!*

At that point, the earl had extracted the entire story from
him.

"Bakámu help Chan-ler!" The Arawak's voice broke into
Devin's thoughts. It sounded imperious, freighted with Arawak
indignation, Devin thought. If he hadn't been so hot and sweaty
and humiliated, he would have grinned. But he knew he was
getting off lightly.

"If ye raise a hand to help him, I'll lop it off!" threatened
the rough voice of Peter Stubbs, the earl's man. He was a
seaman through and through—small and tough, one didn't
have to be a Sir Isaac Newton to see that, and Somerset had
introduced him as his former quartermaster.

Devin bared his teeth in silence, wishing in that moment he
could lop off the man's tongue.

"Chandler is doing quite well by himself" Somerset added
matter-of-factly. Then, in a more pensive tone, "I'm rather enjoying our little sojourn up this mountain. It holds many
memories for me."

Devin grimaced and raised the machete again, freezing in
mid-movement as a brown and black-patterned boa snagged
his startled gaze. It was resting coiled about the bole of a tree

just off to his right, but the familiar aversion to that particula
reptile moved through him like quicksilver, threatening to para
lyze him.

Not in front of the Earl of Somerset! his pride screamee
silently.

Either in delayed reaction to the departed macaws or or
some inexplicable avian impulse, in the same instant Henry
Morgan shrieked, "Kill the bloody Spaniard! Squaaawk!"

Devin jumped, startled out of impending paralysis, and auto
matically began the downward swing of the machete.

He grudgingly blessed the reprobate parrot, momentarily
thinking it more precious than the brightest macaw in the
Caribbee Islands. No one had noticed his slight hesitation, and
for that Devin granted the bird a permanent place in his es-
teem.

He continued trudging up the pathway, deliberately focusing
his thoughts on the stream ahead, its two amphibian inhabi-
tants, and his first meeting with Bakámu.

On Henry Morgan's grave! Even *that* was preferable to thinking about Meredyth and their inevitable encounter.

Meredyth, the woman who'd wed him at the drop of a hat
then just as quickly spurned him; the woman who'd consumee
his daytime thoughts and nighttime dreams, yet had made it
perfectly clear she didn't want anything to do with him; the
woman who loved another, but whom Devin still loved desperately.

"There's something about Jamaica that makes a person just
a bit mad."

Meredyth looked up from where she was working with a
handful of children. It was a small room at the back of the
mission church, which had been built for that specific purpose.

Even in the shadows, the Earl of Somerset stood tall and
confident, and endearingly patriarchal. A thousand emotions

gathered in her breast, momentarily rendering her incapable of speech. She slowly rose from her seat and faced him fully.

He looked her over then, and as his gaze settled on her bare feet, said with a soft chuckle, "Just like your mother, Merry. I never could keep a pair of shoes on her when we were here."

The children sat still as mice, obviously uncertain of what to do in light of this unexpected interruption. Then Carla raised a finger to her lips and motioned the others toward the door.

"Father!" Meredyth finally mobilized her tongue. He walked toward her, a smile curving his handsome mouth, and Meredyth finally found the wherewithal to fling herself into his arms. She clung to him, her feelings suddenly surging to her throat, triggering tears long overdue.

"How's my Merry?" he said softly into her hair.

"Oh, Papa!" she blurted with a sob, just like she had when she had been a child with a cut or scratch or hurt feelings. "I've made such a muddle of things!" At the same time she was mortified by her outburst, but it was impossible to stem, like trying to hold back a collapsing dam with her bare hands.

"Haven't we all at one time or another," he said quietly, half to himself. His arms tightened about her briefly, then he held her away from him and looked deeply into her eyes. "You look more unhappy now than when you left England, Merry. How can that be for one so young?"

A fresh wave of tears pressed against the back of her eyes, and she couldn't speak.

"Your lady mother was so very worried about you, I felt compelled to come see for myself."

"Mother? Is she well?" She frowned, her voice suddenly full of concern.

He nodded. "She was torn. Kerra had a miscarriage, and Brandy wanted to stay with her until her spirits improved. Kerra had also lost a lot of blood, and your mother was feeding her all kinds of rich meat and—believe it or nay—brandywine to build the blood." He raised an eyebrow, his eyes twinkling with amusement. "You know how your mother loves brandywine. I think 'twas an excuse to drink the stuff every time she pushed it on Kerra. Her cheeks were like poppies the last time I saw her."

Meredyth laughed aloud, thinking how her father had fondly continued to call her mother "Brandy" even though her lawful name was Juliana. She hugged him again.

"Are you ready to return to England with me?"

His tone was neutral enough, but Meredyth suspected there was much behind the query. She turned away from his probing green gaze, so like her own. "I'm not . . . certain."

"Do you mean you're not over Luke Pelton yet?"

She swung back to him, essaying to grasp the real meaning behind his words. Then another thought struck her. "How do you know him as Luke Pelton rather than Lucien Pendwell?"

"There's much I know about him, Meredyth, that I didn't reveal to you back in England. I acted the overprotective father, and I regret my secret and melodramatic methods now. Of course, at the time I didn't know I'd be catapulting you into his lap by allowing you to travel to Jamaica." He paused, then said levelly, "Death was too good for a man like him."

She raised her eyebrows and opened her mouth, for her father had never before expressed such a low opinion of any man. "How did you know?"

"Woodrow Kingsley told me."

"You know Master Kingsley?"

"Aye. An associate of mine, you might say."

Meredyth absorbed this for a moment. Suddenly, her look turned dark and her eyes lit with ire. "But better I had fallen in love with Luke Pelton than Devin Chandler!"

"Chandler came to you at my bidding. I retrieved him from Newgate and made a bargain with him."

Meredyth felt her mouth drop open. "You?"

"Your mother and I were worried. We regretted having let you hie yourself off to the Caribbee Islands alone."

"But you had connections here, the Greaveses and—"

"Jackie has his hands full with his family and the plantation."

"But . . . but *Devil* Chandler?"

Keir St. Andrews nodded and walked to the door the children had left ajar. He stood there, eyes narrowed against the afternoon sunlight that wedged through the opening and bathed part of his form. "He's a good man, basically."

"He's a libertine!"

Somerset glanced at her over his shoulder, a half-smile crescenting his mouth. "Is that all? He sounds less of a scoundrel than I was twenty-five years ago." His smile disappeared before he turned his head. "He wed you, when I wouldn't marry your mother until I thought I'd lost her. She'd had a child by then and was forced to face the world alone." He shook his head, squinting into the middle distance of the compound, obviously lost in memories.

Meredyth shook her head stubbornly and walked over to join him at the door. "Don't make excuses for him, and never compare yourself to him!" she said with irritation. "He trapped me! I had little choice but to give in to his seduction and then accept his marriage proposal!"

The earl crossed his arms over his chest, his pensive look turning to a frown of disapproval. "Did he drag you physically down to his cabin?"

"Nay, but—"

"He lured you, you say? Did he tell you there was a chestful of treasure below decks that was yours for the taking if you but laid claim to it?"

She tightened her lips mutinously. "Nay."

"Then I would say, child, that you wanted to be alone with him as much as he did with you. And," he added as she opened her mouth to protest, "his marriage proposition was but a hint of his love for you, his desperation to have you, even if for a few months in name only, all in the hope of you possibly changing your mind and accepting him."

"He told you this?"

The earl shook his head, then turned to face her fully. "Not in so many words. He didn't have to, for I've been that deeply in love myself."

Meredyth stood stunned, disbelief refusing to die within her. "But he killed Luke!" she insisted.

"Who needed killing," the earl said without emotion. "There was much about Pelton that you didn't know, Meredyth. One day I'll tell you. But you can't blame Chandler for striking out in self-defense. Who do you think shot him?"

Reason began to rout disbelief.

"But Devin dealt in slaves. Luke told me so."

"Did Devin admit that to you?"

"Not exactly."

"If you love someone, you naturally give them the benefit of the doubt, daughter. Or did you still love Pelton?"

Meredyth swallowed and shook her head, her eyes glistening with emotion.

Somerset sighed heavily. "Why don't you ask your husband about his involvement with the slave trade? I think after you speak to him you'll wish to apologize, Merry," he said softly. "There are things he was forced to do and say to deflect any suspicion about his real work."

She suddenly went very still, waiting for him to reveal more.

"Mayhap he'll tell you all since you are his lawful wife and I cannot control what he shares with you. But I'm not at liberty to say any more, except mayhap that you'll now see fit to thank him for having been there when you needed him. Then, too, you'll feel better about returning with me to England, where you belong."

The seed had been firmly planted.

Meredyth spent an hour with the earl, then reluctantly went about finding Devin, while her father went to see Father Tomas.

She searched the compound, part of her dreading the encounter out of fear of rejection, part of her unwilling to meet up with him because of lingering vestiges of obstinacy and trampled pride, for her father had implied that she'd misjudged Devin Chandler. And part of her was giddy with longing to see him again.

She passed Peter Stubbs and toyed with the idea of greeting him, but he seemed preoccupied with Dionisio, deep in animated conversation as they compared muskets. She would speak to Peter later.

Devin, however, was nowhere to be found, and no one seemed to know where he'd disappeared to.

Perhaps you'll feel better about returning with me to England, where you belong. . . .

For some reason, the thought was far from appealing, aside from seeing her family once again. But she had grown to love the island of Jamaica—from Father Tomas's peaceful mission tucked away in the Blue Mountains to the raucous and now ruined town of Port Royal, a town she had wished to help rebuild before she had been banished to the safety of the mission by an uncharacteristically angry Devin Chandler.

Meredyth caught a glimpse of Carla and another little girl sitting against the trunk of a tree and peering into Sir Hiss's small wicker basket. Their girlish giggles came to her on the breeze, and Meredyth slowed her steps and watched as Carla tipped the basket on its side and waited in silence.

She was freeing the anole. The lizard had survived all these weeks, and now the child was releasing it back into the wilds. A thrill of satisfaction moved through Meredyth, for whether Dionisio or herself had been responsible, the child had learned a valuable lesson.

A totally unexpected image appeared in her mind's eye: that of her waving farewell to Jamaica and Devin Chandler aboard the earl's *Odyssey*. Her leavetaking would, in a fashion, free Devin from her. Free him to pursue his own life as he saw fit, without being saddled with an unwanted and ungrateful wife, who'd turned his life upside down.

Mayhap her father was right. Jamaica was a beautiful paradise to visit, but she belonged in England.

The other child caught sight of Meredyth and spoke softly to Carla. Carla looked up and smiled, obviously pleased to see Meredyth. Then a fleeting expression of enlightenment crossed her features, and the girl promptly straightened the basket and shut its lid. She stood, her smile widening as she adjusted her crutch, then moved toward Meredyth.

Meredyth wondered what the child was up to, disappointed that she hadn't set the lizard free after all. "Here, Señorita Meredyth," Carla said. "You found him, you set him free."

Meredyth unthinkingly took the basket. "You don't want to let it go, Carla?"

Carla looked at her companion, who was younger than she and appeared puzzled. " 'Tis for you to do. In the same place, *sí?* So he'll not be lost?"

Meredyth hugged the basket to her, feeling a sudden reluctance to part with the creature. "If you want me to, little one."

"Bakámu great warrior! Squaaawk! Cut white man's throat!"

Meredyth looked up at Henry Morgan's squawk. Bakámu was walking toward them, a broad grin on his face. Meredyth returned the smile, in spite of echoes of the parrot's bald revelation in the presence of the children. She'd learned that no matter how outrageous the gray's utterances, the bird was only imitating what he heard, and this latest revelation sounded suspiciously like Arawak braggadocio. It certainly would be in keeping with his protective and proprietary attitude where Devin was concerned.

"How are you, Bakámu?" she asked, reaching out to stroke Henry Morgan's alabaster head.

"Bakámu good."

"Why did you teach Henry Morgan to say such a thing?" she asked as the parrot transferred himself from the Indian's shoulder to Carla's reaching hand.

Bakámu's smile slid from his face. "Englishman took Chan-ler from boat. Tie him and beat him. Almost kill him. Hurt Bakámu, too. Bakámu kill him for Chan-ler."

"Slit his throat! Murdering bastard!" sang the African gray from his new perch.

Meredyth paled in the face of one more misconception she'd harbored, one more misconception that had just been added to the mounting evidence against Luke Pelton. It seemed like everyone else had seen him for what he was but her. Even after he'd treated her so abominably in England.

That said, the Arawak's smile reappeared and he asked, "You look for Chan-ler?"

A shaky sigh escaped her lips before she admitted, "Aye. Do you know where he is?"

The Indian pointed toward the forest, in the direction of the waterfall. And Meredyth's heartbeat quickened at the possibility of Devin having gone to the place where they'd first met.

Silly, she thought, but what reason would he have to go there?

Don't entertain any romantic notions, warned a voice. *'Tis a peaceful and secluded place. A good place to be alone, to sort one's thoughts.*

Or nurse one's grudges, added an imp.

The low afternoon sun was still warm as Meredyth made her way unhurriedly through the woods, but already, because they were up in the mountains, the air was getting cooler. Goose bumps beaded her bare arms, and she wondered if it was the air or the chill in her heart. Her steps were unhurried, she made certain of that, for it wouldn't do to go running to Devin Chandler only to be soundly rebuffed, to have her apology flung back in her face, which she certainly deserved.

Marry come up! she thought. How could she have made two devastating mistakes in a row? She must be flawed somehow, surely she was the poorest judge of character who'd ever lived! She'd fallen in love with Devin Chandler and then betrayed him, just like Luke had betrayed her, only on an emotional level rather than physically.

She reached the clearing and paused at its perimeter, her thoughts whirling. But as soon as she saw Devin sitting cross-legged beside the pool, she was deluged with tender feelings. She knew she loved him beyond a doubt and hadn't really misjudged him until Luke Pelton had poisoned her mind. So mayhap her instincts weren't so inaccurate, 'twas just that she was gullible.

She stepped from the shadow of the trees onto the sun-warmed slate surrounding the pool. His head was bowed contemplatively, as if he were studying the rock slab upon which he sat or thinking. The westering sun wound through the trees and touched his golden head like a benison. She couldn't see his face, but his blue silk head scarf lay on the ground beside him, along with a wicked-looking machete.

Meredyth took a breath of fresh mountain air and moved toward him on silent feet, her heart fluttering about her ribcage like a captured bird. But as she approached, she noted that he didn't appear as contemplative as tired. Fatigue was etched in the lines of his powerful shoulders, and the curve of his spine.

Suddenly, he put one hand on the back of his neck and raised his face to the sky, his eyes closed. Meredyth's breath caught at the unimpeded view of his striking profile, like a Viking deity of old gracing the mountain with his presence. From where she stood, clutching Sir Hiss's basket, Meredyth could see the masculine jut of his adam's apple from the strong column of his neck. And his face, at least the side of it she could see, was free of the ugly bruises that had discolored it after the altercation to which Bakámu had evidently alluded.

But it wasn't a fight, she thought in sudden outrage. It was a beating, and it had been unfair. From what the Arawak had said, Luke had dragged him from the *Lady Elysia*—no doubt with help—and tied him and beat him senseless.

She could have lost him, and he had made light of it at her father's town house.

She opened her mouth to speak, just as he turned his head and saw her.

"Devin . . ." The name hung in the air between them.

"So my mother saw fit to name me," he said with unexpected gentleness as the corners of his mouth lifted. Was there a tremor in his voice?

Her drawing room etiquette deserted her, in spite of her determination to make amends, and she clutched the basket to her ribs as pure cowardice crawled up her backbone. He was so beautiful, so masculine, and so hurt. She could tell now because of the anguish in his eyes, for the instant before he'd covered his true feelings with typical light-heartedness.

It was now clear to her that when he was the most hurt or uncertain he donned his glibbest façade, as he did now, with a lift of his golden eyebrows and a cocky half-smile. "Good evening, my lady wife."

He made to stand, but Meredyth held out her free hand. "Please, don't stand for me. You look tired." She moved toward him, her head tilted consideringly as she fought to hide her sudden, insidious lack of confidence. "Are you ill? Does your wound still trouble you?"

Which wound, Merry-mine?

"Nay. The wound is healed. I'm just fatigued from forging a new path up the mountainside. Single-handedly. Your father is very exacting."

He stared out over the pool at the cascading waterfall, and Meredyth thought of her angry father making him labor all the way up the mountain when hired men could have handled it. Though if the earl were truly furious, the punishment wouldn't have stopped there, and he had seemed more upset with Meredyth than Devin.

"I see you've decided to free the lizard," he said, his frost-blue eyes returning to her face. "Mayhap if you'll let it go, you'll break the spell and we'll both wake up to discover this is all naught more than a dream." He softened the words with a sham smile that didn't reach his eyes. "Or a nightmare, whichever you prefer. You do look much the same as you did weeks ago, you know. Except for that ridiculous hat."

Meredyth closed her eyes briefly and drew in a fortifying breath as memories washed over her. She noticed that he smelled as clean and fresh as the crystalline mountain pool and the evergreens surrounding it. His clothing, now that she was closer, was damp. And his hair . . .

Unthinkingly she reached out one hand toward that blond mane. He caught her wrist in a firm but gentle grip, his eyes cool, distant as he looked up into hers. "I'm sure you didn't come here to stroke my hair," he said softly. "Why don't you let the creature go and then return to your father . . . and England. I've spoken to him about an annulment, and he's agreed."

That was an exaggeration, Devin acknowledged, but she didn't need to know it. He wanted to make it easy for her, but he'd been secretly elated at her unexpected appearance. Until he'd seen the basket and realized she'd not been seeking him out, as he had thought with a brief burst of hope.

"Devin, I've spoken with my father, also."

He returned his gaze to the waterfall, his elbows resting on his drawn up knees, his hands crossed loosely between his legs, but he remained silent.

"I've made some hasty conclusions . . . was too quick to believe the wrong man."

She thought the side of his mouth quirked, obviously an effort at insouciance, but his body was too tense for that. "You didn't do wrong, Meredyth. You're supposed to believe the man you love, although you would have saved me a great deal of trouble if you'd admitted the truth to me instead of toying with my affections. No man—or woman—particularly enjoys playing second fiddle."

Meredyth set the basket on the slate slab and knelt beside him.

"Devin—"

"Why don't we just leave things as they are, Merry?" he cut in. "If you feel better after having certain things explained by the earl, I'm glad for you. But your seeking to make amends is based on what your father told you, not on your ever having given me the benefit of the doubt when Pelton was involved. And yet, you were willing to surrender your virtue to me and take my name." He shook his head, shrugged lightly. "Although it really doesn't matter now, I suppose."

"My father told me to ask you myself about slave trafficking."

"I've already told you."

"Tell me again, Devin."

"I don't deal in slaves."

"Did Luke?"

He gazed into her eyes. "Aye. He worked for du Casse and la Compagnie de Sénégal. But I thought you might have guessed that."

Meredyth sat back on her heels with a thoughtful frown, thinking back to her last conversation with Luke: *I'm not deserving of you, at least in the eyes of your father. . . . Your father was behind my leaving . . . . 'Twasn't my choice to leave you . . .*

"My father must have learned of his activities after we met and somehow induced him to leave me, to make it look as if he'd jilted me."

"Evidently. And you chose to believe him over me, I being a mere privateer." He cocked one eyebrow in feigned condescension.

"You did lie to me about one thing," she accused softly.

"And what was that?"

"The beating Luke gave you."

Devin threw back his face to the kiss of the sun again and released a long sigh. "How many brothers have you Merry?"

"Two."

"And a father."

"Of course. But what—?"

"Don't you know by now that no man would ever wish to reveal that he'd been kidnapped, tied, then beaten by another? Especially by his archrival for the woman he loves?"

"Luke Pelton was never your rival, Devin," she said, her heart in her eyes, for she had to convince him she didn't love Luke Pelton and never really had. "In fact, I told him he wasn't fit to clean your boots."

She got her wish. His head dropped and he turned to stare at her in disbelief. "You said *that* to him?"

"Don't you know that any woman truly in love would defend her man verbally with her last breath? Even to an old beau?"

He sat up straight, his weariness disappearing. "And if I killed Pelton? Slashed his throat?"

She shrugged. "It matters not if or how you killed him, just that the deed was done." She inhaled another deep breath and looked deeply into his eyes. "Devin, forgive me, my love, for doubting you, for allowing myself to think the worst."

He grinned suddenly, the movement of his lips emphasizing the fine lines splaying out from his eyes and mouth. "But I didn't kill him. Bakámu did. Damned, interfering Indian!"

Meredyth wisely feigned ignorance and frowned in delicate puzzlement. "Bakámu?"

"Aye. Pelton challenged me to fight, but when he lost his sword and pulled out a pistol, Bakámu launched himself and dispatched him, almost getting me killed with his exuberance."

Meredyth allowed herself a tentative smile. "I can just picture the great Arawak warrior trying to save you."

But Devin wasn't smiling. He was looking at her with a barely hidden hunger in his eyes, a yearning that he couldn't quite mask. "Ask me where I buried him, Meredyth," he asked, his expression very solemn.

She felt her face warm at the memory of wanting to bury Luke herself, but she went along, fearing to break the tenuous line of communication growing between them. "Where, then?"

"Under a rock, where he belongs."

His eyes suddenly sparkled with mischief, and Meredyth couldn't prevent the laughter that bubbled up her throat and escaped her lips. Its sweet sound was balm to Devin's soul, more pleasing even than the flash of her dimple.

"You're going straight to Hell, Meredyth St. Andrews Chandler."

" 'Tis the only way we can be together for eternity," she informed him.

Their lips hovered a heartbeat apart. "Point well taken, milady."

"Devin?"

"Aye, love?" He caressed one side of her face with his hand, his thumb skimming the flawless flesh of her cheek.

"Father said I should ask you about your real work."

He groaned softly, feeling desire wend through him like liquid heat. "You truly know how to strike a man when he's most vulnerable, Merry-mine!" he said huskily in her ear.

Her hand went boldly, naughtily, to his codpiece, and she knew exactly what he meant. "Tell me, my love," she insisted, stroking him.

"Informant," he said through clenched teeth, his hand moving from her cheek to her breast, resting beneath the thin native blouse she wore.

Just before Meredyth gave in to the answering need racing through her blood, she remembered the earl's exact words: *There are things he was forced to do and say to deflect any suspicion about his real work . . .*

Dear God, he'd been risking his life every day to help put an end to the very practice she'd accused him of, she realized at last.

Tears of joy filled her eyes, and her lusty urges threatened to overwhelm her as her body responded like kindling to flame. "Ah, Devil Chandler, you really know how to strike a woman when she's most vulnerable. But you'll have to change your line of work, for that of husband and father. This informant business is too dangerous."

"Only if you'll remain with me in Jamaica." His fingers found their way beneath the blouse to bare flesh. "Say you will, Meredyth. Say you'll be mine and stay with me forever, for I love you more than my life."

Her kiss was all the answer he needed, her mouth opening and offering him all that she was, all that she would ever be.

They reclined upon the warm stone ground, and Devin unwittingly tipped over Sir Hiss's basket with his foot. Within seconds, the tiny chameleon's head appeared at the opening.

"I love you, Devin," Meredyth murmured between sweet, sweet kisses.

"And I'll thank God every day of my life!" he answered fervently.

The anole skittered across the slate toward freedom beckoning from the trees.

Author's Note

While researching *Tender Pirate* a few years back, I came across an article in an old *National Geographic* describing an earthquake that hit Jamaica in 1692. Its consequences were particularly devastating for Port Royal, and although part of *Tender Pirate* was set in Port Royal and the Jamaican Blue Mountains in 1664, I decided then and there to one day write another story set nearly thirty years later, involving a son or daughter of the main characters in *Tender Pirate*.

According to a brass pocket watch retrieved from the waters covering part of the original Port Royal, the earthquake struck at seventeen minutes before twelve noon on June 7, 1692. Two-thirds of the town sank within two minutes and two thousand people perished. The acting governor, John White, survived the quake; "the *Swan* Frigot was forced over the tops of many Houses . . . She did not over-set, but helped some Hundreds, in saving their Lives." A French ship, a prize of war docked in Port Royal, was actually carried by the tidal wave following the earthquake and set down in a marketplace.

In describing the catastrophe, I've attempted to stick to the facts as much as possible, while weaving in the story elements of *Tender Scoundrel,* including several actual tremors (there were three), a tidal wave, and the actual injury and death of many victims from fissures opening unexpectedly and closing just as suddenly in the earth.

TODAY'S HOTTEST READS
ARE TOMORROW'S SUPERSTARS

VICTORY'S WOMAN   (4484, $4.50)
by Gretchen Genet
Andrew—the carefree soldier who sought glory on the battlefield, and
returned a shattered man . . . Niall—the legandary frontiersman and
a former Shawnee captive, tormented by his past . . . Roger—the troubled youth, who would rise up to claim a shocking legacy . . . and
Clarice—the passionate beauty bound by one man, and hopelessly in
love with another. Set against the backdrop of the American revolution,
three men fight for their heritage—and one woman is destined to
change all their lives forever!

FORBIDDEN   (4488, $4.99)
by Jo Beverley
While fleeing from her brothers, who are attempting to sell her into a
loveless marriage, Serena Riverton accepts a carriage ride from a
stranger—who is the handsomest man she has ever seen. Lord Middle-
thorpe, himself, is actually contemplating marriage to a dull daughter of the aristocracy, when he encounters the breathtaking Serena. She
arouses him as no woman ever has. And after a night of thrilling intimacy—a forbidden liaison—Serena must choose between a lady's
place and a woman's passion!

WINDS OF DESTINY   (4489, $4.99)
by Victoria Thompson
Becky Tate is a half-breed outcast—branded by her Comanche heritage. Then she meets a rugged stranger who awakens her heart to the
magic and mystery of passion. Hiding a desperate past, Texas Ranger
Clint Masterson has ridden into cattle country to bring peace to a
divided land. But a greater battle rages inside him when he dares to
desire the beautiful Becky!

WILDEST HEART   (4456, $4.99)
by Virginia Brown
Maggie Malone had come to cattle country to forge her future as a
healer. Now she was faced by Devon Conrad, an outlaw wounded body
and soul by his shadowy past . . . whose eyes blazed with fury even
as his burning caress sent her spiraling with desire. They came together
in a Texas town about to explode in sin and scandal. Danger was their
destiny—and there was nothing they wouldn't dare for love!

*Available wherever paperbacks are sold, or order direct from the
Publisher. Send cover price plus 50¢ per copy for mailing and
handling to Penguin USA, P.O. Box 999, c/o Dept. 17109,
Bergenfield, NJ 07621. Residents of New York and Tennessee
must include sales tax. DO NOT SEND CASH.*